A
DIFFERENT
DAWN

ALSO BY ISABELLA MALDONADO

FBI Agent Nina Guerrera series

The Cipher

Detective Veranda Cruz series

Blood's Echo
Phoenix Burning
Death Blow

PRAISE FOR ISABELLA MALDONADO

A Different Dawn

"A killer of a novel. Fresh, fast, and utterly ingenious."
—Brad Thor, #1 *New York Times* bestselling author

The Cipher

"The survivor of a vicious crime confronts her fears in a hunt for a serial killer . . . forensic analysis, violent action, and a tough heroine who stands up to the last man on earth she wants to see again."
—*Kirkus Reviews*

"[In] this riveting series launch from Maldonado . . . the frequent plot twists will keep readers guessing to the end, and Maldonado draws on her twenty-two years in law enforcement to add realism. Determined to overcome her painful past, the admirable Nina has enough depth to sustain a long-running series."
—*Publishers Weekly*

"A heart-pounding novel from page one, *The Cipher* checks all the boxes for a top-notch thriller: sharp plotting, big stakes, and characters— good and bad and everywhere in between—that are so richly drawn you'll swear you've met them. I read this in one sitting, and I guarantee you will too. Oh, another promise: you'll absolutely love the Warrior Girl!"
—Jeffery Deaver, *New York Times* bestselling author

"Wow! A riveting tale in the hands of a superb storyteller."
—J. A. Jance, *New York Times* bestselling author

"Intense, harrowing, and instantly addictive, *The Cipher* took my breath away. Isabella Maldonado has created an unforgettable heroine in Nina Guerrera, a dedicated FBI agent and trauma survivor with unique insight into the mind of a predator. This riveting story is everything a thriller should be."

—Hilary Davidson, *Washington Post* bestselling author

Previous Praise

"Maldonado's a writer to watch, and she showcases her own extensive law enforcement background in this tightly plotted police procedural."
—*Publishers Weekly* (starred review)

"Maldonado, a former law enforcement officer, brings her experience and expertise to this gripping police procedural. With its gritty heroine, this action-packed mystery will attract readers who enjoy crime novels about the war on drugs."

—*Library Journal*

"Phoenix may be burning, but Maldonado's star is rising. Gritty and gripping."
—J. A. Jance, *New York Times* bestselling author

"Maldonado's writing always bristles with urgency and authority."
—*Mystery Scene* magazine

"Delivers a brilliant and complicated heroine, accented by a take-no-prisoners plot . . . It's spicy, smart, and entertaining, definitely worth your time."

—Steve Berry, author of *The Lost Order*

"A highly entertaining police procedural . . . Maldonado rises to her written challenge to entertain, enthrall, and engage readers in this high-octane thriller."

—*Suspense Magazine*

"A tense thriller with a strong sense of place and an insider's look at some of the most dangerous work in law enforcement."

—Jan Burke, *New York Times* bestselling author

"The Phoenix sun isn't the only thing burning in this thrilling debut, and I look forward to more."

—Shannon Baker, bestselling author of the Kate Fox mystery series

"An ex-narc leads a war against a powerful crime family. The payoff is satisfying."

—*Kirkus Reviews*

"If you're in the mood for a nonstop exposé of every fear you've ever had about cartel crime, Veranda Cruz is the woman to follow."

—*Kirkus Reviews*

"Finally! A kick-ass female protagonist and an author who knows firsthand the world she writes about. The combination makes for an explosive read that grabs you from page one and doesn't let go."

—Alex Kava, *New York Times* and *USA Today* bestselling author
of *Lost Creed*

"Red alert to all readers of police procedurals with a strong thriller bent: Isabella Maldonado's *Death Blow* delivers nonstop action with substance, grit, and surprises."

—Lisa Preston, author of *The Clincher*

"Gritty, raw, and realistic, Isabella Maldonado's *Death Blow* is the real deal."

—Bruce Robert Coffin, bestselling author of the
Detective Byron mystery series

"A gritty, gut-wrenching, page-turning thriller featuring a woman cop bent on bringing down a twisted cartel leader for reasons of her own, *Death Blow* grabs you from the first jaw-dropping scene to the last, and Maldonado's stellar writing weaves it all together."

—Jamie Freveletti, internationally bestselling author of *Blood Run*

A
DIFFERENT
DAWN

ISABELLA
MALDONADO

THOMAS & MERCER

Text copyright © 2021 by Isabella Maldonado
All rights reserved.

No part of this book may be reproduced, or stored in a retrieval system, or transmitted in any form or by any means, electronic, mechanical, photocopying, recording, or otherwise, without express written permission of the publisher.

Published by Thomas & Mercer, Seattle

www.apub.com

Amazon, the Amazon logo, and Thomas & Mercer are trademarks of Amazon.com, Inc., or its affiliates.

ISBN-13: 9781542022781
ISBN-10: 1542022789

Cover design by Christopher Lin

Printed in the United States of America

For Max:
wherever your path takes you,
always know you are loved.

Chapter 1

Twenty years ago
The Russell House group home for girls; Fairfax County, Virginia

Seven-year-old Nina sat cross-legged on the floor with the others, breathless with anticipation. Every girl at the home envied Angelica, who was spending her final night at Russell House. Angelica had been chosen.

Eleven years old and willowy, with long coltish legs and skin fair enough to pass for white, Angelica had spent the past three months with a foster family who had decided to petition the court for adoption. The process would take many more months, but she would continue to live with her future family in the meantime. Today, Angelica had come back to Russell House to say goodbye to her friends, or bask in her superiority, depending on how she felt about you.

According to Miss Brown, almost no one was adopted past the age of ten, yet Angelica had managed to defy the odds. She had been placed in foster care only six months ago, unlike Nina, who had never known her family.

Nina privately wondered if prospective adoptive parents were told how long each child had been in the system. She pictured her photograph in a police-style mug book, a tag beneath her with the word *lifer* in bright red.

On the other hand, maybe she could make a better effort next time she was placed in a foster home. Why did she have to be so curious? Ask so many questions? Poke around in things that weren't her business? If she'd known the teacher would call the police, she never would have brought the items in the shoebox her foster father stashed under his bed to school for show-and-tell.

As Nina and the other girls sat in a semicircle around her, Angelica leaned forward in her chair, her words taking on a spooky tone. "This is the legend of *La Llorona*, the wailing woman."

Little Samantha, who was only five years old, scooted closer to Nina. The girl's hazel eyes were already wide with fear, and Nina handed over her favorite plushie, a soft stuffed cheetah named Princesa. The only thing Nina could call her own.

Samantha clutched the spotted toy cat in trembling hands as Angelica told the story.

"There once was a woman named Maria. She married a handsome man and had two children, but her husband loved their children more than her. One day, Maria caught her husband kissing another woman and realized he loved the other woman more as well."

Another little girl, Caitlin, edged up to Nina's other side. Caitlin had what the social workers called "special needs." To Nina's way of thinking, the only thing special Caitlin needed was protection from bullies.

Nina thought Caitlin was supersmart, even though some of the older girls like Angelica called her stupid. They teased Caitlin because she wasn't good at speaking. She stuttered and had trouble talking to the other kids, but she could add long columns of numbers in her head, knew how many jellybeans were in a jar without counting them, and had begun to study algebra last month when she turned six.

When Angelica arrived for her final visit earlier this evening, she had hidden Caitlin's new math book. Nina had snatched the brand-new cell phone Angelica's adoptive parents had given her, holding it over the toilet until she returned the stolen textbook to Caitlin.

Nina draped an arm around Caitlin's small shoulders, comforting her as they listened to the rest of the tale.

"Maria grew angry," Angelica said. "And a bit *loca*. She vowed to make her husband pay for cheating on her. To punish him, she drowned their children in the river. When she went home, her husband asked where the kids were, and she admitted she had killed them. Her husband got real mad at her. Told her he could never be with her again until she found their children."

Caitlin began rocking back and forth.

Angelica's voice dropped to a stage whisper. "Maria, sorry over what she had done and missing her lost children, drowned herself in the same river."

Samantha squeezed the stuffed cheetah harder.

"Now she is doomed to walk the earth as a ghost," Angelica continued, "forever searching for her dead *niños*. She wears a white gown and a flowing veil. If she finds children wandering at night, she kidnaps them and drowns them in the river. She is called *La Llorona* because she is always weeping. If you hear her, you will be the next to die."

An eerie voice cried out from behind them: *"¿Dónde están mis hijos?"*

One of the older girls had hidden in the back of the room to scare the little ones.

Samantha screamed, threw Princesa in the air, and raced to the bedroom. Caitlin flung herself into Nina's lap, her slender arms circling Nina's neck. Nina felt warmth spreading onto her jeans and realized Caitlin had peed herself.

Angelica scooped up the discarded plushie, a sly grin on her lips. "What's this?" Her voice took on a singsong quality. "Is this widdle Nina's widdle baby toy?"

Nina gently set Caitlin aside and stood. "Give it back."

Angelica pointed at Nina and shrieked with laughter. "Look, everyone, Nina wet her pants!"

Nina looked down. Sure enough, Caitlin's pee had dripped into her lap. She shifted her gaze to Caitlin, whose small frame shook with terror as she clutched Nina's leg.

She could have pointed out to everyone that it was Caitlin who had peed. She knew what it meant to show weakness in the group home, which was why she held her tongue. She could handle the abuse better than Caitlin. She'd certainly had enough practice.

Angelica lifted up the stuffed cheetah for all to see. "I think widdle baby Nina needs to grow up." She grasped its head and began to twist hard.

Nina took a step toward her. "Stop it!" Caitlin's death grip on her leg prevented her from going any farther.

Angelica looked around the room, playing to her audience. "I'll never have to see any of you losers after tonight. But before I go, I'm going to give you all something to remember."

She ripped the head off the cheetah and began yanking the stuffing out, flinging it all around her in a white cloud of polyester fluff. Her eyes narrowed on Nina. "Unlike the rest of us, nobody ever wanted you. We at least had a family at some point. Your parents threw you in a dumpster. Like trash." Her voice took on the same singsong quality as before. "Dumpster baby, dumpster baby, dump—"

One moment Nina was standing while Caitlin clutched her leg; the next thing she knew, the staff at the group home had rushed in from the kitchen to tug her off Angelica, whose nose bled freely under Nina's flailing fists.

If there had ever been the slightest hope Nina might be adopted, it had ended that night. The night of *La Llorona*.

Chapter 2

He crept inside the dark house on silent feet and scanned the empty foyer, which appeared to him in hues of luminous gray. Cutting-edge night-vision goggles gave him a distinct advantage, especially when the family sleeping upstairs was completely unaware that an intruder prowled the floor below.

He eased the pistol from his waistband and reviewed the plan. Years of planning, months of winnowing, and weeks of surveillance had brought him to this moment. He had left nothing to chance. The couple upstairs would take tonight's secrets to the grave.

He placed a foot on the carpeted stairs and eased himself up to the next step.

Neutralize the husband first. A male would likely present the greatest physical threat, although a mother protecting her child could be formidable. She would also have the advantage of knowing what was coming since she would be last. Which was the whole point.

She would pay for what she had done.

He reached the top of the stairs, stopped, waited, and listened. Every nerve thrummed in anticipation.

The mingled scents of talcum powder and fresh linen brought him up short as he made out the steady *lub-dub* of a heartbeat in the room to his left. After a brief pause, he realized it was one of those gadgets parents put in cribs to mimic the sound of a mother's pulse.

He pushed the thought from his mind. He had plans, and he had backup plans. Nothing would stop the inevitable. Like the Angel of Death, he was deaf to pleas. Blind to tears. Entirely without mercy.

Cloaked in darkness, he slipped inside the nursery and went about his business.

Six minutes later, he inched down the hall to the master bedroom carrying the football-size bundle in the crook of his left arm.

The door had been left slightly open. Better to hear the baby's cries. Better access for him. The parents slept peacefully in their bed, oblivious to what was about to happen. What had already happened.

He elbowed the door wide, giving him a clear view of the king-size bed.

The man slept on the left and the woman on the right. He faced the ceiling and she curled against his side, heads resting on their pillows. Their chests rose and fell in synchronistic rhythm.

He raised the barrel, clicked a switch along the side of the weapon, then placed the tiny glowing dot over the slumbering man's heart.

Time to set things right.

Slowly, he began to squeeze the trigger.

Chapter 3

Two days later; Monday, March 2
Behavioral Analysis Unit, Aquia Commerce Center
Aquia, Virginia

FBI Special Agent Nina Guerrera slid into the sole empty chair at the rectangular black laminate table at the far end of Supervisory Special Agent Gerard Buxton's office. Sheets of rain pelted the tall windows lining the corner office on the second floor of the commercial complex.

Her boss arched a brow. "You're late."

Should she tell him about the disabled motorist blocking the right lane of Route 123 that had backed up traffic for half a mile? Explain how she had gotten out in the deluge to help push the woman's smoking VW Bug onto the shoulder? Mention how she had stayed until Virginia state troopers arrived to set up flares and call a tow truck for the stranded motorist?

"And you're wet," Buxton added. "Did you break down on the way in?"

"No, sir," she said, leaving out the details. "Someone else did."

"Here." Special Agent Dr. Jeffrey Wade, who sat in the chair beside hers, held out a crisp white handkerchief. "You're dripping on the table."

Her mentor and the most senior criminal profiler in the FBI, Wade was the only agent she knew who routinely carried freshly ironed handkerchiefs. In his early fifties, perhaps Wade viewed it as a holdover from a bygone era, but Nina appreciated the gesture.

Flashing Wade a grateful smile, she took the proffered cloth, mopped fat droplets from her short-cropped hair, and swiped at the rivulets trickling down the sides of her face.

She glanced across the table at Special Agents Kelly Breck and Jake Kent, who made up the rest of her newly formed team. Breck's sharp wit and sassy attitude—softened by her southern accent—came as a surprise to those who didn't know her. A contrast she'd used to her advantage in dealing with criminals.

Kent—a former Navy SEAL with a sandy buzz cut, hard muscles, and incongruous black-framed glasses—looked like he would be equally comfortable in a combat zone or behind a podium in a university lecture hall.

Settling into her seat, Nina noticed tension in the lines of their supervisor's features. Buxton never displayed strong emotion, but this morning he sat stiffly at the head of the table, pulled off his glasses, and pinched the bridge of his nose.

Two neatly stacked manila folders rested in front of him. He tapped them with his long fingers. "If this is a pattern, it's right up there with the most disturbing ones I've seen."

They all exchanged glances. Nina waited to hear the briefing.

"ViCAP found a potential match between two triple murders committed in different cities precisely four years apart," Buxton continued. "We've been tasked with determining whether they're related and, if so, assisting with the investigation at the request of the Phoenix police department in Arizona."

The Violent Criminal Apprehension Program's massive database was maintained by the FBI as a repository for crime information entered by law enforcement agencies around the country. The system was designed as a clearinghouse and centralized analysis point, a net created to link crimes committed across states and over time. Nina figured something bad had gotten caught in the net.

"What do we know about the two cases?" Wade asked.

Nina admired how the veteran criminal profiler shifted straight into high gear. Interest lightened his gray eyes as he opened an old-school notepad. Wade had the benefit of a doctorate in psychology and a couple of decades in the FBI to inform his theories about who had committed unsolved crimes sent to the BAU for input. This advantage, however, came at a high price. Continuously delving into the minds of both killers and their victims took its toll. Over two years earlier, Wade's career had been temporarily sidetracked when one of his prior investigations ended with the death of a young girl he had not been able to save.

In response to Wade's question, Buxton pushed his glasses back on and turned to Breck, who had already grabbed her laptop from its soft leather case by her feet. "I sent you an encrypted file with crime scene photos and other information," he said to her. "Can you pull it up?"

Breck, detailed to their team from the Cyber Crime Unit, was never without her laptop, which seemed like an appendage rather than a piece of equipment. She propped it open in front of her, tucking a spiraling lock of long auburn hair behind her ear. "I'll put it on the big screen," she said, her southern drawl betraying a coastal Georgia upbringing.

Nina turned toward the flat-screen monitor mounted on the wall as Buxton continued.

"I'll start with the most recent case, which occurred two nights ago in Phoenix," he said. "An entire family was murdered in their home in the middle of the night." He drew in a breath. "Mother, father, and their newborn daughter."

An image filled the screen. Nina found herself gazing at a sprawling Mediterranean-style estate situated on a lush green lawn surrounded by towering royal palms. A second picture replaced the first. A man who looked to be in his midthirties lay in a king-size bed, his head at an odd angle against the ornate headboard. He wore nothing but boxers, and blood covered his bare chest.

The next screen showed an infant apparently asleep in a crib.

"The baby was suffocated—no obvious injuries or trauma except for petechial hemorrhaging associated with hypoxia caused at the time of death." Buxton swallowed audibly. "She was only eight days old."

Buxton nodded to Breck, who brought up the next crime scene photo.

A woman lay slumped in a bathtub, dressed in a pale pink nightgown. A semiautomatic pistol rested in her slackened right hand, and a single gunshot wound pierced her right temple. She looked like one of the many suicide victims Nina had seen as a patrol officer before joining the Bureau.

"I thought you said it was a triple murder," Nina said, mentally processing the succession of images. "This looks like the mother killed her family before turning the gun on herself."

Buxton's dark eyes met hers. "Because that's how it was supposed to look."

Silent until now, Kent offered a theory. "Someone entered the home, killed everyone, then staged the bodies?"

While Kent had been in the Navy, Uncle Sam had paid for his master's degree in psychology, which he put to use in the field during prisoner interrogations on classified operations. After joining the Bureau, it had not taken him long to find his way into the BAU, where he repurposed his hard-won skills from fighting enemies to hunting predators.

"Phoenix police Homicide detectives suspected a problem right away," Buxton said. "They found a trace amount of blood residue in the foyer just inside the house. It appears the killer may have worn gloves and shoe coverings when he went upstairs, but some droplets must have spilled when he took them off before he left the house."

"He came prepared," Kent said.

"The blood in the foyer was a match for the father and had no logical explanation for being where it was," Buxton said. "The father clearly died in his bed. He couldn't have gone downstairs after getting shot through the heart. That was enough to get the PPD detectives looking for other trace evidence." He gave Breck another nod, and she clicked on the next picture. "That's when they found this."

Nina leaned forward and squinted at the screen. She made out a pale shoe print barely visible on the tile floor in the foyer. "That looks like a ghost print."

"They used an electrostatic lifter," Buxton said. "According to the report, the Phoenix crime scene techs laid a sheet of Mylar on the welcome mat inside the door. Once static electricity raised the dust to the surface, they turned the sheet over, and the shoe print was there."

Nina smiled. "Nice work."

"They sent the image of the tread to their crime lab," Buxton continued. "Ran a comparison with the shoes in our database and came up with a match for a Nike-brand running shoe two sizes larger than anything the father owned."

Breck pulled up a side-by-side shot of the tread from the crime scene and the sample from the database. They were identical except for wear marks on the shoe print taken at the murder scene.

Buxton picked up the second folder. "That's how we got a match to a case in New York City four years ago," he said. "NYPD investigated a case in Manhattan where a mother, father, and newborn baby girl were murdered in their apartment. The deaths were staged to look like a double-homicide-suicide. In that case, the family succumbed to carbon monoxide gas fumes. The father and baby were both found in their respective beds, but the mother was seated in an armchair in the master bedroom. Every window was closed and towels were stuffed under the doors."

Breck closed the digital file from Phoenix and clicked open the one from New York. An image of a four-floor walk-up apartment building popped up on the screen.

"There was a shoe print inside the apartment that didn't belong there too?" Nina asked.

"Not just any shoe print," Buxton said. "The same brand and size as this new case in Phoenix. The wear patterns on the soles could not be conclusively matched, but that's not surprising since it was a running shoe, and those don't usually last four years for a regular jogger. The suspect would have gotten new sneakers before committing the second crime."

"Both crimes were staged to look like double-murder-suicides." Wade looked up from his notepad. "Any other similarities?"

"Just one." Buxton paused until every eye was on him. "The case in New York occurred on February twenty-ninth."

"Just like in Phoenix." Nina turned to Wade. "Why would leap day be significant?"

Wade put down his pen and steepled his fingers. "Same victimology, same MO, if not in the manner of death, then in the way he tried to cover up his crimes by framing the mother."

"Same size and type of shoe print," Kent added. "Same date."

"And leaving no sign of a break-in," Breck said. "The killer would have to make entry in such a way that he wouldn't wake up the family and the police wouldn't find any evidence of his presence at the scene."

Buxton nodded. "I'm willing to concede that these two cases are related."

"The next question is, are there more?" Wade seemed to be thinking out loud. "Has he succeeded in getting other cases closed as homicide-suicides over the years?"

Nina picked up his train of thought. "If he managed to hide his crimes, there would be no further investigation by the police, who probably wouldn't enter the case information into ViCAP because they believed the perpetrator was dead. There's one case near the West Coast and one on the East Coast. That means he could be committing murders misidentified as homicide-suicides anywhere in the country and it would be unlikely anyone would spot a pattern."

"Which would make recognizing a series nearly impossible," Breck said. "This guy is smart." She dragged her finger across the touch screen on her laptop, and Nina could see she was opening a new window. "We need to go back and check every leap day to search for any double-murder-suicides. I'll have to run a simultaneous scan in multiple databases."

"What about non-leap years?" Nina said. "We should check February twenty-eighth and March first on the years in between."

Buxton jerked his chin at Breck. "Expand the search parameters to include the week before and after the end of February."

"How far do we go back?" Nina said.

Buxton looked thoughtful. "Let's start with twenty years."

"On it." Breck tapped the keys. A moment later, she straightened. "I've got another one."

Nina leaned toward her. "Where and when?"

"In San Diego, four years before the one in New York." Breck clicked on one of the text boxes. "That one was closed as a double-murder-suicide." She elaborated, eyes on her screen. "A mother, father, and their infant daughter."

"Nothing between?" Kent asked.

"Nada," Breck said, still typing. "Wait, there are more showing up now in a different system. Older cases on prior leap days that might fit."

Buxton frowned. "Give me a chronological list."

"That should only take a— Oh, no way." Breck's eyes widened.

"What?" Nina couldn't read the scrolling screen fast enough.

Breck kept the cursor moving. "Starting at the beginning, there was one twenty years ago in Philly, then sixteen years ago in Chicago, then twelve years ago in Houston, then San Diego, New York, and now Phoenix."

"Are we sure twenty years ago was the beginning?" Buxton asked. "I chose that as an arbitrary starting point."

Breck resumed her typing. "Let's go back another twenty years before the Philly case." A minute later, she turned to Buxton. "The oldest incident I can find goes back twenty-eight years." She paled. "And you'll never believe where it all started."

Buxton, apparently not in the mood to guess, simply stared at her.

"Phoenix," Breck said. "There was a double-murder-suicide of two parents and their baby girl in Phoenix twenty-eight years ago. The next one was twenty-four years ago in LA."

"Then Philadelphia twenty years ago?" Nina asked, trying to keep the timeline straight.

"Exactly," Breck said.

"Whatever else is going on," Kent said, "we have a clear pattern. He only hits on leap day."

"Maybe not." Wade stroked his jaw. "Perhaps he's killed on other dates of significance to him." He turned to Breck. "Can you reconfigure the search to include the event type only?"

Breck's brows shot up. "You want me to look for all reported murder-suicides in the past thirty years?"

"Only ones that involve two parents and their infant child—and where the mother was the perpetrator," Wade said. "That should narrow the results considerably."

While Breck surfed the databases, Buxton addressed the rest of the group. "We can't be certain all the cases are related until we analyze the situation further. Remember that each one has been investigated and closed by local police years ago."

"True, but we also know this guy is careful," Nina said. "And he's had lots of practice."

Buxton glanced at Breck. "Any results yet?"

"This will take a while," she said, head down and fingers working the keyboard.

He turned to Wade. "What kind of profile would you create for this unsub?"

Referring to the perpetrator as an unsub, the FBI's term for *unknown subject*, made it clear Buxton considered this a series.

"I always like to start with victimology, and I'd prefer to review the rest of the case files before I go into any depth," Wade said. "One thing is for certain, though. We have a person who repeatedly murders entire families, including the most innocent victims of all—newborns."

"He's not schizophrenic, because this level of sophistication and planning demonstrates that he knows exactly what he's doing," Kent said, adding his observations to the mix. "That leaves one overriding conclusion." He looked around the room. "Our unsub is a psychopath."

Chapter 4

Two hours later, Nina stood back to study the whiteboard that covered most of one wall. "Why every four years?" She rested her hands on her hips. "Why leap day?"

No one answered. The keyboard clicked under Breck's fingers, Kent paced back and forth, and Wade cocked his head to one side as he peered over her shoulder at the crime scene collage. After the initial briefing, Buxton had traversed the room to sit at his desk and review expense reports while the team struggled to make sense of the senseless.

Photographs crowded the whiteboard's gleaming surface, held in place by circular magnets. The disturbing mural had slowly taken shape as Nina added snippets of information Breck printed from downloaded police files forwarded from around the country. Kent had devised a color-coded system using dry-erase markers to track their level of confidence about the initial findings in each suspected case.

Breck had completed her search for other double-murder-suicides that had occurred on different dates and non-leap years. Whether due to an eyewitness, a suicide note with confirmed handwriting analysis, or some other means, they had been able to confirm the original findings of the police reports for each of the cases except the ones on leap days. When all other incidents were eliminated, they were left with a total of eight separate incidents in seven different cities spanning twenty-eight years.

Nina examined the new data points. "Hold on a sec. If he committed murders every four years going back twenty-eight years, why do we have eight incidents instead of seven?"

"You're thinking that seven times four is twenty-eight." Breck smiled at her. "But you have to think of the first one as case zero. Then there's seven after that."

Nina felt her cheeks warm.

"Let's approach the unknown by examining the known," Wade said, saving her from the awkward moment. "What patterns are there regarding victimology?"

Kent stopped pacing to face the board. "The victims are similar in that they are relatively young couples with a first child born anywhere from six weeks to one day prior to the murders."

Wade nodded. "Their ethnicity and income levels vary, although none of the families would be considered economically disadvantaged."

"They all lived in metropolitan areas," Nina added. "There were no cases in rural communities. The housing is literally and figuratively all over the map," she went on. "The two most recent cases occurred in a Manhattan apartment and a large single-level estate in Phoenix."

"He has a reason behind what he's doing," Wade said. "If we can figure out what it is, we'll be a lot closer to putting a name to this guy."

Kent took a step closer to the whiteboard. "This is representational targeting."

Nina raised a brow. "Meaning what?"

"He selects victims that stand in for something or someone else. Based on the variety of cases, it's not their location, race, income level, profession, or religious affiliation."

Nina grasped the concept. "What they all have in common is the birth of their first child. That situation must mean something to him."

"Not just any first child either," Kent said. "In each case, it's a girl."

Nina processed that for a few moments. "So the suspect has a specific and symbolic target. He won't deviate from his pattern, which makes him highly mobile and a planner. How does he know the victims, or if he doesn't know them, how does he select them?"

"We need more data," Breck said from behind her laptop.

"Which means we'll have to get the police to reopen several closed cases," Wade said.

Kent blew out a sigh. "We're not going to be popular."

She knew what he meant. Having come to the FBI from a large local police department herself, she understood the resentment they might have toward Feds wading in and questioning their entire investigation and the conclusions they had drawn from it. Police detectives worked a lot more homicides than FBI agents and viewed themselves as the experts. The thought gave her an idea.

"Speaking of the different locations," she said to Breck. "Could you pull up the largest US cities by population going back thirty years?"

Breck's cheeks dimpled. "Lucky for you, I can multitask."

"Tell me if any of the cities where we have suspected cases is *not* in the top ten," Nina said.

"You're right." Breck looked up from her laptop a moment later. "Every city with a potential case is one of the ten biggest US cities."

"Interesting." Kent gave Nina an appreciative look. "Do you think that figures into his choice of target locations?"

Nina lifted a shoulder. "If you're trying to pass off one type of crime as another, maybe it would be better to choose a place where the detectives are trying to keep up with hundreds of murders each year rather than only a handful."

"You're saying he chose places where police would be more likely to take things at face value and move on to the next whodunit?" Kent asked.

She spoke up for her former colleagues. "That's not exactly what I meant. Big-city Homicide detectives can be swamped with cases. On the other hand, they've analyzed hundreds of crime scenes, and know what to look for."

"Which makes it even more curious that they were fooled," Kent said.

"*Might* have been fooled," Nina said. "We haven't confirmed anything yet."

Kent shook his head. "These cases have too much in common for coincidence."

"I don't believe in coincidence," Buxton said, getting up from his desk, where he had apparently been listening as he worked. "We're going to treat this as a series until we know otherwise." He crossed the room and stood next to Wade. "What does the profile look like now?"

Wade gestured toward Kent. "I concur with Kent's assessment of psychopathy."

Nina knew just enough psychology to be dangerous. "I'm not a psychologist," she said. "Although I play one on this team. Why a psychopath and not a sociopath?"

"There's a great deal of debate on the matter," Wade began. "In my opinion, you're *born* a psychopath, but you *become* a sociopath." At Nina's raised brow, he continued, "The term *psychopathy* has fallen out of favor, although Kent and I still use it sometimes. It's now called antisocial personality disorder, or ASPD, by clinicians. To put it in layman's terms, a person with ASPD isn't wired like the rest of us. They truly don't care if someone gets hurt as long as they get what they want. They have no ability to feel for others, although most have learned to mimic emotions to create the appearance of empathy and compassion when it serves them."

Nina was fascinated. "They can fake feelings they've never experienced?"

"Exactly." Wade warmed to what was evidently a favorite subject. "Because they can be well educated and hold steady jobs, they've learned to navigate the world of people who feel. They're not insane, so they can easily adapt to their environment and blend in."

Breck scooted back from her screen, apparently drawn to the conversation. "If they don't care what other people think, why do they bother to fake emotions at all?"

Wade shrugged. "To achieve their goals through manipulating others."

"It's one of the reasons someone with ASPD can pass a polygraph exam when they're lying," Kent said, adding his perspective. "Their autonomic nervous systems work differently. This has been conclusively shown through medical testing. They don't exhibit a stress response or any noticeable arousal in situations where most people would register fear or anger."

"Polygraphs test for involuntary autonomic responses," Wade said, clarifying the point. "Most people find maintaining a deception stressful, especially if the stakes are high, such as being questioned by police. Their bodies will exhibit signs of stress—signs they can't hide. On the other hand, someone without an internal reaction to lying won't move the needle."

Nina considered a practical application. "If I pointed a gun at someone with ASPD, they would—"

"Calmly go through the actions they should take to deal with the situation," Kent broke in. "They don't freeze up in life-or-death circumstances. If you catch them at the border with a hundred kilos of cocaine in the trunk of their car, they will casually answer your questions and won't sweat, stammer, or do anything else to make you suspicious."

"Damn," Breck said. "Cool as a root cellar in July."

Kent grinned at Breck's colorful turn of phrase before he went on. "Although they appear normal to others, brain scans of people with ASPD have verified that their thought processes are consistently atypical. The section of the prefrontal cortex where empathy normally manifests won't light up. In addition, the amygdala doesn't react to what most people would perceive as an alarming situation."

"Got it," Nina said. "So how does this help us?"

Wade was quick to respond. "Because he's been at this for almost three decades, I would put him in his late forties or fifties. His victims come from all races, so I'm not confident on that aspect yet." He paused a moment. "He's been successful at hiding most of his crimes, so I'd say he's highly intelligent. His ability to adhere to a schedule and plan carefully indicates an ability to control his impulses, which many people with ASPD lack."

"A self-disciplined psychopath." Nina gave Wade a sardonic smile.

"Which means he's more likely to have an established career," Wade said. "Probably in some kind of sales position. He's successful because he excels at upselling his customers or clients."

"Would he be a traveling salesman?" Buxton asked. "Is that why his crimes occur all over the country?"

"Possibly," Wade said. "But since he only strikes once every four years, it wouldn't be difficult to arrange time off for travel. His work schedule will, however, be a good way to eliminate suspects as we develop them. We can check to see who's been requesting leave every four years around the end of February."

"Question," Breck said. "You keep referring to the unsub as *he*. Why don't you think it's a woman?"

"There have certainly been plenty of female serial killers." Wade's gray brows drew together. "But I'm going with the research. The majority of women who commit multiple murders target people they know or who are in their care. Of those who attack strangers, most do not stalk their victims and break into their homes." He crossed his arms. "I'm confident this is a man."

"What else can we use to narrow our search?" Buxton asked.

"As a child with ASPD, he would not have developed self-control yet," Wade said. "He'd have had a history of violence toward others. Anyone he perceived as a threat or came between him and something he wanted would be in harm's way. He would have skipped school often, stolen things, gotten in trouble, and likely committed arson or become interested in fires somewhere along the line."

Nina remembered something she had heard about serial killers years ago. "What about bed-wetting and cruelty to animals?"

"I see you're familiar with the killer's triangle," Wade said. "Many have a history of bed-wetting, animal torture, and arson. I wouldn't be surprised if our suspect had all three in his background." He looked at Kent. "Anything to add?"

Kent shook his head. "The profile may not give us a lot to go on at this point," he said. "It's more of a way to narrow down a pool of suspects once we have a list to work with."

Nina kept coming back to the oddest part of the equation. "What is the significance of committing his crimes every four years on leap day?"

"That's a unique pattern," Wade said. "I haven't seen it before."

Breck gestured toward her computer. "I've been researching the number four. It has a lot of references throughout history. The four seasons, the four elements, the four directions on a compass—"

"The four horsemen of the apocalypse," Nina said.

Breck grinned. "That seems about right."

Kent walked over to the whiteboard to tap the various locations on the timeline with his finger. "Technically speaking, if he only kills on February twenty-ninth, he may not be completely disengaging between crimes."

"I don't follow," Buxton said. "There's a substantial time gap after each incident."

"He strikes every time leap day comes around," Kent said. "If all these cases we've identified turn out to be attributable to him, then he's never missed once."

Wade's next comment broke the silence that had followed Kent's observation. "We know for sure there are at least two cases because of the matching shoe prints. I'd like to get eyeballs on the freshest scene so we can get a better feel for what we're dealing with."

"For whatever reason, he's hit Phoenix twice," Breck said. "That's the location of the newest and the oldest cases—provided the one from twenty-eight years ago really is the first in the series."

"Why would he circle back to where he started?" Nina wondered out loud.

Wade turned to Buxton. "I'd like to go find out. Immediately, if not sooner."

Buxton's brows raised a fraction. "You all are scheduled for a Simunition exercise in Hogan's Alley tomorrow."

Their supervisor had arranged the training as the final component in his plan to have the team authorized for a pilot program he had spent the past four months developing. Wade and Kent were criminal profilers with the BAU, Breck was on extended loan from the Cyber Crime Unit, and Nina had previously been assigned as a criminal investigative agent in DC.

With agents normally stovepiped into highly specialized areas of expertise, Buxton had convinced the Bureau's hierarchy to test his proposal of a stand-alone hybrid unit. This new rapid-response team would be deployed in the field rather than analyzing cases from the confines of the BAU offices. If they performed well, similar units could follow, based around the country. If they failed, Buxton's career would take a turn for the worse.

"I'll reschedule the training for the weekend," Buxton said on a sigh.

Breck had apparently opened another window on her computer. "There aren't many nonstop commercial flights to Phoenix," she said, sliding her mouse around. "And they're all booked solid. I'll try to find ones with only one or two stops."

Nina hated waiting. She hated layovers even more. She glanced at the boss. "Given the severity of these cases, maybe you could make . . . other arrangements?"

"BAU profilers fly commercial," Buxton said.

"We're not profilers." Nina swept out an arm to encompass the entire group. "We're a new hybrid team in a pilot program."

Buxton looked like he was fighting a smile. "Don't push it, Agent Guerrera."

Chapter 5

Hermosa Vista Apartments
Springfield, Virginia

The drive home to her apartment in Springfield normally took Nina forty-five minutes in rush hour traffic, but the torrential rain had doubled her travel time. After climbing the stairs to her fourth-floor walkup, Nina had barely taken off her drenched raincoat when she heard a knock at her door.

She blew out a sigh, certain it was her frequent visitor, Bianca Babbage, her next-door neighbor's teenage foster daughter. The girl had an uncanny knack for knowing the instant Nina got home. After looking through the peephole, Nina opened her door to Bianca, who held a slice of cake on a dessert plate.

"Saved you something from my birthday party." Bianca darted a glance over her shoulder before turning back to Nina. "Had to hide it from the roving horde, or there wouldn't be anything left."

Bianca often grumbled about the younger children her foster parents had taken in, but the complaints didn't fool Nina. Mr. and Mrs. Gomez had filled their empty nest with children who needed a loving home, which made their apartment a bit crowded at times. Bianca stopped by Nina's place for a respite but never stayed long. Nina suspected Bianca secretly craved the mixture of bedlam and joy happy little ones brought to a home.

"Feliz cumpleaños," Nina said, aware that Bianca—who wasn't Latina—had studied Spanish for the sole purpose of eavesdropping on her foster parents' private conversations. The girl had a habit of sticking her pierced nose into other people's business.

"Gracias," Bianca responded to the happy birthday wish. "As of tonight, I'm fully cooked—as in, totally done."

Understanding passed between them. Bianca was now eighteen, officially aging out of the foster system. No longer a ward of the state, she was free to make her own way in the world. Or to fail miserably.

Nina opened her arms and waited, knowing better than to force a hug on a foster child with a background of abuse. This knowledge came from her own experience, and Bianca was one of the few people Nina allowed into her personal space.

After the briefest hesitation, Bianca stepped over the threshold and into Nina's embrace, balancing the plate in one hand. The feel of the girl's slight body brought Nina back to the first time they'd met four years ago, when Nina was an officer in the Fairfax County Police Department.

Bianca had run away from yet another foster home, and Nina had spent most of her shift tracking her down. Bianca had an IQ north of 160, which made her a target for bullies at school. Her petite stature made it difficult to defend herself against those who used the system to find victims for other types of abuse. Nina was no genius, but she could read the young girl's story in the dark circles under her eyes and the half-hidden welts on her slender arms. At the time, Bianca had reminded Nina of little Caitlin, and all her fiercest protective instincts had kicked in. The scars crisscrossing Nina's own back bore witness to what she had suffered, and she would not allow the same thing to happen to another child.

Working closely with Child Protective Services, Nina had arranged to have Bianca immediately removed from her current living situation and criminally charged her foster parents. Unwilling to toss Bianca back into the system to take her chances, Nina had been overjoyed to find a caring home for her in the apartment next door. When Nina told Mrs. Gomez about Bianca, it hadn't taken long for Mrs. G to get her husband on board. The middle-aged couple had since taken in three more children and were loving every boisterous, chaotic minute of it.

After releasing Bianca from a gentle hug, Nina was about to close the door when Mrs. Gomez emerged from her apartment, three small children swarming around her legs.

"I knew you'd be here," Mrs. G said to Bianca, her Chilean accent lending the words a lyrical tone. She turned warm brown eyes on Nina. "I was just bringing over some *plateada*." She lifted a small casserole dish with a glass lid.

The rich aroma of the pot roast made Nina's stomach rumble. Her next-door neighbor loved to fuss over her by bringing delicious home-made treats, convinced that Nina needed food, which Mrs. G equated with affection.

Three little blurs raced past Mrs. G into Nina's apartment. Jumping and laughing, they seemed to fill the space from wall to wall.

Bianca gave an exaggerated eye roll as they all migrated into the kitchen. Now eighteen going on thirty, Bianca had nearly completed her undergraduate degree in computer science from George Washington University in DC. She was currently under consideration for a full-ride scholarship to get her master's in biochemistry.

Mrs. G gave her eldest foster daughter a reproachful look. "You should not do that with your eyes, *mi'ja*, they'll get stuck way up inside your head."

Mi'ja. The common term of endearment stirred Nina's heart, as it always did when she heard it. As a child who had never known her own family, she had longed to hear someone call her "my daughter" when she was growing up.

There were times Nina heard laughter in the next apartment. In her innermost core, the place hidden by a layer of carefully constructed walls, she still sometimes longed for a family of her own. For this reason, more than any other, she allowed Mrs. G to dote on her. Maybe a secret part of her even welcomed it.

Mrs. G glanced at the slice of cake now resting on the counter. "It's tres leches, Bianca's favorite."

The gorgeous dessert, with its dense yellow base covered in fluffy white frosting and topped with strawberries, had Nina's mouth watering. The "three milks" involved in making the cake were whole, condensed, and evaporated. In addition, whipped heavy cream was used to make the frosting. Definitely not a dessert for the lactose intolerant.

Little Gustavo, who everyone called Gus, stopped running around long enough to grin up at Nina. At six years old, he was tall for his age, with big brown eyes and thick black hair cut into a flattop-style crew cut that would have made Kent proud.

"My birthday is in five days," Gus said, holding up five fingers. "You can have some of my cake too. It's going to have gobs of sprinkles."

"Lucky I like to bake," Mrs. G said to Nina. "Don't you have a birthday in a couple of weeks? I can make you something special too. What would you like?"

"Don't go to any trouble," Nina said quietly. "I don't celebrate birthdays."

While growing up, she had learned not to expect visits from Santa, the Easter Bunny, or the tooth fairy. Birthdays had been yet another disappointment. If not for the need to fill out forms and applications, she would have long since forgotten the date social workers had assigned to her.

The little boy's excitement pulled her away from dark thoughts. She was happy Gus would have a nice birthday. Happy for him that Mrs. G would bake his favorite cake. Happy that he was with a loving foster family.

No one should be forgotten.

Chapter 6

The following morning, Nina was with the rest of the team at thirty thousand feet on their way across the country. She wasn't sure how Buxton had managed it, but their supervisor had gotten them access to one of the FBI's leased Gulfstream jets for the flight to Sky Harbor Airport in Phoenix.

Nina had already scoured police reports on the recent investigation of the Phoenix murders and had opened her laptop to research news stories about the earliest potential case from nearly three decades ago. Reading through old articles about the incident, she became increasingly fascinated by the details.

Kent caught her eye from across the small table between them. "You look intrigued."

"This case got a lot of media attention at the time," she told him. "I was just watching a TV newsclip from the day the family was found in their home. The reporter interviewed everyone in the neighborhood. The lady next door said what happened reminded her of *La Llorona.* The nickname spread like wildfire, and everyone started calling it the Llorona case."

Breck's head popped up from her computer. "The what-what?"

Nina realized the others had stopped what they were doing to listen. "The legend of *La Llorona,*" she said to them. "It's a combination ghost story and folktale in Latino cultures. I've heard several variations."

"What does *La Llorona* mean?" Breck asked.

"It's Spanish for *the weeping woman* or *the wailing woman*," Nina said.

"I'll bite," Breck said, her southern drawl more evident than usual. "What's the deal with this woman, and why is she crying?"

Nina considered how best to convey the sheer creepiness of the story that had scared her, and so many others, as a child. "Like I said, there are many different versions. The things most accounts have in common are that a wife becomes distraught when her husband falls in love with another woman and drowns their children to punish him for his infidelity. Then, filled with remorse for what she's done, she takes her own life. In some versions, she kills her unfaithful husband before doing herself in."

Breck arched a brow. "You heard this as a little kid?"

Nina nodded. "Mostly from other Latino kids in the foster system. I remember being totally creeped out when the older kids warned us little ones that *La Llorona* is doomed to roam the earth forever, searching for her lost children. If she caught one of us, she would drown us too. For extra drama, one of the older kids would hide in a closet and cry out, *'¿Dónde están mis hijos?'* at the end of the story."

"That means, 'where are my children,'" Kent said to Wade and Breck.

Nina recalled that he spoke four languages. She nodded. "It's what *La Llorona* is supposed to moan as she wanders."

"I swear," Breck said, "the way you grew up sounds like *Lord of the Flies*. I don't know how you turned out so well."

Nina looked away. "Yeah, we all pretty much ran screaming to our beds while the older kids laughed." She avoided responding to the rest of Breck's comment.

"I'm guessing the details of the first case had something in common with the folktale?" Wade asked.

"We still don't have the case file for that incident from the Phoenix police," Breck said. "If we request all the investigative material, they'll have to pull it from their archives."

Nina pointed at her computer screen. "According to media reports, the crime scene investigation revealed a stash of love letters that had apparently been kept in one of the husband's shoeboxes in the bedroom closet."

"I can't believe the PPD would release those kinds of details," Wade said. "They would guard the specifics back then just like they do nowadays."

"The reporter spoke to someone close to the investigation." Nina air-quoted the last few words. "The unnamed source told him the wife had apparently discovered her husband's affair when she was cleaning out the closet. Their newborn baby girl was drowned in the bathroom, the husband shot in the face with a revolver, and the wife died of a self-inflicted gunshot wound to her heart."

"If it's staged, someone did their homework," Kent said. "The scene includes a lot of symbolism. The wife shooting her husband in the face indicates a desire to obliterate him, like she didn't want to look him in the eyes again. Shooting herself in the heart represents what his infidelity did to her."

"And the baby?" Nina asked.

Kent considered a moment before answering. "Water symbolizes the unconscious. Submerging the product of their love into the unconscious could be a way of admitting that she should have known about her husband's inner secrets and was in denial."

"Whoa there." Breck gave him a dubious look. "That's a pretty big stretch."

"I agree," Kent said, apparently unperturbed by the debate. "But the deaths of the mother and father would certainly work even if someone had only a very basic idea of how to stage a crime scene."

Nina tried to put herself in the mind of the unsub. "If this was his first case, do you think he might have studied some literature or other materials to get ideas about how to lead police where he wanted them to go?"

"He's an organized killer," Wade said. "It's highly likely."

"Looks like it worked." Nina glanced back down at the screen. "In a news conference, the police spokesperson said the mother, who had just given birth, may have succumbed to postpartum depression when she killed her husband and child before turning the gun on herself."

"Revenge filicide," Wade said.

Everyone but Kent looked confused.

Wade's mouth flattened into a hard line. "*Filicide* is the technical term for the murder of one's own offspring. Revenge filicide is just what it sounds like—killing your child to get back at someone else. Someone who loves that child dearly."

She thought she knew the answer but asked the question anyway. "You've seen this?"

"Yes." The word came out as a harsh whisper.

Not for the first time, Nina contemplated the inhumanity Wade had observed in his chosen area of expertise. Crimes against children were among the most difficult to investigate. She could only imagine the toll witnessing so much depravity had taken on him after pursuing hundreds of cases.

Kent broke the silence that followed. "Studies have shown that when the child is under eight years old, the mother is usually the culprit. That changes when the children are older."

"I could read a thousand studies on the subject," Breck said, touching her fingertips to her heart. "But I'll never understand it."

Nina agreed. "Children are defenseless against adult brutality." She stopped herself before adding that she had the scars to prove her point. Wade gave her a knowing look. The rest of the team was aware of her background as well. There was no need to elaborate.

"To paraphrase Gandhi," Wade said, "you can measure a society by how they treat their most vulnerable."

"When the victims are infants or the mother has recently given birth, postpartum depression is usually suspected," Kent went on. "Those cases grab headlines because they seem so antithetical to motherhood, but statistically, fathers are far more likely to kill their own children."

"So detectives investigating these cases would have no reason to question the narrative laid out for them?" Nina said.

Wade's voice sounded strained when he spoke. "As you said earlier, these are seasoned Homicide detectives. They've seen it all. Like me, they would view the situation as tragic but plausible."

The starkness in Wade's gray eyes matched the increasingly grim atmosphere inside the plane. To break the mood, Nina clicked on another media report from the old case in Phoenix.

"According to a follow-up news story a few days later, the ME didn't find anything to contradict the police theory and ruled the causes of death to be homicide for the father and child and suicide for the mother."

Buxton, who had been sitting toward the back of the plane, spoke for the first time. "Put your stuff away, people, we're starting our descent."

Nina closed her laptop and peered out the small window to survey the vast beige-and-brown desertscape below, so different from the Virginia foothills in Quantico that it might have been another planet. She was leaving the damp early spring chill of the mid-Atlantic East Coast to arrive in the sun-bleached warmth of the Southwest. Buxton had warned them to pack for balmy weather, and he hadn't been kidding. She shed her sweater, grateful to be wearing a light blouse underneath. As the plane banked, circling lower, she felt an almost tangible shift into a different world.

Chapter 7

Perspiration prickled Nina's scalp as she rode in the black Suburban with her team. After landing, Buxton had opted to catch a taxi directly to the Phoenix FBI field office to set up their workspace while the rest of the team clambered into an SUV with Special Agent Paul Ginsberg, who was assigned to the PFO.

"They call the Phoenix metropolitan area 'the valley of the sun,'" Ginsberg was saying as he steered the vehicle onto the freeway. "I've been assigned here two years, and I still can't take the heat. You're lucky to be coming here in the spring."

Nina looked out the tinted window at the clear blue sky, so different from the cold, rainy gray back east. "The weather is gorgeous."

"That's because it's still winter where you're coming from. I should know, I was born and raised on Long Island." He smiled. "The winters here are fantastic, but the summers . . . yeesh."

This was her second trip to Phoenix—neither had been during the summer. From what she had seen so far, the place seemed like a balmy paradise.

Ginsberg took an exit and headed toward the northeast part of the sprawling city. "I'm sure you'd like to get to your hotel, but we need to swing by the crime scene first if you want to go over it with the lead detective."

"It's still an active scene?" she asked, surprised there would be anything to examine. "The murders took place three days ago."

Ginsberg maneuvered onto a side street. "The initial investigation and evidence collection have been completed, but we've asked the local police not to release the scene yet." He shrugged. "It's not an issue, because nobody lives there anymore. The whole family was killed in the attack, and the relatives are trying to sort out ownership. There's a mortgage on the property, so the bank is wading in. Because of the title question, nobody's hired a crew to clean and decontaminate the house either. Long story short, we have free run of the place for the time being."

Kent looked at Ginsberg. "Has the house been secured?"

Ginsberg nodded. "We reached out to the Phoenix police Homicide Unit to tell them your team is on the ground, and they sent the lead detective to meet us there. Since you're here at their request, the PPD has agreed to work directly with us, starting with taking us through the scene and going over everything in their reports."

She was pleased to jump straight into the investigation. Viewing the space where a crime occurred in person was always better than looking at two-dimensional photos and reading someone else's observations about what they thought was important.

As Ginsberg swung the SUV into a residential area, high-end shops and restaurants gave way to the rolling greens of a manicured golf course. Nina assumed they were headed into the swanky part of town. They stopped at the front gate of an enclosed community.

Nina watched Ginsberg punch in a series of numbers before the gate slowly opened. "PPD gave me the code," he said. "It's different for every user, but the police use zero-nine-one-one for entry."

"Easy enough to remember," Breck said.

They continued down a wide street lined with blooming plants and verdant foliage that Nina was sure would never grow in the desert city without plenty of irrigation. After passing several massive residences, they pulled into the long driveway of a Mediterranean-style estate.

Nina took in the tile roof, stone siding, and graceful arches. "I'm assuming a house like this would have an alarm system. What happened?"

Ginsberg brought the Suburban to a stop next to an empty unmarked police car. "The detective must be waiting for us inside. He can explain about the security better than I can."

They all got out of the SUV and climbed a set of wide stone steps to reach a pair of towering front doors. Four strips of yellow crime scene tape across the entrance had been cut and dangled down.

Kent rang the bell as everyone waited behind him. When the door swung open, the former SEAL's large frame blocked Nina's view inside. She saw Kent's spine stiffen as he stood transfixed on the threshold.

After a moment's pause, Kent's harsh words echoed off the arched interior ceiling. "No. Fucking. Way."

"Special Agent Kent," a familiar male voice carried from inside. "Nice to see you too." The tone oozed sarcasm.

Nina slipped past Kent and held out her hand in greeting. "Glad to be working with you again, Detective Perez."

The Homicide detective's entire demeanor changed, white teeth contrasting with tan skin as his face split into a grin. He clasped her outstretched hand. "I had no idea you were back in town, Nina."

"You two know each other?" Ginsberg asked, evidently noting that Perez had used her first name.

"You recall the high-profile case that brought us to Phoenix a while back?" she asked Ginsberg.

He gave her a sardonic look. "Who doesn't?"

"Detective Perez and I partnered up to check out leads." She didn't add that Perez and Kent hadn't hit it off at the time, nearly coming to blows.

"Why did your team fly all the way out here?" Perez asked. "We know the case might be related to one in New York, but there must be more to it."

Wade responded before anyone else had a chance. "Can you take us through the scene first? Then we'll get into the particulars."

She caught Perez's frown.

"What?" Wade said, obviously spotting the taut expression as well.

Perez crossed his arms. "Let's just say it isn't the first time Feds landed in the middle of our investigation and didn't want to provide any information."

"We'll play nice," Nina said quickly. "I promise. Just fill us in on this case first."

"I'll hold you to that," Perez said, turning toward the interior of the house. "Here's how we think it went down," he began. "The subject entered the home through the front door at about two in the morning. Everyone was asleep."

Listening to Perez, Nina recalled that police tended to use terms like *subject* or *perp*—depending on the department—to describe an unidentified assailant, while the FBI favored *unsub*. One of many small shifts she'd made when changing careers.

"I would expect a place like this to be alarmed," Nina said, reiterating her earlier question before she got sidetracked by other crime scene details. "How did he get in?"

"Defeated a wireless security system," Perez said. "We figure the subject used a remote signal to jam the frequency. That way, when he opened the door, the sensors didn't detect a separation of contact points, so there was no alarm activation."

"That's pretty sophisticated," Breck said, speaking for the first time since they'd entered the home. "He had to know what he was doing, or he could have accidentally overloaded the system and set off the alarm."

"Everything this guy did at the scene indicates careful planning," Perez said.

Breck, who seemed to understand electronics better than the rest of them, pressed the issue. "Was the front door unlocked?"

Perez shook his head. "There is no sign of forced entry. We believed he either picked the lock or climbed inside an unlocked window."

"Is it possible to pick a deadbolt?" Breck asked.

Nina followed her gaze to the circular silver lock above the door-knob. "A few years ago I arrested a burglar who had a set of picks that could have opened this lock in forty seconds," she said. "It's totally doable."

"Well organized, well prepared, well executed," Wade said. "We have reason to believe the unsub had plenty of time to check out his targets and study their security."

Before Perez could start asking more questions about why the team from Quantico was there, Nina redirected the conversation, prodding him for more details. "Speaking of the targets, we read the preliminary report on the flight here, but we don't have any updated information about the victims."

"The couple was living in a high-rise condo downtown until the wife, Meaghan Doyle, found out she was pregnant. She and her husband, Tom, moved into this upscale gated community about six months ago."

Breck perked up. "Does the gate record which access codes were used and when?"

"We already asked the HOA," Perez said. "The system doesn't record that information."

Nina wanted to keep the discussion on the victims. "The report said the Doyles were doctors?"

"He was an orthopedic surgeon, and she was an ophthalmologist, both in their late thirties. They waited to have their first child, presumably due to their professional commitments."

They followed Perez to the bottom of the staircase leading up to the second floor as he continued his narration of the scene. "Crime scene techs found no evidence that the subject went through the entire house. He seems to have zeroed in on his target area once he entered, then left after he finished without taking or touching anything that we could discover."

"Because he was done here," Kent said. "He's efficient and sticks to his purpose."

Nina scaled the steps, glancing at family photos on the wall as she passed. Smiling faces filled with joy. The kind of happy family she had never known. The kind of family that would have been excited to welcome a new life.

"How did the unsub know the parents wouldn't be awake feeding the baby?" she wondered out loud.

"The question we keep asking ourselves," Perez said. "He either took a big chance or he had some way to know what they were up to inside the house."

"This unsub left nothing to chance," Wade said with absolute certainty. "He knew they were asleep somehow."

Nina steeled herself for the grim reality of what the unsub had done. She stopped in the hallway and glanced at Perez. "How did this go down?"

"We're not sure, but we believe he suffocated the baby first," Perez said, grief flickering momentarily in his dark eyes. "Then he carried her body out of the nursery down the hall into the master bedroom. The parents used a baby monitor, but apparently didn't wake up until the killer fired his weapon at the father, which makes me think they kept the bedroom doors open as a backup in case something went wrong with the monitor. That way, the killer would have been able to push each door open without making any noise."

"A lot of people put a newborn's crib in the bedroom with them for the first few months," Breck said. "It's what my sister did."

Wade looked grim. "I don't think he would have changed his plans if that were the case here."

"I don't either," Perez said. "He took out the father with a single gunshot to the heart. We figure he wanted to neutralize the husband quickly."

"Obviously, the sound would have awakened the wife," Nina said. "And probably a few neighbors."

Perez shook his head. "These are five-acre lots, and the homes are well insulated. No one reported any noise that night."

After inspecting the nursery, which appeared undisturbed except for detritus from crime scene technicians collecting evidence, they walked down the hall into the master bedroom, retracing the killer's steps. Nina followed the others inside, taking in the blood-soaked mattress and stained sheets.

"Ballistics indicates the subject was standing about fifteen feet away when he shot the father," Perez said. "Yet somehow, he managed to make a perfect kill shot in the dark."

"Night vision," Kent said. "The technology was used during the Second World War. And maybe a laser sight too. They've been around since the eighties."

"You think this unsub is in the military?" Nina asked him.

Kent's background in special ops meant he had been deployed on many nighttime missions.

"I don't." Kent didn't hesitate. "But I'll bet he's had weapons training somewhere along the line. He could have purchased military-style equipment online or at a private gun club."

She agreed. If the murders had been going on for decades, the killer wouldn't be able to continue in a military career where he had little control over his deployments. Plus, the kind of personality Kent and Wade described would not fit into an institution that demanded self-sacrifice and strict adherence to rules set by others in command.

"What about one of those militias?" Breck asked.

"This guy seems like a loner," Kent said. "And he's cagey enough to keep his gun collection a secret to avoid drawing attention to himself. He probably trains alone too."

"Plenty of places outside the city to set up target practice," Perez said. "Phoenix is like an oasis surrounded by hundreds of miles of desert." He continued to the master bathroom and picked up where he left off. "We believe he used the baby to control the mother, possibly threatened to harm the little girl if she didn't cooperate."

Nina swallowed the obscenity welling in her throat as she put herself in the mother's position. "The poor woman didn't know her daughter was already dead, so she'd do anything the unsub told her to."

"That's what we think," Perez said. "Apparently, he ordered her to get into the bathtub, because there's no evidence that she was dragged in there by force."

Nina looked at the streaks of blood splashed against the smooth white porcelain tiles just above the rim of the oversize soaking tub. The body was long gone, but she could make out the stained imprint of the woman who had died there a few short days ago.

As Wade had taught her, she put herself in the mind of both the victim and the killer. "I wonder if she knew at the very end," she said quietly.

"Knew she was going to die?" Perez asked.

"And that the rest of her family was dead," she said. "Including her baby."

Wade glanced at her sharply. "I was thinking the same thing. I believe this unsub would have wanted her to know."

"Why do you say that?" Perez asked.

Wade walked out of the bathroom, back through the bedroom, and into the hallway as he spoke. "There was no sexual assault, no robbery, no vandalism or destruction of property. The person who did this had another motive." He paused and turned to the others, who had gathered around him. "He wanted to inflict as much mental torment as possible."

"But the father didn't even know what hit him, and neither did the baby," Perez pointed out.

"Exactly." Wade seemed completely confident in his conclusions. "The target of his rage—his fury, his retribution—was the mother."

The house grew silent as everyone considered the theory.

Wade continued his assessment. "After torturing her with the worst pain any mother could possibly feel, he framed her for his crime so she would be further humiliated in death. Everyone would think she killed her own family, a crime so repugnant that it flies in the face of everything we think about motherhood."

Kent nodded. "When we find this guy, he's going to have major issues with his mother."

What kind of soulless creature would do that? Nina had run across many bad people in her life, but now, striving to grasp the dark mind that had committed this horrific crime, she sensed evil in its purest form.

Chapter 8

An hour later, Nina glanced out the SUV's window to see a massive metal sculpture featuring a fingerprint mounted to a cement base standing beside a towering saguaro cactus. Etched into the other side of the cement were the words FBI PHOENIX DIVISION. Ginsberg steered into the parking lot of a boxy five-story cream-and-rust-colored building behind imposing wrought-iron fencing. The exterior was unbroken except for staggered rectangular windows. If Nina had to sum up her overall impression of the structure, she would have called it *postmodern desert*. On the outside, at least.

"This is our new facility," Ginsberg said, pride evident in his voice. "We relocated from downtown to the north part of the city a few years ago. This is much more up to date, and it's farther away from the traffic and congestion."

He led them inside the front doors to a reception area, where he greeted the woman working at the front desk. Apparently expecting them, she smiled and gestured toward a scanner. Nina duly pulled out her creds and access card, waving them in front of the beam along with the rest of her team. Ginsberg held open the entry door to the office area for them.

Trailing him, Nina surveyed the contemporary office space. Members of her former unit at the Washington field office in DC would have killed for this kind of spacious, sleek, well-designed work area. The

WFO was cramped, and no amount of remodeling could create more square footage.

Ginsberg opened a double door that led to a windowless conference room. "This will be your base of operations while you're here. We've set it up as a combination command center and briefing area."

A rectangular graphite-colored conference table occupied the middle of the room and an expansive whiteboard took up most of one wall while four flatscreens were mounted on another.

Breck strode directly to a monitor and keyboard resting on the far end of the table. "Dibs."

No one argued.

After Nina and Wade took seats on one side of the table, Kent and Buxton sat opposite them. Ginsberg, who had disappeared while they looked around, returned a few moments later with a slender Asian woman in her late forties.

"This is Special Agent in Charge Jennifer Wong. She'll be keeping tabs on the investigation."

Buxton stood to shake her hand. "Supervisory Special Agent Gerard Buxton."

Nina had grown accustomed to working with Buxton, but Wong oversaw the entire Phoenix field division, so she outranked him. Nina wasn't sure how this additional layer of managerial oversight would play out. How involved would Wong be? Would she break Nina's crayons and send her home for coloring outside the lines? If the Phoenix SAC turned out to be a stickler for rules and regulations, that could be a problem.

Wong took a seat at the head of the table, and Ginsberg sat to her right. "I won't be present at most meetings, but I wanted an overview of the case," she said, then turned to Buxton. "After that, you can keep me apprised of developments."

Nina glanced at Wade. Hopefully, Wong wasn't going to be territorial.

"Why don't we go to your office and I can loop you in on what we've got so far?" Buxton said. "The team can move forward more quickly without reviewing our progress to date."

As the two left the room, Nina appreciated that her boss had neatly removed management from the space, leaving the field to the players.

Ginsberg watched them go before addressing the rest of the group. "I've been detailed to help your team with whatever you need."

"Much appreciated," Breck said to him. "You know this city better than we do."

"I'm glad you got us into that crime scene before it was cleaned up," Wade said to him, apparently anxious to get started on analysis. "Helped me get a better feel for the unsub."

Wade hadn't spoken much on the trip from the Doyle home to the Phoenix field office, but he had apparently spent the time analyzing what he'd seen.

"The staging was very elaborate," Wade began. "I believe it served two purposes." He raised a finger. "First, to create the story he wanted police to believe." He raised another finger. "Second, to satisfy an emotional need."

"Then you believe the staging is part of the MO as well as the signature?" Nina asked him.

Ginsberg shook his head. "Signature?"

"I can explain it best with an illustration," Wade said to him. "Imagine a killer who abducts random women in Central Park after dark in a blitz attack from behind and strangles them. That's his MO. He draws a circle on their stomachs with a black marker after they die. That constitutes his signature." Wade steepled his fingers, warming to his subject. "Something about those rituals fulfills a need that has nothing to do with how he commits the murders."

"Does he have a compulsion to kill, or to perform the rituals?" Ginsberg asked.

"Both," Wade said simply. "But one element is changeable, while the other is constant." He paused briefly. "Let's say the police increase patrols in the park, so the killer begins breaking into women's homes and strangling them in their beds. His MO has changed, but he continues to draw a circle on their bodies, which is his signature. That's how we can link the crimes even though some involve an opportunistic attack in a public place, while others involve a burglary with a preselected victim."

Ginsberg appeared to consider the information. "Did you come up with that?"

"Wish I could take credit," Wade said. "But the term *signature* was coined by John Douglas, who was one of the first FBI profilers decades ago."

Nina leaned forward, drawing the conversation back to the staged crime scenes. "Applying that concept to our unsub, part of the reason he poses the bodies in certain positions speaks to what spurred him to kill in the first place?"

Wade nodded. "As I said before, this all goes back to his mother somehow."

"You think she abused him?" Breck asked.

"Not necessarily in the way you and I would define abuse," Wade said. "But the unsub has interpreted her actions as a severe injustice or personal insult. What we're looking for is a point of inflection."

"What do you mean?" Nina asked.

"An event that starts a person on a different course," Wade said, moving his hands in the air to illustrate. "A change in trajectory. If it never happened, the person's entire life would have been different."

Nina thought she understood. "If we can figure out what triggered this guy, that would help ID him?"

"Exactly." Wade turned to Kent, who had yet to offer his own opinion. "What did you see?"

"Ritual and undoing, along with a heavy dose of displacement," Kent said.

Nina blew out a sigh. "I speak English and Spanish but not psychobabble."

Kent chuckled. "Those are some of Sigmund Freud's ego defense mechanisms. Basically, the human mind always works to defend itself against inconvenient truths. According to Freud, we've all developed a variety of coping mechanisms."

"Okay," Nina said. "But how did you see that in the crime scene?"

"A husband who gets angry at his boss, then goes home and beats his wife because he can't punch the one who signs his paycheck is using displacement. In this case, the unsub took out his rage over his own family, especially about his mother, on the Doyles."

"What about ritual and undoing?" Nina asked.

"The unsub is trying to compensate for his bad feelings about himself by performing certain rituals that act as countermeasures." At Nina's raised brow, he continued, "Similar to someone who keeps washing his hands to cleanse himself of imaginary stains, the unsub is trying to go back and fix something in his past by reenacting a scenario he's created to represent what occurred. Unfortunately, like all coping mechanisms, it never solves the problem, so he's stuck in an endless cycle of repetition."

A flash of insight struck Nina. "Whatever went wrong—his point of inflection—happened on a leap day. That's why he tries to fix it every leap day. When it doesn't work, he has to wait another four years to try again."

Wade gave her an appreciative nod. "I agree. Whenever we have a pool of suspects, we should look into that date to see what was going on in their lives."

"To do that, we need to develop some suspects," Nina said. "Whatever his deep-seated personal reasons for killing the family were, it looks like he was trying to recreate the Llorona case where he succeeded twenty-eight years ago. Only he failed this time. Why would someone so experienced make errors?"

Breck shrugged. "Maybe he hasn't been keeping up with technology and forensic science."

"Are you kidding?" Nina said. "You can learn enough from searching the internet to get a bachelor's in forensics these days."

"Then what?" Breck looked at the two profilers. "A subconscious desire to get caught?"

Wade snorted. "Not this guy."

"Is he devolving?" Nina asked, recalling the broad categories for killers. "Going from organized to disorganized?"

"I don't think so," Wade said. "I believe he legitimately made mistakes on the two most recent cases, and it caught up to him."

"What will that do to his mindset?" Nina asked.

"Most likely, trigger him to act out in a new way," Wade said. "In the past, he had everything under control, which is essential to this guy. His narcissism and his antisocial personality compel him to orchestrate every part of the drama he's playing out."

Nina wanted a way to turn the insight into action. "Getting back to my previous question. How do we grind up all this sausage to develop a suspect?"

The room grew quiet, silencing even the clacking of Breck's keyboard while everyone gave it some thought.

"He travels to various cities to commit the crimes," Breck finally said. "But we can't check flight manifests going back twenty-eight years, and we also don't know where his home base is, so that would be pointless anyway."

Nina looked at Kent. "Earlier you mentioned night vision and laser sights," she said. "How would he get on a plane with that kind of gear and a gun?"

"I can answer that one for you," Breck said. "I made a spreadsheet. The only murders involving firearms were committed in Phoenix."

"The oldest and most recent cases are the only ones he didn't have to fly to," Nina said, latching on to the idea of the unsub's starting point. She turned to Wade. "You've always maintained that a serial killer's first crime is the most revealing. In this case, the location of his first crime is also the only city he's hit twice. When things went south on him in New York, what if he came back to Phoenix to push the reset button?"

"The place where it all began," Wade said. "A place of comfort, a place of strength . . . a home base." He stroked his jaw in a characteristic gesture of concentration. "Highly likely that he either lives inside the Phoenix city limits or somewhere close by. I would estimate no more than two hours' drive."

Breck connected the terminal where she was working to one of the flatscreens on the wall. In less than a minute, she had pulled up a map of Arizona and generated a red circle in a radius around Phoenix. "The largest cities that fit that description are Tucson, Mesa, and Scottsdale, in order of population," she said.

Wade gazed at the map. "He may have killed people all over the country, but he lives somewhere inside that circle."

Nina stood beside Wade, staring at the map as if she could see the unsub. "We're here now," she muttered. "And we're coming for you."

Chapter 9

Nina zipped her empty suitcase and stashed it under one of the two queen beds. "This place is nice," she said, looking around the spacious hotel room.

"Government rates," Breck said. "Otherwise, Uncle Sam wouldn't foot the bill for pricey digs like these."

Ginsberg had driven the team downtown to the Phoenix Royal Suites after their meeting at the command center in the PFO. SAC Wong had arranged for another agent to follow in a second black Suburban, leaving the keys with Buxton so they would have a Bureau car at their disposal during their stay.

At check-in Nina and Breck had been assigned to share the suite that adjoined Wade and Kent's. Buxton had a room to himself across the hall. They had each showered and changed into casual clothes, not planning to go out again for the night.

A light knock at the door separating the pair of suites interrupted their conversation. They exchanged glances before Nina crossed the room. "Who is it?"

"It's Wade and Kent." The exasperated response came from Kent. "Who the hell else would it be?"

She flipped the lock and opened the door. Kent didn't wait for an invitation, striding straight past her. "Turn on the news."

"I could've been in my undies," Breck said, putting a hand on her hip. "Could've been just out of the shower and buck naked."

Kent made no response, snatching up the remote before Nina could get to it. Wade had trailed Kent into the room, his expression somber.

Everyone stood in front of the wide flatscreen as it flickered to life.

". . . activity at the home of the Doyle family this afternoon," a field reporter was saying into the camera. His graying brown hair ruffled in the breeze as he stood at the end of the driveway, the expansive house in the background.

"That didn't take long," Nina said as the camera cut to footage that had obviously been shot earlier.

The reporter was in the front courtyard of a neighbor's home, speaking to a middle-aged woman. "What did you see today?" he asked before jutting the microphone toward her.

She needed no further prompting. "I've been keeping an eye on the place since it's been empty," the woman said. "Today I saw a car and one of those big black SUVs pull up. A bunch of people got out of the vehicles and went inside. I called the police, and they told me it was one of their detectives and some FBI agents."

Wade shook his head. "Their next-door neighbor is Gladys Kravitz. The only thing she's missing is a beehive and a housedress."

The reporter edged his response with a bit of drama. "The FBI?"

She nodded vigorously. "That's what they told me, so I was watching when they left, and I recognized one of them."

"Who?"

Nina groaned, knowing what was coming.

"That one they call the Warrior Girl."

"Special Agent Nina Guerrera?" the reporter asked.

"That's the one."

The screen cut back to the live shot with the reporter speaking directly into the camera. "We've contacted the Phoenix FBI field office, who confirmed they were working with local police on this case. They would not elaborate as to why a team of profilers would fly across the country to review the case in person."

There were so many things wrong with that statement Nina didn't know where to begin. The reporter looked familiar, and she made a mental note of his name at the bottom of the screen.

James Snead.

The same reporter who had covered the first murder back when he was almost three decades younger and a good fifteen pounds lighter. Snead had interviewed neighbors then, too, and one of them had mentioned *La Llorona*, giving the case its creepy nickname.

"What we do know is that profilers usually only get involved when there are a series of crimes to investigate," Snead continued into the camera. "Which begs the question . . . Were the Doyles victims of a serial killer?"

Kent swore as he clicked off the television. "The story is all over the local news now, but Channel Six had it first."

"So much for keeping this on the down-low," Nina said. "Now the unsub knows we're onto him."

"The PPD put out a news release characterizing the Doyle case as a triple murder before we got here," Wade said. "So he knew he hadn't fooled the police into buying the murder-suicide scenario in that case and in New York, but he had no way of knowing we matched this case to that one . . . or to any others."

"Until now." Kent tossed the remote onto the nearest bed. "He has to assume we've connected the dots. And he has to be panicking."

"We have one advantage still left," Nina said. "The unsub doesn't know we are actually investigating two murders in Phoenix, and neither does the media."

Breck gave her a side-eye. "Yet."

"We need to ask the PPD to sit on that as long as possible," Wade said. "I don't want it getting out until we're ready. The Llorona case was pretty famous locally back in the day from what we've heard. Pairing that with this one will complicate things."

Nina had no interest in being part of another headline-grabbing investigation. "And once word gets out—and it will—that there are also other cases around the country, the story's going to go national, maybe international."

A few months ago, she'd gained notoriety as the Warrior Girl, which was the English translation of *Nina Guerrera*, when she confronted a different serial killer.

"I'm okay with that happening," Wade said. "But I want to be in control of the timing. We can use it to apply psychological pressure at the right moment."

"Well, we have four years to figure this out," Breck said.

Kent folded his arms. "Not necessarily. The unsub had a strict time frame, but now that everything is changing and we're out in the open, he could adapt, make a move earlier to throw us off or regain the sense of control he believes he's lost," he said. "Bottom line, right now is when he will be at his most unpredictable . . . and most dangerous."

Chapter 10

"Ooh, that poor family, isn't it just awful?"

He turned to his clients. "It certainly is." He schooled his features to reflect his best approximation of sympathy mingled with concern.

He had thought the couple would be in the bedroom longer. He'd told them he would wait in the kitchen to give them time alone to discuss things. In reality, he'd seen an alert about a breaking news story on the Doyle murders and couldn't resist pulling out his iPad to watch the coverage on the six o'clock evening news.

The husband treaded into the kitchen behind his wife, glanced at the screen, and scowled. "Seriously, what kind of deranged lunatic would kill a whole family?"

It seemed appropriate for him to express some sort of outrage at this point. "Terrible." He nodded. "Really makes you wonder."

His clients both responded with grave nods, apparently thinking that very thing. They had no idea he could answer that question better than anyone else. Certainly better than the FBI, who had sent the famous Warrior Girl to investigate. She and that profiler, Dr. Something-or-Other, thought they would get inside his head, track him down. "I don't think so."

"Pardon?" the wife said to him.

He hadn't realized he'd muttered that last comment. Better distract them. He folded the cover of his iPad closed and stretched his mouth into a smile. "This is a real bargain. Good value for the money."

"We need to stick to our budget," the husband said. "I'm not sure we need all of this."

"It does seem like a bit much," the wife said. "We're on a fixed income."

"But an exceptionally good income." He glanced at the fruit bowl on the counter. Slightly off-center. He reached out to push it a bit to the left. "And some things are priceless, right?"

"I don't know," the husband hedged. "Won't it be hard to maintain?"

"It's perfect for you." He moved the fruit bowl a fraction more to the left. "What if your children want to come visit? What if they want to bring the grandkids?"

"But this is such a nice neighborhood," the wife began. "We—"

"Exactly," he cut in. "Maybe they'd like to visit you in sunny Arizona when they're sick of shoveling snow. You could offer them world-class golf, gorgeous scenery, and the best spa day they've ever had. All in a lovely, secure, and up-to-date home."

The wife slid her husband a sidelong glance. "What do you think?"

Everyone had a weak spot, a leverage point, and he had just found theirs. They couldn't resist the idea of lording it over their friends and family. They had moved to paradise.

"What would the monthly payments be?" the husband asked.

His smile widened. He would get them to sign today. Right now. "We'll make sure everything fits into your budget."

While the couple jabbered on, he contemplated what he had just learned watching the news. That witless reporter had a point. If the FBI was involved, that meant the Doyle case was no longer just a local murder investigation. Could the police have somehow connected that fiasco in New York City to the Phoenix incident?

"Pardon?" The wife stared at him, a scandalized expression on her face.

He cursed under his breath. The old bat had better hearing than he would have imagined. He'd have to be more careful.

"I said 'luck.'" At her dubious look, he added, "A deal like this is all about timing and luck."

Timing and luck. One he could control, the other he could not. He would find a way to capitalize when fortune favored him. Perhaps this Warrior Girl situation could work out for him. She was practically a celebrity. Would he be able to use that as a distraction? Throw the FBI off its game? He relished the thought of a mental showdown with the best law enforcement had to offer. The question was, what would the famous profilers make of him? He hadn't started himself down this path. Someone else was to blame for what he had done. But now he would be the one in control. To do that, he would have to change the rules of engagement.

First thing tomorrow, he would head for Phoenix.

Chapter 11

The following morning at the command center, Nina posed the thorniest question to the team. "Are we going to tell Detective Perez about the whole series or just the first Phoenix case?"

The PPD had been the ones to request FBI involvement after the ViCAP hit on the matching shoe prints. Before leaving the Doyle house yesterday, they had shared their conclusion that Perez's current case was in fact connected to the one in New York City four years earlier but nothing more.

"I think we should tell him about all of it," Wade said without hesitation. "We'll ask him to inform his chain of command but no one else until we confirm each of the other leap day incidents."

She was pleased Wade had been the one to say it. As the most junior agent present, she would have had a fight on her hands to get the locals fully briefed if the rest of the team disagreed. In her former career as a police officer, she had always been annoyed to discover that Feds had been holding out on them.

Nina glanced up from her bagel as Ginsberg pushed open the conference room door and ushered Perez inside.

"Nice of you to provide breakfast," Perez said, glancing down at the cluster of bagels, lox, cream cheese, and jam in the center of the table. "Figures the FBI would have a budget for that."

"Agent Ginsberg picked it up on the way in," Buxton said, frowning. "At his own expense."

"Aww, now I feel bad." Perez's grin put the lie to his comment.

Nina pointed at the credenza along the wall. "Can you grab the picante sauce on your way to the table?"

Breck looked appalled. "On a bagel?"

Perez picked up the small red bottle. "I see you like to spice things up." He took the empty seat next to hers. "Me too."

She ignored the subtext, deliberately sticking to the literal meaning of her words. "I grew up putting the stuff on everything."

Buxton had called for a working breakfast in their temporary center of operations. Nina had managed to score half of the only salted bagel hidden among the cinnamon raisin, blueberry, and honey bran.

"Let's get to it," Buxton said as soon as everyone was settled. He turned to the PPD detective. "We need to brief you on the rest of the situation."

"This is strictly confidential," Kent said, glaring at Perez. "Not to leave law enforcement circles at this point."

Perez put down his coffee, widening his eyes in mock wonder. "Is this where I get my FBI secret decoder ring and find out what the message inside the cereal box says?"

"I'll save you the trouble." Nina stage-whispered around the back of her hand, quoting from a favorite movie. "It says, 'Be sure to drink your Ovaltine.'"

Buxton ignored the chuckles around the table. "We are investigating the possibility of a serial killer, with two cases in Phoenix."

His comment silenced the room.

"Two in Phoenix?" Perez said, all traces of humor gone. "ViCAP connected the triple murder of a family in New York to the Doyle case here in Phoenix. Both were staged to look like double-murder-suicides. We discussed the matching Nike shoe prints yesterday." He frowned. "But you didn't say anything about another Phoenix case."

"The other Phoenix incident also occurred on February twenty-ninth," Nina said.

"A leap day series," Perez said slowly. "That's something I haven't seen before."

Breck flashed a list of cases up on one of the other screens. "We did some checking and discovered a total of eight cases, each committed on leap day. All but the last two were closed as double-murder-suicides."

Buxton opened the notebook resting on the table next to his elbow. "We've assigned field agents at various offices to work with local police to reopen the cases we believe are related and check to see if there could have been a mistake. Each incident occurred in a different city, except Phoenix, which he hit twice."

"Eight cases." Perez's eyes widened. "That means—"

"This unsub's been operating under the radar for twenty-eight years," Nina said.

"It all started in Phoenix," Wade added. "And now he's circled back around, which is why we came here. This appears to be both the newest and the oldest incident. There's a lot of information to gather."

"If you guys want to know about something that happened twenty-eight years ago, we might have to rely on written reports," Perez said. "The detectives who worked it will be retired or dead by now."

"This investigation received a great deal of attention at the time." Buxton slid on his reading glasses and scanned the page. "It happened in Palomino Villa." He glanced up. "The Vega case."

"La Llorona," Perez said under his breath.

Nina was intrigued to see that Perez knew the case by its nickname. If he'd been in elementary school when it happened, he would have been at the age when kids liked to scare each other with spooky stories. When the adults around them were talking about *La Llorona*, it would have made a big impression on children. Phoenix, with its large Latino population, would have been fertile ground for such a tale to take root.

She pressed Perez for more details. "We saw the news reports, and we understand the locals called it the Llorona case."

"They still do," Perez said, meeting her gaze. "When they talk about it."

Something in his tone made Nina think he had more interest in the case than as a childhood memory. "You have personal knowledge about the investigation?"

He shifted slightly. "I go to the same church as Victor Vega's family, and I also buy food at the Mercado Vecino. That's a Latin market run by the Soto family."

Nina recalled the names from the news stories. "Victor and Maria Vega were the couple who died."

Perez nodded. "I see Maria's family at the market all the time. Her maiden name was Soto, and her sister runs the place," he said. "Don't talk to Victor's relatives much, though. Unfortunately, the two families don't speak to each other. For a long time, the community was divided."

Buxton closed the notepad, obviously more intrigued by the first-hand information he was getting from a local. "Could you fill us in, Detective?"

Perez paused a moment, as if deciding where to start. "Word on the street was that Maria Vega, the wife, killed the whole family because she caught Victor cheating on her right after they brought their newborn baby home from the hospital. Victor's parents accused Maria's family of hiding what they assumed must have been long-standing mental instability."

"Pretty harsh," Breck said.

Nina agreed with the sentiment, but she had seen many instances of grieving survivors lashing out in all directions as if their pain needed a target.

"On the other hand," Perez continued, "Maria's family blamed Victor for cheating on his pregnant wife. They felt that his moral failings were due to his parents."

"Both sets of parents blamed each other?" Nina said.

Perez grimaced. "It all came to a head when the two fathers got into a brawl after the funeral service. Both families objected to having Maria and Victor buried together, so they interred them in different cemeteries."

Nina thought about the littlest victim. "What about the baby?"

"They argued bitterly over where the baby would be buried," Perez said. "They finally agreed to have the little girl cremated and split the ashes between both families."

"You said they still don't speak to this day?"

"And their friends took sides as well," Perez said.

This crime had not only divided the community but devastated two families. What would happen when they found out it had all been based on a lie?

"I don't know Victor's family as well," Perez said. "They had two sons. The oldest was in the military and died in combat overseas a year after Victor's death. They lost both of their children in such a short amount of time, which is another reason they're so angry at Maria, and they mostly keep to themselves. The father owned a construction business he planned to pass on to his sons, but he's since sold it and they're retired now."

"But neither family thought the police got it wrong at the time?" Nina asked.

"Oh, they both did," Perez assured them. "Victor's parents claimed he would never have an affair, that he loved Maria blindly. Maria's family said she would never harm anyone, much less her own baby, no matter how angry she was. They didn't accept postpartum depression as a reason either."

"But the case was still closed with Maria as the perpetrator," Wade said.

Perez nodded. "All the evidence pointed that way. If I remember correctly, the ME didn't come up with anything to dispute it."

"You're right," Buxton said, tapping the notebook in front of him. "He didn't. I wonder if he would change his mind now."

"He died a few years back," Perez said.

Nina figured that might make it easier. She had seen Medical Examiners become entrenched once they'd made a determination. Some were hesitant to change an initial ruling on cause of death.

She knew what she wanted to do next. "We're going to have to contact the detectives who worked the case."

"I know the lead detective," Perez said. "I see him at the police lodge now and then. Got to warn you, he's a crusty old buzzard, and he's not a fan of the FBI. Claims you guys bigfooted him on one of his high-profile cases shortly before he retired. Left a bitter taste in his mouth."

Buxton looked thoughtful. "Agent Guerrera, why don't you and Detective Perez interview him? Detective Perez knows him, and you're former local PD. That might help."

Perez nodded. "I'll set it up."

"We'll make headway faster if we split up," Buxton said, looking around the table as he spoke. "Agent Kent, team up with Agent Breck and go over the Doyle investigation. Agent Wade, you can review the police files from around the country as they come in. Agent Guerrera can work with Detective Perez on the Llorona case."

Kent looked like his breakfast had given him heartburn.

"I'll start making phone calls," Perez said, ignoring Kent's glare. "All our documents have been converted to digital files in the record-management system—we call it RMS. In order to access those files on my computer, I have to put in a request to have that case added to my queue."

Breck's antennae went up at the mention of computer technology. "You mean you can't just access the file in the database?"

"Not without authorization," Perez said. "No detective can freely peruse hundreds of thousands of cases going back decades at will. Access is restricted to investigations the detective has been assigned to work."

"I have an appointment to update the Phoenix police chief this morning on what we're doing," Buxton said. "Would it help for me to ask him to expedite authorization?"

Perez laughed. "That's overkill. I'll call my commander and make the request. Once I tell her you have a meeting with the chief, she'll make it happen. We can get started reviewing the reports a lot more quickly that way."

Buxton turned to Wade. "As the lead profiler, I'd like you to join me in providing an overview to the chief while we wait for the first reports from the other jurisdictions to come in. Everyone else can head out. We'll reconvene here later today."

They had their marching orders. She was grateful for a chance to work on the Llorona case, because to unravel the mystery of how the unsub had waged an undetected campaign of terror over almost three decades, she would have to start at the beginning.

Chapter 12

Nina glanced up at the tiny camera aimed down at her as she stood beside Perez on Detective Martin O'Malley's front porch.

Perez had been able to access the Llorona case file from his laptop about twenty minutes after he called his commander. Nina had reviewed the information briefly, deciding she would rather go over it in detail with the detective who wrote it. During the drive to his house, Perez had repeated his earlier caution that O'Malley was grouchy at the best of times and, unlike most detectives on the PPD, highly resentful of the FBI.

She considered herself warned.

Perez rang the doorbell and knocked three times. Nothing.

After a full minute of silence, she cut her eyes to him. "I thought you said O'Malley was home and was expecting us."

"He is," Perez said. "Doesn't mean he's going to talk to us."

The door jerked inward, taking her by surprise. A barrel-chested man with a substantial paunch, sparse gray hair, and a scraggly full beard stood, blinking in the sun.

Perez dipped his head briefly. "Good to see you, Marty."

Martin O'Malley grunted by way of answer, then glared at Nina with puffy, red-rimmed eyes. "You're keeping some piss-poor company these days, Perez."

Unsure whether this applied to the entire FBI or her personally, Nina tried for diplomacy. She stuck out her hand. "Nina Guerrera." She made sure to leave out *Special Agent*.

O'Malley made no move to take her hand. He turned to Perez. "You don't need Feds to tell you how to run an investigation."

Nina dropped her hand back to her side. "Actually, it's your help we could use right now, Detective O'Malley."

His eyes narrowed as they settled on her again. "I've seen you on TV. You're that Warrior Girl."

"If you know that," she said, "then you also know I was a cop before I went to the Bureau."

He gave her an assessing look. "What made you go to the dark side?"

She shrugged. "Wanted a bigger sandbox to play in."

He let out a croak that might have been laughter. "May as well come in and get this over with." He turned and retreated into the dark recesses inside.

Nina felt like the billy goat who answered the troll's questions correctly and had been allowed to cross the bridge. Perez trailed her as they passed through the foyer and into what looked like a home office. O'Malley lowered himself into a seat behind a scarred desk covered in stacks of papers and decorated with mementos from his law enforcement career.

"What's this about?" O'Malley gestured toward two dusty chairs nearby. "Perez would only say it had something to do with a case from my time in Homicide."

She appreciated Perez leaving it to her to frame the discussion. He obviously knew how important the order of questioning in any interview would be. That included victims, witnesses, suspects, and previous investigators.

She opened with a generic question to see how much O'Malley kept in touch with current events. "You may have seen the news recently about the Doyle murders?"

"Which someone tried to pass off as a homicide-suicide," he said. "Yeah, I heard some stuff."

As far as she knew, the media hadn't reported many details about the Doyle investigation. "How did you know about the crime scene staging?"

"I keep in touch," he said. "Go down to the lodge for lunch at least three times a week and hang out with the guys." He gestured around at the quiet house. "Ever since Connie died, it's not like I've got a lot of things to do."

"If you've been talking to other detectives, then you know the scene was set up to put it on the mother."

"That's what I heard. The woman takes out her husband and child, then does herself in the bathtub."

She was certain the detail about the bathtub hadn't been released to the public. O'Malley's sources were accurate. "Do you recall working a case where the mother killed her husband and baby before committing suicide?"

His bushy gray brows drew together, then shot up. "The Llorona case. That was ages ago."

She leaned forward, watching his reaction. "Twenty-eight years, to be exact."

He cocked his head to one side, considering. "You think that case has something to do with this one that just happened?"

"We're looking into it."

O'Malley gave her a shrewd look. "You don't work out of the Phoenix field office. You work back east with those profilers. You wouldn't have come clear across the country unless there was some reason to believe a serial killer was involved."

"Right now, this is just preliminary," Nina told him. "We're trying to—"

"To figure out if I screwed up the Llorona case." He looked from Nina to Perez and back again. "You're thinking I let some damn serial killer slip through my fingers and he's at it again here in Phoenix."

Nina held up a placating hand. "We don't know if—"

O'Malley shot to his feet. "Out."

She kept her seat, hoping to calm him. The interview would be over unless she took a chance on him and revealed an important piece of the investigation. Right now, she wanted access to O'Malley's memories, not just his reports.

"How about if I let you in on some information we've been holding back?"

"Yeah, right," O'Malley said. "The FBI is like a toilet. They suck all the shit in, and nothing ever comes back out." He crossed his arms. "In other words, it's a one-way flow."

He plainly didn't believe she would be straight with him. She took the plunge anyway. "Look, if this is a serial killer, he's managed to fool a lot of top-notch detectives from some of the best police agencies in the country for years. He's extremely clever and resourceful. He knows how to hide his tracks."

O'Malley narrowed his eyes. "What other departments?"

"New York, LA, Chicago, Houston, Philly, and San Diego." She leveled him with a hard stare. "You need to keep all of this to yourself."

He sat back down heavily. "Damn, how many cases are there?"

"We believe there are eight," she said. "He hits once every four years."

"On the same date," Perez added.

"Leap day," O'Malley said. "I remember it like it was yesterday. It's one of the ones you never forget."

Now they were getting somewhere. "What stands out?" she asked.

"I was going through my second divorce at the time." O'Malley's jaw hardened at the unpleasant memory.

Nina pulled him back on track. "About the case?"

"I'm getting to that." He gave her an indignant look. "Anyway, wife number two, Brenda, was a piece of work. That woman made my life a living hell."

Nina thought she knew where he might be going with this. "You were having marital trouble when you were on the case."

O'Malley's expression darkened. "The day after I got called out on the Llorona case, I had an appointment at my attorney's office to meet with Brenda and her pit bull of an attorney. She wanted half my pension, and we'd only been married two years." He thumped his fist on the desk. "Screw that."

"Getting back to the Llorona case." Nina found she had begun calling it by the nickname everyone in town used. "You might have had some other things on your mind when—"

"Bullshit." He glowered at her a moment before going on. "I know how to compartmentalize. When I'm on a case and something's bothering me, I shut that shit down. Nothing distracts me."

Nina wondered if O'Malley realized how much the mere memory of his bitter divorce had distracted him from describing the investigation to her now.

"We pulled your case files," Perez said, gently redirecting him. "Could you go over them with us and walk us through what you found?" He opened his laptop and turned it toward O'Malley. "These RMS files are scanned and downloaded from the original murder book."

On the way over, Perez had explained to her how all police reports had been digitized. Instead of plowing through dusty and decaying files that were subject to loss, misfiling, or damage, now everything was searchable, safely stored in the cloud.

O'Malley put on his reading glasses. "Can you believe I used to bang out my reports on a typewriter back in the day? Now everything's digital, even my old pencil sketches of the scene. Damn." He leaned close to the screen. "Oh yeah, I remember how this part of town used to be. Palomino Villa. Blue-collar neighborhood, mostly Latino. Pretty quiet, considering."

"Considering what, exactly?" Nina asked, allowing a slight edge to her voice when she posed the question.

O'Malley glanced up, perhaps realizing he was speaking to two Latinos. "Uh, I mean to say that it was a nice starter home." He cleared his throat. "It was their first place. They had just moved in about two months before the murders."

Certain this wasn't what he had been referring to, she made no response. Perez didn't seem to feel inclined to let him off the hook, either, letting an awkward silence build until O'Malley changed the subject, pointing at a copy of one of the crime scene photos.

"There's the open shoebox. I remember that lying on the floor in front of the master bedroom closet."

She followed his gaze. "I believe the report said there were love letters from another woman to the husband hidden inside?"

"Burned," O'Malley said. "Only part of one of the notes was legible."

"It was typed." Nina peered directly at O'Malley. "Didn't you find that strange for such a personal communication?"

"Who am I to say how lovers communicate?" He waved a dismissive hand. "Maybe her handwriting sucked."

"Did you ever figure out who the other woman was?" Perez asked.

"Never did. We dusted the unburned part of the paper for prints and came up with nothing. None of his friends or family knew anything about a mistress either."

Nowadays there would be ninhydrin testing that could bring up prints on many different kinds of surfaces a lot more reliably.

She pressed him again. "Did you find it odd that the woman who sent it never touched it?"

"Not particularly." O'Malley looked defensive. "And before you ask, I also didn't find it strange that she never came forward. Could you blame her, given the media circus? The families might have done her in."

She switched to a new line of questioning. "How were the families when you interviewed them?"

"How the hell do you think?"

She suppressed a sigh. "I mean, did they offer any other theories about what happened that night? Did they go along with double-homicide-suicide?"

"No one ever believes something like that. Of course both families wouldn't accept it. The wife's relatives kept saying she was a good Catholic girl and would never commit murder or suicide. They also made a big deal about how the baby hadn't been baptized yet, so her mother wouldn't have sent her soul to purgatory by killing her."

"What did you think about that?" she asked him.

"I thought they were in denial." He shrugged. "The wife just had a baby. Some women go batshit after childbirth. Then she finds out her man is cheating on her?" He snapped his fingers. "Off the deep end."

"What about the husband's family?"

"They had two children—both boys." O'Malley shook his head. "About a year after Victor died, their older son was killed in combat overseas. When I asked about Victor, his parents told me he was a God-fearing man who was devoted to his family and would never have an affair."

"What about the murder weapon found at the scene?" Nina asked. "Did either family remember one of them having a gun?"

"Everyone we asked said they didn't own any weapons," O'Malley said. "Not even for self-defense." He jabbed a finger at her. "And don't look at me like that. A lot of folks don't tell anyone they own a gun. The neighborhood they lived in could be dicey at times." He raised his hand to forestall any accusations. "I'm not saying that because it was a Latino area either."

Nina stayed focused. "Did you trace the weapon that was found at the scene?"

"We ran it through ATF. It hadn't been used in a crime. Serial number led back to a gun shop in Mesa that went out of business a couple of years before the murder when the owner died. The shop owner's family got rid of all his records, so we filed a request for a hand search through the federal purchase database. Took a few weeks, but we got a response. The buyer turned out to be some lowlife in Mesa who ended up getting shot in a drive-by. No one knew what happened to his gun after the guy was killed."

"Hard to imagine how the weapon would have ended up in Victor Vega's house," Nina said. "He had no criminal record or connections."

O'Malley spread his hands in an elaborate shrug. "Gun might have changed hands sixteen times before it ended up at that crime scene. It's not like there are any records kept when a private citizen sells a firearm to another person."

Nina clicked on a document summarizing the results of a neighborhood canvass. "No one heard a gunshot the night of the crime."

"Small-caliber revolver," O'Malley said by way of explanation. "The house was on one of the larger lots and backed up to a wash. There was only one neighbor close by, and they were out of town."

She figured the unsub, who had proven himself to be extremely thorough, probably knew that fact. She scanned the array of photos scrolling by as Perez swiped the surface of the computer screen with his index finger. The crime scene bore silent testimony to the unspeakable horror that had been visited upon the home that night.

Studying the images of the bodies frozen in time, she reached out to stop Perez. "Wait, let me see that photo again."

He scrolled back to the previous picture.

She used her thumb and forefinger to expand the image. "Look at the wall."

"I don't see anything," O'Malley said.

"Exactly." She heard the excitement of discovery in her own voice.

O'Malley frowned at her. "What are you talking about?"

"I'm talking about a void in the blood spatter."

"A what?"

She zoomed in more. "If you look down near the lower edge of the picture, you can make out where Victor's blood hit the wall. Look closer, and you'll see a blank space inside the area surrounded by blood."

"It's not blank," O'Malley said.

She nodded absently, her mind already racing ahead. "It's got a thin trickle or two of red, but that's from droplets rolling down from their contact point above the empty spot. That blank part never got spattered with blood."

Perez turned to her. "What are you saying?"

"I'm saying someone moved Victor's body after he died."

"Maybe he crawled a bit after he was shot," O'Malley said in a half-hearted tone.

She arched her brow at him. "You know that didn't happen. The round hit him point-blank in the face, just above the nose on the lower part of the forehead. He would have been dead before he took his next breath, with no ability to make any move at all."

It was the kind of shot snipers made when a hostage taker had a gun to someone's head. When the bullet penetrated that part of the brain, it short-circuited all movement. O'Malley knew it too. Every cop did.

She turned back to Perez. "Let me see the autopsy photos."

He clicked another subfolder in the file.

She studied pictures of the husband's nude body taken before, during, and after the procedure. Next, she examined photos of the wife, beginning with those taken at the crime scene.

Realization dawned. "Holy shit."

"What now?" O'Malley looked irritable.

"The wife, Maria." Nina pointed at the screen. "Look at the lividity and blanching on her left arm."

Nina had noticed the pooling of blood, which formed a reddish-purple discoloration called *lividity*, on Maria's left side. Where her body rested on the ground, however, the pooled blood had been forced back, away from the point of contact, causing blanching—whitened skin that contrasted with the dark lividity.

"I don't see what you're getting at," O'Malley said.

"Here." She swiped the screen with her fingers to enlarge the image. "Look at the arm."

Maria was dressed in a long-sleeve winter nightgown, so the lividity wasn't visible in the photo.

Nina tapped the screen, enlarging the image still more. "See, she was slumped on her right side."

Perez caught on quickly. "But the lividity and blanching were on her left side."

O'Malley muttered a curse. "Okay, looks like we've got a problem."

"Damn straight we do," Nina said. "Maria was supposed to be the last person alive. So who moved her?"

"She didn't adjust her position after a fatal gunshot to the head," Perez said. "Someone placed her."

"And he waited a while to do it," she said, growing more animated. "Allowing time for the blood to pool while he did something else in the house."

Perez nodded. "I'm thinking he spent time getting other things rearranged."

"Like the husband's body." Nina felt the certainty of a puzzle piece snapping into place. "The unsub wanted to tell a story, and he had to make the evidence fit the narrative. He had to plant those love letters and partially burn them."

Perez clicked back to a photo file containing pictures of the house. "There were ashes found in the fireplace."

Several images popped up, showing a small brick fireplace with curled black papers in the grate.

Infused with excitement, she clutched Perez's arm. "It's definitely enough to reopen the case, but we'll need more to prove this was a triple murder." She turned to O'Malley, who had gone curiously silent. "Can we pull the original evidence you collected?"

"It'll be stored in the Property Room." He looked down at his hands. "Uh, I gotta say that I'm pretty damned pissed off about this."

Nina ratcheted down her enthusiasm, realizing what her discovery would mean for O'Malley. "Look, we're not trying to make you look bad, we're just—"

"Pissed off at myself," he cut in. "Not you. I should've caught that. My stupid marital problems are no excuse. I failed."

He wouldn't meet her eyes. "I failed those victims, and I failed the community. There's no excuse at all. I'm gonna get my ass handed to me . . . and I deserve it."

Chapter 13

Nina stepped out of Perez's unmarked car and gazed at the festive cream-colored building. Constructed in a mission style, complete with a bronze bell high up on the stucco facade, the Mercado Vecino stretched half the length of a football field.

Perez had explained during the morning briefing that the Sotos, Maria Vega's family, owned and ran the Mercado Vecino. After they left O'Malley's house, he had called the Property Room, requesting the physical evidence preserved from the original crime scene of the Llorona case. When Perez learned it would take an hour to retrieve the material, he had suggested grabbing lunch during their downtime without telling her where they were headed.

"Why are we here?" she asked.

"I saw how you picked at your bagel this morning." He winked. "I know what you're really hungry for."

She didn't let him distract her with humor. "I don't want to risk running into anyone from the Soto family before we have a strategy worked out."

He unbuckled his seat belt and opened his door. "Trust me. I have my reasons."

The exterior of the market looked like a south-of-the-border bazaar, with stands displaying everything from art to clothing to fresh-squeezed juices. Mariachi music piped in through intercoms nestled in the terra-cotta-tiled overhang above the wide glass front doors. The smell of fresh cilantro growing in tiny clay pots along one of the tables blended with the heavenly aroma of scented goat-milk soaps stacked in a tower on a blue porcelain tray. Having come from the cold, gray winter back east, Nina hadn't just entered another state—she'd entered another state of mind.

She reluctantly followed Perez as he strode to an outdoor grill, where two men were flipping pieces of chicken with metal tongs, basting it with a sauce that instantly made Nina's stomach growl when she caught a whiff.

Perez laughed. "See, I know what you need."

One of the men at the grill inclined his head toward Perez. "Nice to see you bringing someone with you besides that ugly partner of yours." His chuckle revealed the humor behind the remark.

They got a paper plate heaped with chicken and Mexican fried rice before walking to the fresh-beverage stand. She pondered the array of choices. Papaya, watermelon, horchata, lemonade, guava, and something she had never seen before.

"What's this?"

"Prickly pear." Perez pointed at a cluster of reddish-pink fruit in a woven-straw basket next to the stand. "It's made from the fruit of a cactus that grows here in Arizona. The juice is delicious on its own, but it also makes the best margarita you've ever tasted. That's for after work, though. I'll buy you one sometime before you go back to DC."

She ordered the prickly pear juice, he got papaya, and they headed toward one of the brightly painted wooden picnic-style benches in the vast eating area inside the store.

Two men with enormous white cowboy hats, plaid shirts, and jeans with huge silver belt buckles ate fresh burritos at the next table over. They were speaking Spanish, laughing at a shared joke. Another table held a family with a father, a very pregnant mother, and Nina lost count of their children, who seemed to be in a constant state of motion, running back and forth on the Saltillo tile floor.

She realized this was what she had missed growing up in a series of foster homes. She hadn't been raised to value her ethnic background. She had taken care to learn Spanish and to hang out with some of the Latino kids when she could. She had even moved into the Latin corridor of Fairfax County as an adult, but nothing was quite like growing up among people who looked like you. In so many ways, she had been an outsider her entire life.

Perez seemed to catch her watching, and his cheeks dimpled. "You should seriously think about living in Phoenix. It suits you."

"I couldn't move all the way across the country. I don't know anyone here."

"And your *novio* would miss you?"

He was fishing, and not bothering to hide it. "I don't have a boyfriend," she said. "And I'm not looking for one either."

"Javier," a feminine voice called from behind her. "Nice to see you."

Nina turned to see who was greeting them and nearly dropped her plastic fork. She looked into eyes she had seen in newspaper cuttings. And in crime scene photos.

Perez cleared his throat. "Good to see you, too, Teresa."

The woman—slender, petite, and in her fifties—leaned forward to clutch Perez's hands in hers. "And you brought a young lady." She smiled at Nina. "How nice."

"Agent Nina Guerrera," Perez said, then turned to the woman. "This is Teresa Soto Marquez."

Nina put it together, recognizing the name from the files she had studied. Teresa Soto was Maria Soto Vega's twin sister. After having scrutinized the crime scene photos for hours, it was eerie to see those same eyes looking at her. Now, though, instead of being lifeless and dull, they were wide with surprise as they returned her gaze.

Nina's cheeks warmed, certain Teresa had recognized her. "Nice to meet you."

Teresa shook her hand. "I saw the news. You are here working with Javier on that horrible murder."

This was precisely the kind of awkward situation Nina had been concerned about when Perez took her here for lunch. She cocked her head and turned to him.

As if understanding the implied question, he responded to Teresa's comment. "The FBI is always willing to help us when we ask. This case is . . . challenging."

"I hope you find whoever did that," Teresa said, a series of emotions playing across her lovely face. "It is a truly dreadful thing to kill an entire family."

Nina looked up at her, aware that perhaps no one else could better understand what relatives of the Doyles were going through. "Whatever else happens, I can promise you that we will not stop until we put the person responsible behind bars."

Teresa choked out her thanks and hurried away.

Once she was out of earshot, Nina rounded on Perez. "Why did you bring me here if you knew I might run into Maria's family?"

"This is what I meant when I told you to trust me." He was not the least bit apologetic. "What better way to get a feel for them?"

"I don't know how you run investigations in the PPD, but in the FBI we don't contact potential interviewees until we are ready."

"Then you probably miss out on a lot of opportunities to learn things about them while their guard is down."

"That's not going to go over well when I'm sitting across from her, asking hard questions about her sister's death."

"Actually, it will work to your advantage. She will have already seen you in a nonthreatening situation. And you've eaten her cooking, which is always a plus." He gestured around them. "All the food here is made using Soto family recipes." He gave her a wry smile. "Look at it this way, do you know any Latina women who like to cook?"

She immediately thought of Mrs. Gomez next door. "My neighbor."

"Food is a bonding experience in our culture."

She wasn't prepared to play along with whatever angle he was working. "Food is a bonding experience in a lot of cultures around the world. What's your point?"

"She's more likely to confide in you now."

"You think so?"

"I know Teresa. I know the whole family. You don't. You'll have to trust me on this."

"You haven't given me much choice."

He had no way of knowing the depth of what he asked. Trust did not come easily for her. He may have thought he was helping, but she had the sneaking suspicion that he had immeasurably complicated things.

Chapter 14

Two hours later, Nina pushed open the door to the center of operations at the FBI Phoenix field office. Perez followed her into the room, where all other members of the ad hoc task force were waiting for their arrival.

"We just got back from the Phoenix crime lab," Nina said. "Perez got authorization to take the archived physical evidence from the Llorona case out of the Property Room for forensic analysis."

Buxton's brow creased with confusion. "I thought we were sending the materials to our lab at Quantico."

That had been the plan, but Nina had made an operational decision in the field. "I called our lab," she told Buxton. "They're backlogged. The estimated turnaround time to process the materials is about two weeks." She drove her point home. "Not including transit time to ship the evidence from here to Virginia."

Perez stepped beside her. "Our lab will have preliminary results tomorrow and a full report a day or so after that."

Apparently satisfied, Buxton motioned her toward the two empty chairs at the conference table. Nina realized the seats were arranged around three sides to face the jumbo flatscreen on the opposite wall.

Buxton had arranged for a virtual interoffice meeting, dividing the screen into six sections, a patchwork of feeds from other field offices around the country filling each subsection. Small banners at the bottom of each read Los Angeles, Philadelphia, Chicago, Houston, San Diego, and New York. Each subsection was occupied by an agent from that city's respective FBI field office. Buxton had all hands on deck.

She turned to their supervisor, scrutinizing the deep lines etched around his mouth and eyes, as he put down his coffee and glanced at Breck, who clicked on the audio link from the terminal to the wall screen.

"Thank you all for joining us," Buxton said, addressing the room at large and the virtual attendees. "After a careful review of the information, we have concluded that all the suspect cases are connected." He looked grim. "We've got a highly meticulous serial killer operating among us, flying below the radar for almost three decades. His crimes were so well planned that they didn't even register as homicides."

"Until the two most recent cases in New York and Phoenix," Kent said.

Buxton nodded. "I believe the only reason the deaths were identified as triple murders in those instances is because of advances in forensic science and technology. It's getting increasingly harder to conceal or eliminate trace evidence."

Nina thought about the shoe print that had connected two apparently unrelated crimes committed four years and over two thousand miles apart from each other.

"Let's begin with an overview of the cases," Buxton continued. "We'll start with New York, then circle back around to Phoenix."

Breck clicked open the digital file sent from the NYPD, splitting the wall monitor's screen with the New York field agent, who filled them in on what he had learned.

"In our case, the crime was interrupted because the mother had complications during her cesarean section surgery resulting in ongoing heart arrhythmia," the New York agent began. "Her doctor had her on one of those monitors that alerts 9-1-1 if the heart stops."

Nina marveled at the way medical technology had interfered with the unsub's plans. "So the moment he killed her, paramedics were dispatched?"

"He must not have been aware of her condition," New York said. "He had already murdered the family and was in the process of staging the scene when an EMT unit responded."

"Looks like he learned from that experience when he came to Phoenix a few days ago," Kent said. "He figured out how to jam a wireless alarm system at the Doyle house."

Nina spoke directly to the New York agent. "Since the case in Manhattan involved a five-floor walk-up apartment building, the unsub must have chosen a knife for the murder weapon rather than a gun to avoid alerting other tenants."

"Only the parents were stabbed," New York said. "The infant was suffocated."

Wade exchanged a glance with Kent. "This appears to be another part of his pattern," Wade said. "He never uses brutality against the child, only the parents. In every case, the baby has no injuries and almost appears to be sleeping."

"I don't think he feels compassion for the babies or has any paternal instincts," Kent said. "He's gentle with them because he knows it would frame the mother better."

Nina turned back to the screen. "What happened when the paramedics arrived?"

Breck tapped the keyboard, displaying a series of grisly crime scene photos as the New York field agent answered the question.

"They summoned the building superintendent to open the locked apartment door with a key," he said. "They found a bloodbath inside. The NYPD noted in their report that the scene was staged to look like a homicide-suicide."

Breck pulled up an image of a butcher knife lying on bloodstained beige carpeting as the agent continued. "He didn't have time to arrange everything like in the earlier cases you sent us for reference. He must have heard the door opening and took off, because he left the knife too far away from the mother's body. Detectives knew she couldn't have used it. Neither could the father."

"Did they see him leaving?" Nina asked.

Breck switched to a photo of a metal railing against the side of the building.

"This is an old building," New York said. "It still has external fire escapes. One of the medics thought he heard metal rattling like someone was climbing down when they first arrived. The police processed the rear window, and that's where they found that Nike shoe print."

"No one got a description then?"

New York shook his head. "It was the middle of the night on a weekday."

"Where did he hit before that?" Kent asked Buxton.

"Four years prior, he was in San Diego," Buxton replied, picking up the narrative as Breck tapped her keyboard. The San Diego police file and a different FBI field agent replaced the images from New York.

"This case—and all the others before it—were closed as double-homicide-suicides with the mother as the perpetrator," Buxton said.

"The SDPD found the whole family deceased from carbon monoxide gas," the San Diego field agent said as Breck clicked through various images. "The father and baby were in their respective rooms, and the mother was in a rocking chair near the crib. In the kitchen, all four gas burners were on and the oven door was open. The exterior doors all had towels stuffed under them."

"No one raised any objections to the suicide conclusion?" Nina asked.

"The wife had been estranged from her relatives and didn't have many friends," San Diego said. "No one contradicted the idea that she was unstable. In fact, there had been a previous suicide attempt ten years earlier when she was fifteen."

"What did the unsub set up as the immediate trigger?" Wade asked. "Jealousy again?"

"Not this time," San Diego said. "He didn't really set anything up."

Wade steepled his fingers. "Which makes me wonder if he knew about the previous suicide attempt and figured he didn't need to bother."

"He has plenty of time for research before he kills," Nina said. "Although he couldn't have found out about a juvenile's suicide attempt through normal channels."

"Wonder if he searched her social media?" Breck said. "Although I doubt she would still be talking about it if she only had one incident ten years earlier."

Discussion of how the unsub knew so much about his victims spurred a thought Nina hadn't considered before. "Here's a random question. Babies tend to come into this world when they damn well feel like it. Once the unsub targets a couple, how does he know when the baby is born?" Another thought followed closely. "What if the baby is stillborn and never comes home with the parents?"

"In each case, the child was born anywhere from six weeks to a day before the attack," Buxton said. "The killer wouldn't need precise information about the date of birth, only that the baby had been born alive and was home from the hospital."

They were all missing something, and she couldn't let it go. "We know the unsub has to plan his attacks well in advance of the crimes. That includes locating and targeting his victims. How is he doing that?"

"Is it possible he is accessing medical information from these women's obstetricians?" Kent asked. "That way, he would know the projected due date for the baby."

"That information is highly confidential," Buxton said. "And there's no national clearinghouse containing all of it."

"What about someone hacking into a medical insurance database?" Breck said.

Wade shook his head. "They didn't have anything like that almost thirty years ago. People used to fill out forms that were kept in file cabinets at the doctor's office." He cut his eyes to her. "You remember pen and paper, Breck?"

"Okay, boomer." She smirked. "But Guerrera is right, babies arrive on their own schedule, unless it's a planned C-section."

"That's it," Perez said, speaking for the first time since the meeting began. "I was at Meaghan Doyle's autopsy. Her C-section incision was still fresh."

"Was it planned?" Nina asked. "Or an emergency procedure?"

"I spoke to her best friend, who threw the baby shower," Perez said. "It was planned. Meaghan told her the delivery date months in advance."

Excitement hastened Buxton's words as he looked at the screen on the wall. "Can all of you forward the autopsy files for the mother?"

"This has to be it," Nina said to her team as the various agents from around the country began typing on their computers. "How would the unsub plan his crimes for leap day if he couldn't be sure when the baby would come home from the hospital?" She paused a moment. "And how would he know the sex of the baby ahead of time?"

"The only answer is that he had to have backup families in place," Kent said. "Since he was methodical and careful and had access to so much information in advance, we can only assume he would have more than one target couple."

"He had to know they were expecting a baby and where they lived ahead of time," Buxton said. "If we can figure out how he knew, we could get a bead on him."

One by one, Breck clicked on the forwarded files from each city, checking the attached autopsy files, all of which confirmed a recent C-section incision on the mother. In each case, the baby had been a girl, and the couple's first child.

Nina felt the familiar tingle of gathering momentum. She wasn't sure how, but this meant something.

Chapter 15

He hefted the empty suitcase and stowed it on the top shelf of the closet. Twenty minutes earlier, he'd checked into the Phoenix Royal Suites. He resented having to burn one of the aliases he had developed over the years. More than simply a fake name, he had constructed several elaborate false identities that included driver's licenses and credit cards needed for travel. If the FBI tried to link the cases together, they would not find his real name—or any recurring name at all—on airline passenger lists to and from cities where the crimes occurred.

While at the hotel's front desk, he'd made it a point to study the security system, including camera placement, room-key procedures, and hotel staff. His lock-picking skills would not work with electronic card readers on guest room doors. He needed a different way to access what he wanted without leaving a trace of his presence. A plan began to take shape when a bellman approached to ask if he needed assistance with his small piece of rolling luggage—an obvious play for a tip.

He had declined the offer, wheeled his suitcase up to the room, then immediately called for room service to request extra hangers for the closet. Ten minutes later, he answered a polite knock to find a uniformed room service attendant holding ten wooden hangers.

He took them from the young man, then made a show of digging around in his pocket as the attendant waited for a tip. He held out a twenty, then pretended to lose his balance. The attendant caught him, preventing him from falling. He clutched at the young man's jacket to right himself and, when the attendant left after accepting the tip, he no longer had his universal electronic keycard.

Now, gazing at his reflection in the long mirror on the back of the hotel door, he weighed his options. He assumed hotel security would deactivate the stolen keycard as soon as the attendant reported it missing but figured he should have at least twenty minutes before that happened, since most people who requested room service were in their rooms to open the door for an attendant.

A uniform would be a useful tool for his purposes, a kind of shorthand by which people read one another. He decided that a bellman's duties would serve his purposes better than a room service attendant. The gray bellman's outfit with red trim would cause people to make certain assumptions about him, allow him to remain invisible as he prowled the halls . . . or entered a room.

He stepped out of his suite and traversed the carpeted hall to the elevator. Once inside, he pressed the circular button with a *B* on it and felt his stomach lurch as he rapidly descended to the basement.

The doors hissed open and he stepped out, scanning the area. He spent the next ten minutes in a determined hunt, telling a startled maid he had mistakenly gotten off on the wrong floor, before he found the hotel supply room.

After checking to be sure no one was around, he began a quick and efficient search of the linens, bedding, toiletries, and towels stacked in neat piles. A hint of red caught his eye, and he made a beeline for a rack filled with hotel uniforms. He pushed aside gray-and-white maid's dresses, black security blazers, and gray valet outfits before finding the bellman's uniforms with their red-striped pants.

He had just snatched everything he needed in the right size when the door opened.

"What are you doing?" A young bellman eyed him with overt suspicion. "Guests aren't supposed to be down here."

He gave a nonchalant shrug. "I wanted to borrow a uniform."

The bellman looked barely old enough to shave. "You're up to something," he said. "I should call security."

The kid had said he *should*, not that he *would*, call security, leaving open the possibility that he might be persuaded not to make the call.

He noticed the young man's worn shoes, cheap watch, and obvious DIY haircut and took a calculated risk.

"I'm looking for a bit of information." He waited a beat before adding, "And I'm willing to pay for it."

He had dangled the bait. Either the kid would bite, or he wouldn't.

"What do you want to know?"

"For starters, what rooms are that famous FBI lady and the other Feds staying in? I'm sure you know who I'm talking about."

"Oh yeah. She's hot." The kid nodded, then his eyes narrowed. "You're not just a random hotel guest, are you?"

The kid wasn't as stupid as he looked.

"No, I'm not."

"You a reporter or something?"

He turned the idea over in his mind, quickly assessing the possibilities. He decided another admission could work to his advantage. He could keep in touch with the kid going forward.

He adjusted his approach. "Guilty as charged. I want to get a scoop on the case they're investigating, and there's no way to get anywhere near them. Their FBI facility is like a fortress, but here at this hotel . . ." He allowed the implication to hang between them for a moment, then lifted the uniform on its hanger. "I can wear this and blend in. Watch what they do without them knowing."

"The bell captain will have my ass if he finds out I'm helping a reporter." The kid gave him a shrewd look. "What's it worth to you?"

He smiled. He had closed the sale, now they only needed to settle on a price. He enjoyed negotiations. "A hundred bucks."

The kid jutted his chin out and adopted a tough tone. "Five hundred dollars and you've got yourself a deal."

He allowed a long pause. "Tell you what. I borrow the bellman's uniform and you tell me what rooms they're in, and I'll give you three hundred dollars."

The kid folded his arms across his scrawny chest. "Five hundred."

He pulled three crisp Benjamins from his pocket. "Three hundred. Cash money. Right now."

"Done." The kid snatched the proffered bills, slipping them into his inside vest pocket.

He stifled a smirk. He would have paid a thousand. The kid had a lot to learn about haggling.

"She's on the thirty-first floor," the kid said. "In the farthest adjoining suite at the end of the hall. There's two G-men in the connected suite and another one across the hall in a room by himself."

"Pleasure doing business with you." He made a show of pausing as if an idea had just occurred to him. "Can I have your cell number in case I need more information in the future?"

The kid rattled off a number, then grinned. "It'll cost you each time."

He nodded, committing the number to memory, then pulled a black garbage bag from the shelf. He slipped it over the hanger to hide the uniform, then walked down the hall to the service elevator.

Ten minutes later, he strode along the thirty-first floor dressed as a bellman, aware the FBI team was out investigating. He scanned the numbers on placards affixed to the walls beside each door. Based on the bellman's description, he figured Guerrera and the other female were sharing a room that adjoined the suite with the two male agents he'd seen with her. Their supervisor was probably the one with a room to himself across the hall.

He arrived at the end of the hall, glanced over his shoulder, and waved the keycard in front of the sensor to room 3110. If anyone ever thought to check the hotel's computer system in the future, they would eventually determine that the room had been entered on this date using a room service attendant's lost keycard. The trail would end there.

He wasn't worried. The young man who brought the extra hangers up to his suite would be blamed—and probably fired—for carelessness. The bellman in the supply room wouldn't connect the incidents. If he did, he certainly wouldn't come forward to admit he'd taken a bribe to point out where FBI agents were staying.

The latch clicked and the tiny light turned green. He pushed the door open and slipped inside. He was not here to take anything. He was here to leave something.

Fortunately, the uniform's matching gray gloves would leave no prints or extraneous fibers that didn't belong in the hotel. He slipped a pouch from his pocket and pulled out a metal disk the size and shape of a nickel. He removed the lampshade, unscrewed the bulb, and pulled out its electrical guts. He spliced a thin wire jutting from the side of the circular listening device to the lamp's internal wiring, giving the bug a continuous power source. He could monitor them for weeks if necessary. He lifted the lampshade back on and screwed down the finial that held it in place.

Now for the backup. He had taken the ballpoint pen the hotel had thoughtfully placed in his room on the desk and retrofitted it for audio. He switched out the pen already on the desk with the one he'd rigged, taking care to aim the tiny microphone toward the room rather than the wall.

One room done, two to go. He considered the pens a double-or-nothing gamble. He'd made sure the ballpoints could all still write, although the shortened cartridge meant the ink would run out quickly. With luck, one of the agents might take it with them. People often did—hotels counted on that for cheap advertising. If they did, he would literally be in their pocket as they investigated. On the other hand, they all might throw the pens away. Unlike the bugs in the lamps, the minuscule batteries in the pens would drain after a few days without a constant power source. If this investigation dragged on, he might have to come back and replace them. Either way, he would have audio from the lamps indefinitely.

It was all about the risk-to-reward ratio. The likelihood of discovery was low, and the potential to gain information was high. He liked his odds.

Chapter 16

Nina had learned from Wade and Kent that part of a profiler's job was to go inside the mind of both the killer and the victim, but she was running headlong into mental dead ends with this one. Unable to fathom why he did what he did, she was left with how. How had he known about the C-sections? How had he chosen his victims?

"Maybe we can find something in his history that will help," Buxton said, steering the conversation back to the past cases. "Four years before San Diego, he successfully pulled off his scheme in Houston." He glanced up at the wall-mounted screen, which Breck had split between the Houston agent and the HPD case file from twelve years ago.

"He mixed bleach and ammonia to make a toxic gas," the Houston agent said, taking Buxton's cue.

"Interesting," Wade said, studying the images on the screen. "Poison has a reputation as a woman's weapon of choice, and he also used household items any woman would be familiar with. He played to stereotypes so framing the mother would be more convincing."

"And that's exactly what the police investigation concluded," Houston said. "The mother in this case had ended her career as a well-regarded attorney shortly after she became pregnant. She told everyone she wanted to be a stay-at-home mom. A rumor started after the deaths that she regretted her decision and became depressed. Local police never could find the source of the gossip, but it fit with what the evidence showed."

"Maybe he helped spread the rumor," Nina muttered, thinking of the Llorona tale. "He's been fortunate in cases where a false narrative helps his storyline along, or he pushes out a convenient theory himself one way or another."

Kent regarded her thoughtfully. "It would all be part of his smear campaign against the mother in each case."

"No sign of a struggle?" Perez asked, taking the discussion back to the crime scene.

"There were a few contusions on the bodies," Breck said, an array of autopsy photos still visible on her computer screen. "But the ME concluded they could have occurred perimortem as the victims thrashed around."

Perez's brows furrowed. "He must have struck the husband and wife hard enough to render them unconscious or at least incoherent while he gassed them."

"I'd like to have one of the forensic scientists at Quantico take a closer look at that autopsy report," Kent said.

"I've directed Agent Breck to compile and forward the information as soon as we're finished," Buxton said before directing his attention back to the wall monitor. "Four years before Houston, he struck in Chicago."

The Chicago agent appeared on the screen. "In our case, he used an organophosphate to poison the victims."

"Pretend I'm not a chemist," Perez said. "Organo-what?"

"The FBI has run across it a few times," Buxton responded for the Chicago agent. "An organophosphate, or OP, is a type of chemical commonly found in pesticides. It can be concentrated to form a nerve gas. Terrorists have been known to do this. Sarin is a type of OP toxin. When it's properly formulated, a single drop of OP on exposed skin can cause almost instant death."

Nina folded her arms. "Okay, so how did this get blamed on the wife? Was she a chemistry professor?"

In answer, the Chicago agent held up a printed image of a panel van with a company logo on the side. "Her husband was a professional exterminator. He had all kinds of poisons stored in containers in his van. During their investigation, the police found a trove of web searches in her computer history researching how to create a fast-acting toxin from the chemicals her husband had."

"This is going back sixteen years," Buxton said. "The subject of sarin was well publicized due to terrorist attacks around the world. I suppose it was easy enough for detectives to assume she had latched on to the idea from watching the news."

"And what was her supposed motive?" Nina asked.

"Nothing obvious," Chicago said. "I imagine the internet searches were the main source of corroboration with what they found at the scene."

"Searches he may have planted on her computer as part of his staging process," Breck said.

Nina had another idea. "If he's as good as I think he is, he might have gained access to the house and run searches on the computer once or twice prior to the day of the murder to create a brief but convincing search history."

Breck looked up from her monitor. "If he was *really* good, he could have taken over her computer using a Trojan horse and put stuff in there for months in the background where no one but police computer forensics would find it."

Nina was convinced there was more information hidden just beneath the surface. She was beginning to get a picture of the unsub but wanted to delve deeper. "Which city was before Chicago?"

"Philadelphia." Buxton nodded to Breck, who switched to new images on the screen.

"Ours was another case of carbon monoxide poisoning," the Philadelphia field agent said. "This time it was a car left running in the attached garage. I've been assigned to Philly for five years now, and February's damned cold around here. Apparently, their next-door neighbor thought they were just warming up the car in the morning. After a while, she went to check it out and found the family dead. Turns out the car had been running in the garage since midnight."

Nina was perplexed. "How does an accidental death get ruled as a murder-suicide?"

"Evidence at the scene indicated the mother had waited until the family fell asleep before starting the car and propping open the interior door leading to the garage," Philly said.

Nina leaned forward. "But car motors are loud, the mother and father would have heard the noise and woken up. The unsub would have had to break in, subdue the family, then set the scene. Was there evidence of trauma to the bodies?"

"The ME found blunt force trauma to the husband's skull and sleeping medication in the mother's system," Philly said. "Detectives concluded the wife hit her husband with a shovel from their garage before taking the sleeping pills. They figured she wanted to die in her sleep after what she'd done to her family."

Nina thought about what they had learned from the Doyle crime scene in Phoenix and grasped the cruel but efficient methodology. "But in reality, the killer could have forced the mother to swallow the pills by threatening her child."

"Highly likely," Kent said, echoing her thoughts. "I believe that's how he got Meaghan Doyle to step into the bathtub in the most recent case."

"I think that's how he's controlled the mother at every scene," Wade said. "Using her child to terrorize her would add an even higher level of torment, which seems to be a main motivation behind his crimes."

Nina felt sick at the thought that someone who was incapable of emotions had learned how to use them against the women he targeted for his sick retribution. Their very capacity to feel love made them vulnerable to him.

"Going back twenty-four years, we have a case in LA," Buxton said as Breck switched to the final agent in the virtual link to the meeting.

The Los Angeles field office agent popped onscreen. "Ours was a stabbing fairly similar to the one in New York. LAPD concluded the wife struck her husband on the head with a metal lamp before stabbing him multiple times in the upper torso. She appeared to have suffocated the baby before jamming the same knife used to kill her husband into her own throat."

The crime scene photos on Breck's screen were in stark contrast to the Philadelphia case, in which everyone appeared to be asleep.

Nina saw blood sprayed all over the walls and carpet. "The mother's alleged motivation this time?" she asked.

"Infidelity," LA said. "The husband had been frequenting a prostitute. The wife found out, confronted him, and it all went downhill from there."

"How did the wife learn about the prostitute?" Kent asked.

LA glanced down at his notes. "The police report doesn't say how she knew, but she left a suicide note indicating a woman she simply referred to as a 'hooker' approached her with evidence of a relationship with her husband. The woman reportedly wanted money for an abortion and the husband wouldn't pay, so she went to his wife."

Nina was skeptical. "All of this was in a suicide note?"

LA held up a copy. "The LAPD had the handwriting analyzed. The wife definitely wrote it."

"Because he forced her to," Wade said. "No doubt he threatened her baby."

Nina could picture the woman writing the letter with trembling hands. "She had to know she was writing her own death warrant. He must have promised to let the child live if she cooperated." She glanced at Wade. "But you believe he would have made sure she knew her baby was dead before he killed her."

He inclined his head in affirmation. "If it's all about torturing the mother, he would have viewed that as the worst pain he could inflict."

"Did they track down the prostitute he was supposedly with?" Breck asked. "I mean, is there any reason to believe he actually paid for sex, or that he had gotten someone pregnant?"

"The police never found anyone they could link to him," LA said. "Everything was circumstantial, and it fit with the scene, which looked like a domestic fight gone off the rails."

"The jealous wife," Wade said. "LA was only the killer's second attack. That ploy worked the first time in Phoenix, so he would have been confident it would work again."

"He was right," Nina said.

"Which brings us back in time to the very first case," Buxton said, turning to Nina. "What did you and Detective Perez find out today?"

"Enough to convince me the Llorona case is part of the series." She quickly brought the team up to speed on their investigation.

When Buxton seemed impressed by the observation of the blood-spatter discrepancies, Perez interrupted Nina's account to make sure the boss understood that it had been her discovery alone.

"We'll need to take a closer look at the crime scene photos in the other cases," Buxton said, then turned to Wade. "Your thoughts?"

"I can draw one firm conclusion." His gray eyes roved around the room and up to the screen, where their fellow agents from around the country watched and listened. "We are dealing with a unique predator. He is severely disturbed yet able to pass himself off as normal, even charming. He is ruthless, manipulative, and completely without con-science. He's a shark swimming in the ocean, and we have to find him because he will keep killing."

Chapter 17

"Let's review the most recent case." Buxton glanced to his left. "Agent Kent, what do you and Agent Breck have to report about the Doyle investigation?"

"They were both medical professionals," Kent said. "We split up the work. Breck looked into Mrs. Doyle's patients and professional contacts, and I checked on her husband's. There were no red flags. Both seemed to have highly professional reputations, and there were no pending malpractice actions or complaints. Everyone who worked with either of them had nothing but praise."

"If I recall correctly, Mrs. Doyle planned to leave her practice after she had the baby," Buxton said.

"She wanted to be a stay-at-home mom," Kent said. "Everyone at her practice told us how much they missed her as well as how excited they were for her."

"Several of the staff from both offices even helped them move into their new home six months ago," Breck added. "People definitely like you if they're willing to help you move. It's the ultimate test of friendship. Even with the help of a moving company, there's still a thousand things to pack up . . . plus the stuff you don't trust anyone else with."

"They had been living in a high-rise condo in downtown Phoenix," Kent said, "but decided they wanted a house and a yard when they started their family. They must have begun looking for a new place right after they found out they were pregnant."

"They purchased the house almost immediately," Breck said, glancing at her computer. "Put the condo on the market. It took about four months to sell, but they made the move quickly."

"Wait a minute." Nina recalled something she had seen in the Llorona case file. "Didn't Maria and Victor Vega move into their home shortly before they were killed too?"

"Let me check." Breck's fingertips flashed over the keyboard. "Found it. They moved in right after Christmas, about two months before the murders."

"And the Doyles," Nina said, not sure where this was going but anxious to follow the breadcrumbs. "Exactly when did they move into their home?"

"September first," Breck said. "About six months before they were killed."

Unconcerned about protocol, Nina took it upon herself to address the agents linked in on the screen. "Did any of you find out or did the police note anything in their reports about a recent change in residence for the victims?"

The agent from the New York office spoke up. "The family in our case relocated from Jersey about three months prior to the attack."

Nina held her breath as the other agents typed on laptops, checking their files.

"They moved into the house just over a month before the crime," the Philly agent said. "They had planned to do it earlier, but there was some trouble finalizing the mortgage. The extended family said the couple worried they wouldn't be able to get settled in and set up a nursery before the baby came."

"Where did they move from?" Buxton asked.

"Across town. They were living in an apartment and bought a house once they found out the wife was pregnant."

Buxton glanced her way. "This is beginning to sound familiar."

"We don't have anything about a recent move in our files, but we'll check on it right away," the San Diego agent said as his coworker stood and walked out of view.

"Same here," the Chicago agent said. "It never came up."

"Ditto," Houston said.

Not surprising. The city police in these jurisdictions believed they had a homicide-suicide on their hands. There would be no reason to investigate how recently they had moved into the house where they lived.

Nina pressed on while their fellow field agents scrambled to fill in the blanks. "So far, several of the couples initiated a move to a larger residence when they learned they were expecting a baby."

"Makes sense," Kent said. "Since it was their first child in each case, it's presumable that they would want more children in the future and needed the extra space."

Nina considered the ramifications. "Selling their home and relocating also makes it public that they are expecting a baby a lot sooner than when the wife starts showing. In other words—"

"The fact that they were having a baby might be widely known," Breck said. "And far in advance of the birth."

"But a C-section date wouldn't," Wade said. "How would the unsub know about that?"

Nina didn't have an answer, so she focused on other clues. "Don't forget he's got four years between each murder to plan. Maybe that's why he targets only big cities. He needs a large pool of victims to choose from in order to meet his criteria with several backups ready."

"So he decides what city he wants to hit, then waits until it's a few months out from leap day and starts checking to see who wants to move houses due to an upcoming baby," Kent said.

Breck frowned. "But realty companies don't put upcoming childbirth announcements in their databases."

"My wife is a real estate agent," the Chicago agent said, drawing everyone's attention. "Realtors always know the background on buyers and sellers. It's part of their job. They might tell a potential buyer that the seller was moving to a bigger place due to a growing family. That way the buyer wouldn't be scared off thinking it's because the neighborhood is bad or there's something wrong with the house."

"That's true," Wade said. "I remember the last time I sold my house. I told the real estate agent I wanted to move closer to work, and I also asked her why the homeowner was selling the place I was buying." He paused. "It all comes back to the Realtor."

"But would that kind of information go into a database?" Perez asked doubtfully.

"My wife puts details like that into the private comments other agents could see," Chicago said. "The public couldn't access it, but another Realtor could. She's also called sellers' agents on behalf of her clients to find out that information in some cases."

"I've just heard back," San Diego said, breaking into the discussion. "Our couple relocated from the other side of the city four months before the murders."

"Us too," Chicago said a moment later. "Our victims sold their house and moved into a different neighborhood five and a half months before the murders."

"I've got something interesting," Houston said. "The couple in our city bought the home five months prior. Get this . . . they relocated from Phoenix, Arizona."

"Who was their realty company?" Nina said.

"Rubric Realty."

Nina had heard of the huge national corporation. Some of her fellow FBI agents from the Washington field office had used them when they were reassigned, having the same realty company deal with both the sale of their previous homes and the purchase of their new ones.

"Did they handle both ends of the move?" Buxton asked.

"Yes, Rubric Realty's Phoenix branch sold their old house, and their Houston office took care of the purchase."

Buxton directed his next comment to Breck. "How many of the cases involve Rubric Realty in some way?"

Breck had previously downloaded police reports from every case, which included the victims' addresses.

"Give me a moment," she said. "I'm pulling the public records for each address."

A few minutes later, she pumped her fist. "Bingo."

Buxton leaned forward. "Let's hear it."

Breck looked up from her computer. "Every single case involved Rubric in some way, either representing the buyer, the seller, or both."

"Were there any real estate agents who were personally involved in more than one transaction?" Buxton asked.

"Thomas Kirk," Breck said, glancing back at the screen. "He works out of the Phoenix branch. He handled the sale of the condo and the purchase of the new home for the Doyles. He also sold the home for the couple who relocated to Houston twelve years ago."

"Run him," Buxton said. "How old is he?"

"Fifty-one," Breck said after a quick check.

They all exchanged glances. Kirk was old enough to have committed the crimes. They finally had a viable lead.

"Guess what?" Breck said, then continued without waiting. "He's got a juvenile record."

"For what?" Wade asked, excitement animating his normally placid features.

"It's sealed," Breck said. "All juvenile criminal history is." She tapped the screen with the back of her pen. "But I've worked with these codes long enough to know that this one means there's an underage conviction."

Buxton frowned. "What else can you find?"

Breck bent back over her keyboard and began typing. "He attended elementary and middle school in Tucson, then got a GED from the state of Arizona, so I'm assuming whatever crime he committed was in Arizona as well."

"Why no high school info?" Nina said.

Wade frowned. "I'm guessing because he was in juvie during those years."

Made sense to Nina. "Is there a youth detention facility in Tucson?"

Breck glanced up. "Yep. And I'll bet that's where our boy was. Give me some time and I'll dig up the dirt."

Nina didn't want to ask too many questions about how Breck would unearth juvenile records, and she noticed Buxton didn't appear to either.

"I want to know everything about him," Buxton said. "Then we need to pay Mr. Thomas Kirk a little visit."

Chapter 18

Two hours later, Nina sat beside Wade in Robert Cahill's living room. Seated in the chair across from them in his Arizona Cardinals jersey, cargo shorts, white knee-high socks, and black sandals, Cahill looked like a cross between an ad for senior singles and a retired football coach.

Breck had run across Cahill's name after confirming that Thomas Kirk had been locked up in a juvenile detention center on the outskirts of Tucson. Kirk had been convicted of robbing a string of convenience stores at fifteen and sentenced to incarceration until his eighteenth birthday.

Cahill had been Kirk's supervisory coordinator during his time at the facility. Luckily, Cahill had retired and moved to Tempe, a short drive from Phoenix. Kirk would have been twenty-three years old at the time of the Llorona case, and Wade was convinced his earlier criminal history would provide insight into his motivations.

Buxton had designated Nina and Wade to conduct the interview while the rest of the team continued their workup on Kirk.

Cahill had been more than happy to speak with them, and Nina had the impression he welcomed any opportunity for visitors.

"You want to know about Tommy Kirk," Cahill said, making it a statement. "I'm sorry to hear he took a turn for the worst."

"Why would you say that?" Nina wanted to know.

"Because the FBI wouldn't be knocking on my door to tell me Tommy's getting a Nobel Prize."

"True," Nina said. "We need your help to understand what Tommy was like when he was younger." She deliberately used the nickname Cahill had called Kirk when he was a boy, referencing the part of his life they wanted to know about. "How would you describe him?"

Cahill leaned back, looking thoughtful. "He was a mean kid when he first came to the center."

"Mean?" Wade prompted.

"Boys will be boys," Cahill said. "But Tommy took it too far. The slightest thing provoked him. He got in more than his share of fights."

Nina refrained from asking what the appropriate "share" of fights for a kid to get in was.

"You'd classify him as violent, then," Wade said.

"To the extreme." Cahill's gray-blond head bobbed vehemently. "He formed a tight-knit group of friends at the facility. They looked out for each other, beating the shit out of anyone they felt threatened them."

"Nice guy," Nina said dryly.

"Actually, he was." Cahill rushed to add, "By the time he left, I mean."

"Could you elaborate?" Wade said.

"Tommy matured over the years before he got out. He became something like a big brother to the younger kids in his clique. He helped a lot of them after they left the center."

"What did he do for them?" Nina asked.

"In a hard-core facility like the one I worked at, the boys usually age out. In other words, if they were convicted as adults, they would be doing a twenty- or thirty-year stretch, but they're juvies, so a lot of the judges give them another shot when they turn eighteen." He grimaced. "The unlucky ones with longer sentences are transferred to regular prison when they come of age."

"Was Kirk released at eighteen?" Nina asked.

"He was," Cahill said. "The problem comes when the kids are released and no one wants to hire them. Their records are sealed, but it doesn't take a genius to figure out where they've been. We try to make sure they get a GED and give them vocational training, but any potential employer with half a brain is going to know they served time."

This was an issue Nina had observed all too frequently with the adult penal system. It was difficult for offenders to go straight after completing their sentences when no one wanted to employ them. Many turned back to crime to support themselves or ended up homeless.

Cahill continued with his recollection. "Seeing how Tommy had turned things around, I called a friend of mine who was a regional director for a security company and asked him to give the boy a chance. Tommy was good with computers and technology, so he could help install home-security systems."

Nina gave Wade a meaningful look before turning back to Cahill. "Did your friend hire him?" she asked.

"Tommy worked for Jexton Security for a few years until he got his Realtor's license and changed careers. I lost track of him after that, but he seems to have done well for himself selling homes."

"You mentioned he helped the other boys?" Wade asked.

"Yeah, after he got his first job in security, he paid it forward, recommending the other boys to work there, too, once they got out of the detention center." Cahill shrugged. "Probably kept a bunch of them off the street and out of jail." He shook his head. "I really thought Tommy was a success story. I don't know what he did to make you two come to see me, but it must have been serious."

Wade leaned forward, intent. "You said you thought criminal activity would not be in Tommy's character anymore. Why do you believe that?"

Cahill considered a moment before answering. "When he first came to us, Tommy was on drugs. The hard stuff. We spent months detoxing him. I wonder how much of his crimes had to do with supplying his habit and how much of his violence inside the center was about going through withdrawal."

"I see your point," Nina said, trying to reconcile this with a cold-blooded killer. "What was his family like?"

Anyone who would slaughter families had to have major issues in that area. Cahill's insights into Tommy Kirk's childhood might bridge the gap between his apparent rehabilitation and the psychopathy of a serial killer.

"This is going back a few decades," Cahill said, "so my recollections may not be perfect, but I don't remember any problems with his family."

Nina waited quietly, giving him time to dredge up any loose scraps of memory.

"His father never came to visit," Cahill finally added. "But his mother and sister did."

"He came from a family of four?" Wade asked. "Father, mother, and sister?"

"That's right."

"Was it a younger sister?"

"I believe so."

"This is important, Mr. Cahill," Wade said. "Did Tommy ever act out in late February or early March . . . especially if it was a leap year?"

After a long pause, Cahill shook his head. "Not that I recall."

Sensing they had pumped Cahill dry, Nina ended the interview with a catchall question. "Is there anything else about Tommy we haven't asked? Anything that might help us understand his personality?"

Cahill's brow furrowed. "Don't think so."

Nina handed him a business card. "Call us if you remember something."

Nina followed Wade out to the black Suburban parked in the driveway. "Cahill seemed genuinely disappointed when we told him we were here to talk about Kirk," she said to him as she hoisted herself up into the driver's seat.

"Cahill thought Kirk had turned his life around," Wade said. "But maybe Kirk just figured out how to hide his propensities better."

She backed out of the driveway. "Interesting that his family consisted of a mother, father, and sister. The exact composition of each murdered family."

Wade buckled his seat belt. "It's like he's the son who's absent in each case. That must be significant, but we still don't know what his original trigger was. Or the precipitating stressor right before he killed the Vega family twenty-eight years ago."

She worked through the profile with him. "The original trigger would have been something involving his family, probably during his childhood, no?"

"Almost certainly," Wade said. "This unsub is obsessed with family."

She noticed Wade still referred to "the unsub," which meant he was not prepared to call Kirk a suspect at this point. "And the precipitating stressor would be something completely different that happened after he got out of juvie. An incident that retriggered him."

"Stressors could include the loss of a job, a relationship, or a health crisis, but our information indicates Kirk had successfully transitioned into his new career in realty. He never had any health issues Breck could find, and he never married." He frowned. "We're missing something important."

Nina wove her way through traffic as she headed to the Phoenix field office, hoping like hell Wade was wrong.

Chapter 19

The next morning, Nina adjusted the visor to block the morning sun as the Suburban glided toward central Phoenix. An evening spent guzzling too many cups of coffee while the team tracked down every scrap of information they could find about Thomas Kirk had left her unable to sleep after they got back to the hotel the night before. She had eagerly discussed the developments with Breck, who was equally wired on caffeine, until almost midnight.

The team had planned to descend on Kirk's house first thing in the morning before he left for work. She followed closely behind Perez's unmarked sedan as they turned onto Kirk's street, Wade in the front passenger seat and Breck and Kent in the back.

"The place looks quiet," she said as they eased to a stop a couple of houses down from the target address.

Perez got out, ambled to the driver's door, and stuck his head in when she buzzed the window down. "Do you want me to request some uniforms?"

She shook her head. "We're not going in heavy. At this point, it's a knock-and-talk." She used the police vernacular she knew Perez would be familiar with for an initial approach to the subject of an investigation under voluntary circumstances.

Less than sixty seconds later, Nina, Wade, and Perez were at the front door while Breck and Kent covered the back of the house. You could never tell when a knock-and-talk would morph into a cut-and-run.

After no response to the doorbell, Nina pounded with her fist. The front door creaked open a fraction. She darted a glance at Wade and Perez before raising her voice.

"FBI. We're looking for Thomas Kirk."

Silence.

"Mr. Kirk, we need to speak to you."

Nothing.

Nina craned her neck to peer inside. A few dots of crimson on the pale gray tile floor caught her eye. "I think there's blood on the floor." She drew her Glock, and both men followed suit.

Wade tapped his ear, activating the com link to Breck and Kent. "The front door is open, and Guerrera saw blood inside," he said. "We're making entry."

Evidence suggesting the possibility of injury to someone inside, coupled with the homeowner being a person of interest in a homicide investigation, was enough to constitute exigent circumstances, giving them the right to make entry to ascertain the safety of anyone in the house.

"FBI," Nina announced again as she surged into the foyer, both men close on her heels. Law enforcement techniques around the country and in different agencies were similar enough that she didn't need to look at her companions to know they were taking up positions to buttonhole around corners and avoid a crossfire as they swiftly cleared the house.

Nina peeled off to investigate the spots of blood she had seen dappling the tile by the dining room near the foyer. Peeking around a wide decorative column, she saw two bare feet sticking out. She recognized the purpling of the legs in the areas closest to the floor and knew that gravity had caused lividity.

"Clear," Wade's voice carried from down the main hall.

She opened her com link and called out so everyone would hear. "I've got a white male lying in the dining room. Obviously deceased."

"Stand by," Wade said. "Everyone else, continue clearing the house."

She waited, gun drawn, for her team to finish and join her in the dining room.

"He's been stabbed," she told them. "Multiple times. Looks like he crawled in here from that direction." She pointed down the hall.

"There's a trail of blood from the master bedroom," Wade said. "He was attacked in bed. Most likely while he was asleep."

Nina bent down to peer at the gaping wounds on the victim's neck. Her eyes traveled up to his face. "It's Thomas Kirk. I recognize him from his driver's license photo." She grimaced. "I'm surprised he made it this far. Those gashes are deep."

Kent holstered his weapon. "Someone slit his throat. Made sure he couldn't cry out or talk on the phone. I'm guessing Kirk was trying to make it out the front door to get help."

"This is now officially a homicide," Perez said, pulling his phone from his pocket. "I've got to make some calls. My department has jurisdiction."

Perez was correct, but Nina forestalled him with a raised hand. "Hold on a second." She glanced around at the chairs lying on their sides, the drawers pulled out from the ornate china cabinet, the artwork dangling askew from hooks on the wall. "What does this look like to you?"

Perez followed her gaze. "A burgoc gone bad."

Police parlance for a burglary of an occupied dwelling.

She narrowed her eyes at him. "I'm not buying it, are you?"

He blew out a sigh. "I agree that it's way more than a coincidence that our prime suspect gets whacked right before we have a chance to interview him." He continued before she could interrupt, "But that doesn't change the fact that Phoenix Homicide has primary jurisdiction here. I need to make notifications, and we've got to stop contaminating the crime scene."

"You know that's what this unsub does," Wade chimed in. "He stages things to look like something they're not." He jerked a thumb toward the hallway. "I was in the master bedroom, which was also ransacked."

"Which means three things," Kent said, holding up a finger. "This wasn't a random burglary." He raised another finger. "Kirk wasn't our unsub." A third finger went up. "Kirk knew something the real killer didn't want us to find out."

"You left out one more key point," Nina said. "Somehow, the unsub knew we were coming here this morning."

Chapter 20

An hour later, Nina was standing outside Kirk's house, conferring with her team, when Perez strode across the lawn to join them, irritation stamped on his features.

"You have a visitor at the perimeter," he said to her without preamble.

Buxton, who had arrived at the scene half an hour earlier, turned toward Perez. "Perhaps you'd better explain, Detective."

"The patrol sergeant coordinating perimeter access told me there's a woman demanding to speak to FBI Special Agent Nina Guerrera." Perez dragged a hand through his thick dark hair. "And she's got a reporter with her."

"Why isn't the reporter in the media-briefing area?" Buxton asked. "And why can't your Public Affairs handle a request for information? There's no need for Agent Guerrera to answer questions."

Perez blew out a frustrated sigh. "It's that same TV reporter who was on the news the day before yesterday. Apparently, the guy covered the Llorona case when it happened, so he knows all the players and a lot of details."

"That's James Snead with Channel Six News," Nina said, recalling the articles and newsclips she had reviewed on the flight to Phoenix. "Who's the woman with him?"

"Teresa Soto," Perez said. "Snead interviewed Teresa about her sister's death . . . and about how the case is being reopened by the FBI."

Kent let out a stream of obscenities. "Who leaked to the media that we were reopening the Llorona case?" He leveled a hard glare at Perez. "No one in the FBI would talk to a local reporter about it."

Perez stepped in close to Kent. "You accusing me of something, Kent? Because if you are—"

"At this point, we don't have time to worry about that," Buxton said, cutting off Perez's rejoinder. "Right now, we need to deal with Maria Vega's sister before she decides to hold her own press conference."

"She wants answers," Nina said. "Can't blame her. We knew this would happen, but I didn't think it would be this fast."

"You'd better go over there and talk to her, Agent Guerrera," Buxton said.

Perez turned away from Kent to stand by Nina. "I'll come with you."

"It's not your place to talk about the Llorona case," Kent said. "That's part of an FBI investigation now."

"That the PPD is assisting with," Perez shot back. "We handled the original case and—"

"You mean *mishandled* the original case," Kent said.

"Gentlemen." Buxton stepped between them. "Stop." He cut his eyes to Nina. "Go."

She pivoted and strode across the lawn. The moment she made her way around the Phoenix police command bus, she spotted Teresa and Snead behind yellow perimeter tape.

Nina still had trouble looking at her despite their previous encounter at the Mercado Vecino the day before. The resemblance to Maria in the crime scene photos was jarring.

Teresa called out to her as soon as she was within earshot. "You're looking into my sister's death, Agent Guerrera." She put a hand on her hip. "Why?"

Nina saw Snead signal his cameraman, who hefted a camera to his shoulder. She ignored the reporter and directed her response to Teresa.

"We are reexamining the evidence in Maria's case because we want to be sure the conclusions reached at the time were accurate."

Teresa jerked her thumb at Snead. "This reporter told me more than that. He said you people suspect someone might have murdered my sister, her husband, and my baby niece. He said it might be the same person who killed that family on the east side of the city a few days ago."

Worse than she'd thought. Above all else, she did not want to lie to this woman whose family had been through so much sorrow. She did not want to add to their pain, but she had to maintain the integrity of the investigation—whatever was left of it.

"We are exploring that possibility."

"That's all you have to say?" Teresa jabbed a finger at her. "My family has carried not only the grief of Maria's death but the shame of having the whole community believing she killed her family." She redirected her finger to point at a Phoenix police van. "They said she was jealous of her husband. They said she went *loca*. They said she murdered her own sweet little girl." Teresa's eyes filled with tears. "My niece. I always knew it wasn't true. I knew Maria could never have done such a thing. No one would listen. And now . . . now . . ." Her trembling hand flew to her mouth, muffling a sob.

Nina could not stop herself from putting an arm around the woman's shaking shoulders. *"Lo siento,"* she whispered. "I'm so sorry for what you have been through."

Eyes brimming, Teresa looked up. "Is it true? Did someone kill my sister and her family?"

Nina knew what she was supposed to say. The company line was that there was an ongoing investigation, and nothing could be released until there was more evidence. Materials from the crime scene were being processed, we'll know more shortly. We'll release the information when we can, blah, blah, blah. Looking into Teresa's eyes—so much like Maria's—she couldn't do it.

Nina nodded slowly. "We believe so."

Teresa threw her arms around Nina in a tight embrace, then pulled back. Her brows drew together. "Promise me you will find the bastard who did this. You hear me? You find him."

Snead, who had been getting every moment of the exchange, poked a microphone toward Nina. "Sources tell me the Doyle family murder is related, and so is the death of Thomas Kirk, which is why you are here now. Can you confirm that the FBI is investigating a serial killer in Phoenix?"

She disengaged from Teresa to face the reporter, responding without taking the bait. "The circumstances surrounding Mr. Kirk's death are under investigation by the Phoenix police, who have jurisdiction in the matter." She gestured toward Perez, who had followed her over. "You'll have to ask them for a comment."

Her assertion was technically accurate. She turned on her heel and began walking away, meeting Perez's dark gaze with a grimace. She'd thrown him under the bus and they both knew it. He stepped past her, prepared to give Snead the party line.

Snead sidestepped Perez to call out to her. "Why is the FBI at the scene of a local Phoenix murder, Agent Guerrera? What are you hiding?"

She didn't acknowledge the question. Snead was right. Their presence at the Kirk homicide made it clear there was more to the case, but how had he figured out the connection between the Llorona case and the Doyle case? The reporter was putting things together quickly.

Perhaps too quickly.

Chapter 21

After another night of unsettled sleep, Perez had picked Nina up at the hotel while the rest of the team rode to the Phoenix field office in the Suburban. Perez had taken her on a brief detour for coffee before parking at the Phoenix police crime lab in the bright morning sun.

The lab director had called Perez late the previous afternoon, indicating she had significant findings to report. After hearing from Perez, Buxton had detailed Nina to review the director's information with him while everyone else spent the morning at the PFO poring over the cases from the other field offices.

The mountain of incoming data provided various points of comparison for Breck, who would consolidate everything onto a color-coded spreadsheet. Nina had never met anyone who loved charts, spreadsheets, and graphs as much as the cybercrime specialist. When Nina and Perez returned from the crime lab, the team would compare notes to see how Thomas Kirk's murder fit into the growing profile.

As Nina pushed open the main entrance door leading into the lab's two-story open foyer, her feet stopped of their own volition. An enormous mobile in the shape of a DNA double helix dangled overhead, suspended on a hook affixed to the soaring ceiling. Petri dishes, beakers, and other scientific equipment glinted in the early-morning light as they gently rotated from wires, creating art from science.

Perez followed her upward gaze. "This mobile has that effect on people the first time they see it. It's not what you expect to find in this setting." He strode past her to the inner door. "Let's go."

As soon as they crossed the threshold, a woman with thick, wavy gray hair and silver-rimmed glasses rushed toward them, her white lab coat billowing behind her.

"Dr. Deborah Ledford." She stuck out a hand to Nina. "Call me Deb."

Perez had texted the lab director to let her know they were coming, and she must have been waiting for their arrival.

"I didn't expect to meet with you personally," Nina said.

Deb smiled as she started toward the back offices. "When I heard what the examiners found, I verified everything myself," she said by way of explanation. "I've never seen anything quite like this."

Nina picked up the pace, matching Deb's strides. "Where are you taking us?"

She knew lab protocols wouldn't allow them into the examination areas due to the potential for cross contamination.

"I've set up a special viewing area," Deb said, pushing through a door on the right side of the wide corridor.

They followed her inside, where they continued down a long hallway until they reached a plexiglass window. Nina peered through the glass to see white-coated technicians with full-face shields and hair coverings working with glistening equipment.

"We're still performing an analysis of the samples from both the old and the new cases," Deb told them. "These results are preliminary since the materials from the Llorona case were only submitted to us late Wednesday, which means we didn't start on them until yesterday morning, but they are highly unexpected. We decided to let you know about these early findings before we completed our full analysis."

Nina realized the lab director had referred to the early case by its nickname. The whole city seemed to have an institutional memory of the crime that had scarred it. How would they react when the story they thought they knew turned out to be a false narrative?

"We performed an expedited DNA and serology examination," Deb said. "I'm hoping your team can provide some context to assist us as we go further with our analysis."

"How can we help?" Nina asked.

Deb gestured toward the technicians. "We analyzed blood samples recovered from the clothing worn by each victim as well as droplets collected from the walls and carpeting in both cases."

Nina pictured the carnage left behind in the two Phoenix homes, then the void in the blood spatter at the Vega house that had prompted them to submit the old material for a new lab analysis.

"I'll start with the Llorona case," Deb said. "The bottom line is that there are four distinct and nonfamilial DNA samples from that scene."

"Four?" Nina instantly grew excited. "There were only three victims. Could the fourth be the killer?"

Perez raised a brow. "Or could the fourth be a friend who came to visit earlier that day, or one of the detectives?"

"Negative," Deb said. "We analyzed only blood samples collected as evidence at the scene. The police were good about documenting exactly where each sample came from, so unless a friend stopped by a short time earlier and bled in the same area where the victims died, that's not possible."

They both took a moment to absorb this.

"You say there were 'four distinct nonfamilial samples'?" Nina prompted, trying to make sense of the statement.

Deb sounded as if she'd been waiting for them to come to this point. "Exactly."

"But they couldn't have been nonfamilial," Nina said. "Their baby girl was—"

"Not their biological child," Deb cut in.

Nina leaned forward, anxious to clarify what the lab director had said. "Copies of the birth records were in the detective's files. I saw them. Maria Vega definitely delivered a live baby girl at Phoenix General Hospital six days before the murders."

Perez rested a hand on his hip. "Are you saying Victor was not the baby's father?"

"No." Deb's tone was firm but patient. "I'm saying that neither Maria Vega nor Victor Vega has any biological link whatsoever to the infant that died in their home."

Stunned, Nina asked the obvious question. "So whose baby was killed?"

No answer was forthcoming.

Perez broke the silence. "Would that play into the motive for the murder, since we believe it was the first one?"

"I analyze evidence," Deb said, apparently thinking the question had been directed at her. "You're the investigators."

"Wait," Nina said, still coming to grips with the findings. "The police took the blood to the lab for analysis at the time. They didn't find any anomalies like this."

"Remember that we're talking about forensic science from almost three decades ago," Deb said. "There was no DNA testing back then. The detectives relied on physical evidence, witness statements, and serology, which is blood typing." She paused, seeming to search for the right words. "In this case, blood found at the scene matched the ones who were deceased. There were no extraneous blood types present."

Nina thought she understood. "So the killer would have had the same blood type as one of the victims."

"That's precisely what happened." Deb seemed relieved they had grasped the concept. "The mother and the baby both had type A blood. The father had type O blood, and the mystery person at the scene also had type O blood."

"If that's the case," Perez said, thinking it through, "when the police analyzed the evidence using only serology, which was standard procedure at the time, they would have typed everyone's blood and assumed all the samples they collected came from the three victims."

"Correct," Deb said. "If the killer had type B blood or an Rh negative factor, or something like that, it would have been obvious that someone else was at the scene."

"But they couldn't tell because the fourth person shared a blood type with the father," Nina said.

"Not surprising, since type O is the most common," Deb said. "O positive represents thirty-eight percent of the population and O negative is another seven percent. Combined, that's a total of forty-five percent."

Nina marveled at the early state of forensic science that had allowed the unsub to get away with his first crime. Even though the scientist had described how it had occurred, Nina considered it a cruel twist of fate.

Deb continued her explanation. "And the original lab techs investigating the evidence at the time also wouldn't have known the baby wasn't related because she shared a blood type with one of the parents. Scientifically, the baby would have to have a blood type in common with at least one parent, and in this case, she did by chance."

Perez groaned his frustration. "What are the odds?"

"Again, not that steep," Deb said. "Type A positive is thirty-four percent of the population, and A negative is six percent. Combined, that makes forty percent. It's all very feasible."

"What about the new case?" Nina said. "The Doyles."

"There was no extraneous blood at that scene. All samples collected matched the three members of the Doyle family who were killed."

"And all three of them are related?" Nina asked, double-checking.

"Yes. We confirmed the husband and wife are the biological parents of the child."

Perez heaved a sigh. "We'll need to go back and check on the relationship between the family members on every case."

Deb's brows shot up. "There are other cases?"

Nina addressed the lab director, distracting her from Perez's inadvertent slip. "Now for the million-dollar question," she said to Deb. "Did you analyze all four of the DNA samples from the Llorona case?"

"We're running the DNA profile through CODIS right now," Deb said.

The Combined DNA Index System, which was the FBI's program containing DNA profiles contributed by forensic laboratories around the nation, included convicted offenders, certain arrestees, crime scene samples, unidentified human remains, missing persons, and relatives of missing persons. This was their chance to finally put a name to a relentless murderer who had been destroying families for far too long.

"How soon will we have an answer?" Perez asked.

"If one of the DNA profiles has already been entered in the system, we'll get a match within a couple of hours," Deb said.

"That works for the suspect," Nina said. "What about the baby?"

"Depends." Deb appeared thoughtful. "If the biological parents are in the criminal database, we could get a strong indicator of a familial match within a few hours as well. If not, we will have to look to external sources like foreign countries or private genealogical companies who are willing to cooperate, which could take weeks. Ultimately, we may never get an answer. There are no guarantees."

"Thank you, Deb," Nina said. "Please advise us as soon as you know anything further."

Perez spoke to her in an undertone as they made their way out of the lab. "I'd like to follow up on that birth certificate in Detective O'Malley's case files. He authenticated it through Arizona state records. With luck, it might be possible to see if the hospital records match."

"I'm going to brief Buxton," she said, coming to a decision. "We need to go to Phoenix General Hospital." She pulled out her phone. "Now."

Chapter 22

Nina sipped from a Styrofoam cup filled with truly awful coffee in the business-annex waiting room at Phoenix General Hospital. She glanced at Perez. "The suit with the expensive briefcase and designer Italian shoes showed up half an hour ago, but we're still sitting out here. This has all the earmarks of a panicked butt-covering session."

Perez drank from his own cup, made a face, then put it down on the end table next to a rumpled magazine. "Agreed. I'm not buying the admin assistant's story about wanting to locate all the files so they can help us." He air-quoted the last two words.

Nina agreed with his assessment. "If I hear the sound of a paper shredder chewing up documents in the back room, I'm pushing past the admin and going in."

Perez leaned closer. "My guess is the hospital screwed up, and they're in there with their boxers in a bunch, trying to figure out what to tell us."

"And avoid a multimillion-dollar lawsuit," Nina added.

The office door opened, and a short man with a neat mustache and a sheen of sweat on his balding pate stepped out. "Please come in."

He ushered them into a spacious conference room, where Nina saw the man who had wordlessly strode past them earlier. His suit looked like it had cost a month's worth of her salary, and the gold cufflinks peeking out at his wrists were embedded with twinkling diamonds. He had just the right touch of gray at the temples of a perfectly barbered Afro, lending him an air of wisdom and experience.

He stood when they entered. "Marcus Johnson, chief legal counsel for the Valance hospital group."

Like many hospitals, Phoenix General was part of a network. Nina was not surprised the hospital director had gotten legal counsel to respond in person. The rapid deployment of their top attorney, however, caught her off guard. The gravity of the situation must have been alarming, although Marcus Johnson didn't show it. The director, however, appeared to be on the verge of nervous collapse.

The director introduced himself as Tim Davies, and once everyone had settled, Nina opened with a shot across the bow. "As I mentioned nearly forty-five minutes ago," she said, emphasizing their extended wait, "we are here to investigate the circumstances surrounding the birth of a baby girl, the daughter of Maria and Victor Vega, twenty-eight years ago on February twenty-third."

She directed the comment at Davies, who squirmed in his chair and turned to the company lawyer.

Johnson cleared his throat. "You indicated to Mr. Davies that this has something to do with an investigation you are conducting. May I ask what the delivery of a baby decades ago has to do with the FBI?"

Johnson was openly fishing for information. Once Davies pulled up the medical files, he would have either recognized the names from the headline-grabbing murder-suicide or found a trove of information about the Llorona case after a quick Google search.

"We can't disclose details at this time," Perez said.

Johnson looked like he had expected as much. "While you've been waiting, we've searched through our archives. I am aware that you could obtain a subpoena duces tecum for the documents, so we are willing to share them with you now. Some of the information contained is redacted due to privacy concerns, as they pertain to medical—"

126

"The two parents and the infant involved are all deceased," Nina cut in. "I'm not sure whose medical information you are protecting."

Johnson leaned back, a closed look on his smooth features. "That remains to be seen."

Nina decided to cut through the legal posturing. "We've been getting a lot of questions from the media. I'm sure we can let them know at our next press conference that our investigation has been hampered due to unnecessary—"

"You've requested information about Victor and Maria Vega and the baby girl they delivered at this hospital," Johnson said. "We can confirm that Maria Vega had a planned cesarean section operation that turned into an emergency surgery when the baby went into distress before delivery."

"What happened next?" Nina asked.

Director Davies dug a finger into his collar. "The infant received standard postpartum care. She recuperated very quickly and was transferred from the NICU to the regular nursery about an hour after delivery. The family was then told they could see her."

Nina narrowed her eyes. "How many other babies were born at Phoenix General that day?"

Davies flicked a glance at Johnson, who raised no objection to answering the question. "Thirty-four babies were delivered at Phoenix General that day," Davies said. "Of those, three were sent to the NICU, the rest went to the nursery."

"Of the three in the NICU, how many were girls?" Nina said, pressing him.

"Two."

She kept up a steady pace of rapid-fire questions. "Of those two, how many were Latina?"

"One. Maria Vega's baby."

Nina processed the information quickly. She concluded that no mix-up had occurred in the NICU. "So after an hour, the Vega baby went to join the other thirty-one babies in the nursery?"

Davies cut his eyes to Johnson, who gave him a subtle nod. He swallowed audibly before answering. "Actually, at that point there were a total of thirty-two newborns in the nursery. The Vega baby made thirty-three."

Perspiration dotted the director's scalp.

Nina, scenting his fear, bore down like a dog after a bone. "But you said thirty-four babies were delivered at the hospital and three went to the NICU, which means thirty-one were in the nursery. Once the Vega baby transferred to the nursery, there would only be thirty-two babies there."

"You asked how many babies were *delivered* at the hospital, and I answered correctly," Davies said. "There was one baby that was born elsewhere but arrived at the hospital shortly after birth."

Nina clenched her fists under the table to prevent herself from shaking him by the lapels until those glistening droplets of sweat flew from his forehead. She tried a different approach. "How many of the babies in the regular nursery were girls?"

"Seventeen."

"How many were Latina?"

"Including the Vega baby? Two."

"Was the other Latina baby the one that was born elsewhere?"

Davies looked at Johnson, who nodded. "Yes," Davies said.

Now she was getting somewhere. "This is important to our investigation, Mr. Davies. What else can you tell me?"

"The other baby was born at home," Davies said after another surreptitious glance at his legal counsel. "Apparently, the mother couldn't get to the hospital in time. A neighbor reportedly called police when she heard screaming next door. Police arrived to find the woman in labor and ended up delivering the baby in the kitchen moments before the ambulance arrived. Rescue personnel brought the mother and child to the emergency room for evaluation."

"And the baby went to the nursery?" Nina asked.

Davies nodded. "We performed routine checks on the newborn while the mother was receiving treatment."

"What kind of treatment?"

Johnson cut in. "We are not at liberty to say. In her case, privacy rules attach."

"Can you provide her name?"

"We cannot," Johnson said. "I'm sure you appreciate the legal ramifications."

Nina tried for any further scraps of information she could finagle. "Can you tell us when she and the baby were discharged and if her baby survived?"

"The mother recuperated quickly," Davies said. "Her baby was healthy. They both left the hospital later that day." He paused to consider his next comment. "Apparently, the mother chose not to spend the night in the maternity ward."

"And Maria Vega?"

"Ms. Vega and her baby stayed in the hospital four extra days due to the mother's surgery," Davies said.

"Four days in the hospital for a C-section?" Nina asked. "Did something go wrong?"

"Standard procedure at the time," Davies said. "Nowadays hospital stays are much shorter."

Nina arrived at the inexorable conclusion. "You do realize this means the two baby girls were switched at the hospital before the other woman left?"

"There is nothing to substantiate that," Johnson said. "And what makes you believe the babies did not go home with their biological parents?"

"They were the only two Latina newborns in the nursery that day," Nina said. "And we have evidence that—" She stopped before revealing that the infant who died at the Vegas' house was not their biological child. "We have to investigate further," she said instead. "We need both parents' names for the other baby."

"As I mentioned before," Johnson said, smoothing his tie, "I am not at liberty to release that information. We have been more than generous in providing the details we have so far."

She leaned forward. "This is a murder investigation, Counselor."

Johnson's brows shot up. "Murder?"

She took the opportunity for a little payback. "We are not at liberty to disclose the details of a criminal investigation." She smiled. "I'm sure you appreciate the legal ramifications."

They had reached an impasse.

"I don't believe there is any more to say until the proper legal documents are submitted." Johnson handed her a business card, effectively bringing the meeting to a close. "You can reach my office with whatever warrants or subpoenas you obtain, and I will comply immediately."

As they walked out into the parking lot, Nina became increasingly infuriated with the legal and bureaucratic logjam that had ground their forward momentum to a halt.

"Johnson and Davies were in possession of information critical to our case," she said. "But they wouldn't hand it over."

"They have rules," Perez said.

"They have their asses to cover." She kept going toward the parking lot. "We'll have to waste hours writing up an affidavit," she said. "And there's no guarantee a judge will sign it."

Perez came to an abrupt stop. "Or you could ask me nicely and I could give you what you need in about fifteen minutes." His cheeks dimpled. "No affidavit required."

"What are you talking about, Perez?"

His grin widened. "Davies told us the woman's baby was delivered by police officers. Since the ambulance took her to Phoenix General, odds are the Phoenix police were the ones who responded to her neighbor's 9-1-1 call."

Nina barely restrained herself from jumping up and down with excitement. "Do you guys keep daily logs for twenty-eight years?"

"Remember when I filled you in on the Records Management System?" At her nod, he continued, "Everything is digitized, going back to the beginning of our department. Every call, every report."

"I could hug you."

Perez chuckled. "All I ask is that we stop by a Starbucks and get a decent cup of coffee on the way back to the PFO. I'll work a lot faster with a bit of caffeine."

Her smile matched his. "I'll buy you anything you want."

Chapter 23

Nina inhaled the sweet scent wafting up from the tall cup sitting on the table in front of Breck. "What did you say that was?"

Nina and Perez had taken coffee orders for the rest of the team before arriving at the Phoenix field office command center.

Breck pulled back the drink, possessive. "A caramel macchiato."

Nina eyed the mountain of whipped cream on top. "Looks more like dessert than coffee."

"This is breakfast and lunch combined," Breck said. "It's got that perfect jolt of caffeine with a shot of sugar that powers me through the day until dinner."

Nina sipped her own café Americano as her thoughts meandered to Victor's and Maria's relatives. How would they react when they learned of the bizarre twist the investigation had taken?

Perez had already opened his laptop on the conference table. Now he navigated to the internal PPD server and signed in. "I'll set up search parameters based on the date of the incident."

Breck, who had propped her computer next to his, pulled up copies of the PPD files Perez had forwarded to her earlier. "We know from Maria's family and Detective O'Malley's report that she gave birth on February twenty-third," she said. "Based on your interview with the folks at the hospital, the bio mom of the baby who was killed in the Llorona case delivered her child on the same day."

Perez tapped the keyboard. "We use a system that generates a case number starting with the date of the report." A long list of numbers appeared on the screen. "I'll look at February twenty-third."

"That's hundreds of police reports to dig through," Breck said. "Can you narrow it down based on the hours of the day, checking around the time Maria's baby was born?"

"There's an easier way," Perez said. "I'll enter a code to select for certain types of calls for service." He paused, considering. "Since we don't have a specific classification for delivering a baby, I'll go with the original complaint, which could be a welfare check because the neighbor said she was worried about the screaming."

Nina had performed many welfare checks in her years on the force. When someone was concerned about another person's safety, they called police and requested an officer to respond. In Nina's experience, this often led to discovering a month's worth of newspapers in the driveway, flies all over the inside of the windows, and a decomposing body inside.

"I've got something," Perez said. "Welfare check on February twenty-third. The address is for an apartment in South Phoenix. Two officers from the South Mountain precinct were dispatched. I'm pulling up the report now." His gaze traveled down the screen. "Hot damn. They delivered a baby."

"Bingo," Wade said from across the table. "Please tell me they recorded the mother's name."

Perez glanced up. "Carmen Cardona."

Breck began typing. "What's her date of birth?"

While Breck entered the data into the FBI system, Nina's mind wandered. Had Carmen Cardona deliberately taken the wrong baby? Not likely. Both were healthy girls, according to hospital records.

"Is there a father listed on the police report?" Nina asked Perez.

Perez shook his head. "The officers asked for the father's contact info so they could let him know about the birth of his daughter, but Ms. Cardona refused to identify him."

Not a good sign. Nina turned to Wade. "Why does a woman not want the father of her child identified?"

Wade considered before responding. "Because she doesn't know who he is, she's afraid of him, or she's involved in an affair."

"Or," Breck said, "because she has substance abuse problems." When everyone stared at her, she continued, "I found her. After her address in Phoenix, the next place she turns up is in jail in Montgomery County, Maryland, about a year later."

"Maryland?" Nina couldn't hide her surprise.

"Convicted for prostitution and drug possession," Breck read from the screen. "She got out after six months."

"What the hell happened in her life?" Kent said to no one in particular. "And what happened to her baby?"

Nina's heart lurched. "You mean Maria and Victor Vega's baby?"

Kent paled. "Shit, that's right."

Breck was still scrolling through databases on her computer. "Uh-oh."

Nina braced herself for more bad news. "What now?"

Breck spoke in a hushed tone. "Her current residence is listed as St. Elizabeth's."

"What's St. Elizabeth's?" Perez said when the room grew quiet. "And why are you all looking at each other like that?"

Nina realized Perez probably wouldn't know about a facility on the other side of the country. "St. E's is a psychiatric hospital in Washington, DC."

"I did an internship there for my doctorate in psychology," Wade said. "They treat patients with serious mental illness who need full-time inpatient care. They also take patients who are committed by the courts."

"If she's a long-term resident, she could be too mentally unfit to answer questions," Kent said, "or too medicated to remember what happened almost thirty years ago, or possibly unaware of who she is."

"Damn," Perez said, expressing the general view of the situation.

"We've got to try." Nina wasn't ready to give up. "Can we get in to talk to her in person?"

"I can," Wade said. "Might be able to arrange for one of you to come with."

Nina was determined to be the one accompanying him.

"I've pulled her criminal history," Breck said. "She's been locked up a bunch of times. Mostly property crimes like burglary and shoplifting, but also prostitution. Likely to support her drug habit." Breck shook her head. "Seems like Cardona was self-medicating with illegal narcotics. Her longest stretch was five years for possession of heroin. The last time she was incarcerated was seven years ago. It looks like she went to St. E's a few months after she served her time."

"Involuntary committal?" Wade asked.

Breck's eyes never left the screen. "Doesn't say."

Nina's thoughts kept coming back to what she viewed as the most important point. "Any information about Cardona's baby?"

"There is no data relating to her having a child." Breck frowned. "Nothing I can find, anyway."

Nina turned to Wade, who would know more about inpatient treatment than the rest of the team. "If she was in jail and later institutionalized, wouldn't Child Protective Services take her daughter away?"

He nodded. "Unless the father came forward or she had other relatives the child could stay with."

The door opened and Buxton entered the room. "I just got a text from the Phoenix crime lab. The rest of the results from the DNA tests are in." Without further comment, he activated the intercom at the center of the table and took a seat. "Go ahead, Dr. Ledford. You're on speaker with the team."

"We completed the search through CODIS, and we have more findings," the lab director said. "The extraneous sample from the

Llorona case we believe is from the perpetrator does not have a match in any criminal database."

"That would be asking too much," Nina muttered to Wade, then spoke into the intercom. "What about the baby from that case?" She wanted confirmation that their theory about the switch at the hospital was correct.

"We got close familial matches for the child," Ledford said. "There was a paternal match with José Salaya, a multiple felon who died in prison in Florence, Arizona, four years ago. Drug overdose."

Nina saw Breck typing furiously, doubtless scouring databases for information about Salaya.

"We also got a mitochondrial match for the mother," Ledford continued. "She was in the system due to a felony arrest for burglary."

They all held their breath. This should corroborate their investigative findings.

"Her name is Carmen Cardona," the lab director said after a brief pause. "I appended her information to the file in Detective Perez's queue in the RMS system. That's all I have for now."

"Thank you, Dr. Ledford," Buxton said. "Your input has been extremely helpful. Please keep us posted on any further developments."

Nina let out a long breath. Now there was no doubt the babies had been mixed up in the hospital nursery. Victor and Maria had taken home Carmen Cardona's child, who had died at the hands of the unsub. But what had Carmen done with Maria's baby?

"I'm searching every database I can access," Breck said. "I still can't find hide nor hair of Carmen Cardona's daughter. There's nothing, no school records, no international travel, nothing in CPS. She's a ghost."

Ghost. Nina didn't like where that word took her. "Look for a death certificate that matches the birthdate listing Carmen as the mother."

"On it," Breck said.

Perez was downloading the information the lab director had sent to his laptop. "What did she do with that baby?" he muttered as he clicked through the files.

Breck looked up. "No death certificate matching any of those search parameters."

Kent grimaced. "We know Carmen has a history of substance abuse. This is horrible, but . . . could she have sold her baby for drugs?"

As everyone else seemed to reel from the very thought, Wade's face hardened. "I know one thing for damn sure. We need to talk to Carmen Cardona, and I want to do it in person."

Nina voiced a thought that had been nagging at her. "The babies got switched at the hospital. No one knew. If it weren't for this investigation, no one would have ever known." She directed her gaze at Buxton. "We're going to have to notify the families."

Wade reacted before Buxton could respond. "We're going to tell both families that Maria was not a murderer, that we can't find any trace of her baby, and that there's a serial killer loose?"

Buxton scrubbed a hand over his face. "We can't tell them anything until we get some answers. And there's only one person who can provide them." He looked around the room. "We're flying back to DC first thing tomorrow."

Chapter 24

Nina jammed another blouse into the suitcase lying open on the hotel bed, unconcerned about its wrinkled state. "I'll be glad to bring some fresh clothes when we come back."

"Amen to that," Breck said, tossing garments into her own luggage.

"I'm packing some running clothes for the trip back," Nina said. "The weather is gorgeous here."

Nina jogged to relieve stress. She relished the time to herself, engaging her body in a demanding activity while freeing her mind to think. For her, it was moving meditation.

A knock at the door separating the adjoining suites interrupted the conversation. Nina pulled it open to find Wade peering down at her.

"We need to be at Sky Harbor airport tomorrow morning at seven," he said. "We'll be in the air five hours, so we're scheduled to land at Reagan National at three o'clock eastern time."

Stepping aside, Nina motioned him into the room. "Will we be able to see Carmen Cardona tomorrow?"

"Already called St. Elizabeth's and made arrangements," Wade said. "We should be able to go visit her right after we land. Tomorrow is Saturday, but her treating psychiatrist agreed to meet us there anyway."

Kent appeared in the doorway. "Buxton asked us to let you two know he's arranged for us to knock out the training we were supposed to complete on Tuesday while we're back in DC." He stepped inside the room. "We'll spend tomorrow night at home, then go to Quantico on Sunday morning and fly back here in the afternoon so we can return to the investigation first thing Monday morning."

Nina pulled lacy dark purple panties from the dresser drawer and tucked them into the suitcase. She reached for the matching bra and noticed Kent's face redden as he became fascinated with the lamp sitting on the desk.

"This thing is crooked," he said, adjusting the shade.

She smiled to herself. Who would have thought a former SEAL would blush at the sight of lingerie?

"I'm trying to keep an open mind," Breck said, oblivious to the byplay. "But there's just no way this story has a happy ending. That baby is either dead or her momma sold her."

The grim thought erased all humor from Nina's mind. She considered the sheer desperation Carmen Cardona must have felt in order to do such a thing. "If you're right, maybe that's what pushed her over the edge mentally."

Breck put down a blouse she had been packing and turned to them. "Here's another disturbing question. What if she's the one who mistakenly switched the babies? I mean, we're thinking it was an accident by the hospital personnel, but suppose she somehow got confused and told the staff the wrong baby was hers?"

"I doubt it," Kent said. "Hospitals have controls in place."

Wade looked thoughtful. "They didn't have as many protocols back then as they do now. There have been many cases of babies being switched at birth in hospitals in the past."

"Either way, Ginsberg and Perez will continue to follow up with the hospital while we're gone," Nina said. "Given the new DNA results from the lab, they'll have no trouble getting a search warrant for their paperwork. They'll give Buxton a report after he checks out the hospital's information."

"You said that hospital administrator was sweating when you interviewed him," Breck said to Nina. "Now we know why he was in a lather. They're in for a world of hurt if it turns out to be the hospital's mistake."

"No matter how it happened, the hospital will take the blame," Wade said. "It's their responsibility."

Nina recalled the information Perez had gleaned from police sources before they left for the day. "We know Carmen left Phoenix by the end of February, because she paid a month-to-month lease on her apartment and the landlord had a new tenant in her unit by March tenth due to nonpayment of rent on March first."

"Why would someone travel all the way across the country with a newborn baby?" Kent asked.

Nina wondered the same thing. A car trip would take at least three days. "Do we know if she flew?"

"Ginsberg is following up on that too," Wade said. "He's trying to find old flight manifests."

"I looked up Carmen's boyfriend's arrest records," Breck said. "One of José Salaya's arrests was for beating Carmen while she was pregnant with their child. I imagine she left town to get the hell away from him."

"Makes sense," Nina said. "Salaya was due for release after a six-month stint in jail at the end of March, so he would have no way of knowing what happened to Carmen and the baby . . . if he cared at all."

"It's quite possible that Carmen did nothing wrong," Wade said. "That she was merely a victim of circumstances and that she'll be able to tell us who raised the baby and where she is now."

Nina realized something else. "We're going to have to tell Carmen that her biological child was murdered only days after she was born," she said to Wade. "If she's already struggling with her sanity, that may well and truly break her."

"We'll see what sort of mental state she's in," Wade said quietly. "Then I'll decide how much to tell her."

Nina considered the human misery involved in this case. Carmen's tragic life and her baby's heartbreaking death were only one part of a tapestry of suffering woven by an evil man who seemed bent on destroying the happiness of others.

She looked at Wade. "Ever have one of those points in a case where you're cranked up with adrenaline because you're getting closer to the truth, but you're also dreading finding out what it is?"

"Since I've been assigned to the BAU?" Wade said. "Every damn case."

Chapter 25

He laid the digital player on the smooth granite countertop, adjusting the volume to replay the previous night's audio recording from Nina Guerrera's room. After pressing the start button, he prepared to shave while he listened.

Eavesdropping on the FBI had been a stroke of genius. Without his foresight, the Feds would have interviewed Kirk. He couldn't allow that. Taking Kirk's computer had been an extra measure of security—probably unnecessary, but prudent. And he was always prudent.

He heard Nina and the other FBI woman's chatter as he smoothed the foamy cream over his jawline. After wiping his hands on a pristine white washcloth, he picked up the disposable razor. When the male agents joined the conversation, he was surprised to learn they were planning a trip to DC to talk to some woman named Carmen Cardona. Then a comment drew his attention.

"Here's another disturbing question. What if she's the one who mistakenly switched the babies? I mean, we're thinking it was an accident by the hospital personnel, but suppose she somehow got confused and told the staff the wrong baby was hers?"

He became so distracted he nicked his upper lip. Switched babies? He stared at the mirror, watching the progress of the crimson rivulet sliding down his face as he listened in dawning comprehension.

From the distant past, when he was only eleven years old, his mother's voice rang in his ears. "Oh, sweetie," she said to him. "Isn't it wonderful? It's a surprise, but a wonderful surprise."

He didn't think it was wonderful. He listened in abject silence as his mother continued her bleating.

"We won't be able to go to Disneyland this year, sweetie, because Mommy will be in the hospital, having your baby sister." She gave him a big smile, fake as a plastic dinosaur. "But we'll go next year. I promise."

Next year, she would tell him the new baby was too young to go to Disneyland. Then she would say the same thing for the next five years. By then, he wouldn't care. He was already eleven. Everything was going to be about the new baby. The little girl his mother had always wanted. The little sister he never did.

He should have been enough for them. Should have been enough for his mother and his father. Now the little brat would be the center of their universe, the orbit around which they all spun.

Or not.

Chapter 26

Nina stopped wheeling her small suitcase through the terminal at Reagan National Airport to glance over her shoulder at Breck, who had lagged behind the rest of the team. "Come on, *chica*. They've got a car waiting for us."

Breck was staring at her phone. "Every alert I have is going off."

Buxton, Wade, and Kent continued ahead of them.

Nina walked back to Breck. "What's wrong?" She watched the color drain from her fellow agent's face.

Breck's eyes stayed riveted to her phone. "Crap."

"That's not helping," Nina said. "Maybe you could elaborate?"

"Crap on a cracker." Breck turned the screen toward Nina. A headline from Phoenix's Channel Six News filled the top.

SWITCHED AT BIRTH: MIX-UP AT PHOENIX GENERAL MUDDLES FBI INVESTIGATION

Nina let go of her suitcase's handle and tugged the phone from Breck's hand. She swiped the screen to scroll through the story, alarm increasing with every line.

"What's the problem?" Buxton had doubled back, Wade and Kent in his wake.

"The problem is James Snead," Nina said. "That reporter with Channel Six News. He just got another exclusive."

"What now?" Kent looked like he didn't really want to know.

"I set up alerts to notify me about any stories in the media dealing with our cases," Breck said. "Snead found out about the switched babies at the hospital. He's gotten an official statement from Marcus Johnson, the chief legal counsel Nina met with."

"How could he have found out this fast?" Buxton said. "It's not like the hospital would want to publicize it. They'd keep it quiet forever if they could arrange for an out-of-court settlement with a nondisclosure agreement."

"Someone leaked," Kent said. "Someone in law enforcement. I'll bet it's Perez."

Nina put a hand on her hip. "Why Perez?"

"He's the only one outside of the FBI who knew."

"And his chain of command on the Phoenix police," Wade said.

"No one on the PPD had a reason to put this out," Nina said. "It calls their original investigation into question and makes them look bad. I'm not buying it."

As Kent launched into a debate with Wade about the source of the leak, a new problem occurred to Nina. "We didn't notify either Maria's or Victor's families." A wave of guilt washed through her. "They're going to learn about this from the news."

Buxton glanced at his watch. "We're on a tight schedule." He addressed Wade. "You and Agent Guerrera can take a cab to St. Elizabeth's while we deal with this." He turned to Breck. "You and Agent Kent need to contact both families and fill them in on what we've learned. Ask them not to speak to the media until we have a chance to meet with them when we get back to Phoenix."

"I still want to know who's feeding information to that damned reporter," Kent said.

"Maybe no one." Breck's eyes widened as she spoke. "He covered the Llorona case, which means he was around back then. That would put him at the right age—"

"To be the unsub," Nina finished for her. "What do we know about James Snead?"

Buxton gave Nina a brief nod of understanding. "We'll profile Mr. Snead while you two interview Ms. Cardona."

"Speaking of Snead, did he identify both parties in his coverage of the baby switch?" Kent asked.

Nina scanned the printed version of the televised news story until she spotted it. She groaned. "Not only does he mention the Llorona case and the Vega family, but he also mentions Carmen Cardona by name as the mother of the other child."

Wade cursed. "We need to get to Carmen before anyone else does. At least she's in a secure facility, but someone on the staff could mention the story, even though it broke on the other side of the country."

"We'll call ahead on the way over," Buxton said. "From now on, we keep everything on a need-to-know basis. That's the only way to control information." He focused on Wade. "What effect will the fact that Maria and Victor's biological child survived have on our unsub?"

"This is going to send him into a tailspin," Wade said. "All these years, he's orchestrated his crime scenes like some sort of drama he feels compelled to act out. He researches his victims well in advance, arranges everything to the smallest detail. Now he discovers the very first scenario he planned was based on a mistake."

She imagined the killer, filled with rage when he learned the happy family he intended to destroy wasn't a family at all.

"He built a house of cards and then someone pulled out the very first one he set up," Wade continued. "Everything else is going to cave in."

She asked the logical follow-up question. "What will he do about it?"

"Until recently, he always operated on a predictable schedule, only killing on leap day," Wade said. "He's already broken his pattern with the murder of Thomas Kirk. That means he's devolving. Given this new information, he won't wait to correct the error."

"Correct the error?" Breck said.

"I predict he will feel a strong compulsion to fix what he will perceive as the original problem with his plan," Wade said. "Someone with his personality type won't be able to rest until things are set right. That, after all, was the whole point of the murders."

Nina made sure she understood. "You're saying he'll try to find the missing baby—now an adult—and kill her?"

Wade nodded. "She's a loose end."

Nina stooped to grasp her bag's handle. "This interview with Carmen Cardona just got a whole lot more critical," she said.

"As has our need to keep the results confidential," Buxton said. "If word gets out when we locate her, she'll be in serious danger."

Nina had grasped the gravity of their mission. "If he finds her before we do, we'll have another murder on our hands."

Chapter 27

Nina and Wade strolled down the long white corridor as the late-afternoon sun angled through the tall picture windows along one side. It was an acknowledgment of the seriousness of the situation that the hospital director had arranged for Carmen Cardona's treating psychiatrist, Dr. Bernice Matthews, to be present during the Saturday interview. Furthermore, they had agreed to delay Carmen's afternoon meds by thirty minutes to be sure she was clear when Wade and Nina spoke to her.

During Wade's previous phone conversation with Dr. Matthews, she had insisted he could only bring one other agent and recommended a female, then also warned that Carmen would lapse into Spanish when she became distressed. Nina had been the logical choice.

They had conferred with Dr. Matthews before the interview, but offered her no more information than she could have learned from a Google search of news reports from Phoenix. Dr. Matthews told them Carmen favored art therapy, spending her days painting and drawing. She was known to be withdrawn, often retreating into the recesses of her own mind. According to the psychiatrist, reality was mutable for Carmen, who could not reliably discern the year, much less the date.

Based on that assessment, Nina doubted any criminal admissions on Carmen's part would result in prosecution. This would be strictly a fact-finding mission.

Dr. Matthews had agreed to help as best she could, warning them to treat the patient with care before escorting them to Carmen's private room.

After they entered, Dr. Matthews approached a frail woman whose salt-and-pepper hair tumbled down past her hunched shoulders.

Whatever Nina had expected about Carmen's living quarters, it hadn't been this. Every surface and wall space seemed crammed with artwork featuring dolls of every size and shape. Watercolors, charcoal drawings, oil paints—all juxtaposed in an unnerving hodgepodge, their glimmering eyes staring at Nina from every direction.

"Good afternoon, Carmen," Dr. Matthews said, gesturing toward Nina and Wade. "These are the visitors I told you about earlier. This is Agent Wade and Agent Guerrera from the FBI."

Carmen peered up at them with owlish eyes but said nothing.

Nina had seen Carmen's date of birth in the police report and could hardly believe the fractured shell of a woman in front of her was only forty-seven years old. Her troubled past seemed to have taken a toll on her body as well as her psyche, giving her the appearance of someone two decades older than her true age.

Dr. Matthews took a seat in the chair closest to Carmen and tipped her head toward two empty folding chairs, indicating they should sit. Nina figured the staff had rearranged Carmen's room, adding the extra seating to conduct the meeting in her own personal space so she would feel more comfortable. Nina was more than happy to let Wade take the lead and follow up with any questions that came to mind.

Wade opened the discussion on a gentle note. "Ms. Cardona, do you know why we're here?"

A silent shake of the head was Carmen's only response.

"Did you ever live in Arizona, Ms. Cardona?"

Nina recognized the technique. Ask the interviewee something you already know to assess how truthful—or in this case, how lucid—they were likely to be going forward.

Carmen looked down at her hands, which were clasped in her lap. "Ages ago, I lived in Phoenix." A slight Spanish accent tinged her words. "That was not a happy time in my life."

"How so?" Wade's tone was deep, calm, and caring.

"I was nineteen years old." She chewed her lip. "I was pretty messed up."

"We're aware there were some difficulties," Wade said. "Ms. Cardona, can I call you Carmen?"

"Sure."

"Carmen, when did you leave Arizona for Maryland?"

Her eyes returned to her hands. "I don't remember exactly when."

"Do you recall *why* you left?"

She picked at her sleeve in silence for a long moment. "I . . . had . . . a baby." Her palm touched her chest. "*Una niña.* I called her Linda because she was so beautiful."

A little girl. *Niña* meant *girl* in Spanish, which was how Nina had gotten her own name from social services in Fairfax County. Carmen had named her baby Linda, the Spanish word for *beautiful.*

"All of this must weigh on you," Wade said. "It's time to talk about it." He paused before beginning the main part of the interview. "Why don't you start with the baby?"

Carmen continued to pick at her sleeve, not making eye contact. She was silent so long Nina was afraid she would never answer.

Finally, in a small voice, Carmen began to tell her story. "I was seeing a man named José, and I got pregnant. I used to do all kinds of things like that—I took drugs, drank too much, got mixed up with the wrong men."

Nina knew better than to interrupt once the floodgates had been opened. She listened intently as Carmen continued.

"José beat me bad when he found out I was pregnant. Put me in the hospital." She gave her head a rueful shake. "I didn't want him anywhere near my baby. A police lady helped me, and I pressed charges. The judge gave José six months, but I knew he'd be out soon after the baby was born. He would come home, and he would be real mad at me." She winced at the thought. "He would blame me for putting him in jail."

As Nina had suspected, Carmen had fled Phoenix to escape her abusive boyfriend.

"I had my baby at home in my apartment," Carmen said. "One of my neighbors heard me screaming and called the cops. I had my little Linda right there on the kitchen floor, then an ambulance took me and her to the hospital."

When she trailed off, Wade gently prompted her. "What happened at the hospital?"

Carmen's voice grew even quieter. "The nurse told me they had to do some tests. I had used when I was pregnant. I was scared they would take my baby away and throw me in jail."

Nina put herself in Carmen's place, imagining her fear of the authorities, of her violent boyfriend, and of losing her baby.

"So I found out where the nursery was," Carmen went on. "And I went to get my daughter before they did any tests. The nurse stopped me, but I walked right over to the bed where she was sleeping and demanded my little girl."

When she lapsed into silence again, Wade gave her a verbal nudge. "Carmen, how did you know the baby you took from the nursery was yours? Was there an identification band on her?"

Carmen scrunched her eyes closed, trying to remember. After a long moment, she straightened and looked at Wade. "There was one of those plastic things around her ankle, if that's what you mean."

"Did it match the one on your wrist?"

"I didn't look," Carmen said. "I knew which baby was mine."

"How could you tell?"

She gave Wade an exasperated frown. "A mother knows her own child. Plus, she was the only brown baby girl in the nursery. The rest were all white or black."

Nina and Wade exchanged glances. Carmen hadn't considered the possibility that her baby might have been taken to another room for testing.

During her research, Breck had found data about thousands of newborns being switched at hospitals over the years, especially in the past. Nina had been shocked to learn that nurses and parents sometimes didn't double-check the bracelets before being discharged from the hospital.

"The nurse wanted me and Linda to stay overnight," Carmen continued. "But we were both healthy. They had to give her to me. I carried her straight out the door and called a friend to take us back to my place."

"You mentioned substance abuse during pregnancy," Wade said, keeping his voice free of judgment. "Your baby could have been born addicted."

"The nurse said she was fine, and I hadn't used for at least two months before I delivered."

Nina wondered if Carmen realized she was contradicting herself. She claimed to fear discovery of trace amounts of narcotics in her daughter's system, but then justified taking her from the hospital because she felt certain Linda had no risk of going through withdrawal.

Wade dropped the subject. "What did you do next?"

"I knew I had to get out of Phoenix. As far away as possible so José wouldn't find me. I had a cousin who lived in Bethesda, so I loaded up my car and headed east a few days later."

"Did you get to Bethesda with the baby?" Wade asked. "Did something happen along the way?"

Nina held her breath, half expecting to hear about a deadly car crash Carmen never reported.

"We made it all right," Carmen said. "Traveled across the country over four days in an old Chevy. After the trip, Linda and me stayed with my cousin for a couple of weeks until the baby's crying got to him. I was looking for a job. I really wanted to go straight. My little girl was depending on me."

Carmen stopped talking again. She scrunched down and seemed to fold in on herself. Nina knew the next part of the story would be critical to their investigation but also heartbreaking for Carmen to relive.

Wade edged closer to her without making physical contact. "What happened to Linda?"

Silence met his words.

He inched closer still. "Carmen?"

"My cousin said we had to leave. Said the baby was ruining his life." Carmen began wringing her hands. "So I went to a shelter. One where I could take Linda too."

Carmen came to a halt again, lips pressed tight together, a clear indication that she did not want to say more. Frustration gnawed at Nina. She had been through root canals less painful and drawn out than this interview. She reminded herself that Carmen was fragile, and nothing could be gained from rushing the process. Wade had the background to take Carmen through her story without causing a complete shutdown, which was probably what would have occurred if Nina had been asking the questions.

"Can you tell us about the shelter, Carmen?" Wade said.

"I got some help there, but I also made friends with a couple of women who used. They knew where to find the good stuff. They gave me a little, just to take the edge off. I thought they were being nice."

"But they weren't being nice, were they?" Wade said.

Carmen shook her head. "I needed more, and they took me to the guy who gave them the stuff. He told me if I was one of his girls, he'd take care of me."

Nina had heard similar tales many times before. Carmen had been targeted. After a while, she had become addicted and fallen into the hands of a pimp. Nina would not judge this woman. She had not lived Carmen's life, suffered her pain, felt her loss.

"I started working for him," Carmen said. "I had to move out of the shelter so no one would find out what was going on."

Undoubtedly, Carmen was aware that if the staff discovered she was taking illegal narcotics, engaging in prostitution, or neglecting her baby, they would call CPS immediately.

Carmen looked Wade full in the face for the first time since the interview began, her eyes brimming. "For weeks, I tried to do it on my own, but I couldn't." A tear spilled over, sliding down her cheek. "I just couldn't."

Firmly but patiently, Wade restated his question from earlier in the conversation. "What happened to the baby, Carmen?"

Carmen's stifled sobs were her only response.

Nina wasn't sure what to do, but she took her cue from Wade and Dr. Matthews, who made no move to touch her. Dr. Matthews had explained that Carmen didn't like physical contact unless she initiated it. Nina could tell she was in a delicate state and didn't want to do anything that might bring the interview to an abrupt end.

Carmen finally sniffed and plucked a tissue from Wade's outstretched hand. Her shoulders slumped slightly, a sign that she had given up resisting. After a shuddering breath, she began again. "One night, I was supposed to meet a guy in Virginia. Just off the beltway. I left the baby in the back of my car while I was taking care of the customer. All of a sudden, she starts crying. The guy got real mad. He hit me hard and left without paying." She dabbed at her nose with the tissue and accepted another from Wade. "I knew I would get beat even worse when I came back without any money. I was still high—it's no excuse, but I wasn't real clear."

"What did you do, Carmen?" Wade prompted after another long pause.

"I took my baby from the car and then I . . ."

Nina's heart pounded as Carmen's head bent down, her shoulders shaking as she sobbed. Watching her, Nina realized that Carmen had stopped calling her child Linda, now only referring to "the baby."

Carmen's mouth worked, but no sound came out. She was trying to say something. Finally, Carmen managed a single word. *"B-besar."* After another round of tears, she said, *"Le d-d . . . besar."*

Wade raised a quizzical brow at Nina, who strained to make out the words.

"¿Qué he hecho?" Carmen said, then let out a wail of anguish that dissolved into tears.

"That's enough," Dr. Matthews said in a tone that brooked no argument. "I trust you two can find your way out." She moved to sit beside Carmen and began speaking to her softly.

Wade waited until they were in the hallway to question Nina. "What did she say?" he whispered.

"After she said, 'I took her from the car,' it was hard for me to understand," Nina said. "It sounded like she said *'besar,'* which means 'to kiss.' Then it sounded like she said *'Le di un beso,'* which means 'I gave her a kiss.'"

"What came after that?"

"Then she said, 'What have I done?'"

Wade appeared to consider the comments. "Carmen couldn't bear to admit what she did in English. She regressed to an earlier version of herself."

"It sounds like she kissed her baby goodbye," Nina said, "then she was finally overwhelmed by guilt."

She read the intensity of Wade's gaze and knew they were thinking along the same lines. They would not get any more out of Carmen Cardona, but what she had told them was as good as a confession.

Chapter 28

A knock at her apartment door interrupted Nina's musing as she dumped the contents of her suitcase on her bed. Relieved for a reason to delay unpacking and laundry duties, she padded to the door to peer through the fish-eye lens. Spotting only the top of a jet-black ponytail, she opened it wide.

"Where've you been?" Bianca said as she stalked past her and into the kitchen. "I've been looking for you."

Bianca had the habit of dropping by shortly after Nina arrived home. Nina was convinced the eighteen-year-old college senior had installed some sort of monitoring system in the parking lot. Best not to ask.

"Come on in," Nina said wryly. "What's up?"

"Can't you hear the noise?" Bianca gestured in the direction of her apartment next door. "Mrs. G is having a birthday party for one of my foster brothers."

"It's not too loud."

"There is a wild pack of seven-year-olds running around an apartment designed to hold a family of four." Bianca was practically bug-eyed. "It's a friggin' zoo. If I didn't get out of there, I was going to go batshit."

"Little Gus," Nina said, remembering their last conversation. "He's turning seven today, isn't he?"

"Hello?" Bianca had set her snark level to maximum. "We talked about this a few days ago when Mrs. G and I brought a slice of tres leches cake over for you."

"Been a little busy." Nina snarked back at her. "What with all the flying back and forth across the country, investigating murders, and chasing down leads, I've had a few things on my mind."

"Tell me you're chasing more than just leads." The corner of Bianca's mouth quirked up. "Tell me you're chasing that hottie on your team." She wiggled her brows. "The one with the muscles and the glasses."

Nina felt her cheeks warm. "Agent Kent?"

Bianca rolled her eyes. "Well, I sure as hell didn't mean the old guy."

"If you're referring to Agent Wade, he's in his fifties." Nina opened the refrigerator. "That's not old."

"Yeah right, well, that Kent dude is closer to your age." Bianca twirled a strand of hair around her finger. "And he's totally worth investigating."

"Not gonna happen." Nina bent to peer inside the fridge. "No fraternization allowed between team members."

Bianca stuck her hand on her hip. "Well, that sucks." A mischievous gleam lit her eyes. "Then what about that tasty Phoenix detective I saw you with? He's easy on the eyes."

"Wait, what?" Nina turned around, two bottles of water in her hand. "How could you have seen me with Detective Perez, he's—"

"It's called the internet." Bianca accepted one of the bottles. "I've been following articles and stories about your investigation in Phoenix, which, by the way, is getting more hits every day."

Nina took a long swig. "I'd rather not talk about the media right now. One reporter in particular is making life extremely difficult."

"I know the one you mean," Bianca said. "But there are plenty of people posting things about the Llorona case being reopened." She unscrewed the top of her bottle. "By the way, how creepy is that story? I can't believe you grew up hearing stuff like that. I would never tell

Gus something that scary—even if he annoyed me, which he does, like, twice a day."

"You're not fooling me," Nina said. "I happen to know Gus is your favorite."

Bianca put a finger to her lips in mock secrecy. "Don't tell anyone. If it gets back to Gus, he'll never let me hear the end of it."

"I think he knows." Nina smiled. "You've already got him doing fifth-grade math, and I saw you putting together a little handheld computer for him when you were over here last week."

"I had to give the little cookie cruncher something for his birthday." Bianca's tone was dismissive. "It's not like I have a lot of funds."

"He's wormed his way into your heart."

Bianca tilted her head thoughtfully. "Foster kids have to stick together."

Pride tugged at Nina's heart. Bianca had been in a desperate situation when Nina had tracked her down as a teenage runaway. Now Bianca was paying it forward.

"I'm glad you're looking after Gus," Nina said to her. "Mrs. G told me he never even knew his parents."

"Yeah, and we don't even really know when his actual birthday is," Bianca said. "We just celebrate March seventh because that's the date the social workers assigned to him."

Nina put down her bottle of water. Something Bianca said had reminded her of the interview with Carmen Cardona. She clutched at the fragment of thought, but it was too ephemeral, too fleeting to grasp.

Bianca, apparently aware of Nina's distracted state, tossed her empty bottle into the recycling bin. "I suppose I should get back over to the party to help clean up. I'm sure those kids have totally trashed the place."

Nina felt another tingle of awareness. "Trash?"

"You know—garbage, waste, a thousand plastic cups and sporks with gobs of frosting all over the floor?"

The tingle grew stronger. "Garbage?"

Bianca's pierced brows drew together. "What's the matter with you?"

Something was bubbling up from her subconscious mind, but she needed peace and quiet to let it surface.

"I'm going to take a shower," she said. "Wash away the travel." She did her best thinking in a steamy bathroom with water pouring over her.

"I can take a hint." Bianca eyed her warily. "But I'm going to check back with you later."

A few minutes after her neighbor left to face the horrors of a seventh birthday party, Nina stood in her shower as the water sluiced down her skin, the interview with Carmen playing on a continuous loop in her brain. She strained to keep up with thoughts ricocheting inside her head, trying to piece what she had learned into a coherent picture. Something about the interview would not stop nagging at her.

An idea began to coalesce. *What if I misunderstood her?* She'd thought Carmen said "*Le di un beso*," which meant "I gave her a kiss." What had she actually heard the woman say, though?

She pictured Carmen, distraught, saying, *"B-besar."* Then, *"Le d-d . . . besar."*

Translated precisely, *besar* means *to kiss*, not *I kiss*, or *I kissed*. A native Spanish speaker like Carmen would not have used the wrong form of the verb. If she'd meant to say "I gave her a kiss," she would have said "*Le di un beso*," or simply, *"La besé."*

Bianca's talk about cleaning up after the kids at the party had shaken something loose. The Spanish word for *trash* is *basura*, which sounds a lot like *besar*, especially if the person speaking is sobbing.

What if Carmen didn't say "*Le di un beso*"? What if she had said "*La dejé en la basura*," but she was choking out the words as she cried?

Nina's mind raced with possibilities. Had Carmen confessed to leaving her baby in the trash?

Like what had happened to her.

Nina grew queasy as something else Bianca mentioned brought random facts together to form a disturbing image. Little Gus had been abandoned as an infant, and the social workers had to estimate how old he was. Assign him a birthday.

Like what had happened to her.

A pediatrician had estimated her age after she'd been found in a dumpster, but what if the doctor got it wrong? What if she hadn't been thriving because she hadn't received proper care? What if she had been cared for by a drug-addicted woman?

She would appear small, perhaps less developed. The doctor might assume she was younger than her actual age by a couple of weeks.

Nina took the next logical step down a dangerous path. Someone who has been celebrating their birthday on, say, March eleventh might have actually been born on February twenty-third.

The water became tepid as she stood motionless under the spray, continuing to the next inevitable conclusion.

In the Llorona case, the baby was born on February twenty-third but died in Phoenix six days later. Except Victor and Maria's baby didn't die at that house. The babies were switched at the hospital. She sucked in a breath as she realized the case had truly become like the legend of *La Llorona*. Maria's child was missing, and no one knew where the baby was.

But maybe she did know . . . now.

Perhaps the baby had been taken to Maryland when she was only a few days old. If Nina had interpreted Carmen's statement correctly this time, she had been in northern Virginia when she left her baby in the trash.

Nina had been found in a dumpster in Reston, which was in northern Virginia.

If the baby had survived, she would have just turned twenty-eight.

Nina's age. Or the age she thought she was about to turn next week.

She shut off the water and rushed from the shower, tugging her satin robe around her. Damp hair dripping on the table as she opened her laptop, she did a Google search for news reports of abandoned newborns in northern Virginia twenty-eight years ago.

Six cases came up—all had made the local news. Fighting a sickening wave of dread, she clicked on each story in turn. Only three pertained to baby girls. Of those three, only one involved a one-month-old baby left in Reston. That case had occurred on April eleventh, the day Nina had been found in the trash.

The trash. *La basura.*

Her case.

Pulse pounding in her ears, she accessed the FBI server and entered the same search parameters. The results were no different.

She had been the only infant girl left in a dumpster in northern Virginia in April of the year she was born. A leap year.

No one had made the connection. No one would have known there was a connection to be made. She felt in her bones, in every fiber of her being . . . she knew it now.

With nerveless fingers, she pulled up the file for the Llorona case and stared at a photograph of Maria and Victor Vega.

People she would never know.

Her parents.

Chapter 29

The following day
Hogan's Alley, FBI Academy
Quantico, Virginia

"Stop, FBI!" Nina trained her sights on the gunman as he clutched the bank teller tight against his body, the muzzle of his pistol against the woman's head. "Drop your weapon."

Nina had intended to use stealth to get closer before announcing her presence, but the bank robber had given her no choice. Now he had a hostage.

His pale eyes narrowed on her. "Throw down your gun, or she's dead." His scruffy beard and mop of sandy-brown hair gave him a generally unkempt appearance. "Do it," Scruffy said.

Negotiation might be her best option, but it wasn't her strongest skill. Fortunately, her partner was a psychologist.

She risked a glance at Wade, who had taken cover behind a low wall across the bank's lobby. Wade could engage the suspect while she figured out her next move. If he didn't get Scruffy to surrender, Wade could distract him while she lined up a head shot. She gave Wade a brief nod, willing him to read her intentions.

"I'm Special Agent Jeffrey Wade," he called out, drawing Scruffy's attention. "Let's talk about this before it goes any further. No one's been hurt yet."

The gunman squeezed his hostage tighter against him. "That's going to change real soon if you don't do what I tell you."

Nina inched sideways, keeping her Glock trained on Scruffy.

He darted a glance in her direction. "What the hell are you doing?"

"She's getting out of the line of fire," Wade said, his deep voice projecting calm.

A not-so-subtle reminder that she had left her position of cover. She hadn't followed protocol, and Wade was apparently trying to rein her in.

"I don't want her sneaking around behind me," Scruffy said. "Tell her to get back over here where I can see her."

With the gunman's attention on Wade, Nina focused on the hostage, who appeared to be Latina. An idea began to take shape. It was a huge gamble, but she would not have a better opportunity to save the woman.

Nina let out a slow, steady breath as she squeezed her index finger a fraction, taking up the slack in the trigger. She flicked a glance at the hostage and gave her a sharp command. *"¡Agáchate!"*

The woman froze, mouth open, for a heart-stopping instant, then pitched forward and screamed as Nina pulled the trigger.

An instant later, Scruffy and the hostage both dropped to the floor out of Nina's line of sight.

Wade rushed out from cover. "What the hell was that about, Guerrera?"

Scruffy sat up and yanked off his helmet. "Damn, that hurt." He rubbed his forehead. "I thought you guys weren't supposed to shoot."

"They weren't." Special Agent Denbry, one of the instructors assigned to the academy, strode into view. "That wasn't part of the scenario. Guerrera was supposed to allow for negotiations."

Instructors at the FBI training facility in Quantico had set up a simulation exercise for the team in Hogan's Alley, which consisted of several storefronts lining the streets of a fake city inside the sprawling academy grounds. For today's scenario, local actors played the roles of bank teller and robber in a hostage situation at the Bank of Hogan, affectionately known as the most robbed bank in the world.

Nina slid her visor up. "I had a shot, and I took it." She gestured toward the actor, who was struggling to his feet. "That was a kill shot. He wouldn't have hurt the hostage."

"Maybe," Denbry said. "Maybe not." He crossed his arms. "The point is, your partner had no idea what you were doing. He wasn't prepared to react because you didn't communicate properly."

Everyone turned to Wade.

He shrugged. "I didn't know what you were up to, Guerrera. I was going to negotiate for the release of the hostage and then for the robber to surrender."

Had she been impatient to resolve the situation? Distracted by what she had discovered the night before? The revelation had made it impossible for her to get a good night's sleep. There had been no time to discuss anything with her team before the practical exercise started, and her nerves were frayed to the breaking point even before the intensive training had begun.

Denbry gave her a hard stare. "I can see why SSA Buxton asked us to set up some scenarios. You all need it if you want to stay in the field."

Nina holstered her specially configured training weapon and glanced out the window to see Breck and Kent enter the faux bank through the glass doors.

"Nice shot," Breck said to Nina.

"Don't compliment her," Denbry said. "She left a position of cover, failed to communicate with her partner, and did not allow for negotiations."

Nina made her case. "But the situation is resolved, no?" She gestured toward the actors. "And the hostage survived. I'd call that a win."

Denbry bristled. "There's coloring outside the lines, Guerrera, and there's scribbling all over the walls." He turned to the woman who had been role-playing as the hostage. "I'm assuming she told you to duck in Spanish?" When she nodded, Denbry rounded on Nina. "How could you be certain the hostage spoke Spanish and the bad guy didn't?"

"I couldn't," Nina said. "I was—"

"Taking a flying leap of faith," Denbry finished for her. "We're using Simunition instead of real ammo. Luckily, the hostage reacted to your command, but there's no way to tell if your head shot would have dropped the suspect before he managed to squeeze the trigger. If those were real rounds in everyone's weapons, the hostage might have been killed." He gestured toward the actors as Nina had done earlier. "I wouldn't call two corpses a win. Not when it could have been avoided by following protocol."

Kent stepped between them. He addressed Denbry first. "There are times when circumstances dictate a different approach. Times when it's not the best move to follow procedure."

Kent's observations carried weight. Everyone knew his background. He had more experience in both simulated- and live-combat situations than anyone present.

Nina felt gratified at his comments. Until he swiveled to face her. "But this scenario was not one of those times. I can see where you might have felt the need to take the shot, but there was no reason to give up cover."

Denbry's smug expression set Nina's teeth on edge. She opened her mouth to object, but Kent wasn't finished.

"And there's room for improvement in your communication skills too," he added.

He *would* focus on that. She had never played well with others. Her childhood had rendered her highly self-reliant, and four years as a local cop before she joined the Bureau had taught her to work independently and make quick decisions in the field. Not a great recipe for teamwork.

"That's why we're here," Wade said, sliding his weapon into a pancake holster attached to his belt. "We need to gel as a team, learn what to expect from each other, anticipate the other's next move."

Breck grinned. "Well, we can pretty much anticipate Guerrera kickin' some ass."

It sounded to Nina like the consensus was that her decision to shoot had been rash.

Two years as a federal agent hadn't fully indoctrinated her into the FBI mode of thinking. They were all about methodical investigations that involved bringing diverse resources to bear on a case and working every angle until it was watertight, everyone contributing their part to get the job done.

As the youngest and least senior member of the newly formed team, she checked her attitude and turned to Denbry. "I will work on my communication."

He gave her a satisfied nod.

"We didn't do so great either," Breck said, jerking a thumb at Kent, who had partnered with her in a different training scenario.

Denbry heaved a sigh. "We're finished here. I'll give SSA Buxton some feedback. You all are clear to go."

Nina could only imagine what kinds of comments he would share with her supervisor.

"Come on," Kent said to Nina. "It's been a long morning."

She looked up at him, curious about how someone with a background in Special Forces would have handled things. "Would you have taken the shot?"

The lines around his mouth tightened. "No, I wouldn't."

Chapter 30

An hour later, Nina sat with her team at a corner table in the FBI's internal lounge and pub, dubbed the Boardroom, which was deserted on a late-Sunday morning. After standing in line for a tray of brunch food in the facility's dining hall, they had retreated to a quiet place to discuss the case. Buxton had texted to say he would join them as soon as he received a critique of the team's performance from the training instructors.

The internal debate continued to rage in Nina's mind about what to share with the others. She kept her silence, giving herself a bit more time to come up with a way to broach the subject. Or to avoid it altogether.

She had stayed awake most of the previous night, mulling over the situation. How would it have been possible, given her career in law enforcement involving two different agencies, for this not to have come to light before now?

Every successful FBI applicant had to qualify for a Top Secret clearance, and an extensive background investigation was part of the process. Nina had been no different.

She recalled that the applicant process for both the Fairfax County police and the Bureau had included running her through the Integrated

Automated Fingerprint Identification System and the National Crime Information Center. The NCIC, which was a massive criminal database, was maintained separately from the FBI's DNA index. A search of IAFIS would only match prints already on file, and NCIC would only reveal involvement in illegal activity.

Neither background check had included a DNA test.

Even if her DNA had been entered into the system, the blood samples collected at the scene of the Llorona case were never submitted for DNA analysis. The case had been closed years before such technology was available. Besides, the police had concluded the culprit was deceased. No need to investigate further.

"That shit show at the Bank of Hogan didn't help our cause," Kent said, interrupting her reverie.

"I thought it went okay," Breck said.

Kent frowned. "Let's just say there were some issues with teamwork."

She felt the weight of everyone's gaze. This was her problem. She had spent too many years relying on herself. And wasn't that what she was doing now?

"I don't think it's sunk in yet for Guerrera that we have her back," Kent said.

Her head snapped up. "What are you talking about?"

"Maybe a real-life illustration will help," he said. "On one of my overseas SEAL deployments, I got pinned down by gunfire during a classified operation. I'd been separated from the rest of my unit when I dropped back to check our six. Sure enough, there were unfriendlies lying in wait, ready to ambush us from behind. I had no way out. Whichever way I moved, hostiles would cut me down."

He had her full attention. "What did you do?"

"We were all on a com system. We'd been trained to give a distress code if we got trapped behind enemy lines. I had to trust them to assess the situation and lay down suppressive fire," he said.

She had learned about suppressive fire in the academy. It involved shooting at an attacker to keep them at bay while a fellow officer escaped from a deadly situation.

"The point is, I could not see my team," Kent went on. "I couldn't be sure exactly where they were or if they'd heard me clearly. I had to have total faith and put my life in their hands."

She had already grasped the point to his story but couldn't resist hearing more. "What was the distress code?" she prompted. "What happened when you used it?"

"The code word was *flashpoint*," Kent said. "There was no time to wait for a response. The instant I said it, I left cover and sprinted as fast as I could toward the team." He lifted a shoulder. "If they did what I expected, I would make it. If they didn't, I would die—or worse, get captured."

"They covered you?"

"Fuckin' A, they did. I've never seen so much lead flying." He leaned toward her. "You have to get to the point where you can trust your team to have your back."

She took a sip of soda, taking in the information. Kent was talking about a tactical situation, but she understood his words on a completely different level. Now was the time for her to decide. Was she part of a team or not?

Her gaze traveled over Wade, Kent, and Breck. They had become more than just fellow agents to her. They were friends. Comrades in arms. Allies. If she confided in them, one of two things would happen. They would either pass the information on to Buxton, as they should, or they would keep her secret, jeopardizing their careers.

Wade gave her an appraising look. "What's on your mind, Guerrera?"

"What do you mean?"

"I read people," he said. "And I'm damned good at it."

She took another sip of her drink, playing for time. "I was think-ing about Carmen Cardona," she said, still unsure how much she was prepared to elaborate.

"I know she was on drugs and all," Breck said, "but how could she hurt her baby—that is, the baby she thought was hers?" She scowled. "Or any baby at all for that matter."

After leaving St. Elizabeth's yesterday afternoon, Wade and Nina had briefed the rest of the team about Carmen's statements. At the time, Nina had translated Carmen's comment as "*I gave her a kiss.*"

Together, they all considered the facts. First, Carmen had expressed regret before she broke down crying, saying, "What have I done?" Second, Carmen admitted to using narcotics again a few weeks after giving birth and was desperate in many ways. Finally, there was zero trace of the baby after Carmen took her from the hospital. Ultimately, the team had concluded Carmen had most likely killed a child that had become a burden to her.

They had agreed to try to find closure for Victor's and Maria's rela-tives through more definitive answers, although the chances of doing so without Carmen's cooperation were slim.

"Let's face it," Kent said. "There's no way we can criminally pros-ecute someone in a psych ward based on mere suspicion that she com-mitted a crime almost three decades ago. Even if we somehow found proof, she would never be convicted."

Nina wanted to look away, but Wade's gray gaze held her trapped as he leaned toward her. "Guerrera?" He would not be distracted.

Time to make her choice. "After we left St. E's, I kept thinking about what Carmen told us," she said.

He made no comment. This was Dr. Jeffrey Wade, psychologist, in interview mode. Before he was through, he would wring the whole story from her.

"At the end, when Carmen began to cry, I thought she said '*besar*,' which means *to kiss*, but now I believe she was trying to say '*basura*,' which means *trash*." She didn't bother going into the intricacies of Spanish grammar involved in her new interpretation. "After giving it careful consideration, I now believe she said '*La dejé en la basura.*'"

"I left her in the trash," Kent said softly, translating for the others.

"The trash?" Wade looked from Kent back to Nina.

Mouth dry, she merely nodded. Wade, who had gone over her psych eval before she became an agent, knew her entire personal history better than anyone else.

"Carmen told us she had met with a client in Virginia," Wade said, dawning comprehension in his expression.

She helped him connect the final dots. "I'm about to turn twenty-eight years old." She let that penetrate before continuing. "But no one knows when my actual birthday is, so I might have turned twenty-eight—"

"On February twenty-third," Wade said.

Breck's hand flew to her mouth. "Wait a minute." She glanced at Wade, then at Nina. "The baby from the Llorona case was born on February twenty-third, then Carmen took her to Maryland. Now you're saying Carmen put the baby in the trash somewhere in Virginia?"

Wade held up a hand, silencing all discussion. "Guerrera, are you saying *you* are Victor and Maria Vega's missing daughter?"

She swallowed. "Last night, I checked to see how many Latina baby girls were left in a northern Virginia dumpster exactly twenty-eight years ago." She finished on a hoarse whisper. "One."

Kent reached out to clasp her hand. "Nina."

Growing up, she had not experienced much in the way of sympathy, tenderness, or any other show of kindness. The compassion in his touch, the warmth in his expression, the gentleness in his tone, were more than she could bear. She pulled her hand away.

"Fate has been especially cruel to you, Agent Guerrera," Wade said. "I don't want to cause you more pain, but you understand that we must have a definitive answer about your status in relation to the victims."

"We've got to go back and reinterview Carmen," Breck said.

Wade shook his head. "Dr. Matthews called me after we left St. E's. Carmen is catatonic now. We won't be allowed back to see her anytime soon."

Nina went straight to the point that concerned her most. "I want to stay on the case. I'm an outsider to both families because I've never known any of them. I can remain objective."

Wade arched a skeptical brow. "You can fool yourself, Guerrera, but you can't fool me."

Maybe she was deluding herself, but she wanted—needed—to investigate this case. She began to regret sharing her secret, then Breck spoke up.

"Is your DNA in any of those commercial genealogy systems?" she asked Nina. "You know, the ones people use to find out about their ancestry or meet their relatives?"

Nina shook her head. "Why would I want to look up people who had thrown me in the trash?"

She realized how hardened she had become regarding the circumstances of her birth and abandonment. She had never thought there could be another reason behind it and walled herself off from further pain by refusing to even think about her biological family.

Breck's mouth quirked up at the corner. "We happen to be sitting in a facility that contains one of the most advanced forensics labs on the planet," she said. "I helped out one of the lab techs with a computer problem when I was in Cyber Crime." Her smile widened. "He owes me a favor. I can arrange to have a sample of your DNA compared with the profile of Victor and Maria Vega that was submitted to the CODIS database by the Phoenix crime lab."

Nina eyed her warily. "This tech is working today?"

"Saw him in the parking lot half an hour ago."

"You're saying he would run the comparison on the down-low?" Kent asked. "Is that even possible?"

Breck's cheeks dimpled. "He'll find a way to keep it off the books." After a brief pause, she added, "But we'll have to wait a few hours for the results."

"We're flying out to Phoenix this afternoon," Kent said.

"He'll call me as soon as he knows one way or another," Breck said. "Probably after we land at Sky Harbor Airport."

"Can we give him a swab from an unknown source?" Nina air-quoted the last two words.

"Sure," Breck said. "But he's not dumb. He'll figure out it's probably somebody in-house, he just won't know who."

"Let's say we do this, and Guerrera's DNA is a match," Wade said. "Now we know for sure she's the missing baby." He paused. "Buxton will put her on the first flight back to DC."

Breck lifted her chin. "*Only* if he knows about it."

Silence followed her words. Nina surveyed her team, all of them apparently lost in their own thoughts. Probably contemplating the effect such a severe breach in protocol would have on their careers. She desperately wanted to work the case but not if it put others at risk.

"I can't let you do it," she finally said to them.

"Do what?" Buxton said. Their supervisor had walked up to their table while they were engrossed in conversation.

Chapter 31

Nina wondered how much Buxton had heard as he sank into an empty chair and gazed at her expectantly.

She scrambled to find something—anything—to divert him from their actual discussion. "I can't let them take the blame for my performance at the training session today," she said after the briefest hesitation. She knew Buxton had just met with the instructors and that they would have had plenty to say about her judgment.

"I'm glad to hear that," Buxton said. "Because Agent Denbry was none too pleased with your operational freelancing."

"Guerrera's still about thirty percent street cop," Kent said, smiling. "She's a work in progress."

"You all aren't helping my cause," Buxton said. "I'm trying to make this a standing unit. Excellent teamwork is a prerequisite."

"So is investigative work," Wade said. "Kent and Breck were just about to explain what they learned about James Snead."

Nina threw Wade a grateful look, fully aware he had changed the subject as an added distraction. She had also been curious to hear what Kent and Breck had uncovered about the Phoenix television reporter who always seemed to know too much.

"Snead kept coming up with information that only either the killer or one of us knew," Kent said. "And he's been obsessed with the case since he reported on the original incident twenty-eight years ago, so he was worth a look."

Breck nodded. "He was the one who interviewed the neighbor who called it the Llorona case, and the name stuck."

Nina recalled the newsclip she had seen on their first flight to Phoenix. It seemed like a million years ago.

"Unfortunately, Snead's not the unsub," Kent said. "He doesn't fit the profile."

"More to the point, we can definitively rule him out," Breck added. "He was in Hawaii on leap day in 1996. That year, February twenty-ninth fell on a Thursday, and Snead landed in Honolulu the day before in preparation for his wedding, which was that Saturday. He did not come back to the mainland for two weeks, after his honeymoon."

Nina had practically memorized the murder schedule. "In 1996 the unsub struck in LA."

"Exactly," Breck said. "There's no way it could've been Snead, but to double-check, we found out that he was in Phoenix on all other leap days, usually on live television, so he couldn't have been out of town committing the crimes."

Nina sighed. "The perfect alibi," she said. "But he still knows way more than he should."

"We reached out to him yesterday evening," Kent said. "He told us he was getting his scoops from a source close to the investigation." He gave his head a small shake. "Which, of course, he would not disclose."

"We explained that the source was probably the killer," Breck said. "Snead quoted the First Amendment to us. It went downhill from there."

"Let's assume the real murderer is feeding Snead," Nina said. "Why would he do that?"

"It's a disinformation campaign like we sometimes did in the military," Kent said. "The info he gives to Snead is strategic. He times the news releases to interfere, mislead, or distract us."

Nina understood the cleverness of the maneuver. "He probably wanted us to waste time and resources investigating Snead as well. That could be why he fed the info to only one member of the media. It would make Snead look more guilty."

"Mission accomplished," Breck said. "We wasted most of the day on that damned reporter."

Buxton redirected the discussion. "Let's move on to the Thomas Kirk investigation."

Even before Snead, Nina had been convinced the Realtor was the murderer. "Another instance of someone who checked all the boxes for a good suspect."

"I liked him for it too," Breck said. "Right up until the actual killer filleted him."

"I want to go back to the scene now that the evidence techs are finished there," Nina said. "The unsub is sending us off on tangents, and I'm anxious to get back on his trail."

Chapter 32

Seven hours later, Nina stepped out of the hotel shower after washing off the travel ick. Bustling airport terminals always made her feel like cattle being herded through a chute.

She cinched the thick belt on the hotel's plush terry-cloth robe and ambled out of the bathroom. "The shower's all yours," she called out to Breck, then came to an abrupt halt as her bare feet hit the dense carpet.

Wade and Kent were seated in a small cluster of furniture, deep in discussion with Breck. Three heads turned her way. Nina strolled over and sat on the love seat next to Wade. Kent and Breck were on the sofa across from her, Breck's laptop sitting open between half-empty boxes of Thai takeout on the low coffee table.

They avoided her gaze. "There's nothing like walking into a room and everyone stops talking," she said.

Wade found his voice first. "We've been having a little chat about you."

Nina waited them out in silence.

Predictably, Breck cracked first. "We've got to tell her," she said to the two men. "Now."

Nina narrowed her eyes. "Tell me what?"

Breck turned away from the men to focus on Nina. "Remember when we ate brunch in the Boardroom at Quantico this morning?"

A sinking feeling formed in Nina's stomach as she got an inkling where this might be going.

Breck grimaced. "I kind of picked up your soda can and took it to my friend at the lab."

"What the hell, Breck?"

"Look, you wanted answers." She swept out a hand toward Wade, who was examining the wall art, and Kent, who appeared to be fascinated by the take-out boxes. "We all did."

"So you had my DNA compared to the Vega family without my knowledge or consent?"

Breck grimaced. "When you put it like that, it sounds—"

"Like a massive invasion of my privacy and a major violation of protocol," Nina finished for her. Not exactly a stickler for protocol herself, Nina still had limits, and she felt Breck had crossed a line.

A red scald spread through Breck's freckled cheeks as her mouth snapped shut.

Wade intervened, his voice soothing. "It's done. Now we need to deal with the ramifications."

"Does anyone plan to tell me what the results were?" Nina heard her own voice rising again.

"You already know," Wade said quietly.

Looking at each of them in turn, she read the answer in their expressions. The lab had only confirmed what she knew in her heart. After a lifetime spent untethered, unwanted, and unloved, she had finally found her parents, only to learn they had been ripped away before she ever even had a chance to know them. Her chest swelled with blinding rage, soul-deep pain, and finally, profound grief.

Since Nina had been old enough to understand how she had ended up in the foster system, she had always known her story would be tragic. A baby doesn't end up in the trash under any but the worst circumstances, and she had assumed it had been a heartless act done out of sheer cruelty.

After meeting Carmen, Nina realized abandoning her child had been an act of desperation born out of mental illness and substance abuse. Carmen had obviously been self-medicating and wasn't in her right mind, but she should have made a different choice. If she couldn't care for her child, she should have taken her to a safe place.

Carmen's reckless and thoughtless actions in a moment of anguish had caused years of suffering. For both of them.

Nina wanted to hate her, but the image of Carmen in her hospital room, surrounded by the accusing eyes of the dolls she painted, trapped in an echo chamber of recurring self-recrimination, hobbled by guilt, tugged at her heart.

Hadn't they both suffered enough? Could she release herself from the burden of hate? Of anger? Of judgment? The fight drained out of her, leaving her bereft and strangely numb. "I'm the missing baby from the Llorona case." She made it a statement. "Victor and Maria Vega are my biological parents." Her eyes drifted down. "I should have died along with them."

"No, honey." Breck reached out to clasp her hand. Then, possibly sensing Nina's discomfort, quickly released it.

"The question is, what do we do now that we know it for a fact?" Kent asked.

She appreciated Kent's use of the word *we*, but this was her load to bear. She would have to deal with it and keep the others from further exposure to career-ending disaster.

"I had an obligation to report my suspicions the moment I had them . . . and I didn't." She dragged a hand through her damp hair and admitted the ugly truth. "Because I want to stay on the case."

"We can't jeopardize the investigation," Wade said. "Or any potential prosecution."

Kent jerked his chin at Breck. "Which is where plausible deniability would have come in handy. Now we have test results, and we can't pretend we don't know."

Still red-faced, Breck defended herself. "No one *knows* we know. There's no report with these findings at the lab. Nothing was entered into any database." She raised her hand, fingers spread wide. "There are five people on the planet—us and the lab tech—who are aware of this right now."

Kent looked thoughtful. "So we proceed like before." He took off his glasses and pinched the bridge of his nose. "And if it comes out for any reason, we act surprised."

Nina realized they were trying to find a way to keep her on the case. "I appreciate what you're doing, but Wade's right, we can't take any risks that would affect the prosecution of—"

"Let's look at what we've got," Wade said. "Things have obviously changed, and we need to adapt."

"What did you have in mind?" Nina asked cautiously.

"We should switch the teams around," he said. "Guerrera will work with Kent on the Doyle case, and Breck will partner with me on the Llorona case."

"Sounds good to me," Kent said.

"If we suddenly change what we're doing, we'll draw attention to the situation," Nina said. "How will we justify it to Buxton? He would never allow us to swap cases in the middle of a major investigation without a good reason." She shook her head. "If we're going to do this, we need to keep going as if we truly don't know. Anything else would look suspicious."

"I agree with Guerrera," Breck said. "We should keep things as they are."

Nina played with a loose thread on her bathrobe. "As long as the public doesn't find out about my relationship to the Vega family until after a suspect is in custody, we'll be fine."

"There's another aspect to this you're not thinking about, Guerrera," Wade said. "Thanks to Snead's news story, both families already know Victor and Maria's biological child is missing. They'll demand to know what kind of progress we've made in locating her, but we cannot divulge that information at this time."

He had a point. She hadn't thought about what it would mean to see the relatives of both victims knowing they were her family. The family she had always assumed had abandoned her. The family she had always longed for.

She shifted uncomfortably. "I'll be forced to lie and tell them we don't know what happened to the baby."

"FBI agents don't lie," Wade said. "We just characterize the situation in such a manner that leaves it open to interpretation."

"Right," she said. "I'm going to have to lie my ass off."

"You okay with that?" Kent asked her.

"Whatever it takes," she said. "I just hope they understand when they learn the truth."

"When should that be?" Breck had posed the thorniest question of all.

"I would say not until after prosecution," Kent said. "But that could take years, and it's too long to let the families continue to suffer." He turned to Nina. "Or Guerrera."

Wade appeared to give it some thought. "I suppose we could come out with it after an arrest is made," he said slowly. "Then Guerrera will recuse herself from the prosecution and trial."

"That could work," Breck said. "But no one outside of this room can ever know."

Nina knew how it would look if everything came out in the open ahead of time. "This was the Phoenix PD's case originally. Perez is going to be pretty damn hot if he finds out we kept this from him."

"So will the entire police department, the victims' families, the media, and the general public," Wade said.

"If this leaks out before we put cuffs on the unsub, I'm holding all of you to a promise." Nina looked at each of them in turn. "I take the fall." She tapped her chest with her fingertips. "None of you. Only me."

Kent stiffened. "Listen, Guerrera, we—"

"No," she cut him off. "I'm not taking anyone else down with me. You all will need to stay on and find this guy." She paused, adding emphasis to her words. "And all the others out there who need to get caught."

It was an acknowledgment of the seriousness of the situation. Withholding this kind of information could get her fired. She regarded Kent. He would be the hardest sell. She figured his desire to keep chasing predators was warring with his intense loyalty to his team and his determination to never leave anyone behind.

Finally, he met her gaze. "Deal," he said simply. For him, duty to his job and his community had won out.

The others nodded their tacit agreement.

They had made a pact.

Chapter 33

He clicked off the digital voice player and flopped back on the hotel bed, stunned. He pressed the button to go back fifteen seconds and listened again as Nina Guerrera spoke the words that changed everything.

"I'm the missing baby from the Llorona case. Victor and Maria Vega are my biological parents. I should have died along with them."

Yes, she damn well should have died. She knew it, and now he knew it too.

Finally, he understood why Phoenix had not provided what he needed. Phoenix was supposed to fix everything. Bring it all into balance. But the city had been tainted from the start, and he'd been forced to keep finding other cities, other families, other leap days, to settle the score.

It dawned on him that he was living the legend of *La Llorona*, forever in search of a way to undo what had been done. Like the woman from the folktale, he seemed cursed to never achieve his goal. Doomed to continue, tormented, for eternity. And now he knew the reason why.

Nina Guerrera.

She was the fruit from the poisonous tree. He had learned the legal term from watching courtroom dramas on television. For prosecutors, it meant any evidence obtained from an illegal search was inadmissible in court. For him, it meant everything he had done after Phoenix hadn't worked because it had been tainted by a critical error from the outset.

At long last, he understood why nothing quieted the rage. Nothing made it right. Nothing ever ended. Because a piece had been missing all along.

Once he put that missing piece where it belonged, things would fall into place.

He pulled open his tablet and began searching for more information about her. Like so many others, he had followed her most famous case with interest. This time, with a totally different perspective, he delved into what the media had reported about her background before she joined the FBI. As he absorbed the lurid details, he realized he was reading a slightly altered version of his own past.

Like Nina Guerrera, he had spent several of his formative years in the care of the state. Like her, no one had wanted him. No one had understood him. Others had tried to cow him, but he was a fighter, like the Warrior Girl.

At sixteen, they had each faced a turning point, and that's where their stories diverged. She had chosen the path of weakness, and he had chosen strength. She worked for justice. He exacted revenge.

She had gained fame, even adulation, while he toiled in obscurity. He should have had her life. Should have been famous, admired. And the Warrior Girl shouldn't even exist.

Each breath she drew was an affront. An imbalance begging to be set right. He began to formulate a new plan.

The reporter would make it easy. He had first seen Snead's coverage of the Llorona case twenty-eight years ago, back when they were both young men. Snead's apparent fascination with the case had made him a useful tool this week. The anonymous tips he had given the reporter had provided the perfect distraction. The Feds were looking for a leak among their ranks that didn't exist. Snead was hungry, and he would continue to feed him well.

It took him about an hour, but he laid out three phases to the plan. For the first phase, he would need some extra equipment from his house, including the special laptop he kept locked in his basement. While he was stopping by, he could take out the trash, collect the mail, and retrieve any packages so his neighbors would think he'd been commuting to work from his home as usual, in case the FBI ever came sniffing around.

He did not underestimate his adversary. He would have to lay the trap with extreme care. Of course, an effective trap required irresistible bait. This new information offered him exactly that. A smile slowly lifted his lips. Nina Guerrera would never see it coming.

Chapter 34

Nina stood in the same spot she had been four days earlier, the morning sun burning off the last of the dew. Unlike before, however, a band of yellow police tape slanted across Thomas Kirk's front door.

Perez hooked a thumb on his belt next to his gleaming detective shield. "I'm not sure why you wanted to come here before speaking to Teresa. She's been hounding me for information ever since the news broke about the baby switch."

Nina had called him late the night before after the meeting with her team at the hotel. As agreed, she had not informed Perez about her discovery in DC, instead asking him to meet her at the scene of Kirk's murder.

"I figured this was my last chance to see the crime scene," she said in answer to his comment. "Besides, it's too early in the morning to knock on people's doors." She didn't add that she wanted a bit more time to prepare herself to confront her family without betraying any emotion.

"You're right about the crime scene," Perez said. He had contacted Kirk's sister, who had inherited his estate, to inform her they needed the house another day. "His sister's not happy. Told me she hired a hazmat-cleaning crew to get this place ready to sell, and now she'll have to reschedule."

"Sounds like they weren't close." Nina lifted the yellow tape so Perez could fit a key into the locked front door. "By the way, did the evidence techs find anything interesting when they were here?"

"They collected their usual five thousand bags of stuff to process. I checked with Dr. Ledford this morning. They haven't identified any extraneous DNA or fingerprints so far."

She recoiled at the chaos that greeted her when she walked inside. Chairs tipped over, drawers pulled out, their contents strewn across the floor. "The killer didn't do a very convincing job staging this scene. I'm thinking he may not be as good at improvising as he is when he has four years to plan his crimes."

"Which implies he rushed out here to silence Kirk on short notice."

Something that had bothered her from the moment they had found Kirk's body. "Thomas Kirk only came across our radar the afternoon before he was killed." She strode into the kitchen, eyes continuously roving as she read the scene. "The unsub took him out just hours before we got to him."

"Someone talked when they should have kept their mouth shut," Perez said. "I filed a report and notified my chain of command about the Kirk lead. Lots of people on the department could have accessed that information. I'm assuming the same is true with the FBI."

They had all filed reports as well. Buxton had briefed the SAC and others at the PFO about the case.

"I don't want to believe it either," she said, "but I can't see any other way. How else would he know our next move?" She walked down the hall to the master bedroom. "And did he ransack the place to make it appear like a burglary, or was it to find something Kirk was hiding?"

"Perhaps both," Perez said, gesturing toward the tall chest of drawers. "Evidence techs bagged and tagged Kirk's wallet, a diamond pinkie ring, and a gold watch that were on the dresser in a wooden tray. His cash and credit cards were still in the wallet, and no one has used the numbers to make any online purchases."

"Whoever did this wasn't after money," she said, glancing around. "Televisions, stereo equipment, the victim's car—all here." She turned to Perez. "What's missing?"

"Kirk's computer." Perez beckoned her. "I'll show you."

She trailed him into the home office. A rectangular clearing in a thin layer of dust on the desk's smooth surface delineated the spot where a laptop had been.

She peered behind the desk. "He took the power cord too."

"That would make it more valuable if he intended to sell it," Perez said. "Our pawn unit is checking to see if it turns up anywhere."

"He's not selling it," Nina said. "He needed to be sure he could plug it in because he's going to search for files, which could take time."

"What files?"

"No idea. This is a hunch, but it feels right. If the only thing missing from this house is a computer, the killer didn't want us to see something on the hard drive."

Perez's dark brows shot up. "Could Kirk and the suspect have been working together?"

"You mean a serial-killing team?" At his nod, she considered what she had learned from Wade and Kent about those who formed partnerships to terrorize and murder. "It's rare, but it has definitely happened before." She recalled the investigative files she had reviewed the previous night. "If that's what's going on here, it would have been obvious who he was hanging out with, but that's not the case with Kirk. He was something of a loner. Never married."

"His last relationship seems to have ended over a year ago," Perez said. "A woman he met when he sold her a house after her divorce."

"So . . . a full-service Realtor, then?"

Perez chuckled. "I suppose you could call it that."

She pulled the conversation back to their surroundings. "Kirk died because he knew the unsub." Thoughtful, she strolled back to the living room. "His house was ransacked in an attempt to disguise the fact that there was something incriminating on his computer." Her eyes came to rest on the fireplace. "Wait a minute. What's this?" She stepped close to the hearth. "The mantel has the same thin film of dust the rest of the house has."

"Welcome to Arizona," Perez said. "Everybody loves the dry heat, but the dust is a constant problem. Any flat surface that isn't wiped down every three days accumulates enough to be visible."

She pointed at the cluster of frames propped on the mantel. "There's an outline where a picture used to be. Did the evidence techs collect it for some reason?"

She studied the remaining pictures while Perez called the crime scene supervisor. After a brief conversation, he slipped his cell back inside his pocket. "They didn't take it."

"Then the killer did."

"The pictures on this mantel go back a lot of years," Perez said, squinting at the collection. "This one is of Kirk when he was a teenager."

"There's a bunch of young men in this one," Nina said, pointing to another framed photo. "They all look like they're between eighteen and twenty-five." Realization flashed through her. "When we interviewed Robert Cahill from the juvenile detention center, he said Kirk had helped some of the other boys find jobs after they got out." Excitement blossomed. "What if Kirk stayed in touch with some of them?"

"Kept photos of his fellow delinquents?" Perez looked doubtful. "Why would he do that?"

Despite Perez's lack of enthusiasm, she knew she was onto something. "Remember how Cahill said he thought Kirk turned his life around? What if Kirk was proud of that? These aren't photos of fellow delinquents to him." She swept out her hand toward the array. "They're pictures of kids he rescued. Kids like himself."

"So he gave them a job and maybe mentored some of them?"

"That's what Cahill thought."

Perez put his hands on his hips. "You're thinking the subject comes in here and takes the computer but also swipes a picture off the mantel because he's in it with Kirk?"

"Why else would he take it?"

"That's a pretty big leap, but let's say you're right," Perez said. "How can we tell who was in the missing picture?"

"Easy." This time, she was the one who pulled out her phone. "I'll take photos of the remaining pictures and forward them to Breck. She'll print copies we can show to Cahill and ask him to ID anyone he remembers from the juvenile detention center."

Perez caught on quickly. "We can eliminate everyone who's in any of the photos that *weren't* stolen."

"Exactly," Nina said. "Then we ask him who else Kirk helped right after they got out. The one that's missing is our suspect."

Perez returned her smile. "Pretty damned smart, Guerrera."

Chapter 35

Twenty minutes later, Nina slipped her cell phone back into her pocket and started down the front walk toward Teresa's house. "That was Wade," she said to Perez. "Cahill's not answering his phone, but they'll keep trying to reach him. Buxton wants us to continue with field interviews while the rest of the team chases down the other leads."

Perez fell into step beside her. "Sounds like Teresa's got company. She didn't mention visitors when I called ahead."

The familiarity reminded Nina that Perez had known this family for years, and his fellow detectives had handled the original case. It struck her that he knew more about her relatives than she did.

Sounds of laughter reached Nina as she waited after ringing the doorbell a third time. She wasn't sure what she had been expecting when she came here—this time aware that Teresa was her aunt—but a noisy gathering wouldn't have been her first choice.

"Come in," a feminine voice called from inside.

Nina glanced at Perez, then shrugged and opened the door to a cacophony of clanking dishes, music, and voices.

She followed the sound to the house's main gathering area, an airy family room that flowed into the kitchen. The space held even more people than Nina had anticipated from the noise. It looked like three generations were setting up for a party.

Nina surveyed the room. These were her people. Her *familia*. Something she had never known. This is what fate had stolen from her twenty-eight years ago. She had barely begun to come to terms with the circumstances of her birth. If Carmen hadn't taken her from the hospital, she would have died with her parents.

It seemed destiny had decreed that—one way or another—she would grow up without a family. Her colleagues and neighbors had become the closest thing she'd known.

Perez stepped around her and approached a lady who appeared to be in her seventies. The shape of her eyes and set of her chin identified her as Teresa's mother.

Nina's own grandmother.

She had to shut down these thoughts. Fast. She would handle this. She would compartmentalize.

"It's good to see you again, Mrs. Soto," Perez said to the older lady.

"Javier." She returned his greeting warmly, clasping both his hands in her frail, birdlike ones. "I've told you to call me Sofia."

Perez appeared to be on a first-name basis with the matriarch as well as the others. She watched as he went to shake Sofia's husband's hand. The older man pulled the detective into an *abrazo*, a hug between Latino men.

After Perez made the introductions, Nina apologized. "I can see we're interrupting something." She surveyed the bustle of activity around them.

"We're having a baby shower in a couple of hours." Teresa had quietly emerged from the kitchen. "Come here, *mija*." She beckoned to an extremely pregnant young woman. "This is my daughter, Selena, and her husband, Tony."

Pride lit Teresa's eyes as she gazed at Selena, who looked like she might have the baby any minute.

Nina scrutinized Teresa's features with fresh interest. This is what her own mother, Maria, would have looked like had a killer not taken her life at such a young age. Teresa was lovely, with pretty brown eyes, tan skin, and thick dark hair streaked with gray.

Nina's chest constricted with unspoken loss. Would Maria have looked upon her with a mother's love in her eyes? Would she have called her *mi'ja*?

"Agent Guerrera?" Teresa said, concern in her voice.

Nina silently cursed the terrible timing. At a moment when the family was preparing to celebrate new life, they had come to talk about death.

"Is everyone here family?" Nina asked, her voice cracking on the last word.

"Guests won't arrive for another hour or so," Teresa said in affirmation. "It's going to be a brunch."

Judging by the amount of food covering the kitchen counters, the shower would be a large affair. What they wanted to discuss involved the entire family, so despite the setting, perhaps this was for the best.

"We saw the story about the switch at the hospital on the news," Teresa said, broaching the subject. "Are you two here to tell us what you found out about Maria's baby?"

Nina hesitated as everyone fell silent, their faces filled with eager expectation. This was not like her. She had never backed down from anything. Not bullies as a child, not violent criminals, and not those in law enforcement who had thought her too petite to pull her own weight. Here she stood, irresolute, in front of a group of people who might welcome her if they knew who she was.

Regret momentarily paralyzed her. She had come here to lie to them. That would be their first impression of her when they looked back on this moment.

This was so much harder than she had ever imagined it would be.

"Thank you all for allowing us to trespass on your celebration," she began. "We wanted to give you an update on our investigation into the facts surrounding the death of Maria and her family."

Nina was careful not to refer to it as the Llorona case. That legend had tormented this family for years. At least that much of their nightmare would finally end today.

Nina began her explanation carefully. "As you all have heard on the news, we've learned Maria's baby was switched with another child at the hospital the day she was born."

"So it's true?" This time Teresa's daughter, Selena, spoke. She was holding her extremely round pregnant belly, looking horrified.

"It is," Nina said. "The baby who died in Victor and Maria's home was not their child. We've confirmed it through DNA."

"Then where is my niece?" Teresa said. "What happened to her?"

Perspiration trickled down Nina's neck as she delivered the words she and Wade had rehearsed earlier. Words that were a lie of omission.

"We are still following up on that part of the investigation," Nina said. "We will give you a full briefing as soon as we can."

Teresa looked up at Perez, obviously hoping for more. "Then another family raised our little *princesa*, and their baby died?"

Nina gritted her teeth. This was a rabbit hole she hadn't prepared to go down. Guilt gnawed at Nina as she heard Perez tell Teresa and the rest of the family what he thought was the truth.

"We are still in the process of gathering all the information about the circumstances," he said to her. "We haven't been able to track her down yet."

Teresa turned beseeching eyes on Nina. "But our little girl is out there? She's all grown up, right?"

"It would seem so," Nina said gently, sick with shame over her deception. She decided to shift everyone's attention with a change of subject. "I do have other important news, though."

That worked. All questions ceased, and everyone looked at her with renewed interest.

"After reopening the case with Detective Perez's help"—Nina tipped her head toward him in acknowledgment—"we now believe Maria and her family were murdered by an intruder." She let that sink in for a moment before adding, "Maria never killed herself or anyone else."

"I knew it." A single tear coursed down Teresa's face. "My sister would never do such a thing." Her hands bunched into fists. "How did this happen?"

"The intruder staged the scene to make it look like Maria killed her husband and child before taking her own life," Nina said.

"But there was a police investigation." Teresa turned blazing eyes on Perez. "An autopsy."

"That was twenty-eight years ago," Perez said. "Forensic science has come a long way and—"

"But we told that detective that Maria could not have done it," Teresa persisted. "He would not listen to us."

"It's quite common for family members to deny their loved one could have committed a crime," Perez said. "Detective O'Malley evaluated the evidence he had at the time."

Nina saw no reason to add that she had found a discrepancy in the blood-spatter patterns at the crime scene. There would be plenty of time for recrimination in the future.

Teresa remained indignant. "That detective only found evidence that told him what he had already made up his mind to believe."

"He found evidence that had been carefully planted to lead him in a certain direction," Nina said. "Including the love letters discovered at the scene. They were faked."

That seemed to take Teresa by surprise. "Victor was not having an affair? There was no other woman?"

"There's nothing to substantiate an extramarital relationship," Nina said. "The notes were put there to provide a motive for the murders."

Seemingly deflated, Teresa plopped down heavily on the couch. Her husband sat beside her, patting her hand. Her brother, introduced earlier as Tito, spoke in a low voice to Teresa's parents, who had been sitting on a love seat the entire time. Nina gave them a few minutes to discuss what they had learned, processing it together as a family. Not only did they need to change their opinion about what Maria had done that night, but they also had to reassess their estimation of Victor.

Teresa's husband, John, spoke for the first time. "How did you figure out the truth?"

"Actually, Agent Guerrera had a lot to do with that," Perez said.

Nina blushed. "I noticed a few discrepancies when Detective Perez and I reviewed the evidence." She did not elaborate about the other cases attributed to the same killer.

"Our Maria is not *La Llorona*." Teresa dabbed at her eyes with a tissue her husband had handed her. "All these years, we have not spoken to Victor's family." She shook her head. "So many hard feelings."

"We're on our way to see his family next," Nina said.

"Thank you so much for what you have done." All eyes turned to Sofia, Teresa's mother. "You have lifted a great burden from us."

Nina's heart ached for the older woman who clearly felt responsible for her brood. Nina could tell it was a release of shame. Shame none of them had ever deserved but carried anyway.

"Who did this?" Sofia continued. "Have you caught him?"

"We have not identified a suspect yet," Nina said, silently praying the team was having luck tracking down Cahill.

Sofia's birdlike hand fluttered to her chest. "He's still out there?"

"Which brings us to an important point," Nina said. "You cannot discuss this part of the investigation with anyone. Do you understand?"

Perez added force to the request. "If you want to catch the one who did this, you must allow us to investigate without media interference."

"And without the suspect learning how much we know," Nina added. "Please don't share this outside the family until we make an announcement to the public." She thought about Snead. "And if any reporters contact you, do not pass on what we've told you."

Sofia's eyes hardened. "I give you my word. None of us will say a thing." She glared around the room for emphasis, and Nina had the feeling no one would dare disobey her.

Chapter 36

Nina's cell blinked with a message from Wade when they left Teresa's house. He had located Cahill, who agreed to come to the Phoenix field office to meet with them in an hour. Meanwhile, she and Perez were tasked with updating Victor Vega's parents.

Sitting inside Ana and Luis Vega's quiet living room for the past twenty minutes as they delivered the heart-wrenching developments about the case, Nina observed that this dark and quiet home stood in stark contrast to Teresa's bright and noisy house.

As they spoke, Nina learned that Ana and Luis were both born in San Juan, Puerto Rico, and had moved to the Bronx in New York as children, which explained their slight Nuyorican accents. They met in high school and married soon after graduating. When Ana was expecting their first child, they moved out west to start their family in a roomier, less-populated city. Construction was booming in Phoenix, and Luis had learned the trade quickly, eventually getting his contractor's license and starting his own business. He had planned to pass on the growing enterprise to his two sons but, tragically, both had died in their early twenties.

Nina crossed the room to look at a pair of portraits in matching black frames hung on the wall above the fireplace. She recognized Victor from the news articles and other photos she had seen.

Ana rose to follow her, drawing near as she studied the one beside it.

"That's Samuel," Ana said, her soft accent lending a lyrical quality to her words. "He was a year older than Victor. They were always close."

Nina took in the portrait of a handsome young man in a military uniform. On the wall next to the portrait, a shadow box contained a folded US flag secured in a triangular section at the bottom. A cluster of colorful ribbons, including a Purple Heart, filled the black velvet background at the top of the display. In the center of the arrangement, a five-pointed gold star hung below an eagle affixed to a blue ribbon with thirteen white stars in the middle.

"The president presented that to us when Luis and I went to the White House," Ana said as her husband joined them. "We received Sam's Medal of Honor and his Purple Heart. He was killed in the Battle of Mogadishu."

Luis stood by her other side. "He was a soldier in the First Special Forces Operational Detachment," he said, then added, "Delta Force."

Samuel Vega had been in the US Army's elite Special Forces. If he were alive, she would have called him Uncle Sam. She would have also called him a hero.

"Victor died in 1992, and Sam was killed in action in 1993," Ana said, her voice strained with emotion. "Now we have no children, no grandchildren." She twisted her hands in her lap. "The rest of our family is back east. We are all alone here."

The Vegas had never recovered from their grief. Nina wanted desperately to hug them, to offer them solace.

There were photographs of both sons all over the living room, documenting their infancy through young adulthood. Nina noticed there were no pictures of Victor's wedding or of Maria. It wasn't until she examined the pictures propped on the mantel above the fireplace that she saw it. A small photograph of Victor at the hospital, holding his newborn daughter.

She picked it up, careful to hide her trembling fingers, aware that it was probably the last picture of her father. "When was this taken?"

Luis answered Nina's question. "About an hour after our granddaughter was born. It was the first time any of us had a chance to see her."

Ana sniffled. "She was so precious. We all adored our little *princesa*." She leaned on her husband's shoulder. "Is that . . . um . . . is that a picture of our granddaughter or the other baby?"

Nina placed the photograph back on the mantel. "There's no way to be sure at this point." She didn't add that there was an excellent chance no one in the family had ever actually seen Maria's child.

Until Nina had arrived in Phoenix.

"Every part of this horrible situation keeps getting worse," Luis said.

But Ana and Luis still didn't know the worst of it. They would soon find out that their son and his family had not only been the victims of a murderer but of a serial killer. When the media inevitably got hold of that piece of the story, the whole nightmare would be revisited in excruciating detail. Scabs would be ripped off, and old wounds would bleed freely again.

A heartbeat passed, and Victor's father asked the question she had dreaded most.

"What happened to our granddaughter?" he asked. "What happened to little Victoria?"

"Victoria?" Nina said.

Luis nodded. "They named her Victoria Maria Vega." His eyes softened. "Victoria after my son and Maria after her mother."

Nina stilled as she heard the name that would have been hers. Not the name assigned to her by social workers, but a name given to her by loving parents. A name she would have carried with her through life with pride. She had seen it on digital copies of the birth and death certificates in Detective O'Malley's files, but it had made no impression on her at the time. Now she found she could not speak.

"Mr. Vega, we don't know," Perez said. "We are doing everything in our power to find her."

"Is she alive?" Ana asked, eyes brimming.

Nina turned away, swallowing the lump that had suddenly formed in her throat. She wanted nothing more than to tell these people—her people—that their long-lost granddaughter had not only survived but stood before them.

She wanted to comfort them, not as a professional but as family. It made no difference what she wanted. She had a job, and she would push down her feelings and do that job. The best thing she could do to honor her parents and their relatives was to put the man who destroyed their lives behind bars. To prevent him from visiting this kind of pain on any more families.

"All these years, we have been so angry at Maria's family," Luis said. "We blamed them for what she did. But now it turns out she did nothing. She was innocent."

Nina found her voice. "I know this must be difficult," she said, wishing she could tell them so much more.

"It's far worse than difficult, Agent Guerrera," Ana said. "I'm reliving the worst day of my life."

Luis wrapped his arm around his wife's shoulders. "But this time, we have new hope." He gave her a gentle squeeze. "We have a granddaughter out there somewhere."

Nina caught the pained look Perez gave her and knew they were thinking something completely different. Perez was under the impression that their granddaughter had died twenty-eight years ago somewhere in Maryland, but Nina knew better.

"Can you find her?" Ana asked.

"We will try," Perez said. "It may take time."

She knew she shouldn't ask the question that came unbidden into her mind, but she could not stop herself. "If you could speak to her now," Nina said, "what would you say?"

Perez's brows furrowed as he regarded her thoughtfully. Her inquiry was not pertinent to the investigation. It made no sense.

"We would tell her how much we love her," Luis said without hesitation. "How much her father loved her. He counted the days until she was born. He and Maria had saved up their money and moved into a house with a nice yard so they could start a family. He was such a proud papa. She was such a pretty baby. We all adored her."

For her entire life, Nina had fantasized about hearing words like those. She had longed to hear someone call her *mi'ja*, my daughter. The other children had tormented her about being a throwaway. Unloved, unwanted, an outcast tossed in a dumpster like so much trash. Tears stung the backs of her eyes. She blinked them away. It had been stupid to ask such a question, and now she was paying the price.

"Excuse me." She cleared her throat. "I need to get something from the car." She spun on her heel, left the house, and walked to the black SUV parked in the driveway. She placed a shaking hand against the fender and tilted her head back, briefly closing her eyes as she drew in gulps of air. The house had seemed claustrophobic, as if the weight of loss and grief had slowly constricted the space inside over the years.

A deep male voice sounded from behind her. "You and I need to talk."

She whirled to see Perez gazing down at her.

"I finished the interview and said goodbye for both of us," he said.

"I needed some fresh air," she choked out. "It's stifling in there."

His dark eyes narrowed. "What just happened, Guerrera?"

"We don't have time for this," she said, redirecting him toward the investigation. "Cahill should be at the field office by the time we get back there."

Perez didn't budge. "I've been a cop for long enough to know when someone's holding out on me. And you have that all over you." He crossed his arms. "What aren't you telling me?"

"I've told you everything I can," she said, hedging. "Everything you need to know."

Nina winced at the phrase every cop hated to hear from a Fed. She'd heard those words herself in the past and resented the hell out of them.

"Typical," Perez said, disdain sharpening the word. "We'll play it your way for now." He leaned in close to her. "But this isn't over."

Chapter 37

Nina took the manila folder Wade handed her. They stood together in the hallway of the Phoenix field office, quietly working out the final details of their strategy for interviewing Robert Cahill.

Buxton had designated her to conduct the interview with Wade while Perez briefed the others on what he and Nina had learned from the two families.

Wade tipped his head toward the closed door of the interview room where Cahill waited inside. "He was none too happy to hear from me. He saw a news report about Thomas Kirk's murder, and he's feeling guilty about talking to us before."

Nina kept her voice low. "Why don't I take the lead? I'll get him to let his guard down."

"Ironic," Wade said, a slight smile playing at the corners of his mouth, "because between the two of us, you're way more dangerous."

"Only when I have to be." She tucked the folder under her arm and opened the door to find Cahill seated at an oblong table, clutching a can of soda as if he thought it might try to escape.

"Thank you for coming in, Mr. Cahill," she began, extending her hand in greeting.

Cahill lurched to his feet and awkwardly shook both of their hands.

Nina laid the manila file on the table and pretended to smooth her slacks as she sat across from him, discreetly wiping his transferred sweat from her palms.

"I feel like if I didn't come in, you guys would track me down anyway," he said, a petulant expression on his ruddy face.

This was absolutely true, but she saw no need to belabor the point. "We won't take up much of your time." Offering what she hoped was a disarming smile, she opened the folder and lifted out a slim stack of photographs, spreading them on the table facing Cahill.

"Do you recognize anyone?"

"The last time I talked to you people, someone got killed," Cahill said, eyes resolutely on her face rather than the array of pictures. "I'm afraid if I say anything else, more bad stuff's going to happen."

"You liked Tommy, right?" After waiting for his curt nod, Nina continued, "Then your cooperation will not only help us identify the person who killed him but will make sure no one else gets harmed."

His shoulders slumped. "Oh, all right." He studied the picture on the far left. A thin smile began to form. "This is Tommy Kirk, the way I remember him years ago." The smile faded. "I can't believe he's dead."

"Who are those two boys standing on either side of him?" Nina prompted.

Cahill scrunched his eyes closed, pulling data from his memory bank. After a long pause, his eyes flew open. "Tye Brennan and Jared Hart." He looked impressed with his own mental prowess.

Wade was thumb-typing on his cell, no doubt forwarding the names to Breck in the command center down the hall.

"How about this picture?" Nina asked.

Cahill laid the first one down, directing his gaze to where Nina pointed. "Ah, I remember him. That's Dante Coleman. We're not supposed to have favorites, but he was one of mine." A look of wistful curiosity softened his features. "I wonder whatever happened to Dante."

Nina tapped the next one, keeping the interview from lapsing into maudlin reminiscence. "And this one?"

"He had a weird name," Cahill said. "Something old . . . really old." He drummed his fingers on the table. "Let me think."

"We can come back to him," Nina said. "What about this last one?"

Cahill leaned toward the photo at the end of the row. "Chuck and Dan. The other kids used to call them Chip and Dale—when they weren't around to hear it, mind you." The corner of his mouth quirked up. "You wouldn't compare them to chipmunks unless you were looking for a beatdown."

Nina circled back to the one he couldn't recall. "Can you remember who this one was? You said his name was something really old."

Cahill bent, fixing his gaze on the image again. "Yeah, but not just old, the name was ancient. It made me think of a gladiator." He snapped his fingers. "Spartacus. Spartacus Spinx." He looked at her. "Is that a weird name or what?"

He had put names to all of them. Impressive. Now that his recollection had been primed and his mind was firmly in the past, it was time to ask the most important question of all.

She gestured toward the collection of pictures. "Is this everyone in Tommy Kirk's group of friends?" Cahill didn't respond, apparently lost in thought, so she gently prodded him. "Is there anyone who used to hang with Tommy who's *not* in these photographs? Maybe someone he helped get a job after leaving juvie?"

Cahill started to shake his head, then tensed. "There was one other boy in the group," he said. "Danny Creed."

Out of the corner of her eye, Nina saw Wade texting the name to Breck. This could be the name of the person in the missing photograph. She turned her attention back to Cahill. "What do you recall about him?"

"I figured I'd be having a conversation about Danny someday," he said. "Just didn't think it would be with the FBI."

"You thought Danny would get into trouble after he got out?"

"Hell yes." He froze, apparently unsure if he'd said too much. After giving it some consideration, he straightened. "I'm probably not supposed to talk about this stuff, but I'm retired now, so I'll tell you this." He folded his arms across his chest. "I worked in that facility twenty years. I saw my share of hardened youth, but I was never afraid of any of the kids . . . until Danny."

Interesting . . . and unexpected. She was anxious to hear what crime Creed had committed to land himself in a juvenile detention facility, but opted to let the story unfold organically in the order Cahill wanted to tell it.

"How did he frighten you?" Nina asked.

Cahill uncrossed his arms to tap his left temple with his index finger. "That boy wasn't right in the head. He fooled most of the staff, the director too. He even had me convinced . . . until one day when he let me see who he really was." Cahill's eyes grew distant as he sank deeper into the past. "He did it on purpose too. I think he knew I was scared, and he liked it."

Nina found herself literally and figuratively on the edge of her seat as she leaned toward him. "What happened?"

"I'll never forget it," Cahill said. "The staff psychiatrist and I called him into the office to tell him his parents were dead."

Nina exchanged a glance with Wade. This was the kind of trigger he had taught her to look for in someone's youth. "How did Danny react?"

"No tears, no sorrow, no emotion at all except anger. He was especially mad at his mother, who he kept calling 'the bitch.'" Cahill's shoulders twitched with an involuntary shudder. "I looked into his eyes, and they were cold and flat. Snake eyes. Not a spark of humanity in them, and here I was feeling sorry for him that he had just become an orphan. Hell, we also had to tell him his other remaining relatives didn't want any more to do with him either."

With Creed's rage toward his mother, Nina was certain they had found a good candidate for the unsub. Now she had to draw out more information, keeping the emphasis on Cahill and his perceptions of Creed since that seemed to stimulate his memory best.

"And how did he respond to that?" she asked him.

"More anger," Cahill said. "Again, purely directed at his mother. Said it was all her fault. She had turned everyone against him." Cahill's ruddy skin paled. "And then he said it."

"Said what?" Nina spoke as little as possible, keeping the flow of information coming.

"Before he arrived at our facility, I got a copy of the transcripts from his trial in juvenile court," Cahill began. "Wanted to read through it to see what I was dealing with because he'd been assigned to me. All through the trial, he never admitted what he did to his sister. At first, I thought it was on the advice of his court-appointed attorney, but he never copped to it from the very beginning. Kept saying it was some sort of an accident, but people wouldn't believe him. Claimed he was tried for a crime he didn't commit."

Nina held her excitement in check with effort. Now was the proper time to ask the critical question. "What crime was Danny Creed convicted of?"

Cahill swallowed audibly. "He killed his baby sister the day after she was born."

Chapter 38

Nina schooled her features, hiding the impact of Cahill's words, which had caused a seismic shift in the investigation.

"Danny Creed was convicted of murdering his baby sister?" She wanted to be sure she hadn't misunderstood.

Cahill nodded. "But he claimed she died by accident." He shrugged. "Hell, he was so convincing I began to wonder myself. When he came to the detention center, he maintained his innocence to everyone." He paused a beat. "That is, until the day we told him his mother shot his father before turning the gun on herself. Only Dr. Novak and I were in the room, and we didn't have an internal video system in the psychiatrist's office. Danny must have been shocked or something, because he finally admitted what he'd done. Told us he'd killed his sister in cold blood." Cahill shuddered again. "I'm telling you, the hairs on the back of my neck stood up when he broke into a big grin as he described smothering that little baby."

Nina kept the horror from her expression. "What did you do?"

"What could we do?" Cahill said. "Danny went right back to his usual self the next day, like he'd never said a thing. Even when Dr. Novak brought it up, Danny insisted we both misunderstood him. Denied he ever confessed to anything."

"He gaslighted you and the doctor," Wade said, speaking for the first time since the interview began.

Cahill nodded vigorously. "That's what he used to do all the time. Started a lot of fights with the other kids that way. Got to the point where we felt like we had to record everything he said. You could never pin him down on anything. Never took responsibility, never helped anyone unless it was to his advantage, never showed an ounce of compassion to another living soul."

Nina caught Wade's meaningful look as he silently communicated that this tallied exactly with his assessment of the unsub's character back when they had first been assigned to investigate. She inclined her head in tacit respect. His profile had been spot on.

"Once, a kid came in who had both legs amputated after a car crash," Cahill continued. "The boy had become addicted to painkillers, which led to a series of thefts to support his habit when his doctors tried to wean him off the opioids. After he shot someone in a botched armed robbery, the court sent him to us for rehabilitation while he got treatment for his addiction. You'd think Danny might have given that boy a break." Cahill let out a disgusted snort. "I caught Danny sitting on top of the disabled kid, pinning his arms to his sides while he poured water over a washcloth spread across the boy's face. I pulled Danny off and asked him what the hell he was doing. You know what he said?"

When they both shook their heads, Cahill leaned forward. "Danny wanted to try waterboarding someone. Called it an experiment." His lip curled. "I didn't believe him for a second. He wasn't just doing some random experiment. He tortured that other boy because he was jealous of all the attention the new kid got."

"What did you do?" Nina asked.

"I went to Dr. Novak with it. By that point, he was the only one who would believe me. Danny's victims were too scared to admit what he did to them, and he was careful to do things in places like the bathrooms, where there were no cameras. Dr. Novak told me Danny had antisocial personality disorder and there was no cure. We just had to try to keep all the other kids safe."

"Dr. Novak was right," Wade said. "There's no cure, but there is treatment. Some people with ASPD have learned to get by without causing overt harm to others, but they have to be motivated to change. Unfortunately, many don't understand why they should bother to put in the effort. People with ASPD only make up about one to three percent of the overall population, but they constitute anywhere from forty to seventy percent of those in prison."

"Maybe some antisocial people do okay," Cahill said. "But not Danny. Dr. Novak told me something I'll never forget. He said you can't train a snake, but you can cultivate certain responses using behavioral conditioning. That's how I thought of Danny from then on. We had no way to fix his brain, but we could try to cultivate better conduct."

Nina took a moment to absorb that Danny Creed's treating psychiatrist had compared him to a snake.

"I don't know what you're investigating besides Tommy Kirk's death," Cahill said. "But the fact that I'm sitting here means Danny must have done even more than that. Tell me what else I can do to help."

"Actually, you're doing it now," Wade said. "We appreciate the insight you've been able to provide into his character during his developmental years."

"To be honest, I stayed the hell away from Danny as much as possible after that day. Every so often, he'd give me that same evil smile and a wink, like we shared a secret. He wanted to see me flinch, and sometimes I did. He seemed to enjoy scaring the other kids, scaring me." Cahill grew distant again. "Still creeps me out when I think about it."

"How did a boy like Tommy Kirk end up being friends with Danny Creed?" Nina wanted to know.

"Simple," Cahill said. "Danny viewed everyone as either a victim to bully or a useful fool to manipulate. Tommy was a few years older, so

Danny never targeted him for abuse. Instead, he conned him. Sucked him in like he did most everyone else. I also think Tommy took Danny under his wing because he thought maybe he did get railroaded by the system." When Nina didn't interrupt, he elaborated. "Danny could be very charming when he wanted to."

"Anything else you can tell us about him?" Nina asked.

"If he's up to something, be careful," Cahill said. "Danny's smart and he's slick as snail snot."

"I'll keep that in mind, Mr. Cahill," Nina said. "Thank you for coming. You've been very helpful."

"What's he done?" Cahill looked as if he really didn't want to hear the answer.

Nina didn't take the bait. "Let's just call him a person of interest and leave it at that."

Looking as if that confirmed his worst suspicions, Cahill got up to leave. Nina and Wade escorted him out before making their way into the command center.

As soon as she pushed the door open, Nina saw Buxton on the phone and Perez going through his notes before her gaze landed on Breck, who sat in front of her computer terminal, face flushed, hair mussed as if she'd dragged her hand through it a hundred times. Kent was leaning over her, peering at the screen as she typed.

"I did a quick Google search on Creed while you two were interviewing Cahill," Breck said to her.

Kent straightened. "There were plenty of hits."

Nina was impatient for verification. "And?"

"This is an archived news article from the *Arizona Daily Star*." Breck read from the screen, "A Tucson police spokesperson characterized the death of Darlene Creed, infant daughter of Patricia and Stanley Creed, as a homicide. The couple's twelve-year-old son, Daniel, was taken into custody this morning. Sources at the Office of the Prosecutor indicated they cannot try the boy as an adult because he is younger than fourteen."

Nina felt her jaw slacken. She hadn't asked Cahill how old Creed was when he first came to the facility.

"What was the date of that story?" Nina said.

"March first, 1984," Breck said. "It said the murder had occurred the previous day."

Nina did the math in her head. "Ah, 1984 was a leap year, so—"

"He committed the murder on a leap day." Wade's gray eyes darkened. "I believe we've found our point of inception." He stroked his jaw. "Now we look for the precipitating stressor."

"Twelve years old." Breck shook her head. "Damn."

"There have been many instances of children even younger than that committing premeditated murder," Kent said, adding his assessment to the discussion. "It's rare, but definitely not unheard of."

"Wait a minute." Nina was still working out the timeline. "What was the exact date of the homicide-suicide of Daniel Creed's parents?"

After a few staccato taps on her keyboard, Breck had the answer. "February twenty-ninth, 1988."

Another leap day. Another puzzle piece fell into place.

"The next leap year was 1992," Nina said. "The year of the Llorona case. Creed would have been twenty years old."

"And all of those murders were committed not just during leap years but on a leap day," Kent said. "They were exactly four years apart."

"And every single one after that leading up to the present," Buxton said. He had disconnected from his phone call to join the discussion. Perez, too, had stopped what he was doing to listen.

"The Llorona case was a shooting," Nina said. "Would Creed have been able to legally purchase a gun after he turned eighteen if he'd been convicted of murder?"

"The case would be part of his juvenile record," Buxton said thoughtfully. "Perhaps it was sealed, but I'm no expert on Arizona law."

All eyes turned to Perez.

"In Arizona, a juvenile convicted of murder can't apply to have his gun possession and ownership rights restored until he's thirty years old," Perez said. "Creed obtained the weapon illegally."

"Not surprising," Wade said. "Someone with his personality would skirt the law without breaking a sweat."

"Where is Creed now?" Nina asked. "Does he have an adult criminal record?"

Breck clicked open another tab, then scrolled down the screen. Her russet brows drew together, and she clicked open another tab. Then another.

"What's wrong?" Nina asked.

"I'm hitting a dead end. There's no record of him after he left the juvenile detention facility when he turned eighteen." She glanced up at them. "Daniel Creed is a ghost."

Chapter 39

Nina put her hands on her hips. "There has to be a way to find Creed. What happened to him after he got out of juvie? He had to support himself somehow. His relatives sure weren't going to help him."

"Wait," Wade said. "Cahill told us Tommy Kirk got a job at Jexton Security for his band of friends—and Creed was one of them. We could start there."

Buxton perked up. "I've seen some commercials for Jexton Security. They have offices nationwide."

Perez walked around the table, moving closer to the group. "I've seen their Phoenix branch downtown. It's a newer building overlooking one of the canals."

"This is their website," Breck said after a quick internet search. "They install alarm systems. They claim to have over two hundred thousand corporate and residential clients coast to coast."

"There." Nina pointed at Breck's computer. "Look at that emblem on the bottom of the screen."

Wade stepped closer and squinted. "Jexton is a wholly owned subsidiary of Rubric Realty, Incorporated."

Nina smiled. "Boom."

"Do the two companies share clients?" Buxton asked.

They all waited for an interminable two minutes while Breck clicked open case files from the crime scenes going back twenty-eight years.

"I was able to confirm that the residences had an alarm system from Jexton in four of the eight cases," Breck said. "Three more didn't mention the name of the company, but the house was alarmed. The only home we don't know about is the first case." She hesitated, avoiding eye contact with Nina. "The Llorona case."

"Perez can look into that," Nina said, too caught up in the gathering momentum to be put off by the case's nickname. "Maybe the original detective didn't make a note of it or didn't ask." Detective O'Malley had been more than a little distracted during his investigation.

Perez pulled out his phone. "I have O'Malley's cell number. I'll send him a text."

"And I'll add that to my list of things to ask the field agents from the other cities," Kent said.

Nina wanted a work-around. Something that would give them a hot lead to follow. "Can we contact Jexton Security's Human Resources department and ask them to confirm whether Creed is a current or past employee?"

"HR for a big company like that may not cooperate," Buxton said. "At the very least, they'll want to know why we're asking."

"This will be a simple request," Nina said. "We don't have to spend time getting a subpoena. If they don't want to cooperate, they don't have to, but we won't say why we're asking."

"What if he's working there now and HR notifies him we asked about him?" Kent said.

"If Breck can't find any sign of him, there's an excellent chance he's not there anymore," Nina said. "Hell, someone with his kind of mental health issues may have gotten worse over the years. He could have left the job and is now living off the grid, only coming out every four years."

Kent tilted his head in apparent confusion. "If you don't think he works there anymore, why would we ask them about him?"

"Because Jexton is our only starting point right now," she said. "If they can confirm his employment when he was eighteen, we could subpoena their records and get his address, date of birth, and social security number." She jerked her chin at Breck. "With that kind of information, Creed would be easy to track."

Buxton turned to Breck, who was still hunched over her keyboard. "Have you found anything yet?"

"I'm running him with just his general age and legal name, but Guerrera's right. His DOB and social would be nice. I'm trying to pull that from the records, but since everything was in the juvenile court system, there's an extra barrier to get through."

"I've got another idea," Nina said. "We call the main number and ask for Creed. Don't go through HR with an official request from the FBI—instead, just ask like any ordinary person who's trying to get in touch with someone at the company. We're not violating anyone's rights, and we don't need any kind of warrant to ask to talk to someone."

"And if he's there and they put us through to him?" Buxton asked.

"We disconnect the call and strategize how we're going to interview him." Nina shrugged. "At least we'll know where he is."

Wade stroked his jaw. "We won't be acting under color of authority if we don't do any more than ask for him."

After a long pause, Buxton turned to Nina. "Go ahead."

She pulled out her phone and googled the company, then their Phoenix branch. She tapped the screen to connect the call, then touched an icon to put it on speaker so everyone could listen in.

On the fifth ring, the voice of a twentysomething female answered. "Jexton Security." The words came out on a bored sigh.

Nina kept her voice brisk and light. "Could you put me through to Daniel Creed, please?"

"Who?"

"Daniel Creed. I believe he works out of the Phoenix branch."

"Hold on a sec." Loud gum-chewing followed the words. After a long pause, the voice came back. "We don't have anyone by that name here."

Nina tried a different approach. "Can you see if he works out of another branch, maybe in Flagstaff or Tucson, or perhaps in another state?"

"I dunno."

"You don't know if he works out of another branch or you don't know if there's a way to check?"

"Both." More gum smacking. "Look, this is only my third day."

"Could you find out if there is a way to check your system?"

"How?"

Nina stifled an eye roll. "Maybe . . . ask someone who's worked there awhile?"

"Hold on." The receptionist let out another world-weary sigh before putting them on hold.

They waited for a full minute. Breck resumed her computer search, Perez got a bottle of water from the small fridge in the corner, and Wade conferred with Kent and Buxton. Nina almost gave up and disconnected when a resonant male voice came on the line.

"This is Clay Forge. Can I help you?"

Nina went back into polite, professional mode. "I was trying to get in touch with one of your employees, but I'm not sure what branch he works out of. Is there a way to find out?"

"Certainly," Forge said. "I have access to the entire employee database. Who are you trying to reach?"

"Daniel Creed."

After some keyboard-clacking in the background, he came back with a response. "Our records show Jexton Security has never employed anyone by that name."

"Really? I just met him last night. Said he was some kind of big shot in your sales department." She adopted the disappointed tone of a woman led on yet again by a man with less-than-honorable motives. "Thought the guy sounded too good to be true."

Forge's response was sympathetic. "It's hard to know who to trust, Miss . . ."

She did not fill in the blank when he trailed off. "Thank you for your time, Mr. Forge. You've been most helpful."

She disconnected and looked at the team. "If Creed never worked for Jexton, and Breck can't find any trace of him elsewhere, what has he been doing since he turned eighteen?"

"Besides killing people, you mean?" Breck said.

Wade looked thoughtful. "Maybe we should consider the possibility that Creed isn't the unsub." When five pairs of eyes sent him questioning looks, he lifted a defensive hand. "Okay, okay . . . it has to be Creed. No one else would fit the profile so perfectly."

"Why can't we find him?" Buxton said. "Let's consider the options. How does someone disappear?"

"He's not dead," Nina said. "He's been actively preying on families for decades. Maybe he keeps relocating."

Breck's long, red spiral curls swayed as she shook her head. "Even if he moved away, I'd find a trace of him somewhere."

Nina reflected on her own history. She'd legally changed her name as soon as she was able, drawing a bright line between her past and the new course she intended for herself. The day she walked out of the courtroom as Nina Guerrera had been a fresh start for her. Perhaps Creed had done the same thing.

She addressed the group. "Think about what he was going through when he got out of juvie. His immediate family was dead. His extended relatives wanted nothing to do with him. He was a pariah in the community. He would want a reboot."

"You're saying he assumed another identity?" Kent asked.

They all knew her history. "It's what I did."

Buxton frowned. "If we had his exact date of birth and social security number, Breck could find evidence of a legal name change."

Breck didn't appear daunted. "Let me check the circuit court records in Tucson for the year he turned eighteen to see if there were any petitions for a legal name change. It won't help if he filed in a different jurisdiction, but we might get lucky."

Buxton glanced down at his notes. "While Agent Breck is checking on that, let's consider our next steps."

"Detective O'Malley just answered my text," Perez said, putting his phone away. "He says the Vega house had a residential alarm—apparently the previous owner had been burglarized twice. According to O'Malley, Maria and Victor never activated it when they bought the place. He doesn't know whether the company was Jexton or not."

"We keep coming back to the victim families moving houses and having security systems," Kent said. "There must be something to it."

"Which is why I was so sure Creed worked for Jexton," Nina said. "Too many connections to be a coincidence."

They fell silent, each of them deep in contemplation.

A few minutes later, Breck pumped her fist. "Jackpot." Excitement lit her features. "I've got a petition to the Pima County court for a legal name change for Daniel Creed."

The rest of the team gathered around her.

"The record will contain his DOB and social too," Breck said. "I'll be able to track him." She clicked on a scanned document. "Holy shit."

Nina looked at Breck's flashing cursor. A surge of adrenaline kicked in. She glanced over her shoulder at Wade, who hovered directly behind her. "His birthday"—she pointed at the computer—"is February twenty-ninth."

"Bingo," Wade said.

They were making real progress. "What's Creed's name now?" Nina asked.

Breck scrolled down the screen, then froze, sucking in a breath.

"What?" Nina and Wade said at the same time.

Breck's eyes drifted up to focus on Nina. "Clay Forge," she breathed.

Chapter 40

Clay Forge hung up the phone on his desk. Time to execute his emergency plan. He opened his desk drawer and pawed through its contents in a rushed search for his standby fake ID. A letter opener jabbed his finger.

Cursing, he withdrew his hand and watched a fat red droplet blossom. He sucked his fingertip, the scent and taste of blood bringing back a long-buried memory. It was his sixteenth birthday, and the little shithead squirming beneath him on the wet tile floor needed a lesson.

In his mind's eye, he could see the boy pinned under him as he pulled back his fist to deliver another bare-knuckled blow. The little wuss's screams brought Mr. Cahill to the boys' bathroom, the door banging against the wall as he burst inside.

"What the hell are you doing?" Mr. Cahill's face was as pink as a pig's butt.

The stupid kid was bawling his fool head off.

"I was defending myself," he said, delivering the story he'd prepared in advance. "He attacked me."

Mr. Cahill looked at the other kid. "Is that true?"

The boy stopped his crying but refused to answer.

He swiveled his head away from Mr. Cahill to stare directly into the boy's terrified eyes, barely moving his lips as he silently mouthed the word *yes*.

"Well?" Mr. Cahill said.

"Uh . . . yes," the little shithead finally said.

Mr. Cahill separated them and sent the other kid to the medical unit. Then those weird pale eyes of his narrowed. "Come with me."

He knew Mr. Cahill wasn't inviting him to a surprise birthday party. No one ever remembered his birthday around here anyway. Fine with him. Had Mr. Cahill bought his claim of self-defense? What would happen if he didn't? Probably no television privileges for a week. If he'd broken the little weasel's nose, maybe a month.

Mr. Cahill escorted him into the office and closed the door.

When he turned, he saw Dr. Novak, the facility's resident shrink, already seated in the corner. If nutty Novak was there, that meant Cahill must have been looking for him when he heard the ruckus in the bathroom. Something was up.

He slouched into a chair, crossed his arms, and gave both men his best "fuck you" glare.

Cahill sighed and dragged a hand through his hair. "I should put you in segregation again, but under the circumstances, I'm going to overlook what just happened."

He straightened. "What circumstances?"

Novak took over. "There's no easy way to say this, so I'm going to give it to you straight."

"Well?" He hated the hesitation. Any hesitation was a sign of indecision. Of weakness.

"Your mother and father both died this morning," Novak said quietly.

The statement took a moment to penetrate. "Was there a car crash or something?"

"Word is going to get out," Novak said. "I'm sure you'll hear about it."

More waffling. He clenched his teeth. "Hear what?"

Novak finally met his gaze. "I'm afraid your mother killed your father before taking her own life."

He sat, momentarily stunned, processing the information. Novak moved toward him, extending a hand as if to grasp his shoulder.

"Don't fucking touch me."

Novak's hand shot back as if he had been burned.

He focused on the shrink, who had obviously been chosen to give him whatever information he was going to get. "How did the bitch do it?"

"Your mother," Novak corrected.

"The. Bitch." He enunciated each word, making his point clear.

Novak continued as if he hadn't heard. "Your mother used a revolver your father had apparently purchased a long time ago."

He remembered the gun. His father had kept it in the nightstand.

He reached for an explanation. "Did she shoot him by accident and then off herself out of guilt?"

"Uh, no." Novak looked away again. "She left a note explaining why she did it."

And then he knew why. "I can guess what the note said."

Novak seemed surprised. "Can you?"

"Today is February twenty-ninth," he said. "That's what finally pushed the bitch over the edge."

"I don't understand," Novak said.

"Then you're either a piss-poor headshrinker or you don't bother to read anyone's files," he said. "February twenty-ninth is the day my sister died exactly four years ago."

The two men exchanged meaningful looks.

Novak cleared his throat. "I can see how that would upset your mother, she—"

"The bitch's note would have blamed me for all of this. Blamed me for what *she* did."

"Well, you do bear some responsibility," Novak said, adopting a soothing tone. "You need to accept responsibility for your actions. It's part of the process of—"

"My actions?" He shot to his feet. "My actions were an accident."

"That's not what the court ruled," Novak said, standing to face him.

"Which is why I'm here. No one believes me."

Cahill interrupted, his face going from pink to red as he got to his feet. "You held the pillow down on an innocent baby for more than ten minutes. That's no accident."

He wouldn't put up with their judgmental bullshit. "I was twelve years old!"

"Old enough to know what you were doing," Cahill shot back. "Like just now when you were in the bathroom, beating the crap out of that boy. You were making an example out of him."

He almost smiled. At least someone had gotten the message.

"This is the whole problem," Novak said. "You have never taken responsibility for what you did. If you would simply own up to it, then—"

"Then what? You all would let me walk out of here?" He threw up his hands. "You want a confession? Fine. I killed my baby sister the day after she was born."

The words—so long held in check—spilled from him in a heated rush. "The first chance I had ten minutes alone with her, I held that little pillow down until she stopped squirming. Then I waited a few more minutes just to be sure she was good and fucking dead." He got close enough to smell the stale coffee on Novak's breath. "There. That make you happy?"

"No." The blood drained from Novak's face. "No, it does not."

Stinging from his fingertip brought Forge back to the present. He wiped the letter opener clean before dropping it back into the desk drawer. That had been the first and only time he had ever copped to anything. A mistake he would never make again.

His words to Novak and Cahill that day had served a purpose, however. From then on, they steered clear of him. All the other kids at the center were afraid of him too. They were a herd of sheep, huddling in a flock, seeking protection against the wolf among them.

Thanks to the bitch's suicide note, even his so-called extended family feared him. All his relatives had made it clear he'd better not come around when he was released two years later.

The rest of the staff hadn't heard what he'd told Cahill and Novak, and he used his new status as an orphan to his advantage, playing on their sympathies. Sometimes he would even squeeze out a tear when he wanted extra privileges. That facility had been his training ground, and he had learned everything he needed to know.

That was the day he had begun to make plans for after his release. Plans that he now understood had veered off course by a twist of fate.

His free hand closed on the wallet with the fake ID. He pulled it out of the drawer and got to his feet, stuffing it into his back pocket. The bloodhounds had caught his scent. They were scratching at his door, but he was still one step ahead of them.

He picked up the desk phone and punched the button connecting him to the brainless receptionist in the lobby. "Emma," he said to her after she finally picked up, "hold my calls. I'll be going out of town for the next week or two."

"Will Ms. Garner be handling your—"

"Yes, refer everyone to her in my absence."

He grabbed a tissue to stanch the still-flowing trickle of blood, then got out the bottle and rag from his kit and carefully wiped down every surface. Satisfied, he grabbed his briefcase and headed out the office door, probably for the last time.

He had no idea how the Feds had zeroed in on him, but he was glad he'd moved into the hotel under another name several days ago. He'd have to add more layers to his disguise. He still had advantages they had no idea about, and he would use them all.

Phase two: throw the FBI off their game.

Chapter 41

Dread stole over Nina. "Did you say Daniel Creed changed his name to Clay Forge?"

Breck, apparently stunned into silence, simply nodded.

Nina glanced at the others in the room as the enormity of her blunder sank in. What had she just done?

Buxton spoke up before she could muster an apology. "You made the call, Agent Guerrera, but it was my decision. Any blame rests with me."

"I'm the one who pushed it, sir."

"We all wanted to advance the investigation," Kent said. "Look, if the military has taught me anything, it's not to waste time figuring out how the war started when you're in the middle of a battle. You fight your way out and analyze later."

"He's right," Wade said. "The reality is that Forge knows somebody called his place of business asking for Daniel Creed, his original name. At this point, it's safe to assume he murdered Thomas Kirk, which means he knows we figured out the connection between them."

"Based on the phone call, he probably believes we still haven't uncovered his current identity," Kent said. "But he has to suspect we'll figure out his name change soon."

"Then he knows he's on borrowed time," Nina said. "What's his reaction going to be?"

"Someone with his personality would want to be in control, and he's sensing the net closing around him," Wade said. "Killing Kirk shows he's capable of breaking his pattern when he feels threatened. This will increase that feeling exponentially."

"And we just showed our hand," Kent said. "He's probably in the wind. I would be."

"Should I ask for a patrol unit to swing by his office?" Perez asked Buxton. "I could have a uniform there in less than five minutes."

"No." Buxton responded without hesitation. "We don't have enough legal probable cause to detain him at this point. We don't have a warrant yet either. A premature arrest—or even police contact—will compromise the entire investigation."

"I've hauled suspects in for questioning on a lot less," Perez said.

Buxton's tone was firm. "Mr. Forge may be responsible for murders in Phoenix, but many other deaths have occurred in cities all over the country. We need to take every precaution to make an airtight case that will withstand scrutiny in any jurisdiction."

Perez looked like he might argue the point, then thought better of it. "Let me know if you change your mind. The window of opportunity to nab this guy is closing fast—if it's not already shut."

"I found his home address in Mesa," Breck called out from her seat in front of the computer. "It's in the suburbs outside of Phoenix. I'm pulling up his driver's license photo now."

"I vote we drive to Mesa and pay him a visit right now," Nina said. "If he's on the move, I don't want to give him more time to run while we write affidavits and hunt down a federal judge."

"I'm with Guerrera," Kent said. "If he's home, we can ask for a chat. If he's not home or he won't talk, we may find out something from his neighbors."

"I'd hate to think he's left town before we even have a chance to make contact," Wade said. "This guy has managed to slip between every crack in the system for almost three decades."

Buxton held up a hand. "This will take planning and preparation," he said. "We can't just go barreling out the door after this guy."

"We need to get eyes on him ASAP," Nina said. "Why not ask the Phoenix field office HRT to watch his house until we get the warrants?"

Centrally headquartered at the FBI Academy in Quantico, the Hostage Rescue Team had units at every field office in the country. Despite their name, they could be deployed for a variety of reasons, including surveillance.

"I like it," Kent said. "Forge is probably on his way home now, ready to pack up and run. Even if the HRT doesn't approach him, they could at least track his movements."

"I'll put a rush on it," Buxton said, pulling out his cell phone.

While Buxton murmured over the phone in the background, Breck shared her screen with the wall monitor. Nina looked up to see an enlarged Arizona driver's license. She studied the photograph. A part of her expected to see something demonic. Instead, she saw a good-looking man. The only hint of the depravity within was the eyes. She recalled Cahill's words and had to agree—they were flat and soulless. Devoid of any warmth. Snake's eyes.

"He's a *leapling*," Wade said to no one in particular.

Nina looked at him. "Come again?"

"It's a term for babies born on leap day," he said. "They're also sometimes called *leapers*."

She recalled that Breck had mentioned Forge's DOB when she located the petition for a name change. It had been another connection to the murders, but the team had not had a chance to explore the meaning behind it.

"So why does Forge commit his crimes every time his birthday rolls around?" she asked. In the silence that followed, a flash of insight hit her. "Cahill told us his parents died when he was sixteen, but he apparently didn't remember the homicide-suicide occurred on his actual birthday. Since leap days occur every four years, that means—"

"His mother killed his father on a leap day," Kent cut in. "Sixteen is a multiple of four."

Wade turned to Breck. "You said Forge killed his baby sister when he was twelve, right?"

Breck nodded. "On February twenty-ninth."

"Forge's twelfth birthday," Wade said. "There must have been some precipitating stressor that triggered him to act out and kill his sister on that specific day."

While Wade considered the psychology behind the events, Nina focused on the timeline. "On Forge's very next leap day birthday, his mother kills his father." She paced across the room, the repetitive movement helping her think out loud. "That sets the pattern, because on his next leap day birthday at twenty years old, he kills the Vega family."

"And he's been repeating the behavior ever since," Kent said.

"We should be grateful he's a leapling," Breck said. "Otherwise, he would have killed a family every year, and we'd have a lot more victims."

Buxton ended the call, spared a quick glance at the screen, then addressed the group. "HRT will head out to Forge's house within minutes. They'll be in plainclothes. I instructed them to keep him under surveillance but not to approach."

Nina wanted the solid evidence they needed to slap cuffs on Forge. "I'd like to get a warrant for a buccal swab to compare his DNA to the unknown sample found at the Vega-family crime scene." She thought for a moment. "I'd also like to search his house to see if he owns a pair of Nike running shoes that match the ones from the two most recent cases."

"We'll handle this strictly by the book." Buxton reiterated his earlier sentiment. "We dig until we gather enough evidence to support a search warrant. The search warrant will yield the evidence we need for an arrest warrant." He looked around the room. "Ladies and gentlemen, we have a suspect." He began firing off orders, beginning with Breck. "I want everything there is to know about Clay Forge, from diapers to divorces."

He turned to Kent. "Reach out to all the field agents around the country who have reopened the earlier cases and fill them in. Have them check to see if Forge's name showed up in any of the police reports, if they interviewed him for any reason. Also, see if you can find any evidence that he was in each city around the time of the murders. Hotel stays, rental cars, airline flights, traffic tickets, arrests for minor violations." He waved a hand in the air. "Anything at all. Some of this information will be quite old and may not be possible to nail down, but do the best you can."

"We should check in the months prior as well," Kent said. "He might have traveled to the locations he targeted in advance to do some recon. His crimes required research and planning. He would have had to familiarize himself with the neighborhoods where they were committed as well as local police procedures, which vary from city to city."

"Agreed," Buxton said.

Breck frowned. "I wonder if the location history from his cell phone would put him anywhere near the Doyles' house on February twenty-ninth. Or in the weeks before that, if he was watching them."

Nina had been down that road before. The legal barriers were tough to overcome. "We can track his recent movements using data from his vehicle and his cell, but we'll need to write a separate affidavit to get that information from the carriers."

The FBI could track his whereabouts using his vehicle or his cell phone GPS, monitor his banking activity to see where and when he accessed funds or used credit cards, and issue an all-points bulletin so police all over the country would be on the lookout for him. Forge would suddenly find himself without the ability to communicate, buy goods, or move around.

Impinging someone's freedom to that degree, however, impeded their constitutional rights, and therefore, the legal standard to do so had a high bar. They would have to write an affidavit outlining the probable cause to arrest Forge and charge him with murder. Once that arduous task was completed, they would have to give testimony and convince a judge to sign the warrant. A separate affidavit and a search warrant would then be required to fully exercise the options Breck had in mind.

"Everything we have is circumstantial," Nina said. "There is nothing tying him directly to any crime scene."

They were in that catch-22 situation every law enforcement officer dreaded. They needed evidence to secure a warrant, but they needed a warrant to find the evidence.

Breck switched tactics. "Speaking of accessing info, back when we thought Thomas Kirk was the unsub, we had theorized that he used the Rubric Realty database to locate victims since his company was involved in each home purchase, but what about Clay Forge? How has he been selecting target families?"

An excellent question.

Breck, still at her computer, pressed the issue further. "According to Forge's LinkedIn profile, he's been working for Jexton Security since he was eighteen." She gestured toward the large monitor on the wall, where Forge's driver's license photo flipped to his LinkedIn picture when she clicked her mouse. "He's worked his way up to Phoenix-branch Sales Director now."

"Sales," Wade said. "Just as I thought. I'll bet he's damned good at it too."

"A nationwide company like Jexton would have a database that included sites around the country," Nina said. "Forge could have started his initial research right from his office."

"That would explain how he defeated the alarm system at the Doyles' house," Breck said. "He has skill with electronics. He might have even figured out how to access existing alarm systems to monitor the people inside. He would know when they were home, who was there, and when they were asleep."

Kent reddened. "I've got an alarm system. I don't like the idea of someone hacking into it to spy on me."

"I don't like it either," Buxton said. "But it could explain a lot about how these crimes were committed."

Nina had an alarm, too, but her backup system consisted of a nosy eighteen-year-old genius with major boundary issues living in the apartment next door who kept tabs on things. "Forge starts off installing alarms. Eventually, he realizes he can make more money selling them because he's a natural salesman."

"Which brings up another point," Breck said. "Now we'll have to get subpoenas for Jexton's files if we want to show Forge was accessing their database and potentially their monitoring systems."

"We aren't even there yet," Wade said. "I'd still like to approach Forge in a noncustodial interview setting to see if we can move the ball farther down the field before we go to a judge."

Buxton shook his head. "We're coloring too close to the lines. A few minutes ago, I called Forge a suspect. He's gone past a person of interest at this point. We'll talk to him after we've got everything sewn up tight."

Buxton was playing it carefully. For an interview to be considered noncustodial, they would have to make it clear from the outset that he was free to leave at any time. It was a legal dance, and Buxton wanted to be sure they did not misstep. They would interview Forge after they laid paper on him.

Buxton turned to Breck with an expectant look. "What else have you got on Forge's personal history?"

"He was divorced four years ago," Breck said. "His ex-wife's name is Gail Howe. She's ten years younger than he is. She left him the house in Mesa and moved to Scottsdale. Looks like she remarried but Forge did not."

"I wonder what Ms. Howe has to say," Wade said. "We'll have to pay her a visit too."

"The assignment is yours," Buxton said, then gestured toward Nina. "Take Agent Guerrera with you." He looked at the others. "While they're interviewing Mr. Forge's ex-wife, the rest of us will look under the sofa cushions to see if we can find enough probable cause to write an affidavit. After you two get back, we'll debrief, fill in the gaps in our profile, and put our best case together."

Nina picked up her bag and turned to Wade. "Interviewing someone who once shared a bed and a home with a ruthless serial killer should be . . . enlightening."

"I've done it many times before," he said to her. "I'm always amazed but never surprised."

Chapter 42

Thirty minutes later, Nina and Wade sat in Gail Howe's sleek state-of-the-art kitchen. Gail, a tall blonde with the physique of a ballet dancer and the demeanor of a frightened rabbit, had ushered them inside the expansive midcentury-modern home she shared with her new husband of two years.

After handing them each a bottle of French sparkling water from a chiller beneath the counter, she took an empty chair at the kitchen table. "It's a good thing my husband isn't home," she said. "He gets upset anytime I mention Clay's name."

"Upset?" Nina wondered if Gail had been unlucky in marriage more than once. "What do you mean?"

"Not what you're thinking." Gail seemed to have read the concern in Nina's tone. "He doesn't hit me or anything like that. He just . . . well, I've told him stories about my time with Clay. Stories that weren't so nice. I've been in therapy since the divorce."

Four years of therapy indicated Gail had a lot to deal with. "Would you be willing to share some of those stories with us?" Nina asked.

Gail winced. "Not if it means I'll have to testify against him or anything."

"Then he's committed crimes that you're aware of?" Nina said.

"Oh, this is going all wrong." Gail flapped her hands. "Look, why don't you start by telling me what this is about?"

Nina gave her the standard nonanswer. "His name came up as a person of interest in an investigation. We need some background information."

"Person of interest." Gail grimaced. "I know what that means."

"Mrs. Howe—" Wade began.

"Gail, please."

He started again. "Gail, whatever you can tell us about Clay would go a long way in helping us understand him."

She pursed her lips. "Good luck with that. It took me five years of marriage to truly understand him, and another full year to get away from him once I did."

"Let's start with that," Wade said. "How did you meet and how did you come to understand him?"

"We met when one of my friends was buying a house. The real estate agent recommended Jexton Security for the alarm system."

"Was the real estate agent with Rubric Realty?" Nina asked.

Gail tilted her head in thought. "Yes, he was. I went with my friend when she met the rep from the alarm company, which turned out to be Clay. This was ten years ago, before he climbed the corporate ladder."

She paused for a moment, but no one interrupted, letting the silence stretch. After half a minute, she sipped her water and went on.

"Clay was handsome and charming. He said all the right things, was very attentive, and had a great sense of humor. We hit it off right away. Before I knew it, my friend had a house with a new alarm system, and I had a fiancé."

"How long did you date before you got engaged?" Wade asked.

Nina figured he was trying to tell if it had been a whirlwind romance.

"About a month, maybe less." Gail lifted a shoulder. "Everyone liked him at first. My family thought he was nice. We got married a few months after our engagement and he found a great home for us in a lovely community in Mesa. I wanted to start a family, but he kept putting children off."

Wade leaned forward, intent. "What did he say about having a child?"

"He said babies were a lot of trouble, and that he needed my help to get ahead in the company. He used to tell me we would start a family once he was in charge of a branch and had lots of people working for him."

Nina understood why Wade had asked the questions. Whatever he told his wife at the time, Forge undoubtedly didn't want to compete with a baby for her affection.

"I knew that would take a while," Gail said. "I'm a lot younger than he is, but my biological clock was ticking. After I passed thirty, we began to have serious arguments about it."

"Did he ever get violent?" Nina asked gently.

"Not physically, but he messed with my head."

"How so?" Nina prompted.

"He would say something and then deny he said it," Gail said. "Sometimes about important things, like our finances, and other times about stupid little things that didn't matter, like the laundry."

When they continued to look at her, she blew out a sigh. "Okay, I'll give you an example."

Nina waited while Gail took another sip of water, apparently summoning up the best representation of her relationship with her ex-husband.

"One time he sent me to the store for milk and eggs," Gail began. "I got a couple of other things and came home a half hour later with the groceries. He starts screaming at me about his beer. Says I forgot to buy his stupid beer. There is zero chance I forgot about it. I would never make that mistake. Well, he works himself into a rage and puts his fist through the drywall right next to my head. I apologized and rushed out to buy the beer." Her voice dropped. "That's also when I realized I needed to get the hell out of there."

"That's very helpful," Nina said, then pivoted to a subject she hoped would provide more fodder for a warrant. "What were his birthdays like?"

She had worded the question carefully. If Gail described intimate dinners or giving him presents when he woke up in the morning, their case would be in serious jeopardy. On the other hand, if she indicated her husband was out of town on his leap year birthdays, that would add credibility to the idea that he traveled to various cities during the time frame in which the crimes were committed.

"He acted real weird about his birthday," Gail said. "He's a leap day baby, you know." When they nodded, she continued. "He was sensitive about it. Never wanted to celebrate with me. In fact, he was always out of town on business over his birthday. After a while I realized he only did that on his actual birthday, every four years—not on March first, which is when he normally celebrates on non-leap years."

Gail had corroborated a key element of the case they were building against Forge. Nina barely managed to keep herself from smiling. She knew damn well what Forge was doing every four years, but she wondered if Gail had any idea.

"Where would he go?" Nina asked her.

"No clue," Gail said. "He just seemed anxious to get out of town. I think he did that on purpose so I couldn't make a fuss on the actual day. I would have a cake and a present or something for him when he came home."

"Did he behave differently when he returned from his trips?" Wade asked.

Gail tapped her chin with a slender finger. "A bit calmer, maybe. It's hard to describe. He wasn't quite as particular about things when he got back."

"Particular?" Wade said in a clear invitation for her to elaborate.

"He would get all cranked up about the tiniest things. When he came home, the carpet had to be freshly vacuumed. But—get this—he insisted on lines in the carpet."

"Lines?" Nina asked.

"You know, the marks a vacuum cleaner makes, stripes in the carpet. Kind of like when you cut the grass and there are stripes in the lawn? That's what he wanted every single day. There could be no footprints, he wanted to see straight lines in the carpet."

Nina silently added *control freak* to her mental description of Forge.

"The furniture had to be arranged precisely too," Gail said, finally warming to the subject. "He would measure after I vacuumed to make sure every piece had been perfectly replaced so it was back where he'd left it. Every day I had to move the furniture to vacuum under it, then carefully replace it to line up in the room precisely. There had to be an even amount of space on each side."

Nina cut her eyes to Wade, who looked like he was literally and figuratively biting his tongue.

"My therapist told me Clay was obsessive-compulsive," Gail added.

"Do you know if he had access to any property out of town?" Nina said, looking for information about places Forge might hide out if he decided to run. "Somewhere he might go to get away for a while?"

"Not that I'm aware of. He only ever traveled for business, and he stayed in hotels when he did."

Nina came back around to her previous question. This time, she asked it directly. "Did you ever get the impression he was involved in anything criminal?"

"Never."

Nina wanted to know if Gail had been aware of Forge's background. "Did you ever meet any of his family?"

"Both of his parents died in a car crash," Gail said. "I felt so sorry for him. He didn't have any other family in the area."

So this is how Forge had explained the lack of a family to his bride. Nina found it interesting that Gail never questioned it further. It seemed that Forge had her completely under his control.

Nina changed the subject. "Could you draw us a layout of the house in Mesa?"

"Sure, but I can't help you when it comes to the basement."

"Why not?"

"I was never allowed in the basement."

Nina dropped her voice to a conspiratorial whisper. "You never got curious and took a peek?"

"Are you kidding? Clay would have known, and there would have been hell to pay. He always knew what I was doing somehow."

Nina had a hunch that Forge's seeming omniscience had more to do with electronic surveillance installed in his own home than anything else. She waited while Gail borrowed Wade's notepad and sketched out the floor plan for the house she had once shared with Forge.

Gail finished and handed the pad to Nina. "This is the best I can do. I'm no artist."

Nina assured her the drawing would be helpful as they thanked her and made their way to the front door.

After providing her with a business card, Nina gave Gail's hand an extra squeeze on her way out. "Call if you remember more details."

Gail tugged her closer and whispered, "I'm still not sure what this is all about, and I understand that you can't tell me, but I will say this. I learned the hard way that behind Clay Forge's perfect smile is a cold, calculating mind. I don't think he ever loved me. I'm not sure he even knows what love is."

Nina repeated Gail's words to Wade when they were in the SUV.

"That woman has suffered a tremendous amount of abuse, and I doubt she told us everything that happened with her ex," Wade said. "She still seems terrified of him."

"I'm glad she's in therapy," Nina said. "Because she'll need it even more once this goes public and she learns she was married to a psycho killer."

Chapter 43

Nina briefly took her eyes off the road to glance at Wade when she noticed him checking his phone. "Have you gotten any texts from Buxton? Did the surveillance team catch up to Forge?"

"They detailed half the team to his office and the other half to his house," Wade said. "According to the receptionist at Jexton Security's front desk, Forge left less than two minutes after our phone call. Said he was heading out of town." He gave his head a rueful shake. "We never had a chance of catching him at work."

The phone call to Jexton had been a losing gamble. "And his house?"

"They've been sitting on the place, but Forge hasn't shown up."

Nina passed a slow-moving truck. "So they're confident he never went home?"

"As much as they can be."

"This guy thinks ahead," she said. "Do you think he has bolt-holes and fake identities set up in advance?"

Wade gave the matter some thought. "His kind of planning takes place months in advance of his murders. He's not good at improvising. Look what happened with Thomas Kirk."

"Forge made critical mistakes," she agreed. "Which ultimately led us to his identity."

"I'd like to visit his neighborhood before we go back to the command center," Wade said. "We won't knock on his door or anything, but I can get a better sense of him from his living environment."

She didn't think the boss would go for it. "Buxton will probably tell us to have the surveillance team upload photos and video to our server."

"I'll handle Buxton. Nothing is like being *in situ*."

"Yeah, definitely use Latin." Nina gave him a wry grin. "That should impress him."

Wade chuckled and pulled out his phone. Nina took the ramp for the 202 Red Mountain Freeway toward Mesa, anticipating Wade winning the argument.

After a lot of back-and-forth with the boss, Wade disconnected. "We're supposed to stay away from the plainclothes surveillance team so we don't blow their cover. They'll be one street over from the target location, parked in a blue sedan."

After driving in silence for a while, Nina caught Wade studying her.

"How are you holding up, Guerrera?" he asked her gently.

"What do you mean?"

He didn't dignify the question with a response, instead lifting a salt-and-pepper brow. Dr. Jeffrey Wade, psychologist, was making a house call. She thought about deflecting but decided maybe a sounding board wouldn't be a bad thing.

"Seeing my family was tough." The words *my family* tasted foreign in her mouth. "I looked at Teresa's face, and it was exactly like Maria's. Like . . . my mother's."

Wade said nothing.

She pictured her father's parents, their house dark and empty compared to Teresa's. "And the Vega family, *ay, dios mío*, they are so grief-stricken." She tightened her grip on the steering wheel. "Their whole house is like a mausoleum. I can't imagine how terrible it's been for them to lose both of their children so young."

Wade finally spoke. "Then you coming back into their lives is a blessing for them. You can give them something that was taken from them."

She gave voice to the worry that had been eating at her. "How will they feel about me when they know I lied to them? They wanted to know what happened to their missing granddaughter, and I stood right there in front of them and twisted the knife in deeper. Reminding them of everything they'd lost and offering no hope at all."

"We talked about this when we agreed to keep your relationship quiet for the time being," Wade said. "Sharing that information with them wasn't an option."

"I'm not sure if they'll accept that explanation." Her throat began to tighten. "If they'll accept me."

"Families overcome a lot of challenges." Wade spoke with a certainty she didn't share. "You're not accustomed to that because you've never had a family of your own." He hesitated. "You've never experienced unconditional love, have you?"

She shook her head, not trusting her voice.

"You're their blood, Nina," Wade said quietly. "I know it's not something you can easily understand, but trust me, it means one hell of a lot."

She swallowed the emotion clogging her throat and moved on to another concern. "Perez is getting suspicious."

"How so?"

"He's a detective," she said. "He sensed something when I was at the Vegas' house. He asked me about it, but I blew him off."

"You can tell him about it when the time is right. When the investigation is over."

"He'll be angry with me."

Wade eyed her. "And this matters because you . . . care for him?"

"Stop psychoanalyzing me, Wade."

"It's fairly obvious to me that he has feelings for you, but I can't get a read on what you think about him."

"I'm not interested in romance right now."

"That's not an answer, but I'll take it," he said. "Now wouldn't be the right time to start a cross-country relationship . . . or any other relationship, for that matter." When she flicked a glance at him, he continued. "You've got a full load in the wash . . . no room to cram in more stuff."

They lapsed into a silence again as Nina surveyed the office complexes and shopping centers with their tall arches and stone facades. She spotted their exit and took the ramp off the freeway. "This is a nice city."

"From what I've found online, Mesa is a combination of new and old. It's in a state of transition. This area is one of the newer neighborhoods."

"The addresses go up," Nina said a few minutes later as she turned onto Forge's street. "Odd numbers on the right and even on the left."

"We should be getting close to Forge's house. Do a slow roll."

Nina gave him a look. "You do realize that in an upscale neighborhood like this, someone will probably call Mesa PD to report a suspicious vehicle if we hang around too long."

"Look." Wade pointed. "That's his next-door neighbor."

They watched a heavyset, balding man wheeling a large blue bin from the side of his house toward the street.

Nina had noticed most of the other houses had similar receptacles standing upright at the ends of their respective driveways. She squinted at the three arrows configured into a triangle on the side of the bin.

"Must be collection day for recycling tomorrow." She watched the neighbor awkwardly make his way toward the street, the cumbersome load bumping along on the cobblestone walkway. He struggled to keep it from tipping as it swayed side to side.

The neighbor yanked the bin out onto the street, rolling it beside an identical blue receptacle next to Forge's driveway, then trudged back into his house and shut the door.

Nina recalled how Breck had pilfered her soda can at the Boardroom back in Quantico. "Forge lives alone, right?"

"According to Breck's research, yes." Wade's eyes narrowed. "What are you thinking?"

"That it's time for a good old-fashioned trash run." She held up a hand to forestall his objections as soon as he opened his mouth. "Legally, we can't go onto his property," she said. "But his trash can is on a public street." She paused for emphasis. "He's relinquished control of the contents, which means he has no expectation of privacy for anything inside."

"Technically, that's true, but—"

"Buxton will be more than happy when we turn up with a sample of Forge's DNA to match to the one collected in the Llorona case," she said. "Forge has ghosted. There's no better way to get what we need for a warrant than a solid DNA match. Who knows how long we'll have to wait to get a subpoena to search his office? And even if we got evidence techs in there today, there's a lot of cross contamination to deal with."

"And what happens when that neighbor of his sees us rooting through the trash like a couple of wayward raccoons and calls the police?"

"We make sure we're gone before they get here," she said. "Hand me the evidence kit. I need a couple of bags and some latex gloves."

Wade heaved a resigned sigh and opened his door. "It's been a while since I've been proned out at gunpoint while a uniform yells at me to show my creds." He made a mock wistful expression. "I kind of miss it."

He lifted a duffel from the floor of the back seat and handed it to her. She pulled out the supplies she needed, and they sauntered toward Forge's driveway.

Nina nudged Wade's elbow and pointed at the mini camera system aimed straight at them. "So much for stealth mode," she said, snapping on the gloves. "He's probably watching us from his cell phone right now."

Wade didn't appear concerned. "Given what happened at Jexton today, I'd say we lost the element of surprise as soon as we made that phone call."

She noticed he said *we* and appreciated the gesture, though she still felt personally responsible.

Ten minutes later, they climbed back into the SUV with four evidence bags to show for their effort.

Nina stripped off her gloves and tucked them in a small plastic baggie before sanitizing her hands and starting the car. "Why don't we call and see if Perez can meet us at the lab to put a rush on this?"

Wade pushed the speed dial button and put his cell to his ear. "We've either just made the entire case . . . or screwed it up beyond repair with this little stunt."

Chapter 44

Despite her earlier comments to Wade, Nina had prepared herself for an angry rebuke from Buxton. After their explanation of the circumstances, however, he had agreed that their dumpster-diving episode had been both legal and efficient.

Perez had called the Phoenix crime lab and spoken to Dr. Ledford, who accepted the specimens Nina handed her and agreed to rush the comparison with the unknown sample from the Llorona case.

Throughout the drive from the lab back to the Phoenix field office, Nina had contemplated the trail of devastation Clay Forge had left in his wake as he traveled through life. Everyone who came near him suffered—his baby sister, his parents, the man who had befriended him, and his ex-wife.

After arriving at the command center, she listened as Wade briefed the rest of the team on the interview with Gail. When he finished, Nina summed up her observations. "Personally, I think Forge is a black hole that sucks in everything and everyone that gets too close," she said, then gestured toward Wade and Kent. "But I'll defer to the forensic psychologists."

"A black hole is an accurate description of an untreated psychopathic narcissist," Kent said. "Emotionally, he's a void, and yet he has a powerful ability to attract victims who are ultimately destroyed if they cannot escape his orbit."

"I thought narcissists were self-centered people who think they're better than everyone else," Perez said.

"That's a common misconception because they appear to exhibit arrogance," Kent said. "Truth is, they're so deeply insecure that they overcompensate."

"Narcissism is a disorder of self-esteem," Wade added. "They live in constant fear that people will see through their act. They can't stand it when someone else gets attention or is recognized for achievement, because they fear it diminishes their own accomplishments. They cannot stop talking about themselves because they want to be sure they are viewed as the best at everything. They gaslight other people because they cannot ever—under any circumstances—admit they are wrong or that they made a mistake. Not even about the tiniest thing. They are scared to show weakness of any kind."

"So you're saying that underneath all the bragging and the lying is a frightened individual who is terrified of rejection?" Perez asked.

"Bingo," Wade said. "But you couple that with antisocial personality disorder, and you've got a real recipe for disaster. Take the traits we just described and infuse them into a highly intelligent person who is incapable of remorse, does not have the slightest sympathy for others, and has no compunction about eliminating anyone who gets in his way."

"Don't forget to add the ability to charm and manipulate others," Kent said. "It's their superpower."

"How does this apply to Clay Forge?" Buxton asked.

While Nina and Wade interviewed Gail, Buxton had directed the team, along with Perez, to flesh out the disparate facts from the sprawling investigation that incorporated components from around the country and spanned close to three decades.

"With those personality traits in mind, we can postulate about some of the things that made him go off the rails." Wade steepled his fingers. "First, the initial stressor, which we now know occurred when he was twelve years old. His parents brought home a baby sister he did not want. He saw her as a threat and eliminated her."

"Damn," Breck said. "This guy puts the *antisocial* in antisocial personality disorder."

"After he's sentenced to juvie until his eighteenth birthday, it's not surprising to learn that he continues his selfish and abusive behavior in that setting," Kent continued. "In fact, he might see it as more of an imperative to act in a way that promotes his own well-being above everyone else's."

"He wins over the staff and bullies the other kids," Wade said. "According to Cahill, he gets away with it, managing to fool most of the adults, until the second stressor occurs, which causes a crack in the facade."

"The second stressor being that he is told both of his parents are now dead at the hands of his mother," Nina said, then added, "on his sixteenth birthday, which is the next leap day."

"I suspect leap day was also a trigger for his mother," Kent said. "The anniversary of her son's birth and her daughter's death must have been overwhelming for her. She had essentially lost both of her children on that day and couldn't cope."

"The mother whose affection he was so jealous of when his sister was born had turned against him, but she's dead, so he cannot retaliate against her directly," Wade said. "Instead, he uses a proxy, staging his crimes to portray the mother as the villain of the piece. He ensures everyone in the community will blame her, and her own family will turn against her. She will be hated and reviled by all, just like he was after what he did."

Nina could see the parallel nature of the revenge Forge's warped mind had concocted. She listened with a growing sense of outrage as Wade continued.

"At the same time, while he is at the scene, he torments the women, who stand in for his own mother. He makes sure that before each one dies, she knows that everyone she loves, everyone she holds dear, is dead."

Nina thought about how Maria Vega had suffered, emotionally and physically, before Forge killed her. As she pictured Maria's face, she thought of Teresa's identical features. Teresa had suffered, too, along with the entire community when word of *La Llorona* spread. Forge must have been ecstatic when his plan worked so well. Nina stiffened as she realized Wade had been talking about her family. Her mother.

She noticed Wade regarding her. "The kind of revenge he takes is beyond cruel—it's sadistic," he said.

Understanding passed between them. Everyone in the room was listening to Wade's observations, but she felt as if he were talking to her alone.

"As the saying goes," Wade said, "the opposite of love is not hate. The opposite of love is apathy. Forge is about as far from apathetic about his mother as you can get."

Kent drew his own conclusions. "What Forge felt for his mother in the first place wasn't love but the fear of losing her or sharing her. From what you two learned from his ex-wife, Gail, he was quite controlling and did not want to share her affection with any potential children, even his own."

Wade turned to Buxton. "When we do catch this guy, we can't focus on what he has done to the families, because they do not matter to him. They are stand-ins. He has as much feeling for them as he would mannequins he was staging for a show."

"So what do we focus on?" Nina asked.

"The only thing that matters to him," Wade said. "Himself."

Kent inclined his head in agreement. "We ask how this affected *him*. We want to hear what *he* has to say. It's all about *him*."

"Well, we're not going to get a chance to interview someone we can't find," Buxton said. "Let's focus on locating Mr. Forge."

Nina appreciated the change of subject. She valued the insight into Forge's mind, but she preferred action to analysis. "We can assume he's actively evading us now," she said.

"There's no point in wasting manpower and resources by maintaining surveillance on his house," Buxton said. "I'm calling off the undercover detail and replacing them with a few strategically placed cameras. Doubtless, he's seen us at the door with his monitoring system, and he knows we're looking for him." Buxton paused. "We have a lot of resources at our disposal, but only if we have a warrant for his arrest." He glanced at Perez. "Any news from Dr. Ledford at the lab?"

"She just texted me." Perez's straight white teeth contrasted with his tan skin as he grinned. "The samples you two got from his trash are a match for the DNA sample collected at the Llorona case twenty-eight years ago."

"We've got him," Nina said. "Now we can write that affidavit."

"I should do it," Perez said. "My department has jurisdiction over both Phoenix cases." His grin widened. "I can take the paperwork to the Maricopa County Attorney's office. They know me there. Once I get their buy-in, I'll go before a county judge to get an arrest warrant as well as search warrants for his property and devices. Again, they've worked with me for years, and they know I'm solid."

Buxton looked hopeful. "How long do you think that would take?"

Perez lifted a shoulder. "If we all work together to get the writing done quickly, I could probably turn it around in a day."

Buxton gave a rare smile. "That's one hell of a lot faster than we could do it going through the US Attorney's office and a federal judge." He pointed at Perez. "Do it." He turned to Breck. "While Detective Perez works on that, could you put together an APB with a couple of photographs of Forge with different appearances? Be sure to include his previous name as an alias. That should get us some media attention when the time comes to put it out."

Kent snorted. "Once word gets out, this guy won't be able to take a dump without us getting a phone call."

Nina caught Wade's sidelong glance and guessed what he was thinking. Without knowing it, Perez's assertion of his department's precedence in the case had made it so her name would not appear on any of the arrest documents.

The team's plan to keep her secret was working. If their luck held, Forge would be in custody soon, and she could orchestrate the discovery of her connection to the Vega family at the appropriate time.

"Get busy, people," Buxton said, interrupting their silent communication. "It's going to be a long day."

Chapter 45

After an exhausting but productive afternoon with the team at the PFO command center, Nina had been ready to head to the hotel. Driving back together in the SUV, the FBI team had agreed to change into casual clothes and check out a local Mexican restaurant Perez had recommended.

The conversation had veered onto the topic of which beverages went best with spicy food as they pulled into the parking lot. Nina was sharing what Perez had told her about how prickly pear margaritas were made from the fruit of a cactus when Kent interrupted her.

"What's going on?" He was looking out the vehicle's side window.

Nina followed his gaze to see a familiar figure rushing toward their vehicle.

"It's that reporter," she said. "James Snead."

Snead bore down on them with long strides, cameraman in tow.

"This looks like an ambush," Buxton said, opening the driver's door. "I'll handle it."

Buxton got out and stood his ground as the others followed suit, flanking their supervisor.

"James Snead with Channel Six News," the reporter said to Buxton. "I'm here to get your comment on a story we're putting together for this evening at six."

Nina glanced at her watch—five o'clock.

"What story is that?" Buxton asked.

Snead directed his gaze at Nina. "I received information about Special Agent Guerrera. Apparently, she has a personal connection to the Llorona case."

Nina's pulse ratcheted up. What had Snead found out?

Buxton flicked a glance at her before returning his attention to the reporter. "What connection?"

She forced her expression into what she hoped appeared politely inquisitive, as if she had no idea Snead's finger hovered over a nuclear detonator.

"Our news team double-checked my source's information," Snead said. "We're confident in its accuracy, and we're going forward with the story. I'm only giving you an opportunity to comment." He signaled to the man behind him, who hoisted the camera to his shoulder and aimed it in their direction.

Buxton looked guarded. "I cannot comment until I know what you're talking about."

Nina paid close attention to how Buxton dealt with the situation. He wasn't blowing the reporter off. He evidently wanted the information and therefore seemed willing to put up with Snead's tactics.

The reporter spoke into his microphone. "As you know, we've been covering recent developments in the Llorona case closely, including breaking the story about the switched babies at the hospital. This morning my source told me the current identity of the switched baby who survived."

Nina glanced at each of her teammates in turn, finding her own shock reflected in their blank expressions.

Buxton's brows shot up. He refrained, however, from admitting that this was information the FBI did not know. "How can you be sure your source is correct?"

"First, he has been reliable in the past," Snead said. "Second, he forwarded documents to us substantiating his claim."

"What kind of documents?" Buxton said, echoing her first thought.

She realized that Buxton was looking for an opportunity to explain away whatever documentation Snead had received. Documentation the FBI had somehow overlooked. Anything to avoid embarrassing the Bureau.

"Birth records, for one," Snead said. "They are available online. My source provided the birth record for Maria and Victor Vega's baby girl. He also sent a copy of the birth record for Carmen Cardona's baby girl. In addition, he gave me Ms. Cardona's current address in Washington, DC, with the information that she took her baby to the DC-metro area shortly after she gave birth."

Snead allowed a dramatic pause in his recitation. Nina felt a prickle of sweat at her hairline. A freight train was barreling straight at her and she was tied to the tracks, unable to get out of the way. She could do nothing but listen in silence.

"My source claimed Ms. Cardona left her baby daughter in a dumpster in northern Virginia," Snead said. "And finally, he shared local newsclips about an infant Latina baby girl who was rescued from a dumpster in Reston twenty-eight years ago."

Nina couldn't help but appreciate that law enforcement used the same methods to corroborate information they received from confidential informants. This reporter had a great deal of experience and was not about to stake his reputation on a baseless rumor.

As Buxton's jaw tensed, she knew he was coming to the same inexorable conclusion she'd arrived at on Saturday night.

"It's common knowledge that Agent Guerrera was rescued from a dumpster in Reston twenty-eight years ago," Snead continued. "We all know her story from the media coverage she received recently. How many infant baby girls of Hispanic descent were in that exact predicament during that precise time frame? We did the research. The answer is one." He gestured to her. "Nina Guerrera. The FBI's famous Warrior Girl."

Buxton took a step back when Snead tilted the microphone at him. "I cannot confirm any part of your story," Buxton said. "I do not know who your source is, but we will need time to—"

Snead checked his watch. "I'm putting the package together now, and we're going live in fifty-five minutes." He edged closer. "If you have anything to say, this is your chance to get in front of it."

"I have no comment at this time," Buxton said.

Snead pushed the mic in her direction. "How about you, Agent Guerrera?"

Since calling him an obscenity wasn't an option, she gave the only response she could. "No comment."

Snead pulled back his mic and reached inside his jacket pocket. "Let me know if you change your mind."

Buxton accepted the proffered business card. "Would you consider holding off on airing this until we have time to look into it?"

"It's an exclusive right now," Snead said. "It won't be for long. I'm going live at six."

After parting company with Snead, the team entered the hotel and rode the elevator up to their floor in a tense silence. Nina and the others followed Buxton's ramrod-straight back as he marched to his room. Apparently, he'd decided to hold an ad hoc meeting there.

Buxton checked to make sure the door was closed before rounding on Nina. "Is there any truth to this?"

Another decision point. Her eyes reflexively darted to Wade, Kent, and Breck. She would not lie to her supervisor, but she could sure as hell phrase things to protect her team. She recalled their earlier conversation. Plausible deniability. She realized she could provide cover for Buxton as well.

She chose her words carefully, keeping her toes a hair's width behind the line. "What he said seems accurate, sir. When we interviewed Carmen Cardona, she spoke Spanish. I thought she mentioned kissing her baby, but she might have used the word for *trash* instead.

She was sobbing, and it was difficult to understand her. If she meant she threw her baby in a dumpster, that would have occurred in Virginia while she was meeting a . . . customer."

Everything Nina said was true. She merely left out the timeline for her realization.

Buxton frowned. "How could anyone possibly have known that?"

This time, she didn't need to hedge. "I have no idea, sir."

His dark eyes bored into her, taking her measure. "Agent Guerrera, you will report to the Phoenix crime lab first thing tomorrow morning," he said after a long moment. "You will take a DNA test, and we will find out whether any of this is true."

She did not argue.

"While we wait for the results," Buxton continued, "you will not conduct any more interviews or write any affidavits for this case."

She studied her shoes. "Yes, sir."

"Agent Guerrera," he said, waiting for her to meet his gaze. "If your DNA is a match, you'll be on the next flight back to Washington."

Chapter 46

Nina's feet fell into a rhythm as she jogged north along Seventh Street in downtown Phoenix. Instead of going to her room to pack for her inevitable departure the next day, she had grabbed the running outfit she'd brought back and headed out, hoping a long run through the heart of the city would settle her frayed nerves.

The farther she got from the hotel, the more her thoughts strayed to her two new families. How would they react when they saw the news on television? She had wanted to visit them in person, to warn them about the story before it aired, but Buxton had put the kibosh on that. She winced inwardly, picturing Teresa Soto's kind face and Ana Vega's haunted eyes. Would she admit how she had lied to them? She could always pretend she didn't know about her background when she had last spoken to them.

All at once, she realized she was done with shading the truth. With plausible deniability. With lying.

Even if Breck had never secretly checked her DNA, Nina had known the truth in her heart without the need for lab results to confirm it. She had made a conscious decision to trust her new team, and they had made it clear they wanted her to continue investigating with them. She could have gone to Buxton and confessed her suspicions, and he would have taken her off the case immediately—as he had just done. But she hadn't told her boss. The team had figured out a way to keep her biological connection separate from the investigation until it no longer mattered.

It had worked . . . until the moment it blew up in her face.

She wouldn't blame either family if they never wanted to see her again. She had put her determination to catch the unsub before any other consideration. In the process, she'd probably ruined her only chance at having a real family of her own.

Frustrated, she rounded a corner heading west on Van Buren Street and began the last leg of the run. She hoped to have made peace with herself by the time she arrived back at the hotel, but her self-recrimination still occupied her thoughts.

A high-pitched buzzing sound pulled her attention upward. She tilted her head back to see a small drone hovering above her. She had no idea what kind of regulations the city of Phoenix placed on such devices and wondered if it was permitted to fly around in such a heavily congested area. She followed its progress as it zipped away, disappearing into an alley between two buildings across the street.

A deep male voice called out from behind, startling her. "You're dogging it, Guerrera."

She almost stumbled. Silently chastising herself for becoming distracted by the drone, she directed a frown over her shoulder at Kent, who caught up to her with an easy, loping gait.

"What part of 'I want to be alone' don't you understand?" she said to him.

He gave her a sardonic smile. "Apparently, all of it."

Annoyed he had capitalized on her momentary lack of situational awareness, she sped up. He merely lengthened his stride, effortlessly matching her quickened pace. Outrunning him wasn't an option. "Why are you here?"

"Because of my training."

She played along with his game. "What training is that?"

"Being a SEAL is more than just bragging rights and cool tattoos."

She held immense respect for his elite military background but had no idea where he was going with this, so she waited for him to elaborate.

"Our group has been together for a few months," Kent said. "But that hostage scenario in Hogan's Alley yesterday shows me you still don't get it."

"Get what?"

"Why Breck ran your DNA, why Wade figured out a way for you to stay on the case, why we all agreed to the plan . . . and why I'm out here with you now."

She flicked a glance at him, genuinely curious. "And?"

He huffed out a sigh. "Do you remember the distress code I told you about?"

How could she forget a story like that? "Flashpoint."

He nodded. "We are part of a team. We have each other's backs. We trust each other with our lives . . . or—more importantly—our careers."

"Your priorities are a bit backward," she told him. "But I get what you're saying. Besides, I'm not sure what teamwork has to do with me, since I'm heading back to DC tomorrow. Alone."

"The killers we pursue don't have any rules or regulations to follow. We do. Sometimes we have to balance those restrictions with our own humanity, or we risk becoming what we hunt. We're not robots, we're people. We feel, we care, we love."

She considered his words before responding. "You're saying you all found a work-around to let me stay on the case because you understood what it meant to me?"

"I've studied people, learned how to read them." Kent held his pace steady as he navigated around a streetlight. "When I was in spec ops, my life and the operation often depended on it."

"And what are you reading now?"

"Pain." He softened his tone. "I'm sorry for your loss, Nina."

"That's what we say when we speak to surviving relatives of the victims when we're conducting interviews." She glanced up at him. "I-I don't . . . that is, I never knew them."

"That's just it, Nina." His cobalt eyes filled with compassion. "It's not only the loss of the parents you never met but of the life you never knew. A life that should have included love, kindness, and the warmth of family. Instead, you were abused, neglected, and shuffled from one foster home to another."

She looked away, focusing on the street ahead of them. As his words seeped in, the enormity of what she had missed washed over her. He was right. She was another victim in this scenario. She searched for a clever remark to hide the heartache his observations had caused, but no words came to her. He had summed up her childhood in a couple of sentences, distilling all the grief, loneliness, and longing in a way that succinctly explained her situation—yet left out so much.

He reached out to her, lightly brushing her bare shoulder with his finger as they ran side by side. Instinctively, she veered away, uncomfortable with expressions of warmth and compassion. He had also come far too close to touching one of the many scars that marred her back.

"I have scars, too, Nina." He dropped his hand back into position, his arms moving in cadence with his footfalls. "And I happen to think yours are beautiful. They are an outward symbol of your inner strength."

Those simple words almost undid her. If only he were telling the truth. Instead, she sensed the emotion underlying his kindness. The motivation behind it.

Pity.

She would neither accept nor tolerate anyone feeling sorry for her, nor would she listen to lies. She was not beautiful. Her scars were hideous reminders of a past she could not escape no matter how far or how fast she ran.

She steeled herself. "I don't want your pity, Kent." She deliberately used his last name, distancing herself.

"You think I pity you?" He looked incredulous.

How could she describe feelings she barely understood? How could she explain the carefully constructed walls she had built up around herself? She had always felt unwanted. Thrown away by her family to be raised as one of the thousands of nameless children in an uncaring system. She had been bullied by bigger kids, abused by adults, and attacked by a predator as a teenager. As of two days ago, she learned she had a family and parents who had loved her before they were killed. Now Kent was expressing feelings she couldn't fully comprehend. It was too much. Too fast. Too overwhelming.

"Trust me," Kent said. "You're reading the situation all wrong."

He reached out and clasped Nina's elbow, pulling her to a stop. His eyes met hers. "Nina, I—"

His words were cut off by the crack of a high-powered rifle.

Chapter 47

Instinct took over. She slammed into Kent, knocking him sideways as a second shot thudded into the side of the building directly behind the place where they had just been standing. An instant later, she felt his heavy frame on top of her as he drove her to the ground, using momentum to roll them toward a cement planter the size of a garbage can nearby.

Still pinned under Kent's bulk, she craned her neck to peer around the planter's smooth cylindrical side, pulling back when another round tore off a chunk of cement, sending rubble cascading down on her face.

"Neither one of us has a gun or a vest," she said. "And my tactical pen won't do a hell of a lot in a gunfight. We're sitting ducks."

Cars screeched to a halt on the street beside them. Pedestrians scattered in every direction, screaming as they rushed into nearby stores, desperate to get out of the line of fire.

"That's a large-caliber rifle," Kent said. "He'll keep shooting until he demolishes this cement barrier. If we don't move, we're dead."

Kent had more experience with urban warfare than anyone she knew. She squinted through the powder that had dusted her face, scanning the area for better cover. "If we can make it to that building across the alley, we'll be out of the kill zone."

Kent followed her gaze. "Roger that. He's shooting from somewhere on the opposite side of the street. I'll go first and draw his fire. You stay on the other side of me. We'll go on the count of three."

He intended to use his body as a human shield to protect her while she ran for cover.

Fuck that.

He hefted himself off her, rising slightly to a crouched position behind what was left of the pillar, and began the count. "One."

She tucked into a runner's stance beside him.

"Two."

She made up her mind. If anyone would draw the sniper's fire, it would be her. She was smaller and harder to hit. "Three," she said before he could finish, and sprang forward.

She sprinted toward the corner of the building surrounded by a hail of gunfire coming from the shooter and a barrage of obscenities coming from Kent as his big feet pounded the ground behind her.

They made it to the building together and pressed their backs against the wall.

Kent looked furious. "What the hell, Guerrera?"

She panted, adrenaline coursing through her. "You're the size of a wildebeest. I was the better choice for a distraction."

"And did you notice he was aiming at you the whole time? You're the primary target."

So not a crazed gunman or one of the random mass shooters that had begun to plague so many cities and towns. She may not have her service weapon, but she would damn well do whatever it took to put a stop to this asshole before he killed an innocent bystander.

Another round dinged a nearby metal streetlight pole. Sunset had given way to dusk, and this time she spotted the muzzle flash. Despite the echoes of the rifle's report off the surrounding buildings, she had pinpointed the shooter's location.

She jerked her chin toward the spot. "He's in the alley to the right of that building."

"The police are on the way," Kent said as sirens cut the air. "The sniper is leaving."

A silhouette backlit by the fading light jumped to his feet from a kneeling position. The figure abruptly pivoted, and she caught a brief glimpse of his retreating back before he disappeared into the depths of the alley behind him.

She glanced up at Kent. "We have to see where he's going. If he has a car, we can provide a description and direction of travel."

He clutched her arm, his big hand circling her biceps. "And if he doesn't, he'll finish what he started before we have a chance."

Her eyes darted to his hand on her arm, then back up to his face. She raised a reproachful brow.

He released his grip. "Fine, but we do this together."

She wasted no time. "He's already made it to the far end of the alley. Let's head across the street before he gets into a vehicle."

He trotted beside her as she ran through the traffic, which had come to a total standstill in the wide boulevard. No wonder police were having trouble responding.

They raced to the building adjacent to the one where she had spotted the muzzle flash. The next building over was also tall, throwing the alley where the sniper had hunkered moments ago into complete darkness. She heard Kent curse and had no trouble guessing what he was thinking.

The fatal funnel.

All law enforcement officers are trained to beware of choke points, places where an armed assailant can hide unseen and lie in wait. This dark alley provided an ideal opportunity for ambush.

She prepared to move forward when a heavy hand came down on her shoulder. This time, Kent's grip was not gentle as he whispered in her ear, "We go in together, Guerrera. As a team. Understood?"

She had the distinct impression he would have held her in place if she didn't agree. She gave him a quick nod and surged forward. She heard his deep, steady breaths as he ran close beside her.

As they made their way along, her eyes adjusted to the gloom, and she saw a figure getting into a car parked across the street from the other side of the alley. When he started the engine, Nina began to sprint toward him. He threw the sedan in gear and looked in her direction. For a split second, their eyes met, then he accelerated, leaving a plume of acrid smoke behind the car's squealing tires.

"Did you get a look at the driver?" Kent asked.

"Yes." She looked up at him. "Clay Forge."

Chapter 48

Flashing red and blue lights cut through the gathering darkness as police converged on the area.

Nina pulled her cell phone out of a side pocket on her spandex running shorts. "We need to give the police a vehicle description, suspect information, and last-known direction of travel," she said to Kent.

"I'll call 9-1-1." Kent was already tapping the numbers on his phone. "You notify Buxton."

As Kent gave a rapid-fire account to the dispatcher, Nina pushed the speed dial button programmed for her supervisor.

"SSA Buxton."

"Sir, you're probably hearing the sirens." She forced herself to slow down. "Kent joined me on my run. Someone shot at us with a high-powered rifle."

Concern hastened Buxton's response. "Are you both okay?"

She assured him they were both uninjured and filled him in.

Buxton waited until she had finished before speaking. "I'm heading down to the parking lot with the team. Meet us where we were before." He disconnected.

Kent ended his call with the dispatcher at the same time. "PPD is setting up a command post in the hotel's west parking lot. We're supposed to report there and give a statement. Patrol officers are setting up a perimeter around this sector of the city."

Turning to walk back through the alley, she spotted something lying on the ground in a crumpled heap. "What's that?"

Kent followed her gaze. "Looks like a drone."

She squatted to get a closer look. "This thing was buzzing around right before you caught up with me. It must have crashed."

The device's white plastic body had shattered, its metallic guts hanging out. Red-and-black-striped wires lay on the asphalt like brightly colored coral snakes. Thoughts of venomous serpents reminded Nina of what Robert Cahill, the staffer at Forge's juvenile detention center, had said.

"I looked into his eyes, and they were cold and flat. Snake eyes."

She looked at Kent. "This drone belongs to Forge. He used it to spot me."

"We need to take it for analysis." Kent bent to pick it up. "We can get a lot of forensic information off—"

"No!" Nina grabbed his arm. "Don't touch it."

"You're right." Kent pulled out his phone again. "We'd better get EOD out here just in case."

She doubted an Explosives Ordnance Disposal unit would find a bomb, but it paid to be careful where Forge was concerned.

Within minutes, a pair of uniformed patrol officers approached them. They cordoned off the area and took up posts at either end of the alley to keep curious onlookers away until EOD arrived.

After thanking them, Nina turned and began to walk back to the hotel parking lot. "He knows I saw him," she said to Kent. "He'll probably ditch the car and the weapon and blend in with pedestrians once he's out of the immediate area."

Kent fell into step beside her. "Still, this is our best chance to catch him before he gets away. What did Buxton say?"

"We'll be meeting our team close to where the PD is setting up their command post."

When they made their way to the hotel parking lot, they found the FBI team, along with Perez, in a huddle near the same corner where they had encountered the reporter earlier.

Breck waved them over. "Are you guys okay?"

"We're fine," Nina said. "Turns out it's tough to hit a moving target."

Nina remembered how Kent had unexpectedly grabbed her arm, halting her a split second before the first shot rang out. If he hadn't done that, she would have been squarely in Forge's crosshairs when he pulled the trigger.

"They want us at the command post," Kent said to Buxton. "We're supposed to give a statement to the police."

"Give me your statement now," Perez said before Buxton could respond. "Then I'll go to the command post and fill them in so you can stay here with your team. They're reviewing video from city cameras set up around this area and using traffic cams to try and track down his vehicle, so they're pretty busy right now working on apprehension."

Nina appreciated not having to leave her team while they processed the new developments as a group. Bouncing ideas off each other could lead to better insights about what Forge might do next. Ideas that might provide police with additional search parameters.

After listening to their account of the incident in detail, Wade directed a question at Kent. "Did Forge target both of you?"

"He completely ignored me," Kent said, adamant. "Every single shot he took was aimed at Guerrera."

Nina wasn't so sure but realized Kent had been in a better position to see where each round had hit relative to their positions. His prior combat training and experience would have also afforded him more expertise with detecting the trajectory of incoming fire.

Wade nodded as if he had expected Kent's answer. "You said Forge appeared to have taken a position of ambush near the hotel?"

"He was lying in wait," Kent said. "He must have set up between those two buildings after he saw Guerrera start jogging and used the drone to zero in on her. A sniper would station himself in a place where he knew his target would be unprotected and on a predictable route. He knew she would come back to the hotel. What he didn't factor in was that I would join her."

"Then Guerrera was the intended target." Buxton made it a statement rather than a question.

"But how would he know I was going for a run?" Nina tapped her chest for emphasis. "I didn't know until five minutes before I went out."

"Maybe he's been watching the hotel," Breck said. "Look at how Snead waylaid us in the parking lot. It's apparently common knowledge this place is where out-of-town law enforcement stays."

For Nina, it didn't add up. "I have trouble believing he's been parked down the street, living in his car, running a fleet of drones outside the hotel day and night, watching for this type of opportunity. It doesn't make sense."

"You're right about that," Breck said. "Drones have a limited flight time. He'd have to keep sending them up on a constant rotation. Eventually, someone would report him." She glanced at Nina. "He knew you went out by yourself, but I can't figure how."

Buxton lowered his voice. "Maybe he's paying someone at the hotel to report on our comings and goings."

"Whatever he did," Kent said, "he didn't just get lucky. He staked out Guerrera somehow, and he damn near killed her." He rested his hands on his hips. "We'll figure out *how* eventually, but I'm more concerned about *why*."

"There's only one reason that makes sense, given his personality and the nature of his crimes," Wade said. "Guerrera represents unfinished business, a loose thread that has to be cut."

Nina heard someone shout her name.

"Agent Guerrera!" Snead beckoned to her from across the parking lot behind the perimeter tape. "Could you comment on the shooting? Was this related to the Llorona case? Was the gunman targeting you?"

"Is this guy for real?" Kent said. "How did he know you had anything to do with a random shooting downtown?"

"Because he was probably listening to a police scanner," Nina said. "A lot of reporters do. When we were talking to those two uniforms by the alley, I could hear their radios. The police dispatcher broadcasted a lookout for the suspect saying he was wanted for attempted murder of a federal agent and also—"

Snead yelled out another question. "Is Clay Forge the prime suspect in the Llorona case?"

"Identifying him by name," Nina finished dryly.

"So much for coordinating the release of information to the public," Buxton muttered, then turned toward the command bus. "We need to ask them to transfer all police communications to a secure channel for this operation going forward."

"I see their Public Affairs officer on the scene," Breck said. "PPD will field all media questions about the shooting in general, but they'll want comment from the FBI since two agents were involved." She turned to Buxton. "How do you want to handle that, sir?"

"We'll put out a joint statement with the Phoenix police department once we have accurate information about the nature of this incident," Buxton said, then turned to Nina. "Agent Guerrera, why don't you head back to your room to shower and grab a change of clothes? Get a couple of uniformed PPD officers to escort you. I need a word with Agent Kent. He'll be right behind you."

No one commented on their supervisor's order. Buxton was a stickler for a neat appearance, but she knew the real reason behind his sudden desire to have her gone from the scene, and it wasn't so she could clean up.

She had become a distraction to the investigation.

Chapter 49

Nina stepped out of the shower to find her cell phone buzzing on the granite counter. Was Buxton calling to tell her the police had caught Forge? Still dripping, she snatched the device without checking the caller ID.

"Guerrera here."

Bianca's voice sounded shrill. "What the fuck, Nina?"

She couldn't help but smile. The more obnoxious her teenaged neighbor acted, the more worried she was.

"It's late on the East Coast, way past your bedtime, Bee."

"Bedtime?" Bianca's volume raised with indignation. "Some psycho uses you for target practice and you're asking me whether I've brushed my teeth and put on my jammies?" There was a brief pause. "Seriously, what the hell is going on in Phoenix?"

"How do you know about what happened all the way across the country in less than an hour?"

"Two words," Bianca said. *"Google. Alerts."*

She shouldn't have been surprised. It was the same tactic Breck used to keep apprised of stories about their investigation in the news and social media. Unlike Bianca, however, Breck was a special agent assigned to work the case.

She tried to lighten the mood. "You ever think of working for the CIA?"

"Yeah, right," Bianca said. "I'd never pass their background check."

"I'm not even going to ask why."

"Getting back to the point—which is you, not me—what's going on?" Bianca said. "Mrs. G's going to crack open her emergency bottle of tequila when she hears about this."

"She doesn't have to hear about it," Nina said. "If you don't tell her."

"You're already all over social media. Somebody uploaded video of you and that hot *G.I. Joe*–looking dude dodging bullets."

"What?" Nina never ceased to be amazed at the instantaneous spread of critical information via the internet. People would never think of providing vital footage to law enforcement when it could score social media hits for them. "I need that video, Bee. The police may not have seen it yet. They're busy trying to track down the shooter."

"I'll send you a link and you can check it out."

"Okay, text it to me"—she remembered who she was talking to— "and any other uploaded livestreams, if you can find more."

"Now you're just insulting me."

"Thanks, Bee."

A light knock sounded at the door dividing the adjoining suites. She threw the hotel robe around herself, made her way across the room, and opened it to find Kent, freshly showered and already dressed.

He pointedly kept his eyes on her face. "How are you holding up?"

Rifle rounds zinging past her ears had rattled her, but she wasn't a delicate flower. "I'm fine, Kent. Was just getting ready to put on some clothes and head downstairs."

"I'll wait for you over here on the sofa." He stepped past her without invitation. "You can get dressed in the bathroom, and we'll go down together."

Had Buxton ordered Kent to stick to her, or had he taken that task upon himself?

"I don't need a babysitter," she said. "Or a bodyguard."

He raised his hand to show her a black plastic device that looked like a cell phone on steroids. "Got this from Perez so I could monitor the police radio traffic. I'll turn it up so you can hear it in the bathroom." He sauntered over to the cluster of furniture in the corner and planted himself on the couch.

She considered insisting that he leave her room, but he turned on the radio, and she heard a cacophony of voices in staccato bursts as the PPD blanketed the downtown area, searching for Forge. Kent had deftly hooked her in.

Ignoring him, she padded to the closet, where she contemplated the collection of conservative business suits she'd brought back with her. Would it be gray, black, or navy? So many choices. She lifted the hanger with the gray pantsuit and paired it with a silky red top, then fished a set of underwear out of the drawer on the way back to the bathroom, leaving the door ajar to hear the police radio as she got dressed. It didn't sound like the police were having any luck locating Forge.

Thoughts of Forge brought the shooting to mind. How had he known she would be out alone and vulnerable to attack? As Breck had pointed out, he couldn't have had drones flying around, hoping for an opportunity that would likely never come. And as Kent had observed, he could not have set up with his rifle in time to intercept her on the way out, but he could catch her on the way in.

Forge seemed to know far too much, and he was clearly feeding Snead. But how did he know to look into her past to connect her to the Llorona case? First, he had successfully sidelined her from the investigation, then he had tried to kill her when she was by herself.

She finished putting on her clothes and pushed the bathroom door all the way open. Kent was still on the sofa, holding the radio, monitoring the barrage of transmissions. A frisson of awareness traveled through her as she watched Kent listening in on what the police were saying.

Something about the whole situation bugged her. She froze as the last two words ricocheted through her mind.

Bugged her.

Forge was an electronics expert. He installed security systems that incorporated audio, visual, and other means of surveillance. Everyone in the city knew where they were staying. How hard would it be to gain access to her hotel room?

Kent noticed she had come out and got to his feet. "You ready to go?" He switched off the portable police radio and silence filled the room.

She stood, transfixed. If Forge was eavesdropping on the team somehow, perhaps they could trace the signal or lure him into a trap. She couldn't do anything to alert him and cut off their best chance of pinpointing his location.

Where would Forge plant a device? She scanned the room. Shortly after becoming an agent, she had posed as a cleaning lady to hide bugs in the office of a CEO under investigation for funneling money to terrorist organizations through his business. As instructed by the techs, she had used a smoke alarm, a corner lamp, and a desk clock to create a steady power source so the devices wouldn't need batteries that might die at an inopportune moment.

"Guerrera?" Kent took a tentative step toward her.

What if Forge had installed a pinhole camera and could also watch them? How could she signal to Kent that she wanted to look for a device without making it obvious?

She couldn't. And everything depended on the next couple of minutes.

She faced Kent and hitched her lips into a smile. "I need to . . . uh . . ." She glanced at the desk, noting the lamp. "I need to leave a note for the cleaning crew. We're out of toilet paper."

She strolled over to the desk and sat down. Lifting the pen and pulling the small notepad with the hotel crest in front of her, she leaned forward and pretended to try to turn on the lamp.

"Something's wrong." She peered under the wide brim of the shade. "The light won't turn on."

"Let me see," Kent said, moving behind her.

She wanted to throttle him with his tie. "It's just a loose bulb, I've got it." She stuck her head up higher and twisted the base of the light bulb with her fingers, deliberately loosening it. She figured she had about ten seconds before Forge would become suspicious—if he was listening or watching.

When she tilted the lamp, something caught her eye. A tiny red-and-black-striped wire was sticking out of the metal housing next to the lamp pull.

A cold chill crept down her spine. The wire looked like a coral snake.

Mind racing, she tightened the light bulb, straightened the lamp, and switched it on. "Problem solved."

The distinctive coloring of the exposed wires was as good as a signature. But how would Forge have gained access to the room when they weren't around? She had posed as a cleaning lady to plant a device. What if . . .

It hit her with the force of a physical blow. Hotel staff. She recalled the bellman who had quickly bent to tie his shoe when she'd gotten out of the elevator a few days ago, averting his face. FBI agents occasionally used the same tactic. People in uniform were anonymous—they blended in like wallpaper.

"Did you finish your note?" Kent asked her. "We should get going."

She scrawled out a few words on the pad for show and stood. "I'll grab my gun and my creds."

She pulled her duffel out of the closet and geared up while she considered the situation. Did Kent have devices in his room as well?

Highly likely. There was nothing she could say until she was sure they were not only out of the room but out of the hotel.

Forge had known everything about the investigation from the outset, and they had been looking at it all wrong. They didn't need a plumber to fix a leak—they needed an exterminator to eliminate bugs.

Chapter 50

Nina rushed down the hall on the thirty-first floor to the elevator, barely letting the doors close behind Kent before repeatedly pounding the *L* button for the lobby.

As they descended, Kent regarded her with mounting concern on his chiseled features. "Nina, what the hell is going on with you?"

"Nothing. I'm just anxious to get back to the team."

"You seem anxious in general."

She waved a dismissive hand. "Don't psychoanalyze me."

The elevator doors slid open and she hurried out. Kent matched her strides, appearing as if he wanted to say something but was keeping silent with difficulty.

She found her team beside the idling Phoenix police command bus, which took up a corner of the parking lot. Portable lights had been set up, allowing an overflow of detectives and patrol officers to share incoming reports from the field in the search for the gunman.

She waited impatiently while Buxton finished speaking to a patrol supervisor, who thanked him and went inside the packed command bus.

"Any sign of Forge?" she asked, hearing the breathlessness in her own voice.

"He's a ghost," Buxton said. "City cams show him abandoning his car on Grand Avenue. Patrol just checked out the empty vehicle, which was illegally parked along the side of the street. He left the rifle inside.

Video shows him on foot heading westbound on Roosevelt Street. He went inside a homeless shelter. PPD is checking everyone inside, but it looks like Forge grabbed someone else's jacket and slipped out before they locked the place down."

"EOD checked out the drone," Breck added. "No explosives. Forensic techs are going over it now to see what we can recover, but it doesn't look promising."

Nina couldn't wait any longer. "I know how we might be able to flush him out." She motioned for the rest of the team to follow her to a quiet corner of the parking lot away from the bustle.

She glanced around, making sure they were alone, then dropped her voice. "I found a listening device attached to the desk lamp in our hotel room. There was a red-and-black-striped electrical wire sticking out of it, exactly like—"

"The one in the drone," Kent said. "That's why you were acting weird."

"Where is the device now?" Buxton asked. "Did you deactivate it?"

"I figured we could use it to lure him out, so I left it where it was," she said. "Where it's probably been since we checked in." She let it sink in that their investigation had been compromised from the start. "We've been trying to figure out how he could have set up an ambush attack when I made up my mind to go jogging less than ten minutes before I was out the door." She turned to Breck. "The only person I mentioned it to was you."

"In our room," Breck said on a groan. "I also told Kent where you were when he came looking for you a few minutes later."

"That works," Kent said. "If Forge was eavesdropping, he would have had enough time to send up a drone so he would know when you were getting close to the hotel. He would also assume you wouldn't have a weapon. You were alone, unsuspecting, and vulnerable."

Buxton looked at Nina. "You mentioned a way to flush him out?"

She was certain her supervisor had planned to bench her earlier but now seemed to have granted her a stay of execution. Time to push her luck as far as it would go.

"Forge wants to finish what he started with my birth family twenty-eight years ago. He's watching and listening in the hotel room. Why not use both of those facts to our advantage?"

"What exactly do you have in mind?"

"After we clear this scene in a couple of hours, we go back to our rooms. We all talk about the shooting, and discuss how I'll be featured on the eleven o'clock news tonight. SSA Buxton will order me to catch a flight back to Washington tomorrow. I'll argue against it."

"At least you'll be true to character," Buxton muttered.

"Tomorrow morning, the rest of you will leave for the PFO, but I'll stay in my hotel room to pack for my flight." She hesitated, making sure she had the details worked out in her mind. She would get only one chance to convince the others. "After everyone else is gone, I'll take a phone call from a CI, and I'll put it on speaker so Forge can hear the conversation."

Buxton looked as if he might have expected anything but this. "How would you have a confidential informant in Arizona when you work out of Virginia?"

"I wouldn't," Nina said. "But Forge doesn't know that. We can pretend that an informant provided information to me when I was in Phoenix a few months ago. Forge would know I was in town on a big case recently. It would be plausible."

"And why is this mystery CI calling you, Agent Guerrera?"

"The CI will say he has time-sensitive intel on a new case, but he doesn't want to talk about it over the phone." She waved a hand. "Make it domestic terrorism or something, doesn't matter."

Buxton pursed his lips. "Keep going."

"I tell him I'm leaving soon and ask him if he wants to drive me from the hotel to the airport so we can talk on the way. He's too scared to be seen with me in public, so he wants to meet me somewhere on the way to Sky Harbor where there aren't many people around instead."

Buxton closed his eyes and tilted his head back as if summoning patience. "Let's say—for argument's sake—that I approve of this . . . plan." He leveled his gaze on her again. "What happens next?"

"We choose a location between the hotel and the airport where there won't be much foot traffic," she said. "Like a warehouse district. Then we get our people in place and do a takedown."

"We wait until Forge heads toward the location, then pick him up?"

"Yes, but I have to actually go to the meeting spot myself in case he's watching." She thought about Forge's technical skills. "He probably has more than one drone, and he'll make sure he can see me at all times, or he won't show."

"Let me get this straight," Kent said, looking every bit as skeptical as Buxton. "You want to dangle yourself out there as bait?"

She shrugged. "What better way to lure a fish than by baiting a hook?"

"He isn't a fish," Wade said, entering the fray. "Like Cahill said, he's a snake, and he'll sense a trap."

"It's up to us to sell it," Nina said. "If it doesn't work, he doesn't bite, and we haven't lost anything."

Kent rested a hand on his hip. "What if he sends someone else to kill you?"

"Forge always operates alone." Nina looked to Wade for verification.

Wade nodded his agreement, then said, "What makes you think he'll go for it?"

"From his perspective, it's the last time I'll be alone before I fly out of town. If he doesn't get me tomorrow morning, he'll have to chase me all the way to DC, and there are now outstanding felony warrants out for him. He couldn't board a plane, rent a car, or even get a bus ticket without setting off alarms. His mobility is now severely limited, and he knows it."

Kent didn't look convinced. "He probably has a fake ID or two, and he'll hide out until he can get to you when you're not expecting it."

"You've made my point for me," Nina said. "I'd rather take him down now when I'm ready and have a plan in place than spend the next year or two of my life looking over my shoulder."

"She's right," Wade said. "He's not finished with her." He turned to Buxton. "There are two ways this can go down. On his terms or on ours. I'd rather surprise him than have him surprise us."

Buxton frowned. "Agent Guerrera cannot participate in the investigation until we have the results of her DNA test tomorrow morning."

"Technically, I'm not investigating," Nina said. "This is a separate tactical operation."

Buxton's dark features tensed as he considered the situation. Nina was asking him to weigh the potential for issues with the prosecution against the potential for future harm to one of his agents.

When Buxton gave her a reluctant nod, she knew the matter was settled.

"We get our best people on this, and we do it in conjunction with the PPD," Buxton said. "I want every asset we can get." His eyes narrowed. "This plan had better be tight enough to squeak."

Nina suppressed a smile. There was one good thing that had come from this shooting. She wasn't going back to Washington anytime soon. Her testimony as the only eyewitness who could definitively put Forge behind the rifle would be needed for the upcoming criminal prosecution. If they caught him.

She gave herself a mental shake. *When* they caught him.

Chapter 51

Nina met Special Agent Brad Harper's gaze, fully aware the Phoenix FBI Hostage Rescue Team leader was not happy with her. Approval for the operation had worked its way through the chain of command, and they had gathered with the PPD's Special Assignment Unit at their facility to work out the details. Unfortunately, Harper had spent the past hour becoming increasingly annoyed by those details.

"There's not one part of this operation I'm comfortable with," Harper said. He cut his eyes to Breck. "Are you having any luck tracing the transmitter signal from the listening device?"

"Forge is smart," Breck said. "He's got the wireless signal bouncing all over the place. I can't pinpoint a source without physically testing the unit. Since we also know he's thorough—he'll have more than one bug in the room. He'll know what we're up to and shut it down immediately. It's called redundancy, and it's what we do when we're planting . . ." Her face flamed as she turned to Nina. "Holy shit, what if he put a pinhole camera in our bathroom?"

Nina was way past caring if Forge saw her naked. Thanks to her last major investigation, almost everyone with internet service already had. "Frankly, that's the least of my worries," she said to Breck, then directed her attention to Harper. "This operation is the only chance we have of catching up to Forge before he kills someone else."

She made the stakes clear.

Harper didn't look convinced. "We're giving up the high ground," he said. "Puts us at a tactical disadvantage."

Nina argued her point. Again. "Forge has already used a drone once. There's every possibility he will deploy another one for recon. If he does, we'll catch him."

Nina had proposed a two-mile perimeter around the meeting spot since commercially available drones had maximum range of less than a mile from the controller. If Forge came in person, they would take him down. If he sent a drone, they would close the net around the area, catching him inside. She liked the logic of the operation, but Harper seemed determined to point out flaws.

"I understand why we can't put countersnipers on the roof, but I still don't like it." Harper rubbed the back of his neck. "He used a high-powered rifle earlier. The sonofabitch probably has another one, and he could reach out and touch you at over twelve hundred yards. He's shown a propensity for a long-range attack."

"No operation is perfect," Buxton said, coming to her defense. "What sold me on this plan is that it's proactive." When Harper gave him a quizzical look, he crossed the room to point at a photo of Forge that had been taped to the wall. "Our profile indicates Mr. Forge will continue to pursue Agent Guerrera."

"So why are we offering her up on a platter?" Harper asked.

"Because he already ambushed Agent Guerrera once," Buxton said. "He's still at large, so he could strike at any time or place, but if we lay a trap, we can lure him into a position where we control his movements." Buxton swept a hand out toward the cadre of black-clad tactical personnel on the other side of the room. "We take him down now, when we're prepared, rather than giving him another opportunity for a surprise attack when we don't have all these resources in place."

"Why don't we put a detail on Guerrera?" Harper said. "I can assign some of my team to—"

"Are you going to guard me around the clock for the next four years?" Nina cut in. "Until recently, that's how long Forge has waited between kills. He's demonstrated that he's patient, and a meticulous planner."

Buxton stepped close to Harper and spoke in a low voice. "I've made my decision. Will your team assist us, or do we rely on the Phoenix police SWAT team for tactical support?"

Nina hid a smile. She had never seen Buxton play dirty. His ultimatum had the desired effect, as he no doubt knew it would.

"We'll help," Harper muttered, then raised his voice to address the room. "We believe Forge will only fall for the ruse if everything appears exactly as expected. The teams must be in place and concealed before Guerrera receives the decoy phone call from Detective Perez."

They had agreed that Perez would play the role of her confidential informant. Kent had volunteered for the assignment, but Buxton felt Forge would recognize him from the downtown shooting incident. Perez, on the other hand, could easily disguise himself to blend in with the local Latino population.

The police SWAT leader affirmed his support. "My team can maintain position for hours if necessary."

"It won't be," Wade said. "When Perez calls Guerrera, she will make it a point to say when her flight leaves. We'll make sure there's an actual flight at that time in case Forge checks. That way, we narrow the time he has to act to a small window."

"We'll block all ingress and egress points as soon as his vehicle is past our zone of control," Harper added. "He can go in, but he can't get out."

Nina grinned. "Like a roach motel."

The others chuckled, but Harper's scowl remained firmly in place. "We'll have stop sticks, bull's-eye perimeters, and the air unit up a few miles away. He's not going anywhere."

"Let's go over safety precautions for Agent Guerrera," Buxton said.

"We'll have two wireless transmitters on her," Harper said. "A primary and a backup. One is voice activated, and the other will be hot at all times. She'll also be able to hear SSA Buxton through her earpiece."

She looked at the tiny device. There was no telltale curly cord to dangle along the side of her neck. Once tucked inside her ear, the transmitter would be invisible.

"Keep the equipment zipped inside this bag until you get out of the hotel in case Forge has a way to watch you," Harper told her as he handed her a small black duffel. "Put the com unit on in the car on the way over, where he can't see you."

Once she took the bag, Harper continued, "We've already scoped out a location for the operation. Guerrera and Perez will make contact by the side of the building. There's a concrete post there they can use for cover if necessary." He looked around the room. "As soon as anyone spots the subject, we allow him into the perimeter, where we will initiate takedown procedures."

A police sergeant spoke up. "If a civilian enters the area, the Bravo team will move in to intercept."

Some of the tactical team members would be dressed in Phoenix municipal-worker coveralls over their SWAT gear. It would be their responsibility to redirect anyone coming into the area without drawing suspicion, explaining that gas company employees were repairing a gas main and the area would be closed for the next hour or two.

"Let's divide up," Buxton said. He tipped his head toward Harper. "You and the PPD sergeant can fine-tune your deployment while we rehearse the phone call."

Nina and Perez had sketched out a script for the phone call Perez would make to Nina posing as an informant asking her to meet with him. The call would have to take place in the hotel room, where the bug could pick it up.

Perez held an imaginary cell phone to his ear, and they began to practice their lines.

"Ugh," Wade said a minute later when they were finished. "We're going to have to work on that script."

"Yeah, I'm having trouble buying it," Kent said.

"This isn't Shakespeare." Nina put a hand on her hip. "All we have to do is convince Forge I'm going to be at a certain location at a specific time, that I'll be alone and there won't be a lot of witnesses around."

"I don't like it," Kent said. "I want to be on the ground with Guerrera."

"Ginsberg will be there, posing as the cabdriver," Nina pointed out. "And Perez will be with me too."

"But you'll be out in the open," Kent said.

"I'm going to be exposed anyway." She refused to put more people than necessary in danger. "That's the point. It makes me a more tempting target."

"We're going to dominate the space," Wade said. "We'll be in control of every aspect of the scene."

"Let's look at the time frame," Buxton said when Kent showed signs of continuing the argument. "We need to give Mr. Forge enough lead time so he can get to the location from wherever he's hiding."

"I'm guessing his hidey-hole is close by if he's still determined to target Guerrera," Breck said.

"How about we give Forge half an hour, then?" Nina suggested.

"Might be cutting it too close," Wade said. "He's abandoned his vehicle and knows we're looking for him. We need to give him time to get transportation to the location. I'd say give him an hour—any less and he might feel like he can't make it. He wants Guerrera, but he's also a control freak. He needs to feel like he has some ability to coordinate his assault, or he may not take the bait."

The bait. Meaning her.

"Make it an hour," Buxton said, closing that part of the discussion. "All of our plans have to be completed here, because when we get back to the hotel, we have to assume he's monitoring us the moment we pass through the front doors."

A sobering thought. "We should lay the groundwork for the ruse tonight," Nina said to him.

Buxton nodded. "After we get upstairs, I'll go to Guerrera's room to tell her she's off the case and order her back to DC in the morning."

"As we discussed previously, I'll argue because I want to keep investigating," Nina said. "And because nobody would believe it if I didn't."

A ghost of a smile played across Buxton's lips. "After I leave the room, you can talk smack about me to Breck. Tell her how much you want to stay on the case. That will help sell the idea that a call from a CI would be something you would jump at for an excuse to stay involved."

Breck pursed her lips. "Creeps me out that Forge will be listening— and maybe watching—while we're in our room."

"Try to act natural," Nina said.

Breck cocked her head to one side. "You'll forgive me if I don't take a shower tonight?"

Nina shrugged. "If there's a pinhole camera in the bathroom, he's already gotten an eyeful."

Breck reddened. "You would have to point that out."

Nina, distracted by her conversation with Breck, balked when a slender man wearing latex gloves approached her. "What are you doing with that thing?" She glared at a long white swab in his hand.

Buxton answered before the man could respond. "He's here at my request, Agent Guerrera." He motioned for the man to continue. "He's taking a buccal swab for processing at the lab."

She may have forgotten about Buxton's order to submit her DNA for comparison with the Vega family, but her supervisor had not.

Reluctantly, she opened her mouth and allowed the tech to scrape the inside of her cheek with the plastic tube.

Buxton made a point of watching the proceedings. "We might be in the middle of planning a tactical operation, but we still need answers."

Unfortunately, she already knew what the answer to this particular question would be.

Chapter 52

At precisely eight o'clock the next morning, Nina sat alone at her hotel room's desk under the glow of the lamp with the listening device. The rest of the team had departed for the FBI's Phoenix field office building thirty minutes earlier. Her phone vibrated with a call. Showtime.

She tapped the icon to put the call on speaker. "Guerrera."

Perez's voice came out clearly. "*Hola*, Agent Guerrera, it's me."

"Who is this?"

"It's Pablo," Perez said, flavoring his speech with a Mexican accent. "You remember the last time you were in Phoenix and I gave you that info? I kept your number."

"How do you even know I'm in town?"

"I watch the news. You're here on that Llorona case."

Nina stuck to the script. "Listen, Pablo, I don't have time to talk. I'm leaving for the airport soon."

"You'll want to see me before you go."

"Why is that?"

"I have information."

"About what?"

"I don't want to talk about it over the phone. This is serious shit. These guys are terrorists."

"I can have someone on my FBI team interview you."

"No. I only talk to you."

"Pablo, my flight leaves in three hours."

"Plenty of time to meet me first. There's an industrial park near Sky Harbor Airport. Come and hear me out. If you don't think it's legit, you can catch your flight."

Nina let out a theatrical sigh. "Okay . . . where and when?"

"There's a warehouse at the corner of Jasper and Arroyo Streets. Nobody's around in the mornings. I'll meet you there in an hour."

"I'll be there, but I can't stay long."

"You won't regret it," Perez said and disconnected.

Chapter 53

Forty minutes after her phone call with Perez, Nina rolled her small suitcase down the sidewalk next to the hotel to avoid the taxi stand. The Phoenix police had scrounged up an impounded yellow cab for Agent Ginsberg from the FBI field office to drive her to the meeting location. She spotted him waiting by the curb on Second Street and hopped inside, tossing her bag on the seat beside her.

"There's a bottle of water in the cooler if you want any." Ginsberg's eyes met hers in the rearview. "I always come prepared."

She nodded and provided the response that would confirm everything was a go. "Nothing like Phoenix heat to make you thirsty."

They had agreed to the wording of the exchange last night at the ops-planning meeting, operating under strict countersurveillance protocols until verifying they could speak freely.

Nina bent to open the cooler and pulled out a black device the size of a deck of cards and switched it on. Breck had shown her how to use the signal detector at the briefing. Since Forge had gotten inside their hotel room, he might have planted listening devices, trackers, and cameras in her luggage or tactical gear as well.

She discreetly passed the scanner over her bag and clothing, getting a response only when she got near the back of Ginsberg's head.

He tapped his ear. "I'm off now."

The beeping stopped. She gave Ginsberg a nod. "We're clear."

He tapped his ear to switch his transmitter back on. "We're clear," he repeated for the team's benefit, then turned to her. "We installed dark tint on the cab's side and back windows early this morning. Go ahead and mic up."

As Ginsberg turned south onto Seventh Street, threading the taxi through light traffic, she fished out the zippered bag Harper had given her last night.

"Did everything go okay?" Ginsberg wanted to know.

She hadn't put on her audio equipment but knew Ginsberg was asking on behalf of everyone listening on the com system. In operational terms, she'd been "dark" since the team had left the hotel an hour earlier, and the others would be anxious to hear how her end of the phone call with Perez had gone.

"Pablo came through loud and clear." She spoke with enough volume for Ginsberg's equipment to pick up her voice. "We're good to go."

After her well-rehearsed conversation with Perez, she had gone through an equally well-rehearsed performance when she left the hotel. In case Forge was somehow observing, she wanted to appear as if the phone call had suddenly altered her plans. There would be no other reason for her to change into operational attire.

She had rolled her suitcase through the lobby decked out in black BDUs, a black T-shirt, and a webbed belt with a pancake holster. A Glock semiautomatic, a ballistic vest, and black tactical boots completed the ensemble.

Nina pushed in the earpiece and activated it. "Mic check."

Buxton's deep voice resonated. "I copy, Agent Guerrera."

"I copy, too, sir."

"Good. We're already in position. From this point forward, we'll use our com system."

Ginsberg drove in silence as she listened to chatter from various members of the tactical and surveillance teams. As they coordinated last-minute position adjustments, Nina recalled Perez explaining how the media used scanners to listen to police-radio traffic. Forge was adept with electronics. Could he do the same?

"He can't intercept our transmissions, can he?" she asked no one in particular.

"We're on a secure channel." She recognized Harper's voice in her earpiece. "And it's scrambled."

Relieved, yet wary, she continued to listen as they approached the industrial park. Ginsberg pulled to a stop at the deserted intersection where Perez, a.k.a. Pablo, had told her they would meet.

She got out, walked to the corner of the building she had seen in photographs during the briefing the night before, and spoke in a low tone. "I'm in position."

"We've got eyes on you," Harper said. "What do you see?"

She continued to speak softly, avoiding moving her lips in case Forge had a visual on her. "No movement. No vehicle in the vicinity, but he could have parked somewhere nearby and come on foot, or he could have hailed a cab."

"Okay, keep me apprised of any developments."

"Copy that."

She ambled around, periodically gazing down the street as if looking for Pablo to arrive. As she glanced around, she tried to spot any sign of FBI or PPD tactical operators. They had done an excellent job—the street appeared deserted. If Forge was watching, he wouldn't see any obvious signs of law enforcement presence.

Fifteen minutes went by. She pretended to scratch her nose, covering the movement of her mouth as she spoke. "Maybe he's waiting to see if my CI shows up."

Perez responded immediately. "I'll head your way."

"No." She did not want the detective exposed to danger. "Let's give it more time. If he sends up a drone, I want him to see me alone."

She paced back and forth, doubt filling her mind. Where the hell was Clay Forge?

Chapter 54

Forge stepped on the gas as he turned into the residential area in Central Phoenix. He shook his head in disgust. It had all been a setup. Did they think they were dealing with an amateur? Did they believe hiding in the shadows a few blocks down the street would be enough to evade detection?

When he had listened in on Nina Guerrera's phone call, he had prepared a drone to do a flyover of the meeting area. He'd hesitated because it was close to the airport. People tended to call in complaints about drones near flight paths, and he didn't want to draw attention to himself.

Then he remembered.

Jexton had the security contract for one of the buildings in the sprawling industrial complex adjacent to Sky Harbor. He pulled out the special laptop he had taken from his house and accessed the portal that had served him so well over the years. The portal that gave him back-door access to Jexton's extensive database and the ability to remotely manipulate its systems.

In less than thirteen minutes, he was maneuvering roof-mounted security cameras close to the intersection where she was supposed to be waiting. He had seen SWAT vehicles vomiting out teams of men wearing tactical black, talking into earpieces. That was all he needed to know. Now he would turn the tables on all of them.

He glanced at his watch. Nine o'clock in the morning. She should be up by now. He rang the doorbell and heard shuffling feet inside the house.

The intercom buzzed on. "Who's there?"

He raised the brown-wrapped parcel toward the lens, using it to obscure his face. "Delivery for Selena Fernandez." He made a show of glancing down at the side of the box. "There's a note on the side that says it's a belated baby shower gift."

The door opened and a very pregnant woman peered out at him. "Who's it from?"

He provided the one name certain to gain her trust. "Teresa Soto."

"Why would my mother send me another gift for the baby?"

He shrugged. "You have to sign for it." He held up his phone, turning the screen sideways to display an empty signature line with her name in block lettering underneath it.

She heaved a sigh, shooed the cat from the doorway, and waddled outside, closing it behind her to prevent the little beast from escaping.

They were alone in the secluded courtyard. He knew her husband was at work. She was all alone. Vulnerable. A fat, juicy worm for his hook.

Nina Guerrera had laid a trap for him. Now she would be the one to fall into his. The difference was that his snare would prove deadly.

Time for phase three. The final phase.

Chapter 55

Nina did not want to admit defeat. Nearly an hour had passed, and she could only conclude that Forge either hadn't taken the bait or hadn't overheard the phone call.

"He's not coming," Buxton said into her earpiece. "Let's pack up and regroup."

She glanced at her watch. "Another five minutes."

This time it was the HRT leader who spoke through the com system. "You said that fifteen minutes ago. And thirty minutes before that." Exasperation sharpened his tone. "The operation has been compromised. I'm calling it."

Buxton convened a quick debrief at the command post they had set up inside a city-owned building down the street. After going over the morning's events, both SWAT teams loaded their gear and departed for their respective bases, leaving the FBI team and Perez to figure out their next steps.

"This is on me," Nina told them. "I take full responsibility. We'll have to wait for another opportunity to find Forge."

Buxton shifted uncomfortably. "That's no longer your concern, Agent Guerrera."

She stilled. "What do you mean?"

"I received a phone call from the lab a few minutes ago," Buxton said quietly.

All eyes turned to her. Knowing the results of her DNA comparison in advance didn't make it any easier to hear her boss relay the news.

"You are the biological child of Victor and Maria Vega," Buxton said. "You cannot work this case anymore. As I said before, you need to go back to Washington."

The analytical part of her understood the reasoning, but the emotional side railed against the injustice of it. "Sir, I can still help. I'll stay at the PFO and—"

Buxton held up a hand. "This is not up for debate. You are to report to the hotel and wait. There's a flight leaving for Dulles Airport in four hours. You will be on it."

"Sir, I'd like the opportunity to confirm the news reports for my . . . families."

"I understand, Agent Guerrera, but your life is in jeopardy. For your own safety, as well as for the integrity of the investigation, you cannot visit any of your relatives until Mr. Forge is in custody." He rested a hand on her shoulder in a rare display of emotion. "I'll notify them personally. Without alarming them about your situation, I'll explain that you will be able to visit them soon."

She had wanted to be the one to tell them. And to explain. Now even that would be taken from her.

Buxton removed his hand. "The rest of us will head to the command center while Agent Kent drives you back to the hotel. You can grab a bite at the bistro there and make sure you didn't leave anything in your room when you packed earlier." A look passed between her supervisor and Kent. "He'll take you to the airport and see you onto the plane."

As she had suspected, Kent had been assigned bodyguard duty. She bristled but held her tongue.

"Speaking of the hotel," Breck said, "what about the bug in our room?"

"Leave it there," Buxton said. "We aren't sure why Forge didn't show. We may still be able to use the device to lure him out of hiding."

After transferring her suitcase from the cab to the Suburban, Nina rode back to the Phoenix Royal Suites with Kent in relative silence. They both tried to make small talk, giving up after each successive attempt at conversation fizzled.

They got out after Kent parked in the side lot, and Nina walked toward the back of the SUV. She had packed all her belongings to keep up the ruse in case Forge had been watching, and now she was conveniently prepared to leave town.

"Forge is probably halfway to California by now," she said to Kent. "I'm the last thing on his mind. I can take my bag into the hotel so you can get back to work with the rest of the team. I'll catch a cab to the airport in a couple of hours."

"You're not getting rid of me, Guerrera."

Resigned to the situation, she left her suitcase in the vehicle and walked to the hotel's main entrance.

"You hungry?" Kent asked when they were inside the expansive lobby. "We can eat at the bistro on the mezzanine level."

Before she could respond, someone spoke from behind her.

"Excuse me, are you Agent Guerrera with the FBI?"

Nina turned to see a bellman. He looked young, maybe early twenties. His red-and-gray uniform hung from his bony frame.

"I am," Nina said.

He eyed Kent warily. "Can I speak to you alone?"

"No." Kent drew closer to her. "You cannot."

"This is Special Agent Kent," she told the bellman. "Whatever you have to say, he can hear too."

With evident reluctance, the young man pulled a silver cell phone from his pocket. "A guy handed me a hundred dollars and told me to give this to you."

She reached for it, but Kent stayed her hand. "What guy?" he said. "When?"

The kid looked like he was ready to bolt. "I don't know the guy. It was about an hour ago. He told me to hang around the lobby and watch out for you. Said if you showed up, I should give you the phone and tell you to hit speed dial number one."

She pulled her arm free of Kent's grasp and took the phone. "What did the man look like?"

The bellman shrugged. "White, about fifty. I don't know. Just a regular guy."

Kent narrowed his eyes. "Has he been paying you to keep tabs on us?"

The bellman's Adam's apple bobbed as he swallowed audibly. "N-no, sir."

While Kent was busy scaring the crap out of the kid, Nina examined the cell. There was no screen lock.

"What are you doing, Guerrera?" Kent turned away from the bellman. "That thing could be programmed to explode. We should call EOD."

"He didn't leave a package for me," she said, pivoting away as he grabbed for the phone. "He left me a communication device. That means he wants to talk. If he had wanted to kill me right now, he would have already done it."

Kent stopped trying to take the phone from her. Heart pounding, she opened the screen and pressed number one on the keypad, activating the speed dial feature. The call connected almost instantly.

Nina put the phone to her ear. "Who is this?"

A slight pause. "This is Clay Forge, Agent Guerrera. I have something that might interest you."

Kent tilted his head toward hers, trying to listen in. "Forge?"

"Is that the Viking you were jogging with yesterday?" Forge said. "Get rid of him."

"He's my partner," Nina said.

"This is between you and me. He's not welcome."

"Can't make out what he's saying," Kent whispered to her. "Put him on speaker."

Nina looked pointedly at the bellman.

Kent took the hint, rounding on the kid. "Go stand by the front desk. I'm not done with you."

Nina tapped the speaker icon. "What is it, Forge?"

"Check your text messages. I sent you an image."

She clicked over to messages and opened the only file. "I can see the photo. It's . . ." She leaned closer and sucked in a breath.

"What?" Kent said, crowding her.

"It's Selena," Nina whispered. "Forge has Teresa's daughter."

Chapter 56

"Let her go." Nina barely managed to choke out the words as she extended her hand to show Kent an image of Forge holding a gun to Selena's head.

"Do what I tell you," Forge said, "or your cousin gets hurt."

Her cousin. Of course. That's what this was all about. That's why he had targeted Selena. She forced calm into her voice. "What do you want, Forge?"

"A trade."

"Trade?"

"For you, Agent Guerrera." He paused for emphasis. "Her life for yours."

"I'll do it," Nina said without hesitation. "But you'll have to let her go first."

She saw Kent's entire body tense as he stood next to her.

"Do you think I'm stupid?" Forge said. "You have five minutes to go out front and hail a cab. I have people in the hotel watching you. Once you are in the cab, call me and I will give you an address. Have the driver take you there."

Too bad the fake taxi they had set up earlier was already back at the police impound lot. There was no time to get it back.

"Oh, and Agent Guerrera"—he paused a beat—"leave the Viking at the hotel. I'll know if you're in the taxi alone." He disconnected.

Kent went straight to DEFCON 1. "There's no way you're doing this."

"He's holding a gun to my pregnant cousin's head." She deliberately mentioned the family connection, reminding him that Forge had chosen Selena for a reason. "There are two lives at stake here."

Even if he couldn't condone her actions, she hoped he could admit he would react the same way under similar circumstances.

She turned toward the door, and Kent latched on to her arm. Hard. She looked up at him. His mouth had flattened into a tight line. She considered her options. He could easily overpower her physically. This was a fight she could not win using conventional warfare.

So she fought dirty.

She redirected his protective instincts from her to where they belonged. An innocent woman and her unborn child.

"Kent, I have to do this. He took Selena because of me. I'm the only one who can save her . . . and the baby."

"We don't have time to set up an operation like we did this morning," he said. "I won't let you walk in there with no plan, no backup, and no exit strategy."

He had unwittingly given her an opening.

"Then be my backup."

"How am I supposed to do that? He's going to make sure you come alone."

"We still have our com systems." She tapped her ear. "All you have to do is call Buxton and Harper to have them reactivated."

He appeared to give it some thought. She saw the wheels turning and sensed the moment he caved.

"Buxton is going to have my ass," he said, then released her arm. "I'll have the com links up and running ASAP. In the meantime, stall long enough for me to get in the car. I'll follow you from a distance. Once you hear someone in your ear, find an excuse to repeat your destination."

She didn't wait for him to change his mind. Turning, she marched past the young bellman on her way out to the taxi stand. Her five minutes must almost be up.

The valet ushered her into a yellow cab idling at the curb. As soon as he closed the door, the cabbie glanced at her in the rearview mirror.

"Where to?" he said in a dense accent she couldn't place.

"Hold on a sec." She pulled out the phone and tapped the speed dial.

"The meter's running," the driver said over his shoulder.

She held up a finger, silently asking the cabbie for one minute while the call connected.

"I hope you didn't waste time planning any surprises," Forge said. "I wouldn't like that. Neither would your cousin."

She glanced through the rear window to see Kent across the parking lot, getting into the Suburban, cell phone to his ear, talking fast.

She made sure her earpiece was on, ready to pick up transmissions when it was reactivated. "The cabdriver wants an address," she said into the phone. "What do I tell him?"

"Tell him to take you to the intersection of Mariposa Avenue and Saguaro Street. Once you get there, call me." He disconnected.

She repeated the instructions to the driver, who pulled away from the curb, a quizzical expression pinching his features.

Within five minutes, she heard Buxton's voice in her ear. "Agent Guerrera, do you copy?"

She didn't want the cabbie to think she was talking to herself, so she put her phone to her ear. "Glad you called, boss."

He picked up on the situation immediately. "All right, I understand you're not alone. We'll play this like a phone call."

"Sounds good."

"Agent Kent filled me in. He's a few car lengths behind you. I've contacted Agent Harper, and he's got the HRT rolling. You'll be able to hear him on the com system shortly."

"Got it."

"Where are you headed?"

She gave him the cross streets. "I'm supposed to call when I get to the intersection."

The cabbie's bushy brows snapped together as he glanced at her in the rearview again.

"Copy that." It was Harper's voice this time. "That location won't be the final destination. Sounds like the subject is going to use countersurveillance measures."

She agreed and pretended to end the phone call.

"We are here, miss," the cabbie said a few minutes later. He pulled to the curb near the corner of the two streets and idled. "That will be sixteen dollars and—"

"I need to go somewhere else," she cut in. "Let me make a quick call."

Forge picked up almost immediately. "Tell the driver to take you to 1312 Paseo Drive," he said. "Call me when you're standing in front of the main entrance to the building."

She repeated the address for the driver and for the team.

"You'll be there in less than three minutes," Harper said. "We're going to run on parallel streets, so he won't see us. As soon as you stop, we'll set up a perimeter. We have hostage negotiators with us ready to take over."

A hostage situation. Damn. Her mind went back to the bank at Hogan's Alley. She'd had no idea she would end up in a real scenario a few short days after her training fiasco.

When the taxi pulled to a stop, she pushed thoughts of Quantico from her mind and tossed the driver thirty dollars.

She stepped out and stood in front of a sleek, modern office building with a glass front. After watching the cab pull away, she took out the cell phone and held it up so Forge's voice transmitted over her mic, but on the opposite side of her head from the earbud so he couldn't overhear what Buxton or Harper said to her.

"Where are you, Forge?" she said, looking around.

"Your cousin and I are waiting for you inside."

She stalled for time, giving the team an opportunity to set up. "I'm not going in until I know Selena is okay."

After a momentary pause, she heard a loud slap followed by Selena's voice screaming obscenities in the background.

"As you can hear, she is alive and will stay that way if you follow my instructions."

She used every ounce of self-control she possessed to quell an angry response. "Let me talk to her." The words came through gritted teeth.

"You can talk to her when you come in."

He wanted her in that building, and he wanted it now.

"How do I get inside?"

She tried to provide the responding tactical team with as much intel as possible about the building in case they had to make a rapid entry.

"I have temporarily unlocked the main front doors," Forge said. "All you have to do is walk up to the sensors. They'll open automatically."

She kept up her delaying tactics while pretending to comply. "What happens when I go inside?"

"You will drop the phone, place your handgun on the floor, and kick it away. Then I will give you further instructions."

That meant he would be within talking distance once she got through the door.

"How do I know you'll let Selena leave after I go in?"

"The only thing you know for sure is that I will definitely kill her if you don't," Forge said. "I'm going to count to ten, and then I will begin by shooting her in the abdomen."

Nina heard Selena's panicked shriek in the background. Forge was tormenting both of them.

Harper spoke into her earpiece. "This was not part of the plan, Guerrera. You were supposed to lead us to the suspect so HRT could make the apprehension. Do not, under any circumstances, exchange yourself for a hostage."

"I'm pointing the gun at her belly now," Forge said, then began a slow, deliberate count. "One, two, three, four—"

According to accepted hostage crisis protocol, Harper was correct. Acceding to Forge's demand would involve disarming herself and probably ending up as an additional victim.

Because such exchanges only served to bolster the hostage taker's position, law enforcement officers were never supposed to swap themselves for a hostage. The rules were sound, and they had been created for a reason.

This was not a practical exercise in a scenario, however. This was her cousin. Part of a family she had longed for. Someone whose sole crime was being related to her. Inside Selena was a precious life. Another life put in jeopardy because of her.

Fuck the rules.

Nina drew her gun from its holster and stepped toward the wide glass front doors.

"Six, seven—"

The doors slid open and she stepped onto the threshold.

Buxton's voice halted her. "Agent Guerrera, I am ordering you not to—"

Static filled her ear. Forge had jammed the transmitter. She had no communications, no way to call for backup, and—once she entered the building—no weapon.

"Eight, nine . . ."

She walked inside.

Chapter 57

As Nina crossed the threshold, the static in her earbud dropped to a barely perceptible hum. While effectively cutting her off from the team, Forge had also saved her from disobeying a direct order. She was grateful for that small favor because she had made up her mind to go in.

"Your gun, Agent Guerrera."

The voice had come from her left. She whirled to see Forge step out from behind a lush indoor green space filled with flowering shrubbery and tall palm trees in the building's large atrium. He held Selena tight to his body, the muzzle of his semiautomatic pistol pressed against her swollen belly.

In one fluid motion, Nina dropped the phone to the floor and raised her Glock, training the sights on Forge.

He narrowed his eyes on her. "Don't try it."

She performed a rapid mental assessment of her situation. She had no idea what the team was planning, what Forge would do, or how Selena would react. The only thing within her control was her own actions.

Forge seemed to be thinking along the same lines and was doing everything he could to reduce her options. Taller than Selena, he hunched down enough to keep his head behind hers. He didn't discourage Selena's panicked thrashing, which kept her body in a constant state of motion, shifting around in front of him. Eliminating any hope of a clean shot.

If Nina fired her weapon, she risked either hitting Selena or failing to incapacitate Forge, who would then pull the trigger. Forge was forcing her hand, but she knew the drill.

Never give up your gun.

Relinquishing a weapon only made a bad situation worse. Law Enforcement 101.

"You can tell your FBI friends outside to back off too," he said.

So he knew she wasn't alone. She had wondered why he hadn't already shot her. Now she had her answer.

The soft glow of monitors emanated from the reception desk beside him. Forge had watched her arrival, then spotted HRT personnel setting up on the building.

"I took the precaution of jamming all signals inside the building in case you brought company," he said. "Because it pays to have a backup plan."

The mention of a plan made her wonder what his original strategy had been, and how she might thwart it. She sought to draw his focus away from Selena and onto her.

"What's your endgame, Forge?" She kept her gun on him as she spoke. "Why go to all this trouble to get me here?"

"To separate you from your team, of course," he said as if the answer were obvious. "If you had come alone, I would have killed both of you and gotten away clean." His expression hardened. "But you lied to me, so now I need one of you with me to make sure your friends out there don't get trigger happy when I walk out the door." He jerked his chin at Selena. "This one would slow me down, which is why I'm willing to make a trade. That offer will, however, expire soon." He paused a beat. "What's it going to be?"

If Nina surrendered, what would stop him from shooting Selena? Compassion? The idea was laughable. She thought about Forge's profile. Only one thing would motivate him. Self-interest.

"If you fire a single shot, the tactical team will make immediate entry," she said. "They already have the building surrounded. There's no way out for you unless I cooperate. And I won't do that until you release Selena."

The *snick-snick* of a hammer cocking was his only response. He didn't need to cock the hammer to fire the weapon. The trigger was double-action, which meant it only required a slightly stronger amount of pressure to pull it the first time. The move had been a threat. An unmistakable signal of deadly intent.

She tried to view the situation from Forge's perspective. Using his cold, calculating logic, she arrived at an inescapable conclusion. He had two objectives. First, to get away, then to kill her. He needed a hostage to escape. He had expressed a preference for Nina, but if she refused, he would use Selena. Either way, his plan involved Nina's death.

Looking into his eyes, she had no doubt he would pull the trigger without the slightest remorse. She saw the flatness that Robert Cahill had described.

The eyes of a snake.

He could not feel or understand human emotion. Love, compassion, and empathy were a dark void in his soul, notable only by their absence. Like a computer programmed with AI, he had the ability to calculate how someone might react to a situation and adjust his strategy, but he could not account for the unpredictable. The illogical. He expected human behavior to fall within certain parameters he had observed over a lifetime. Realization erupted to the surface, breaking through the logjam in her mind.

Forge had a blind spot.

Nina reflected on what she had learned from Wade and Kent. Forge would do whatever possible to manipulate the situation to his advantage. He planned to get out of this alive. The only way she would have the upper hand is if she did the opposite. If she made a deliberate choice to sacrifice herself, she would have a chance at saving Selena and her baby. Forge lacked the capacity to anticipate such a move because—like a snake—he would never willingly give up his life to save another.

Once she made her decision, a plan quickly took shape. Had she stalled long enough for the team to get in place? For her next move, she counted on Forge's well-honed survival instincts. It was in his best interest to release Selena after Nina was disarmed, then take Nina hostage. He would not shoot Selena while she was still inside the building, knowing a swarm of tactical personnel would rush in before he could grab Nina.

For the plan to work, she had to give up her weapon. Steeling herself, Nina took her finger off the trigger, squatted, and laid her Glock on the floor, keeping it within reach. Time seemed to stop. She was a trapeze artist flying through space, blindly clutching for the other bar.

"Okay," she said to Forge. "Now aim your gun at me and let Selena go."

He kept the muzzle against Selena's protruding abdomen. "On your knees."

Forge apparently knew action was faster than reaction. He could pull the trigger faster than she could grab her weapon from the floor, aim it, and fire.

She sank to her knees.

He swiveled his arm to point the gun at Nina and used his free hand to shove her cousin away. Selena stumbled, then regained her footing.

Nina cut her eyes to Selena. "Walk out the front door with your hands in the air," she instructed her. "They'll take care of you once you get outside."

She did not want Selena suddenly bursting through the front doors, unwittingly drawing fire.

Selena clasped her hands protectively around her belly. "Agent Guerrera, I—"

"Go." Nina watched her cousin take several ungainly steps toward the front door before she turned her attention back to Forge. He had used her momentary distraction to silently close the distance between them and now stood at point-blank range, looking down at her.

"Up on your feet."

She stood. Her gun, which now lay at her feet, might as well have been in another room. She faced Forge, returning his gaze.

His voice was deadly calm. "Time to go."

He clutched her elbow and pulled her in close. She offered no resistance when he wrapped a muscular arm around her midsection and yanked her backward until her spine touched his chest. She felt the sights of his gun dig into her temple as he jammed the barrel against her head.

Her pulse pounded, but Forge's heart thudded a steady rhythm against her left shoulder. She recalled Kent explaining how people like Forge did not experience a physical fight-or-flight response when faced with imminent danger.

She could be unpredictable, but Forge had the advantages of ruthlessness and rock-solid nerves.

Panic was the enemy, and she could not succumb. She had accomplished her objective. Selena was safe. Whatever happened next, Nina could die knowing no one else had paid the price for Forge's obsession. It would end here and now. When she made her move, he would pull the trigger, but those outside would do the same.

Forge had intended to kill her twenty-eight years ago. She had been destined to die with her parents that day. Fate had intervened in the form of Carmen Cardona, who had discarded her and counted her as dead. Twice, she had escaped what seemed to have been preordained for her.

With a sudden rush of clarity, Nina realized she had been living her entire life on borrowed time. Now the moment had arrived when her story reached its end.

Destiny had finally caught up to her.

Chapter 58

At least she would have sacrificed herself for something worthy. Selena and her baby would go on. Teresa would not have to bury her daughter and granddaughter as she had buried her sister and the ashes of the baby she thought was her niece.

Nina was new to both families. An outsider they barely knew. They would heal and move on. The thought absolved her of any guilt for what she was about to do.

Forge's breath blew hot against her ear as he spoke. "Move."

She let him force her forward. The glass doors hissed open at their approach. The wide expanse of concrete in front of the building was empty. If she didn't know otherwise, she would assume it was deserted.

He gave her another shove and she stepped over the threshold. Instantly, her earpiece crackled to life. Apparently, Forge's jamming device only worked inside the building.

A burst of static resolved into a clear transmission. "Repeat. Agent Guerrera, if you copy, stomp your left foot."

She had never appreciated how wonderful Buxton's voice sounded until that moment. Pretending to stumble, she lifted her left knee and brought her boot down hard. Forge—head on a swivel, trying to spot the police—merely pushed her ahead again.

"I want a car," he called out.

The words reverberated off the walls of the buildings around them, the last echoes dying into silence.

Nina let out a contemptuous laugh. "They're not going to give you a car."

"Then you're about to sustain some serious bodily injury," he said to her, then shouted, "Bring a car around to the front of the building. Now."

She braced herself for what was to come. The FBI would not let Forge escape any more than he would set her free. She was every bit as trapped as he was.

In the silence, she considered the differences between them. Forge operated on base instinct while she answered to a higher calling. She was a protector, a guardian. To her, there were things that mattered more than her own survival. Forge, on the other hand, was only concerned with his own needs and desires. A self-contained entity, he had no friends, no family, no tribe.

Despite the cruelty she had faced in her life, she was still capable of compassion, of love. That was how she had been able to sacrifice herself for Selena and the baby. She had also learned to be part of a team, which was why she had tried to shield Kent from the sniper's bullets during their jog.

As the memory flashed through her mind, an idea took hold. She had come out with Forge planning to go for his gun, even with the knowledge that he would be able to pull the trigger before she could stop him. The team would drop him where he stood the instant he fired. She had come to accept that neither of them would survive.

But what if there was another option? Something she would never have considered only a few months earlier. Her life was already forfeit. She had nothing to lose by trying.

Fully aware everyone was listening through her transmitter, she asked Forge a question. "Have you ever been pinned down by the enemy with no way out?"

She spoke on two levels, simultaneously directing her comments to Forge and to her team, hoping her message would be received.

"That's where you are right now," she continued. "More importantly, that's where I am."

"Shut up," Forge said, still scanning the area around them.

This was the moment. She would have to be strong enough to put her life in someone else's hands. It would require perfect timing on his part and total faith on her part. If it didn't work, so be it.

Every muscle in her body tensed as she uttered the one word that was her last hope. "Flashpoint."

She instantly bent her knees, allowing her back to slide down Forge's chest. At the same time, she lowered her head, doing her best to expose his forehead for a split second. A small target, but any other shot would leave Forge capable of pulling the trigger as he collapsed, ending both of their lives.

Forge reacted with surprising speed, repositioning the barrel of the gun to push against her head again. She closed her eyes, preparing for the explosion of a hollow-point round inside her skull.

She was the Warrior Girl. From childhood, she had fought for others. No one had ever fought for her. She had been let down so many times it had been hard to trust anyone. To have faith in anyone.

Kent was a warrior as well. A warrior who had learned to put his life in someone else's hands. This time, she would have to do the same. Either she would live or she would die, and she had to accept that she could not control the outcome.

She had made her choice.

A single gunshot split the air. She felt Forge's body jerk, then slump. She had experienced a man's deadweight pressing down on her before and recognized the sensation even before the blood and brain matter spattered the ground in front of her.

Her body bowed under the strain as a phalanx of black tactical boots thundered toward her. Forge's bulk suddenly disappeared when he was roughly yanked away and hurled to the ground. HRT members would treat him as armed and dangerous until they confirmed his status, but she already knew his reign of terror was over.

Calloused palms clasped her cheeks. "Nina." Kent tilted her head back to peer into her eyes. "Are you okay?"

She nodded. "You heard the code? You're the one who took the shot?"

"Fuckin' A."

Chapter 59

The wail of a siren drew her attention. Nina turned toward the sound. "Where's Selena?"

"The team medics called rescue to check her out," Kent said, pointing toward the edge of the building. "HRT has vehicles staged around the corner."

She took off at a dead run, desperate to see that no harm had come to Selena during her captivity. Who knew what Forge had done to her?

She rounded the building and saw an ambulance stopped in the parking lot next to a lumbering black beast of a SWAT vehicle. Two EMTs leaped out and hurried to where Selena lay on a cot a few inches off the pavement.

Nina caught snatches of conversation as she reached their vicinity. Words like *blood pressure*, *contractions*, and *labor* floated to her ears. She came to a halt at Selena's side and squatted down to grasp her hand.

Selena's terrified eyes locked with hers. "I—" She let out a howl and clutched Nina's hand with bone-crushing force.

One of the paramedics tapped Nina's shoulder. "We need to get her in the ambulance. We may not get to the hospital before the baby comes, but I'd like to try."

"I'm coming with," Nina said to him.

"Only family can ride inside with a patient." The medic looked apologetic. "Sorry, but that's our policy."

A mixture of awe and unfamiliarity swelled within her. "I *am* family." She pointed at Selena, who was already inside the ambulance. "That's my cousin."

He nodded, apparently satisfied. "Suit yourself."

A new objection came from another direction.

"I need you here, Agent Guerrera." Buxton had materialized beside her.

She stood and turned to face him. "I can provide my statement later."

"I've called SAC Wong," he said. "She's on her way here. I'm sure she'll want to speak to you right away. She's planning a news conference in a couple of hours."

The special agent in charge of the Phoenix field office was the least of Nina's concerns. The ambulance crew was preparing to close the vehicle's rear doors, and she was determined to be inside with her cousin when they left for the hospital.

"Sir, I can't add anything you don't already know."

Kent stepped forward. "I fired the fatal shot, not Guerrera. I'm the one who has to be here to answer for my actions when SAC Wong comes."

Buxton regarded Kent a long moment before turning to Nina. "Go."

Without another word, she hoisted herself inside the back of the ambulance seconds before the doors thudded closed.

Nina perched herself on the short bench seat opposite the EMT, who began hooking Selena up to equipment to check her vitals as the ambulance started to roll.

"Hold her hand and help her through the contractions," he said to Nina. "I'm going to see how far she's dilated."

Nina focused on Selena. "I'm here for you, honey."

The EMT slid down to the end of the bench closest to the doors. "All right, Selena, I'm going to have a look and see how things are going, okay?"

When Selena nodded, he draped a crisp white sheet over her lower body and got to work.

"I need to call my husband," Selena said. "And my mom."

The EMT's head came up. "No time for that now. You need to concentrate on your breathing. We'll call them as soon as we get to the hospital."

Nina smoothed a sweat-soaked tendril of hair from Selena's reddening face. She murmured words of encouragement between the spasms that racked her cousin with pain.

A few minutes into the ride, the EMT called out to her. "This baby is coming right now, get ready." He glanced at Nina. "When I give the word, tell her to push."

Like all law enforcement officers, Nina had taken a course in basic first aid, which included delivering a baby. She had never thought that small amount of training would be needed.

"Now," he said.

She got in close to Selena, breathing with her. "Push."

Selena released a low groan that crescendoed as her entire upper body tensed and reddened with strain. As Selena curled upward, Nina placed a hand on her back, urging her on. She cut her eyes to the EMT, who hunched at the juncture of Selena's splayed legs. She wanted him to tell Selena to stop, to give her a chance to catch her breath before trying again.

The EMT's eyes darted up to meet hers. He shook his head as if reading her thoughts. "We're almost there. Don't stop."

Nina understood. The baby was making its way out. Stopping at this point was not an option—doing so would put her at risk. Now that the child had started through the birth canal, Selena's baby needed to complete the journey.

Nina turned back to her cousin. She could tell Selena was spent. The ordeal of being kidnapped, of having a gun to her head, and of having that same gun pressed against her belly had taken a massive toll. She hated to demand more of her, but that was exactly what she did.

"Push, Selena. Don't stop."

Selena gazed at her, wild eyed, and strained with effort again. This time, they were rewarded with a shout from the EMT.

"Got her!"

Nina looked down to catch a glimpse of the tiny baby as the paramedic clamped the umbilical cord, cut it, and worked quickly until a mewling cry filled the space around them.

He swaddled the baby and leaned forward to place her on Selena's chest, then returned to his previous position to take care of Selena as the two women focused on the new arrival.

"She's beautiful," Nina murmured.

Tears streamed down Selena's cheeks as she cradled her baby. "Come here, *mi'ja*."

The words brought a familiar bittersweet feeling to Nina. Her own mother had never had the chance to call her *mi'ja*, had never even been able to hold her. A twist of fate had taken Nina from her family, and another twist had returned her to them.

The ambulance lurched to a stop, and Nina realized they had arrived at Phoenix General's emergency room. Both doors popped open, and a swarm of medical personnel surrounded them. Apparently, the driver had radioed ahead to notify the staff, who made short work of wheeling Selena and the baby out of the ambulance and inside the building.

Nina started after them but stopped short when she heard her name. SAC Jennifer Wong was walking toward her at a fast clip.

"SSA Buxton told me what happened," Wong said. "I dropped by on the way to the scene to pick you up and take you there. You can brief me in the car."

"But my cousin—" She paused. Had SAC Wong been apprised of her DNA results?

"After you check on your cousin, of course." Wong smiled. Evidently Buxton had filled her in on that development as well. "Looks like you have a new addition to your family."

Her family. She still had trouble adjusting to the concept. "Yes, a baby girl." She stiffened, remembering Selena's request in the ambulance. "I'd better call her husband and her mother."

"Already taken care of," Wong said. "Agent Wade had their contact info. They're on the way to the hospital."

They both walked inside the ER, where they found the two EMTs standing in the hallway.

"They're being checked out," the one who had delivered the baby told them. "You can't go any farther until they're cleared for visitors, which could take a while."

"But they're both okay?" Nina asked.

The ambulance driver nodded. "Mother and baby are doing fine." He gestured to his partner. "And we get a sticker."

Nina looked from one to the other until the driver explained. "When a baby is delivered in an ambulance, we put a stork sticker on the side. This one will be holding a pink bundle in its beak."

Nina grinned. "Nice tradition."

Wong pulled her attention away from the men. "Unfortunately, we don't have time to wait around for visiting hours. I'm sorry, Agent Guerrera, but duty calls."

Duty. That had been Nina's sole credo for years. She hadn't experienced much in the way of a personal life. It was all about the job. She accepted that this was part of what it meant to be in law enforcement. But her calling had never caused her this much pain before. She had never felt so torn. Then again, she had never had a family before.

The brief feeling of elation evaporated when she realized her professional obligations may have ruined any possibility of having a relationship with her newly discovered relatives. When they had asked her about the investigation, she had put duty first, not disclosing her own connection to the case. She could have provided answers they had desperately wanted. Instead, she held back key information because of the constraints of her job.

Would a family who barely knew her understand? Would they forgive her?

"Time to go," Wong said.

Even in this moment, Nina was being asked to choose duty above all else. She cast a wistful glance down the corridor where her family would soon be gathering, then turned and followed the SAC out of the hospital.

Chapter 60

Several hours later, Nina was with her team at the Phoenix Royal Suites, where they had returned to meet with hotel security. Within minutes of their arrival, the security chief located a room service attendant who had reported his universal electronic room key missing a few days earlier. Once they knew when it had been lost, they reviewed the front desk video for that date and saw Forge in disguise booking a suite under a false name with a matching credit card. The security chief had let them into the room before returning to the lobby.

"Forge has been busy in here," Nina said after the team was alone.

Kent looked around. "We've found his base of operations."

Breck strolled over to the desk. "This is a different computer than the one he left at the scene." She bent to peer at the devices resting beside it. "Looks like this one is dedicated to his monitoring equipment."

Before they'd left for the hotel, Breck had spent the past few hours using her cybercrime skills to datamine the computer Forge had left behind in the building.

A chill swept through Nina. "That equipment will contain files that could land us all in a world of trouble."

The room stilled. When FBI evidence techs eventually listened to the recordings, they would hear Nina and her team agreeing to hide information from their supervisor.

"I don't think so," Breck said, pointing at a red rectangular device with a tapered metal tip attached to one side.

"What's that thing?" Wade asked.

Breck grinned. "A degaussing wand." She sighed when no one appeared to understand. "Let's just say it's a powerful magnet designed to permanently wipe data. Forge obviously used it to cover his tracks before he left."

Nina caught on. "He planned to escape, so he destroyed any possible cookie crumbs for us to follow."

"Exactly," Breck said. "No one's going to find any files—or hear any recordings—on this computer. Problem solved."

Nina felt a surge of relief. She continued to search through the room, confirming another suspicion when she opened the closet. "Look at what I found." She lifted a hanger and turned to show the others a red-and-gray bellman's uniform.

Wade crossed the room to have a look. "Between the universal keycard and this outfit, he would have been able to access our rooms anytime he wanted."

"What do you want to bet he had help from that young bellman who handed me the cell phone in the lobby earlier?" Nina said. "The kid was downright hinky. He knew more than he let on."

"As soon as we're done here, I'm going to have a little chat with him," Kent said, irritated. "I'll have the truth out of him in ten minutes."

Nina gave him a sardonic look. "I'm betting he'll crack in less than five."

Wade glanced at his cell. "Buxton just texted me. He wants us all in his suite for a meeting."

They took the elevator to the thirty-first floor and made their way to the end of the hall, where they found a countersurveillance specialist leaving Buxton's suite.

"All done with your sweep?" Nina asked him.

He nodded. "Found a total of six bugs, two in each room. One in the lamp and the other in a pen on the desk. The guy was consistent."

"Have a seat," Buxton told the team after they filed inside and closed the door. "Not that anyone is likely to be on the other end of Forge's listening devices anymore, but I wanted them gone before sharing some news with you."

Nina strolled across the spacious suite, eyeing the sofa, love seat, and armchair clustered around a glass-topped coffee table. As expected, Buxton chose the armchair. She plopped down next to Breck on the love seat, leaving the sofa to Wade and Kent.

Buxton waited for everyone to settle before filling them in. "I was just on the phone with SAC Wong. Agents from the PFO located Mr. Forge's vehicle parked in the rear of the building. He had a military-grade night-vision system and visible infrared laser, dark camo, and Nike running shoes stashed in the trunk."

"Now we know how he got the drop on the families," Nina said. "Did they find a burglary kit too?"

Buxton nodded. "A complete lockpick set. Looked like it had seen a lot of use." He turned to Breck. "Did you discover anything during your preliminary examination of Mr. Forge's two laptops?"

"He wiped the one he left in his hotel room," Breck said. "But the one he left at the crime scene was a gold mine. I figured out how he targeted his victims." She grew animated, as she always did when discussing computer forensics. "He had encrypted files for all the past cases. It's fascinating how he slowly and methodically winnowed an ocean of potential victims down to a small pool."

Buxton leaned forward. "Can you provide an overview for us . . . without too much computer-ese?"

"He's high enough up in Jexton Security to have access to their entire national client database," Breck said. "Since Jexton is a wholly owned subsidiary of Rubric Realty, they share information. Forge used that cross-connectivity to devise a kind of back door into Rubric's computer system."

"He's shown he's tech savvy," Wade said. "But I still don't understand how he used the systems."

"From what I could tell, he cross-referenced Rubric's clients with Jexton's," Breck said. "Then he mined Rubric's database for couples who had recently purchased a home or were currently looking for one. That yielded tens of thousands of data points across the country. Next, he set up search parameters with keywords like 'nursery' or 'baby.' Then he narrowed the search further by accessing notes the real estate agents put in their client files. That's where he would find details about couples moving to have more room for a growing family. As we suspected, he kept several couples under observation as backups to his primary choice."

"But how did he know those couples didn't have other kids?" Kent asked. "Each of the victim families had a firstborn child."

Breck frowned. "Once he found couples that met his criteria, he checked for past birth announcements, information about schools, Little League sports—anything that would indicate they already had other children."

"How did he access that information?" Nina asked.

Breck shrugged. "It's not that hard. Most people freely post all kinds of stuff about their families on social media sites. In the days before the internet, there were birth announcements in the papers for him to look up. Once he developed a list of potential targets, he began to spot-check them."

"How did he do that?" Nina asked.

"The older cases indicate he did the kind of surveillance a private investigator might do. Once camera systems became more common, he used their own home-security system's video-surveillance capabilities to monitor them."

"He used their own security systems to spy on them?" Kent said.

"It gets worse." Breck pursed her lips. "Some of the newer systems are controlled through the client's home computer. You know how you can use your smartphone to turn on the lights or see who's at your door when you're away?"

Everyone nodded. Nina was appalled at Forge's ability to invade people's privacy using technology.

"He used that feature to introduce a Trojan horse into their computer," Breck said. "From that point on, he was in the background, monitoring every keystroke, using their televisions and computer terminals to watch them."

"He broke into homes without anyone ever knowing," Kent added.

"What about Thomas Kirk, the real estate agent with Rubric?" Wade asked. "Was there anything about him in there?"

Breck nodded. "Thanks to the bugs, Forge overheard us talking about interviewing Kirk. Turns out Kirk frequently referred high-end clients to Forge, so that must have been why he stole Kirk's computer. He wanted to hide any digital evidence connecting them."

"I still don't understand about the Llorona case." Kent gave Nina an apologetic look. "I mean, the Vega case. According to Detective O'Malley, they never activated their alarm system."

"I checked that file and found a record of the alarm system the previous owners had," Breck said. "It was one of Jexton's earlier models. We're talking 1992 here. Back in those days, security systems could be either wireless, wired, or a combination of both. The Vega home's system was hardwired from the house to a main control box and was connected to a central monitoring station using telephone lines."

Nina made the next logical leap. "So all Forge would have to do was physically access the wiring, which he could have done if he showed up trying to sell them the service for the existing alarm. After that, he learns that tapping into alarm systems can make his job easier going forward."

Breck nodded. "He adapts as technology improves," she said. "It didn't take long for cameras to be integrated into home security."

"Anything else we need to know?" Buxton asked.

"It's like digging in a field, looking for seeds," Breck said. "I'm still going through everything, but I'll keep you updated."

"Thank you, Agent Breck," Buxton said. He looked uncomfortable, as if he didn't want to broach the next subject. "Before we get to the rest of the agenda, there is a personnel matter to discuss." His somber gaze fell on Nina. "Agent Guerrera, you violated numerous policies and procedures in the process of this investigation. Your insubordination has put me in an awkward position, and I intend to deal with it here and now."

Chapter 61

Nina's eyes slid down to her folded hands. "I will accept whatever discipline is recommended, sir."

Buxton frowned. "That may not be necessary."

Her head snapped back up. "Isn't that what this meeting is about?" She figured he wanted to make an example of her in case anyone else on the team thought they could flout the rules and get away with it.

"That's not how it's done," he said patiently. "Besides, SAC Wong tells me you've become a hero in Phoenix. She hasn't received so many requests for comment in quite a long time. And never for anything favorable to the Bureau."

"Then why—"

"I had planned to place a letter of reprimand in your file, Agent Guerrera," he said. "SAC Wong, however, proposed submitting you for a commendation. We had a discussion and decided they canceled each other out." A ghost of a smile momentarily lifted the corners of his mouth.

She blinked in confusion. Somehow, she had escaped career annihilation.

"The next point of order is the lab results," Buxton continued. "I personally reached out to both Maria's and Victor Vega's families to confirm Mr. Snead's television report," Buxton said. "They needed to know we had verified the information."

Nina imagined Teresa sharing the news with the rest of the family. Then she pictured Ana and Luis Vega in their grim, dark house, learning they had a granddaughter . . . a ray of light in their bleak existence.

"There's another reason I asked you all here for this meeting," Buxton continued after giving Nina a searching look. "SAC Wong and I had a lengthy conversation about an hour ago. She has a proposal for us."

The team exchanged glances. Apparently, Nina wasn't the only one out of the proverbial loop.

"SAC Wong has assigned most of her agents to work a case with national security implications."

Nina understood that to mean *terrorist cell operating in the area.*

"Sounds serious," Kent said. "What does she want us to do?"

"Regarding that investigation?" Buxton waved a dismissive hand. "Nothing. SAC Wong is handling it. Yesterday, however, the Phoenix police approached her requesting assistance with a series of disappearances. She feels our team would be best suited to tackle that investigation due to our unique combination of skills."

Nina was perplexed. "Why does she want our help?"

"Because SAC Wong's resources are stretched tight right now, and this new case has the potential to grow hair." Buxton leaned back. "If we're willing to work out of the Phoenix field office for the next few weeks, the assignment is ours."

She recognized the offer for what it was. SAC Wong could have requested assistance from any number of different assets the FBI had at its disposal. There was no specific need for her team to work the Phoenix disappearances. Buxton knew it too. They were providing her an opportunity to stay in town and get to know her family for an extended time. Overwhelmed by gratitude, she wanted to accept, but it was a big ask for her team, who had lives of their own back home. She had no right to uproot everyone else.

Before she could formulate a response, Kent shot to his feet, back ramrod straight, arms tight against his sides.

Buxton looked as baffled as Nina felt. "What are you doing, Agent Kent?" he asked.

Still keeping his rigid stance, Kent spoke in clipped tones. "Volunteering, sir."

"I don't understand," Buxton said.

Kent continued to stare straight ahead. "In my unit, every member of the platoon stood to show their acceptance of a new mission."

Kent's gesture let all of them know he understood what this meant for Nina and was willing to make the sacrifice for her.

The idea that a member of her team was willing to put his personal life on hold in order to give her a chance to come to terms with her new identity as a member of a family—of two families—tugged at her heart.

The cushion beside her shifted as Breck rose to her feet as well. Moments later, Wade followed suit. Buxton gave her a long look before he, too, stood.

She glanced at the four people around her, all standing at attention in a silent show of solidarity. With the backs of her eyes stinging, she got up to stand with those who stood with her.

Chapter 62

Nina lingered on her aunt's doorstep the following morning, nerves roiling her stomach. Repeated calls to Teresa the previous evening had gone straight to voice mail. At first, she'd assumed Teresa was busy with the arrival of her first grandchild, but as the hours went by with no response, Nina had concluded her aunt did not want to speak to her.

She didn't blame her. Because of Nina's involvement in the investigation, the same killer who had taken her sister's life had nearly murdered Teresa's daughter and granddaughter. Nina had brought the specter of death back to their family. She hadn't bargained for the pain her return would bring into their lives. Or her own.

Finally, after hours of no response, Teresa had texted Nina's cell phone half an hour earlier, asking her to come to the house without further explanation. Kent had offered to accompany her, but this was something she had to face alone.

She didn't expect virtual strangers who had just learned of their biological connection to understand what she had done, but she hoped they would at least hear her out. All she could do was apologize, which was what she had come to do.

Thoughts of the twenty-eight-year separation from her relatives made Nina realize today was March 11, her designated date of birth.

Now she knew her actual birthday had been February 23. The pediatrician at the hospital where social workers had taken her had probably underestimated her age due to her small size and undernourishment. What the doctor had no way of knowing was that her undernourishment would continue in various forms. The next several years of her life involved starvation of the soul that had wrought damage she was still in the process of repairing. Given her total lack of experience as a member of a family, she was completely out of her depth in her current situation.

Expecting the worst, Nina had lifted her hand to knock when the door swung open. Teresa stood in the foyer, eyes wide. "I saw you through the living room window. Why are you standing there?" She stepped aside. "Come in."

Nina trailed Teresa into the kitchen, where the countertops were heaped with food, as they had been before.

"Everyone's out in the backyard." Teresa waved a hand toward the rear of the house. "Go on through."

Nina hesitated. "First, how is Selena?"

"She and the baby are both doing fine." Teresa's features warmed. "They're out back too. You can see for yourself."

Nina wanted to clear the air with her aunt before facing the rest of the boisterous clan. "Teresa, I owe you an apology."

"For what?"

"I'm the reason your daughter was kidnapped," Nina began. "Clay Forge knew he could use her to get to me. If it weren't for me, Selena and the baby would never have been in danger."

Teresa frowned. "I don't understand."

If this family was going to be angry with her, to reject her, they might as well know the full extent of her guilt.

Nina straightened. "I was the one who came up with the idea to lure Forge out of hiding by using myself as bait. I thought I was taking all the risk, but Forge outmaneuvered me. My plan backfired, and it almost cost Selena and her baby their lives."

She finished with a dry mouth, unable to look in her aunt's eyes. "I wanted you to know the truth about what happened yesterday—and where to put the blame." She started to turn toward the front door.

Teresa's warm hand wrapped around her wrist, stopping her. "Where do you think you're going?"

"Don't you see?" Nina asked her. "What happened to Selena"—she placed her palm on her chest—"is all on me."

"You did what you thought was right," Teresa said gently. "You had no way of knowing what would happen." Still clutching her by the wrist, she drew Nina toward the french doors leading to the backyard. "Come celebrate with us."

Nina shook her head. "I don't want to intrude."

An interloper, she had no right to join the party as they celebrated the birth of their newest family member. She might be biologically related, but she felt separate. Apart.

Realizing Teresa wouldn't be denied, Nina relented and allowed herself to be tugged outside. As soon as the doors opened, the sounds of animated chatter reached her ears. Long picnic tables festooned with decorations dotted the yard. Paper garlands hung from a gazebo in the center of the property. At least fifty people milled around, gradually turning in her direction as they took notice of her arrival.

"Everyone." Teresa's voice carried, bringing the last vestiges of conversation to a stop. "For those of you who haven't met her, this is Nina Guerrera . . . Maria's daughter."

Several family members approached with smiling faces. Nina started to shake their hands, but they seemed to prefer rib-crushing hugs.

Selena nudged her way toward Nina through the crowd, a tiny pink bundle in her arms.

"I thought you might like a better look at your new cousin," Selena said, angling the baby to face Nina. "Her name is Victoria Maria

Fernandez." Selena smiled as she glanced up at her husband, who had made his way to her side. "We named her after you."

Nina didn't understand. "Me?"

"Didn't you know?" Selena's eyes widened. "Your birth name was Victoria Maria Vega. You were named after both of your parents."

She blushed as she recalled Luis Vega telling her that when she stood in his living room with Perez, pretending she didn't have a clue he was her grandfather.

"I'm going to call her Tori," Selena said, nuzzling the sleeping baby.

"I like that name for her." Nina spoke through a clogged throat. "I'm so grateful to all of you for letting me join your celebration. It's really—"

The words died on her lips when the french doors opened again, and Teresa ushered two latecomers out to the backyard. A hush fell over the party as all eyes fell on the new arrivals.

"It's been too long since we've been together," Teresa said to Ana and Luis Vega.

Luis nodded. "Thank you for inviting us."

"We wouldn't have missed it," Ana said, her brown eyes misting as they found Nina in the crowd.

Everyone seemed to be looking at her. Overwhelmed with a tidal wave of unfamiliar emotions, Nina shifted on her feet. Nothing in her life had prepared her for this. What should she say? What should she do?

Sofia, matriarch of the Soto family, stepped forward to clasp Ana's hands in hers. "*Bienvenidos*. Welcome."

As the two women embraced, Nina wondered if they had spoken at all since their respective children's funerals.

"We are a family again." Teresa gestured toward Nina. "Thanks to our guest of honor."

"Guest of honor?" Nina blinked in confusion. "I thought the party was for baby Tori."

Teresa's soft chuckle was echoed by the others. "Look around. What do you see?"

Nina scanned the happy faces beaming at her, then surveyed the decorations, noting details she hadn't processed before. Every tree was wrapped in wide bands of fabric tied with enormous bows.

"Yellow ribbons," Nina whispered.

"This is a homecoming party," Teresa said. "For you, Nina."

"Teresa invited us," Luis said. "Thanks to you, we are having a reunion."

Sofia, still holding Ana's hand, pulled Luis closer. Teresa and her husband, John, joined the group hug. One by one, the embrace expanded as cousins and spouses joined in.

Nina watched from a few feet away as a rift born of grief and misunderstanding began to heal. After many sniffles, the group parted enough for Ana to reach out a hand in her direction.

"We cannot have our Victor back," Ana said. "But we can have his daughter in our lives again."

"I-I thought you would all be upset with me," Nina said, her feet still welded to the ground.

"Are you kidding me right now?" Selena frowned at her. "I told them how you offered your life for mine and then helped deliver my baby yesterday. How could any of us be mad at you?"

Nina cast a glance at Teresa, who had heard her full confession a few minutes earlier. A single tear tracked down Teresa's face. "Do you think I could do anything other than love my own sister's child?"

Luis reached out to cup her chin. "I can see it so clearly now. You look like both of them."

Ana nodded. "You are so beautiful."

She had never felt beautiful. Had never felt loved. Had never felt accepted. They were offering her what she had always wanted but never dared hope for.

She clasped Teresa's hands. "I'm not sure how to be part of a family."

Teresa pulled her into the center of the throng. "You'll learn." She paused a single heartbeat, then added the word Nina had been waiting her whole life to hear. *"Mi'ja."*

ACKNOWLEDGMENTS

My husband, Mike, has been amazingly supportive through it all. The best partner and friend anyone could have, he is my rock.

My son, Max, lights up my life and brings joy to my heart.

Family, whether related by blood or the bonds of friendship, means everything. I am forever grateful for their enthusiastic support and understanding over the years.

So much more than an agent, Liza Fleissig shares my vision and makes miracles happen. Her advice, support, and outstanding professionalism have been life changing for me and many others.

My other agent, Ginger Harris-Dontzin, has been wonderfully helpful. She lends her sharp eyes and equally sharp mind to every endeavor.

I am extremely grateful to Ret. Phoenix Police Homicide Detective Sandra Rodriguez, who shared her considerable expertise as I developed this story. Brainstorming is always better over delicious Mexican food.

A very special thanks goes to Martin B. Richards and Penny Lovestedt, who each provided essential input that kept the plot on the straight and narrow. Writers rely on fresh eyes and thorough readings, and the complexity of this particular tale required plenty of both.

I have a deep admiration for the pioneers in the FBI who founded modern criminal profiling: John E. Douglas, Robert K. Ressler, Patrick

Mullany, Howard Teten, and Roy Hazelwood. These agents sacrificed a great deal to delve into the darkest recesses of the human mind.

One of the bright, shiny lights in the world is Megha Parekh, my acquiring editor with Thomas & Mercer. Her insight, generosity, and guidance through every part of the process have made all the difference. I am humbled and blessed by her support.

My developmental editor, Charlotte Herscher, put her considerable talent toward making this story come together. There is nothing like an editor who really "gets" your character.

Every manuscript is a diamond in the rough until copyeditors polish it to a shine. Laura Barrett, Rachel Norfleet, Sarah Vostok, Karin Silver, Kellie Osborne, and Sandra Cebrián Gil all worked diligently to bring sparkle to this story. From timelines to translations and from colons to commas, this incredible team went above and beyond to ensure a smooth reading experience.

The amazing team of marketing and artwork professionals at Thomas & Mercer does a fabulous job of getting books into the hands of readers. I am incredibly blessed to have such talented professionals on my side.

ABOUT THE AUTHOR

Photo © 2016 Skip Feinstein

Award-winning author Isabella Maldonado wore a gun and badge in real life before turning to crime writing. A graduate of the FBI National Academy in Quantico and the first Latina to attain the rank of captain in her police department, she retired as the Commander of Special Investigations and Forensics.

During Ms. Maldonado's more than two decades on the force, her varied assignments included hostage negotiator, department spokesperson, and district station commander. She uses her extensive law enforcement background to bring a realistic edge to her writing.

Ms. Maldonado is a member of the FBI National Academy Associates; Fairfax County Police Association; International Society of Latino Authors; International Thriller Writers; Mystery Writers of America; and Sisters in Crime, where she served as president of the

Phoenix Metro Chapter in 2015 and sat on the board until 2019. The author of the FBI Agent Nina Guerrera series and the Detective Cruz series, she lives in the Phoenix area with her family. For more information, visit www.isabellamaldonado.com.